9/1/12

21/5/12

In comn
children'
for litera
very earl
the Swin
trail, but
IT consu
Literatur
2006. Th

MIRACLE BOY

Michael Reilly

Book Guild Publishing
Sussex, England

First published in Great Britain in 2011 by
The Book Guild Ltd
Pavilion View
19 New Road
Brighton, BN1 1UF

Typesetting in Baskerville by
Norman Tilley Graphics Ltd, Northampton

Printed in Great Britain by
CPI Antony Rowe

A catalogue record for this book is available from
The British Library

ISBN 978 1 84624 615 9

Miracle Boy has been saved for something special. And the communication I have got to make is that he has great expectations.

Open Your Eyes

July 1961

The face looking down at Raymond had a red, swollen nose, split lips and two perfect black eyes. Raymond blinked hard and then sighed with relief. It was Brian.

'At last,' Brian cried. 'Do you know how long you've been out for?'

Raymond tried to shake his head, but it wouldn't move.

'Two flipping days,' Brian said, as if it was something to be envied. 'They've just brought you in here. You've been in a special ward. You've missed all the fun. We've had welfare people here. We've had police here. They've been asking questions about what happened at Hillcrest, but I told them nowt. Guess what? While you've been spark out, we've become film stars. They've taken photographs of me and you!'

Raymond didn't need to interpret Brian's words to know they were in hospital. The strong smell of antiseptic and the fact that his friend wore unfamiliar blue and white striped pyjamas was confirmation enough. He could also see they were in some kind of side ward, with two beds and a metal-framed window through which mote-filled rays of sunlight streamed.

'I told you Uncle Richard would lose his marbles, didn't I?' Brian crowed, sounding as if he had a heavy cold. 'I knew I'd get him. He's in for it now. I didn't mean for us to

1

get brayed so bad, but you should be proud of yourself. He's gonna get what he deserves.'

Sleep, where dreadful dreams awaited, pulled at Raymond like quicksand, but he did his best to resist. The image of Squeaky Dave hanging by the neck on the rope-swing in the desolate woodland ditch behind Hillcrest, the children's home where they lived, flickered in his head like a bad film reel at a Saturday matinee. As Brian chattered, Raymond tried to focus on some of the happy times they'd shared over the past year: times when they'd laughed so much that Raymond almost wet himself. The last few months, though, had been a cycle of forbidden adventure and inevitable retribution. This was far more serious than the sprains and cuts he'd suffered in the rough and tumble of reckless boyhood games during his thirteen years.

His reverie was interrupted by a nurse in a crisp uniform and starched cap, who bustled into the room striking invisible cymbals together with her hands. He recognised her as Nurse Goode, who'd treated him for minor accidents in the past.

'Come on, Brian, give Raymond room to breathe,' she breezed. 'You'll have to go to the dayroom for a while. Raymond's got a visitor waiting to see him.'

'Who is it?' Brian asked, sounding peeved.

'Sergeant Tomlinson,' Nurse Goode replied. 'He's already seen you, Brian, and now he wants to see Raymond on his own.'

She began to plump up Raymond's pillows and help him sit up, while Brian stood at the foot of the bed. Although Raymond winced at being moved, he was soothed by her soft hands and the clean scent of her dark hair, which was scraped back from her broad face into a large bun.

'You'll be just fine, Miracle Boy,' she said to Raymond in a tone as warm as buttered toast. 'Just tell Sergeant Tomlinson what he wants to know.'

Behind her back, clutching a comic book to his chest, Brian mouthed to Raymond, 'Say nowt.'

The homely nurse ushered Brian from the room and a large policeman entered. A knot of apprehension grew in Raymond's stomach as the sergeant pulled a chair up to the bed and sat down.

'Hello, Raymond,' the bobby said, removing his helmet and sitting it on his lap. 'How are you feeling?'

Raymond was afraid and in pain from the welts on his back and the stiffness in his neck, but he said, 'I'm fine, sir.'

'No need to call me *sir*,' the sergeant said, laughing deep down in his throat. 'I haven't been to see the Queen yet. Now then, I just need to ask you a few questions. No need to be worried.'

Raymond was worried, although the sergeant's florid face and bright eyes shining beneath bushy eyebrows radiated benevolence. Judging by his large frame and the tightness of his uniform, he didn't look as though he spent too much time on the beat clipping boys round the ear.

'How long have you been at Hillcrest?' the sergeant asked in a conversational tone.

'Since I was five,' Raymond replied. 'So that's eight years. Before that I was in another home.'

'That's a long time,' the sergeant said. 'Uncle Richard would've been your house-father all that time, then. How long have you known your mate, Brian?'

Raymond felt cagey. He knew Brian hated coppers, but there was nothing wrong with these questions, was there? 'The last year,' he said.

'I know you're good mates,' Sergeant Tomlinson said. 'He told me. He said you and him were always in trouble with Uncle Richard. Why did he larrup you and Brian like this?'

'We kept breaking the rules,' Raymond admitted, thinking of all the trouble that madcap Brian had led him into, and all the punishments they'd suffered.

'How?' the sergeant encouraged. 'It must've been summat bad?'

'I can't say,' Raymond said.

Sergeant Tomlinson gave him a broad smile. 'You're a good mate and mates don't snitch, eh? I know you and that scamp Brian got up to some larks and got punished for it, but this is different. This is serious and it's not your fault.' He paused for a moment and stared at Raymond, which made Raymond feel uncomfortable. 'I've got a lad of my own, grown up and moved away now. He was dead smart like you.'

He picked up a book from the bedside cabinet and looked at it. Raymond recognised it as *Great Expectations*, the most special book from his own treasured collection, which he kept in his locker at Hillcrest. How had it got there?

'He was a big reader as well,' the sergeant said, putting the book back on the cabinet. 'I would hate for anything like this to have happened to him. You can tell me, lad.'

Raymond gave in. This benign bobby invited trust and, besides, who else could he unburden himself to?

'After David Bleasedale died,' Raymond said in a low voice, 'Brian was really angry and blamed Uncle Richard. He wanted to get back at him.'

'That's the lad Brian calls Squeaky Dave,' the sergeant said, 'the one that hanged himself in Millacre Ditch. Do you know why he did it?'

A painful lump swelled in Raymond's throat and he blinked twice before saying, 'He was little for his age and he had a funny voice, and he was frightened about being moved to a home with bigger boys.'

'Aye, lad,' the sergeant sighed. 'So I heard. I also heard that Uncle Richard gave him a hard time. Is that right?'

Raymond thought back to the time just before Squeaky

4

Dave's death and how Uncle Richard had treated the fearful little boy so badly, scolding him without mercy. A deep sadness overcame him and he could only nod, afraid that his voice wouldn't hold if he tried to speak.

'I understand how you feel, lad,' the sergeant said. 'What did you and Brian do to get back at Uncle Richard?'

Guilt, an unwelcome companion during the last few months, squeezed Raymond's throat and made his voice crack. 'We just kept breaking the rules,' he said. 'Then we found the rope, the one Squeaky Dave used, in the outhouse and we tied it to the branch of a tree in the orchard and put a noose on it so Uncle Richard would see it. He caught us and went mad.'

'Then he used the rope on you,' Sergeant Tomlinson said. 'I understand, lad. We'll talk no more about it. There is just something else I need to ask you about. Did you ever see Uncle Richard go into the girls' bedrooms?'

'No,' Raymond said. The girls' dormitories were on a different floor to the boys' and were strictly out of bounds.

'And you never saw him alone with any of the girls?' the sergeant continued, leaning forward and adopting a conspiratorial tone.

'Not really,' Raymond said. What did he mean by *alone*? Everybody had been alone with Uncle Richard at some point, usually for the purposes of interrogation.

'Did any of the girls say anything to you about Uncle Richard?' Sergeant Tomlinson pressed. 'About things that might have happened when he was alone with them?'

'Not to me,' Raymond said. The girls never told him anything. Why would they? He was a boy.

The sergeant shifted in his seat, picked up his helmet and stared at the silver badge on the front. Raymond got the distinct impression that he had something else to say. After a moment or two the sergeant put his helmet on his head, pulled the strap under his chin and spoke.

'I have to tell you this because you'll hear it soon enough when you get back to Hillcrest. It's going to come as a shock. Uncle Richard is dead. After what happened to you and Brian, he disappeared. Last night, two lads found him hanging from a tree in Millacre Ditch.'

Raymond's stomach churned. It was unbelievable. He swallowed hard as a question rose into his mind. Was it the same rope?

'Bad business,' the sergeant said, clapping his hands on his meaty thighs and rising. 'You just concentrate on getting better and put all this behind you.'

*

When the sergeant left and Brian returned to the ward, the first thing he asked was, 'What did you tell that bobby?'

'Nowt,' Raymond replied, wondering how he was going to tell Brian about Uncle Richard. He feared his friend might gloat once he heard the news and he couldn't stand that just now. He needed to get things straight in his own head first.

'Good,' Brian said. 'Me dad always says you should never trust a copper. Hey, I didn't tell you, did I? Me dad's back home and he's coming to get me. I'm not going back to Hillcrest.'

At that moment, Raymond decided not to tell Brian at all.

Brian clambered into his bed and picked up an *Eagle* comic. After a moment of staring at the front page, he asked, 'What did that nurse mean when she called you Miracle Boy?'

'I don't know,' Raymond said, just as perplexed. 'Maybe she's been reading your comics.'

Comings and Goings

The sunlight streaming through the windowpanes painted elongated golden boxes across their beds and onto the drab walls, but Raymond's soul clung to the shadows. He looked at Brian, who was illuminated like a saint, sitting on the edge of his bed with his back to the window, dressed in his regulation Sunday-best.

'I'm not gonna miss Hillcrest, but I'm gonna miss you, Raymond,' Brian said. 'You've been a good mate. You might be clever and go to a posh school, but you never backed down or snitched. I wish you could come with me, but me mum can't cope with all our lot as it is. I'll come and visit you if they let me.' He looked down at his scuffed shoes, so that all Raymond could see was the top of his sandy-coloured thatch. 'I wish *you* could go home, Raymond,' he said. He raised his head and stared at Raymond with his bright blue eyes. 'Is it true what you told me, that your mum and dad are dead?'

'Yes,' Raymond lied, as he always did when asked about his parents; the ones he himself had never asked about. Well they must be dead, mustn't they, if they'd never been to see him?

'Flippin' heck, mate,' Brian said, squeezing his hands together. 'I'm really sorry. To be honest, I wish I was staying with you. Having parents is not exactly a barrel o' laughs. Dad always goes a bit mad on the booze when he gets out and I just seem to rub him up the wrong way.'

7

Raymond struggled with the urge to tell Brian about Uncle Richard's demise. For days he'd tried to fight off the unwelcome images in his head, which alternated between the lifeless forms of Squeaky Dave and Uncle Richard swinging from the tree in Millacre Ditch. He and Brian were bound together by that place: their playground, battleground and finally burial ground; well, not exactly burial ground, but a place of death. He had to tell him.

At that moment, Mr Walker, Brian's father, appeared in the doorway. He was rugged and shifty with nicotine-stained fingers and, although Raymond could see Brian in him, he could also see that Brian was blessed with the best of his features.

'Get yer skates on, Brian,' Mr Walker rasped, shuffling his feet and fingering the half-smoked cigarette behind his ear. 'Yer mum's waiting in reception with the kids and they're running amok.'

Brian's slipped his blazer on and retrieved the duffel bag with his few possessions from the side of his bed. Mr Walker gave Raymond an exaggerated wink and swaggered through the door, followed by his son.

The room echoed with emptiness. Despite the scrapes Brian had got Raymond into, he'd also changed his humdrum life and brought excitement and adventure into it. More than that, he'd taught him how to stand up to oppression, which he'd always accepted as the norm before Brian arrived at Hillcrest.

The sigh had barely left his lips when the door opened and Brian's head reappeared. Brian was grinning and, although Raymond was dismayed to see him leaving, he just had to smile back. Looking at Brian's beaming face with his gap-toothed grin, the bump on his nose and the yellow, fading bruises around his eyes reminded him that Brian's brave, confrontational approach came at a price – a price he was brave enough to pay.

'Them books you're always reading,' Brian said, 'I reckon there's a secret code in one of them that's gonna make everything better for you. Just keep reading, mate.'

He winked just like his dad and the door closed. The shafts of sunlight disappeared as abruptly as if someone had switched off the light.

*

For the next two days Raymond read *Great Expectations*. Most of the books in his precious collection were gifts or school prizes, but he had no idea where this one came from, except that he'd had it longer than he could remember. The thing that fascinated him about it, apart from the story of Pip, the young orphan boy, was what was written in the flyleaf.

Miracle Boy has been saved for something special. And the communication I have got to make is that he has great expectations.
A Well-wisher

Raymond had read the inscription enough times to know that the second sentence was a quotation from the book. He had no idea what the first sentence, or the name Miracle Boy, meant, though. But that was what Nurse Goode had called him. He was mulling this over for the umpteenth time when he had a visitor, Mrs Noble, his Pictorial Auntie, a term coined by a Sunday newspaper for people who were persuaded to visit 'forgotten' children in care. She'd been visiting him for almost a year and often brought books for him to add to his prized collection.

Mrs Noble always dressed like a lady, but on this day she was especially resplendent in a lilac ensemble and broad-brimmed purple hat, with a spectacular spray brooch of silver and amethyst pinned near her left shoulder. Raymond could never work out whether her hair was silver and reflected the colour she was wearing, or subtly dyed to match her outfits. She began talking while placing a large basket of fruit on the bedside cabinet, before easing herself onto a chair by the bedside.

'I went to visit you at Hillcrest and found out you were here, Raymond,' she said. 'What a shock. I always thought something was wrong there. The children never looked happy and your house-mother always seemed shifty to me, like she was covering something up. As for her husband, well, I never liked him. He seemed stiff and cruel. I should have realised something was seriously wrong, but it's too late now. I can't bear to think that that poor little boy was driven to take his own life in that way. He was a mere child and he was your friend. I am so sorry, Raymond.'

She blew her powdered nose on a crisp white handkerchief and looked at Raymond with moist eyes. He liked her and sympathised with her genuine distress. In front of others she played the lady of the manor, but he knew from their trips out together that her airs and graces were soon put aside to reveal a warm heart and a surprisingly plain way of speaking. He smiled to show that he was coping well.

'You're a good boy, Raymond,' she said, placing her handkerchief in her broad lavender lap. 'I don't understand how people like that get into such positions. How could he beat you so badly? It's criminal. Anyway, you do know that he and his wife will not be there when you get back, don't you?'

'I know about Uncle Richard,' Raymond admitted. 'The policeman told me.'

Mrs Noble looked shocked. She'd clearly believed the news of Uncle Richard's death was best left for another time.

'It's time to put these things behind you,' she said, regaining her composure. 'What's done is done. You must now look forward. You'll be going back to Hillcrest where your friends are when you're better. In fact, one of the boys there, the one with the birthmark on the side of his face, gave me a note for you.' She lifted her shiny purple handbag from the floor at the side of the chair and rummaged inside. 'Here it is,' she said, handing him a folded page torn from an exercise book.

Raymond opened the note and read its brief contents.

This is just quick wile that lady is here. We hope you lads are all right. Me and Alan have been wurid sick. We have got new people here. Something has happened to Uncle Richerd but we don't know what. Police have been here loads.
Strawberry Paul and Itchy Alan

He couldn't help his smile and, seeing it, Mrs Noble brightened and said, 'He's a nice boy. He's got a brother, hasn't he?'

'Yes,' Raymond confirmed. 'His brother Alan is the boy who wears gloves all the time to stop him picking at his eczema scabs. They were at Hillcrest even before me.'

'I thought so,' Mrs Noble said. 'There was also a girl with big blue eyes and blonde frizzy hair who asked about you, but, of course, I couldn't tell her anything until I'd seen you. How are you feeling, Raymond?'

'I'm feeling a lot better,' Raymond assured her, while thinking about Shirley, the girl he'd known the longest at Hillcrest. She was a year older than him and often teased him about his ignorance of the mysterious world of girls. She was right about him. He was a reader, dreamer, name-shifter and word-shaper and he'd often imagined himself valiant in battle against the evil Hardric of Chillrest. The way things were now, he'd had enough of being a hero.

'You've got friends waiting for you,' Mrs Noble said, 'and new house-parents. They seemed like a nice couple when I spoke to them. You've got something to look forward to.'

Raymond never imagined he would look forward to going back to Hillcrest, but he now realised that he was. A children's home wasn't so bad, if you were used to it, and he'd known nothing else. Besides, his friends were there and there would be no Uncle Richard to rule them with a rod of iron.

His Pictorial Auntie gave him a rare fleeting gift of one of her most tender smiles, before turning her attention to her handbag and reaching inside.

'Now, Raymond, let's talk about something else. I've brought you a book. It's *A Kind of Loving* by Stan Barstow. I've really enjoyed it and I think it will appeal to you.'

For the rest of her visit she made no further reference to Raymond's troubled past and present. She left him with the touch of a dry hand, the lingering scent of lavender, the basket of fruit, his new book and a ray of optimism.

*

Two days later, during a terrible thunderstorm, Raymond watched the sky through the window turn almost green before a barrage of hailstones, followed by heavy rain, battered the glass. It was almost as if nature's orchestra was heralding the stranger who entered the room. The person, who dropped his umbrella in the corner of the room and sloughed off his dark raincoat, was a sharp-featured man with ginger hair in a crew-cut style. His grey suit was smart and his black shoes were highly polished. As Raymond watched, puzzled, he pulled a chair up to the bed, like a dancer sweeping his partner across the floor, and sat down, making sure that his trouser creases were in perfect alignment before he looked at Raymond with his peculiar green eyes.

'Raymond,' he said, 'it's good to meet you. You and your friend have been the talk of the office. My name is Mr Leather and I'm from the Welfare Department. I bring

12

good news. You must be nervous about going back to Hillcrest after all that's happened. Well, you're not going back.'

Raymond couldn't take in what he heard from the ginger stranger with the odd eyes and flinched as a peal of thunder boomed outside and the window rattled.

'Hard to take in, eh?' the man said, acting delighted to be the bearer of such good news. 'Believe it or not, there's more. We've found you a foster home. It wasn't easy at such short notice, but we've managed to find the perfect placing for you. It was a combination of hard work and good luck. The family is called Marsden and she's a schoolteacher. They have three children of their own: two young girls, and one boy a year older than you.'

Raymond gaped in horror, as a flash of lightning lit up the room, making the harbinger of his fate look like the Joker in one of the Batman films he'd seen at the Saturday matinee at the local cinema. He wanted to close his eyes. He wanted to be unconscious again. Wind the clock back. Let him wake up again. Let it be Brian staring at him.

'I thought you'd be pleased,' Mr Leather said. 'I can understand you being shocked. You must have been dreading going back there after all that's happened. Best for all concerned if you ask me. There are just a couple of other details. Your new home is in Huddlesford and because of that you'll be going to a new school.'

It seemed like the end of the world had arrived. For the next few minutes nurses and porters ran up and down, past the open door, as the hospital seemed to be engulfed by flame and fury. Cries and screams echoed down the corridor. An almighty crash shook the building to its core. Then immediately afterwards, the sun came out and pierced the room like a flaming sword. Shocked and incredulous at the cataclysm, Raymond was amazed to see Mr Leather wearing a serene smile.

'Now that was interesting,' Mr Leather said. 'Where were

we? Ah, yes, Huddlesford. Not too far from here. Another town, but it'll be more than worth it. Here's the best news yet.' He paused and glanced at Raymond, who imagined he must look like a shell-shocked escapee from the trenches of the First World War. His ginger nemesis didn't seem to see him like that.

'Are you ready for this?' Mr Leather crooned, straightening the collar of his suit. 'This is the best news of all. You'll be going to Slevin Grammar School. You've done well at Ramsden College, but Slevin is one of the best schools in West Yorkshire. Only the top pupils go there. It's a boys-only grammar and its reputation is second to none. It's a real privilege, but everybody says you're more than clever enough to excel. The best thing of all, though, is that Roger, the Marsdens' son, also goes to Slevin.'

Mr Leather pushed his chair back and scrutinised the knife-edged creases of his trousers. If he was expecting a response from Raymond he would be disappointed. Raymond had lost the power of speech. He had, from time to time, imagined a moment like this and the elation he would feel, followed by the thrill of gathering his possessions together, before walking through the door into the world without looking back. Yet here he was, lying on his back in a hospital bed, having just been told that he would never be going back to the life he'd always known. Not now, please. Please.

'Are you all right, lad?' he heard Mr Leather ask. 'You've gone really pale. Let me get you some water.'

He poured Raymond a glass of water from a pitcher on the bedside cabinet and Raymond took it with gratitude and pressed it to his lips. Glancing at the window, where raindrops now sparkled in the sunlight, Mr Leather suddenly seemed eager to conclude his duty. He withdrew a sheet of paper from his jacket pocket and unfolded it before handing it to Raymond.

'I should make a break for it while the weather's good. This is a list of all your things. It should have everything. Have a look and make sure nothing's missing. All your books are there. Everything will be packed up and transferred to the Marsdens' house for you, so they'll be there when you arrive.'

Raymond looked at the list, which was laid out in meticulous handwriting. He knew that nothing in that meagre catalogue was going to help him step into the unknown, but he wouldn't want to be without his books.

'That's all right,' he said, almost gurgling into his glass of water.

'Well, that's it, then, Raymond,' Mr Leather said. 'I'm certain this move is going to be good for you. You'll be able to put things behind you. I'm sure you'll do well at Slevin Grammar School. Goodbye.'

He threw his raincoat over his arm and retrieved his umbrella, before rushing out of the room, leaving Raymond floundering in a sea of emotions.

Raymond lay back on his pillow and watched the dust specks dancing like fairies in the startling sunbeams streaming through the room. Had there really been a violent storm and a strange man with dramatic news? In the breathless calm, a nurse passed along the corridor singing Cliff Richard's latest hit, 'Travelling Light', softly to herself.

Of course it had happened. *He* was travelling light, to another town, another school and another home. Not just another *Home*, but a home with a family. The boy who didn't know who he was would be a stranger to everyone he was about to meet. This time there would be no Brian to help him through what lay ahead. He was on his own.

*

In the twilight hours, when the ward went quiet and the voices of patients and nurses seemed to melt away, Nurse

Goode often popped in to chat to Raymond. On the eve of his departure she came into his room with a beaming smile on her face.

'At last, Raymond, you're going home,' she exclaimed. 'I'm so pleased for you. You're all mended. This time next week you'll be playing football and climbing trees as if nothing had happened. Just don't come back here too soon, mind.' She stopped in her tracks and stared at him in surprise. 'Hey, why so sad?' she asked.

He had to tell someone, so he told her everything Mr Leather had told him.

'Never!' she burst out when he'd finished. 'He thought that was good news, did he? How could they? You poor, poor lamb.'

Before he knew it she had enveloped him in her arms and was crushing him to her ample chest.

He never cried, ever, not for anything. She was squeezing him too tight, that's all, and his back was still a bit sore.

The Shrinking House

Raymond read the letter again.

Dear Raymond,

I am sorry I can't come to see you before you leave hospital. The hot weather we're having doesn't seem to suit me and I've not been well. I'm so excited for you. The Marsdens sound like a good family and the fact that their son goes to the same school you'll be going to is perfect. I'm sure everything is going to work out well. All you have to do is be yourself and you'll be fine.

I became your Pictorial Auntie because the newspaper said that forgotten children needed someone to visit them. I'm glad I found you. I have so much enjoyed my visits and the trips we've taken together. The thing is, Raymond, you're not a forgotten child anymore. Now you have a family! Because of that I won't be coming to see you anymore. You need to concentrate on your new life and it wouldn't be right for me to interfere. I'll be thinking of you though and hoping everything turns out well, which I'm sure it will.

I think I'll retire from being a Pictorial Auntie now. I don't think I'll find another boy like you.

Good luck Raymond,
Mrs Noble

Crumpling the last link with his past in his hand and stuffing it into his jacket pocket, Raymond looked at the

17

back of Mr Pickup's grizzled head. He'd seen the dark-suited corporation driver, who had the bearing of a military man, many times before when he transported new inmates and leavers to and from Hillcrest, and had always wondered what it would be like to be ferried around in his immaculate Austin Princess. Now he knew.

The ten mile journey from Barfield to Huddlesford under scudding clouds was unfamiliar, but somehow Raymond sensed that they were nearing their destination when they turned into a long road, flanked on either side by new semi-detached dormer bungalows. The road sign proclaimed it as Coupland Road.

The gossamer wings of the butterflies in Raymond's stomach turned into pounding drumsticks as the car pulled up outside a neat bungalow, which seemed to be more roof than house, and he saw a stout woman wearing a fluttering floral pinafore standing on the doorstep.

It was a picture of suburban bliss, the like of which he'd gazed at many times before with envy. Vibrant rose bushes flanked the path to the front door and clean white lace curtains framed the windows. The red door stood ajar in welcome to the stranger. Mrs Marsden – it must be her because no one could look more like a schoolteacher – was the centrepiece of this idyll and she smiled and waved as Mr Pickup got out of the car and opened Raymond's door.

'Raymond, come in, come in,' she cried out as he followed Mr Pickup down the garden path.

The driver nodded at Mrs Marsden and said, 'He's all yours,' before turning to go.

'He's a man of mystery,' she mused, watching as the laconic driver climbed into his car and glided away. 'Still, here you are, Raymond. Welcome to your new home.'

Two young girls dressed in plain pastel cotton frocks and white knee-length socks appeared in the doorway and stared at him.

'Come on now, girls,' Mrs Marsden said. 'Stand aside and give Raymond room.'

His foster-mother guided him into a small vestibule, where he took in his first impression of the interior of an ordinary family home. The hall and stairs were covered from wall to wall in a dark-red carpet, with a pattern of even darker whorls like clotted blood; the walls and woodwork were soft matt cream. He was sure he could detect the aroma of a freshly baked sponge cake behind the more prominent odour of furniture polish and, if so, it smelled good. This was far removed from the world of echoing corridors, cold linoleum and pallid gloss paint that Raymond was used to.

He flinched as Mrs Marsden clapped her hands, as if she was announcing the beginning of a lesson. 'Right,' she chimed. 'Introductions.' She indicated the oldest girl, who was dark-haired, plump and wore spectacles. 'This is Janet, my eldest daughter. She's eleven.'

Janet blinked like an owl and gave Raymond a shy smile.

'This,' she said, touching the other girl's shoulder, 'is Mary. She's nine.'

'Hello,' the girl said, fluttering her fine lashes.

'Hello,' Raymond replied and had to stop himself from staring. Surely this pretty, fair-haired girl came from different stock. The owl looked like her mother, but the princess must have been left on the doorstep as a baby by a stork.

'We'll show you your bedroom first, Raymond,' Mrs Marsden informed him. 'Come on girls, lead the way.'

The girls scampered up the flight of stairs in front of them and Raymond followed, while Mrs Marsden brought up the rear. At the same time, she explained to Raymond that Roger, her son, was out with friends and Mr Marsden was at work, but both would be back by teatime. Raymond heard her, but his mind was on the marvel of carpet-cushioned stairs. Maybe the stairs in children's homes were uncarpeted so the staff could hear who was moving about.

They crowded into a bedroom with a sloping ceiling, where the light from a dormer window spilled onto its crowded contents. There were two single beds; one between shelves overflowing with piles of board games and magazines in the main part of the room; the other under the window.

'This is the room you'll be sharing with Roger,' Mrs Marsden said. 'Your bed is the one by the window. I've already put your clothes away in the wardrobe and in the bottom two drawers of the chest here by the wall. I've put the suitcase with your books in under your bed for the time being, so you can sort them out for yourself later. I must say, you've got some very sophisticated reading there, Raymond.'

Raymond looked around, conscious that the two girls were watching his reaction. He tried to look as if this was what he was used to, although he was thinking about how confined it was compared to the dormitories he'd always slept in.

'Right,' Mrs Marsden said, 'let's show you round the rest of the house and then we'll have a cup of tea.'

Raymond followed as they trooped around the various upstairs rooms like tourists visiting a stately home, although it could only have been in Lilliput. As well as Roger's bedroom, there was the girls' bedroom and a combined bathroom and toilet. The floor was in the roof space, so the rooms were all strange shapes. As they toured the living room, dining room and kitchen on the ground floor, he kept thinking about how odd it all seemed. He'd always imagined that houses were designed by first deciding how many rooms of what size were required, not by building an odd-shaped house and then trying to cram as many rooms into it as possible.

The only room they didn't go in on the ground floor was

Mr and Mrs Marsden's bedroom. There'd be no reason for him ever to go in there.

Later, as he was sitting at the dining table with the two girls, while their mother made tea in the kitchen at the other side of an open serving hatch, the thought that it was impossible to be more than a few feet away from another person in this house preyed on his mind. He was used to space. Would he be able to cope? However, the worry wasn't allowed to take root because the two girls began to ply him with questions: Was he happy? How did it feel to have a new home? Was his suitcase really full of books and had he read them all?

Raymond tried to give positive answers to the barrage of personal questions, but the smile on his face began to feel frozen. It was a relief when Mrs Marsden poked her head through the serving hatch and intervened.

'Now then girls,' she said. 'Give Raymond some breathing space. He's only just got here.'

She joined them at the table with a tray of tea and sponge cake and, while he sipped and nibbled, she extended her welcome.

'This is your home now, Raymond,' she said. 'Feel free to go where you please. There's no need to ask.'

'You've got to knock before you come into our bedroom, though,' Janet said, looking solemn and blinking behind her spectacles.

Raymond had never entered a girls' bedroom in his life and had no intention of starting, but he nodded his assent. Nodding and smiling became automatic responses to everything, but, eventually, as the afternoon wore on in the company of the tactful Mrs Marsden and her talkative daughters, he began to relax.

He was playing cards with Janet and Mary, while Mrs Marsden prepared the tea, when Mr Marsden returned from work through the back door leading into the kitchen.

'Is the lad here yet?' he asked his wife in a loud voice.

'He's in the dining room with the girls,' Mrs Marsden replied.

He came straight through. In a tight-fitting, greasy, blue boiler suit and oily, slicked-back, black hair he looked like a stoker on a steam train; his glowing face bore the marks from where he'd wiped his brow with an oily hand. The odour of machine oil and stale sweat emanating from him made an unpleasant combination that almost overwhelmed Raymond's senses, but he did his best to look amiable.

'Hey up, lad?' Mr Marsden boomed. 'Settling in all right? Don't let me stop you playing your game. I'm off to get cleaned up and changed before tea. It's mucky work in engineering. If you and Roger play your cards right you'll go to work in smart suits.'

Raymond was left staring at the wall, as he heard the thump of his foster-father's work boots on the stairs. Before he could turn back to his cards, he heard the back door open again and the sound of what was obviously Roger's voice as he greeted his mother. Raymond felt a tremor of nervous anticipation as Mrs Marsden whispered something to her son. His new foster-brother was the one he needed to get on with most.

He managed a diffident smile as Roger, a much cleaner and better looking version of his father, entered the dining room, but all he got back was a curt nod. Raymond felt the smile slip from his face like the sloppy fried eggs used to slide off the plate at Hillcrest and he looked down at his playing cards, feeling foolish.

'Are you going to play cards with us, Roger?' Mary trilled. 'We're playing Twizzle and I'm winning.'

'Naw,' Roger replied, working his thumbnail on the edge of his teeth. 'I've got some things to do before tea.'

Like his father before him, he turned on his heel and left the room. Roger's mother called out to her son, but he either didn't hear her or he ignored her as his steps receded upstairs.

*

During tea, Raymond felt ill at ease with all the talking going on around him. It was the sort of homely meal he'd often dreamt of, but the delicious meat pie stuck in his throat, even though the pastry melted in his mouth. He tried his best to be natural, but he didn't know what to say, in case he said the wrong thing, and he didn't know when to laugh or smile, in case it was out of place.

After tea, Roger went straight up to his room. By force of habit, Raymond began to clear the plates and cutlery from the table, but Mrs Marsden put a hand on his to stop him. Her skin was as rough as sandpaper.

'Don't worry about the dishes, Raymond,' she said. 'Go up to your bedroom and spend some time with Roger while you sort your books out.'

Raymond crept up the cushioned stairs without a sound and entered the bedroom. Roger was sitting on his bed, but as soon as he saw Raymond he threw himself back and lay on his side with his legs crossed and his head propped on one fist. His cheerless face looked as though it had been held close to a fire.

'You do know this is my room,' he said when Raymond opened up his suitcase on his bed. 'There's no room for that lot in here. You'll have to keep that stuff under your bed. I know where all my things are so don't touch owt without asking.'

Raymond's bed suddenly looked like an afterthought, wedged in the shadow under the angle of the lowest part of the ceiling and wall. He began to stuff his books under the bed, catching a disdainful look on Roger's face when he glanced behind him. Roger made an odd, disapproving sound, swung his legs off the bed, and left the room.

Raymond didn't know what to do. Should he follow him?

23

He sat on his bed and waited; for what he wasn't sure. He could hear talking downstairs and began to feel panic rise within him. He couldn't just stroll around somebody else's house, could he? He imagined himself going downstairs on his own and felt the sweat prickle under his shirt collar. What were you supposed to say if you walked into a room in a family home? Maybe you didn't have to say anything. What did they think he was doing? Did they think he was avoiding them?

The light was beginning to fade and he was wringing his hands when he heard a soft footfall on the stairs. He stiffened and waited.

Grey-haired Mrs Marsden poked her bespectacled face around the door.

'Raymond, what are you doing up here?' she asked in a soothing voice. 'You don't have to wait for permission to come down. This is your home now.' She sat on the bed beside him. 'In fact, now we're alone I wanted to say something to you. You don't have to rush, but when you're ready it would be nice if you called us Mum and Dad.'

Raymond's smile flickered like a dying candle, but he did his best to keep it alight. She seemed as awkward as he felt and she stood up and began to plump his pillows before saying, 'Come on. We're about to have some supper.'

He followed her downstairs for a supper of cocoa and muffins with the family, speaking only when spoken to. Afterwards, he waited until Roger was in the bathroom before changing into his pyjamas and slipping into bed. He suffered no pain now, but there were still marks on his body he didn't want others to see. When Roger came into the room he stopped and looked at Raymond lying in the shadow beneath the low ceiling, as if he was viewing a corpse in a coffin. He made no attempt to hide his look of distaste, before climbing into bed to read a magazine by the light of a bedside lamp.

Raymond closed his eyes and berated himself for not knowing how to behave in these unfamiliar surroundings. He'd kept telling himself to act natural, but somehow he'd done the complete opposite. His limbs felt stiff and his voice sounded odd when he tried to speak, so he'd fallen back on what had always been instilled into him: be polite and speak only when spoken to.

After a while, Roger switched off the lamp and plunged the room into near darkness. Raymond was lying on his back and staring at the box of pale light painted on the ceiling by the moon, when a disembodied voice floated out from the dark interior of the room.

'Who are you?'

'Raymond.'

'I know that,' Roger scoffed. 'Haven't you got a family?'

'No.'

'That's rubbish. Everybody's got a mum and dad – biological fact.'

Raymond didn't know what to say and remained silent.

'I heard me mum talking to me dad,' the taunting voice said. 'You got sent here because you were involved in some trouble and someone died. She also said you were a miracle. Well, you must be if you got here without a mum and dad.'

Raymond clung to silence and silence won the night.

*

Over the next few days Raymond was so well-mannered that even he found it excruciating. Mealtimes were the worst. He always waited until everyone else started eating and then ate furtively, as if to be seen chewing and swallowing was a hanging offence. He was always the last to finish and didn't speak unless he was spoken to. Mrs Marsden was always encouraging, but when Mr Marsden was at home in the evening, Raymond was intimidated by his foster-father's bluntness. His advice was uncluttered and to the point:

'Relax lad, nobody's going bite you.'

'Speak up, lad, if you've got summat to say.'

'Don't wait to be told, lad, just help yourself.'

Raymond didn't know how long it would take for him to feel at home, but he couldn't imagine helping himself to anything he wanted. It was impossible to get away from the lifelong notion that helping yourself was stealing.

Somehow, routine, which he'd always resented, became a compulsion. He kept his belongings neat and tidy and his bed was a pristine pallet with precise boxed corners when he wasn't in it. He scrubbed his face each morning until his cheeks glowed and brushed his teeth like a soldier polishing his boots before going on parade. He latched onto every chore he could find like a drowning man clinging to flotsam. He couldn't usurp Mrs Marsden's place at the kitchen sink, which was her domain, so instead he picked up the tea towel to dry the dishes she washed. The first time he did it she said he didn't have to, but then, with a resigned smile, she gave in.

Roger was unimpressed.

'What are you trying to do?' he asked Raymond one night in their bedroom. 'Are you trying to make me look bad? Your stuff's always tidy and you're always helping out in the kitchen. Me mum does all that and if anybody helps her it's the girls. You're not a girl, are you?' Without waiting for an answer, Roger broke wind with unrestrained force and accompanied it with a derisory chuckle.

Raymond rolled over in bed to face the wall.

Why was Roger treating him like this? It wasn't Raymond's fault he'd been sent there. He wasn't there to steal Roger's place. He didn't *ask* Mrs Marsden to make a fuss of him and there was no way he was going to call her *mum*. In fact, he'd made a point of not addressing Mr and

Mrs Marsden by any name at all, which was a lot easier if he didn't speak until he was spoken to.

A gloomy dormitory, full of boys who dreamed the same dreams as he did, was better than this.

*

The start of the new school term was only days away when Mrs Marsden asked Raymond to come into the front room for a chat. Roger was out with his father, who was in the Territorial Army, at some military event and Raymond was drawing pictures in the dining room with serious Janet and twittering Mary. He followed Mrs Marsden into the front room and, at her invitation, sat down in an armchair, while she sat on the settee.

It was the kind of chintz and mahogany room in which Raymond always imagined families spending their time. Over the fireplace, an olive-skinned woman with a long, swan-like neck seemed to stare at Raymond with melancholy brown eyes from a framed picture. He wondered what his foster-mother wanted to talk about. He hadn't adapted very well to their family life so far and he was nervous about what she was about to say.

'I wanted to talk to you about school,' Mrs Marsden said, leaning forward with her hands clasped in her lap. Her eyes seemed to search his face from behind the thick lens of her tortoiseshell spectacles. 'You'll be going to school in a few days and there's something you need to know.' She paused and swallowed. 'Although Roger's a year older than you, he'll be in the third year with you when he goes back to Slevin.'

Raymond couldn't comprehend what she was saying. Had Roger been a late starter?

'It's not his fault,' Mrs Marsden said, 'but he's not happy about it. Last year he had glandular fever and he was off school for weeks. He was very ill and missed most of the first term. He tried to catch up when he got back, but he was too far behind, so he's going to have to do the year again. He's very sensitive about it, so I want you to give him all your support. Do you think you can do that for me?'

'Yes, of course I will,' Raymond said.

This was a seed of hope. In Raymond's world the name of the bridge on which friendships were formed was 'Misfortune'.

'Good,' she said, smiling. 'He's going to need a friend. It's not an easy thing to have to do. Boys can be cruel sometimes and make fun. If it wasn't for his illness, he wouldn't be in this situation. In fact, he's only just getting his full strength back.'

That night, Raymond was already in bed when Roger came into the room. He looked at Roger with compassion, but then noticed his foster-brother looked angry. With his broad, flushed face and his shiny black hair brushed back, he looked like Elvis Presley after he'd been stung by a wasp.

'I know me mum's told you about school,' Roger spluttered. 'It's not my fault. If you think that puts you on a par with me, then forget it. You're not me brother and I don't need any help from you. Me mum's full of soft ideas. I bloody hate it.'

Raymond wasn't offended. Disaffected children with hurt feelings and battered pride had been his brothers and sisters all his life.

'I don't want to interfere, Roger,' Raymond said. 'It's not your fault you were ill, but we'll be going to school together, so we might as well be friends.'

'Get lost!' Roger snarled.

*

The first day of school arrived. Everybody in the household rushed around with such urgency that Raymond felt he was getting in their way. Mr Marsden left for work early, but everyone else was preparing for school, including Mrs Marsden, who taught at the school Mary attended. Raymond waited until last to use the bathroom. When he came down in the school uniform he'd been supplied with, Mrs Marsden, who was fussing in the kitchen while her children were eating breakfast, glanced through the serving hatch at him and said, 'Very smart.'

He was sure Roger pulled a face, but as the older boy had a spoonful of cornflakes raised to his mouth, he could have been mistaken.

Raymond left early with Roger because they had two buses to catch. Fanned by a light breeze, it felt good walking side by side down Coupland Road wearing the same uniform. Surely they'd be mates, if not brothers, in school?

As soon as they were out of sight of the house, Roger stopped and turned to face him. Raymond looked into his brooding face with hopeful expectancy. Roger returned his look with one of total disdain.

'I don't care what me mum says, but when we're outside the house you don't exist,' he said with a sneer. 'You don't talk to me or come near me. You're not *my* brother and I'm not yours. If you say owt, me dad'll have you back in a children's home before you can say Jack Robinson.'

Raymond stood transfixed, as Roger hitched his satchel over his shoulder, wheeled round, and marched off down the road. The ground beneath Raymond seemed to sway. It was only with difficulty that he persuaded his feet to move and follow the receding figure of Roger to the bus stop.

By the time he got there, the bus had arrived and Roger was on it, looking pious and staring straight ahead. Raymond clambered onto the bus and sat down in a seat some way behind him. His throat hurt, as rows of houses flew by; houses he'd always imagined were filled with happy families. He was in a trap. How could he tell Roger's mother or father? He didn't tell tales and, besides, he didn't want to come between Roger and his parents.

He could understand Roger protecting his rights in his home, but out here they were supposed to be equals. He swallowed hard, as if trying to force down a fishbone. His foster-brother's spiteful rejection felt as bitter as spurned and unrequited love.

Snivel

Huddlesford town centre, bustling with workers scuttling between tall grey buildings under a patchwork sky, reminded Raymond of a painting of an industrial town by L.S. Lowry he'd once seen on a day out with Mrs Noble. Roger had abandoned him, but he found his way to the bus station, where he saw that his stop was crowded with jostling Slevin Grammar School boys. Young lads in school caps and stiff blazers, who were clearly new boys, huddled together, while all around them older pupils milled around, calling to each other and clapping each other on the back like long-lost friends.

Raymond stood at the back of the queue and scanned the throng in vain for Roger, until two double-decker buses pulled into the stop. They were motor buses and they growled impatiently, unlike their docile counterparts, the electric trolley buses that were used in Barfield. Raymond held back while the older boys piled forward, elbowing their way past the timorous new flock. When the majority had boarded, he climbed onto the second bus and found a seat upstairs, in the thick of a group of noisy Slevinites. He glanced at the boy sitting next to him, who with his pinched face and diminutive features reminded him of Squeaky Dave, and, with a lurch, the bus pulled away from the stop.

The conductor appeared at the top of the stairs and swayed his way to the front, where Raymond saw Roger in animated conversation with another boy. A small tremor of uncertainty descended on Raymond as he juggled his bus fare in his pocket, while the conductor worked his way towards them.

Snapping tickets out of his machine and ignoring the smart remarks of the boys whose fares he took, the conductor was almost upon him and Raymond started to sweat. When his turn came, Raymond kept his fist clenched as long as possible, before dropping his fare into the palm of the conductor's large hand and looking into his face with a silent plea. The conductor, a burly man in his thirties with long dark sideburns, peered into his hand; his look of irritation brightened and his eyes gleamed.

'Hey up,' he crowed, 'welfare tokens, eh?'

He held a bright yellow plastic token up to the light from the window, before placing it between his teeth and biting on it as if he was testing a gold coin. He had the attention of everybody on the bus and was enjoying his charade, until he caught Raymond's crestfallen look and turned tack.

'S'all right, lad,' he mumbled, punching out a ticket. 'Next.' But the conductor's about-turn was too late to save Raymond.

'He can't be trusted with proper money,' someone shouted, which was received with a general round of raucous laughter.

Raymond felt his cheeks burn, especially when he saw Roger laughing louder than anyone else. It never occurred to him that morning when Mrs Marsden handed him the tokens that this would be the outcome. She'd told him that they'd been given to them by the Welfare Department for him to use, but if he wanted, he could have money. He'd assured her that it was no problem as he'd used them often, but he'd never had this reaction before.

'Leave him be, you lot,' the boy next to him called out and the din subsided. 'Take no notice,' the lad said to him. 'They're a right stuck-up bunch. You must be new. My name's Graham Rich, but everybody calls me Titch, for obvious reasons.'

'I'm starting in the third year,' Raymond said, grateful for an ally of any stature. 'I went to Ramsden College in Barfield before.'

A boy behind them must have been eavesdropping because he cried out, 'Hey up, we've got a Ramsdenite amongst us.'

The roar of derision went up again.

'Ignore them,' Titch said. 'They're all snobs. I don't care where you went to. I am in the third year too. What's your name?'

'Raymond Rawnsley,' Raymond said, trying to shut out the cacophony.

'You'll be in my class, then,' Titch said. 'Three Alpha. Three A is for the lads with surnames in the first half of the alphabet and ours is for the second half. In fact, with your name you should be sitting in front of me.'

Raymond chatted with Titch until the bus finally stopped in the village of Slevin and everyone piled off. After Roger's spiteful snub it was a relief to have found someone amiable to talk to. They followed the herd past quaint shops and cottages and descended a steep, winding road under overhanging trees, while around them older boys advertised their superiority by knocking the caps off the heads of new boys.

'They'll keep that up for a while until the novelty wears off,' Titch said. 'Caps are only compulsory for first-year boys, which makes them a target for a while. You'll soon find out first-years are treated like scum of the earth.'

Slevin Grammar School stood on the lower slope of a picturesque valley. Surrounded by towering oaks, the ivy-covered buildings looked majestic. Raymond could see why Slevin boys, who his new friend seemed to have no time for, had delusions of grandeur. It made him think of *Tom Brown's Schooldays*.

A tall, gaunt man cloaked in a black gown and an air of self-importance stood outside the entrance and ordered all new boys to wait to one side in the yard while the other students entered the building.

'Is Rawnsley here yet?' the master called out in a voice whose authority was undermined by a nasal whine.

Titch nudged him and Raymond stepped forward.

'Good,' the master said. '*You* will need to join the new boys for induction.'

Raymond waited with the nervous pack until they were ordered to follow the master into the cool and gloomy interior, along wood-panelled corridors and into a large gymnasium. Raymond stood at the edge of the group. Facing them, the master began their induction.

'My name is Mr Hanson,' he announced, 'and I am the deputy headmaster. Welcome to your first day at Slevin Grammar School; the first day of the most important part of your educational lives. Today you will be divided into classes and receive your timetables for the term ahead. You will also be shown around the school by your form master. You will adopt a quiet and dignified manner during these proceedings, as you will be expected to do throughout your time here. We do not want other pupils, who will be going about their studies diligently, to be disturbed by a gaggle of geese.'

While he was speaking, Raymond watched three other men in black gowns and mortars file in like silent priests.

'I would now like to introduce Mr Thompson, the head-master,' Mr Hanson said, stepping aside to let one of the other men take his place.

This man was clearly used to having the complete attention of his audience. He was an ancient, hulking scholar in a voluminous gown, with a craggy face that wouldn't have looked out of place carved into the weathered stone above the entrance to the school. The black mortar perched on top of his head was slightly askew, which somehow suggested to Raymond that he wasn't a practising master. He folded his large hands inside his black gown and addressed them. When he spoke, his voice was as deep and rich as that of a Shakespearean actor.

'You boys are amongst the privileged few,' he intoned.

Raymond listened, while at the same time his eyes took in the climbing bars on the walls and ropes tied up to keep them out of the way. He had a reason to dislike ropes and turned his attention back to the speaker.

'Slevin Grammar has been in existence for over three hundred years,' the headmaster continued, 'during which time generations of young pupils like you have stepped through these ancient portals and gazed around in awe, just like some of you now.'

Some boys were indeed gazing around and, as the headmaster's all-knowing eyes swept over them, they lowered their heads. Raymond, however, was used to being preached to; he stared straight ahead and let the headmaster's words wash over him. For the next few minutes, only certain words like 'centuries', 'tradition', 'academic', 'excellence', 'credo', 'dignity', 'decorum' and 'privilege' filtered through to his subconscious. He normally feasted on words, but was on the verge of giving in to the epidemic of feet shuffling. When the headmaster finished his speech, he took a final sweeping look at his timorous new flock, folded his gown around him and glided out of the hall.

'Rawnsley,' Mr Hanson called out, 'you come with me.'

*

Raymond sat at his desk in Three Alpha's dingy form room. Sure enough, his new friend, Titch, occupied the desk behind him, which was comforting, as was the realisation that Roger was in class Three A. Ignoring the stares of the boys around him, he studied his desktop, which was engraved with names, dates and initials testifying to its many previous owners, and tried to decide where he would leave his own mark when he got the chance. He didn't look up until the form master, Mr Dyson, a stoop-shouldered old man with wild white hair and half-moon spectacles on the end of his nose, began the register and boys went forward to pay their dinner money for the week.

'Raymond Rawnsley,' Mr Dyson called out when Raymond's turn came.

'Yes, sir,' Raymond replied, just loud enough to be heard.

The master looked at him over his spectacles and said, 'You, of course, do not have to pay dinner money. That is taken care of by the Welfare Department.'

Raymond's felt his cheeks burn for the second time that day as all eyes turned on him. At the same time, his heart sank as he realised that this ritual would be repeated every Monday morning.

The rest of the morning was straightforward and familiar to Raymond. Ramsden College might not have been so grand, but it had a similar curriculum.

After a bland school dinner, which had been pre-cooked elsewhere and delivered to the school that morning, Raymond was swapping first impressions with Titch in the yard, when a slight commotion broke out; a small delegation of older boys led by a tall young man was heading their way.

'They're sixth-formers and that's Symonds, the head boy,' Titch whispered. 'Watch out for him. He's a snake.'

'Which one of you is Rawnsley?' Symonds called out.

Raymond stepped forward, while the head boy, slim and imperious, looked down on him with a benign smile.

'Look, Rawnsley,' he said. 'It is not your fault you've come from a much lesser school. Even so, I still expect you to be given a decent welcome. I have heard about the disgraceful behaviour of the boys on the bus, tormenting you because you have to use plastic coins for bus fares. It's unacceptable and I do not condone it.' He paused for a moment, the midday sun illuminating his fine blond hair, while the sixth-formers stood around him with solemn faces. 'Don't let it upset you,' he continued. 'After all, they're only token gestures.'

His cruel punch-line brought guffaws of laughter from his cronies, while Raymond stood helpless in front of them and seethed with frustration. With a disdainful look, Symonds turned and, surrounded by his cohort, swept across the yard. Titch, standing close by, reached up to put a consoling hand on Raymond's shoulder, but Raymond shrugged him off and glared at those around him who dared to look at him – so much for the Slevin badge of honour.

Slevin? 'Snivel' more like.

*

Raymond felt trapped between prejudice and malice as he sat downstairs on the homeward bus. He already knew he hated the elitism of Slevin Grammar, but he didn't relish going home to the Marsdens' to face his foster-brother's secret animosity either. At least he'd made a friend in Titch and been introduced to his friends in turn, Rollo and Poggy. They called themselves the Legion of the Dis-enchanted; none of them conformed to the regime of bullying and sneering cronyism that was so prevalent at the school, which suited Raymond just fine. He saw Roger climb aboard and glance in his direction before hurrying upstairs.

Raymond made sure that he was the first to disembark when they reached Coupland Road and began to make his way home with a bowed head. His satchel felt as though it was full of heavy stones rather than new textbooks and the strap dug into his shoulder. He could hear Roger's footsteps right behind him, but he didn't look round. Just as he was about to put his hand on the gate at the front of the Marsdens' house, Roger quickened his step and beat him to it. Raymond stood aside, while Roger opened the gate and headed along the side of the house to the back door. Roger entered the kitchen first and adopted a bright and breezy demeanour in front of his mother, who was stirring something in a bowl.

'Hiya, Mum,' Roger called out.

Wiping her hands on her apron, his mother turned around with a concerned look on her face.

'Well, Roger,' she asked, 'how was your first day?'

'It was great,' Roger replied with feigned enthusiasm. 'No problems. I'll soon leave this lot behind.'

He glared at Raymond and disappeared upstairs. When he'd gone, Mrs Marsden gave Raymond a warm smile.

'Thank you for helping Roger through such a difficult day, Raymond,' she said.

Rom

Raymond was like a soldier in a hostile city during his first few weeks at Slevin Grammar. As a new boy, a welfare boy and a former Ramsdenite, he was the target for icy stares, muttered insults and naked antagonism. There were, however, two consolations to relieve his discomfort: he had acquired an acceptable nickname and become an established member of the Legion of the Disenchanted.

His nickname came from a lesson with Mr Dyson, otherwise known as Dimwiddy, when Raymond and Titch were summoned out to the front of the class to act out the story of the legendary founders of the city of Rome. Raymond was Romulus and Titch was Remus. Playing a different part to the one he was forced to live released Raymond from his shackles. At the point in the story where Romulus kills his brother Remus with an axe, Raymond attacked Titch with theatrical ferocity and followed it up with such anguished remorse that even Dimwiddy was delighted. From that day Raymond was Romulus, although as contraction was the norm, it was soon shortened to Rom. If he had to have a nickname, and everybody at Slevin did, this was a name he could build an identity around.

Raymond learned that Titch, Rollo and Poggy all lived in corporation houses and regarded most of the other boys in school as posh. During their time at Slevin they'd banded together in a common cause and decided to stand up for their working class heritage. Their loud greetings when meeting each other at the bus stop in the morning were a deliberate pastiche.

'Hiya, Rom. Is your mother still bricklaying?'

'Yeah. How about you, Rollo? Have they let your dad out yet?'

His new friends' self-parody was a statement to those around them that they couldn't be intimidated and Raymond was happy to join in. He was also sharp-witted enough to be a master at the game, although they didn't appreciate that deriding his non-existent family had no effect on him.

Some of the masters were also beginning to discover that he was a decent scholar. Angus, the beanpole, Scottish, English master, had a reputation as one of the hardest masters in the school, yet Raymond felt an immediate affinity with him. One afternoon, he asked Raymond to stay behind after an English Literature class.

'You interest me, laddie,' Angus said when they were alone. 'The rest can't hold a candle to you. How long have you been reading seriously?'

'Since I was little, sir.'

'I thought so,' Angus said, stroking his pointed chin. 'What do you think of this?'

He held out a book and Raymond took it from him and studied the cover. It was *Erewhon* by Samuel Butler.

'I don't know, sir. I haven't read it,' Raymond admitted.

'I didn't expect you to have, but what do you think of it?'

Raymond looked at the book again. 'It means "Nowhere" sir,' he said.

'Aye, laddie,' Angus said, a smile lighting up his gaunt features. 'It's yours to keep. Welcome to the University of Unreason.'

*

While Rom was finding his feet at Slevin, Raymond was picking his way through a minefield at the Marsdens'. His

40

escape was to linger as long as he could over his homework in the dining room each evening. Roger did his in his bedroom and took far less time, which he laughed off by saying he'd covered the ground in the previous year. In the long, lonely evening hours Raymond pretended to stare at textbooks, while the sound of the television and laughter drifted from the front room. Television had never been part of his life and he didn't yearn for the flickering black and white images he sometimes glimpsed when passing the living room.

The laughter was a different matter.

Only Mrs Marsden, who often went backwards and forwards from the kitchen, showed any interest in what he was doing.

'Everything all right, Raymond?' she often asked. 'What's your homework tonight?'

Raymond would pick a random subject, while covering the novel he was reading with a textbook.

The weekends were symbolised by a freshly ironed Territorial Army cadet uniform laid out on Roger's bed and a Sacred Heart mounted on the dining room wall. Saturday mornings were filled with chores and in the afternoon Roger and his father went to TA meetings. Seeing his foster-brother strutting around the house in his uniform, Raymond began to imagine him as a swaggering member of the Hitler Youth.

While the two toy soldiers fought their imaginary wars, Raymond played games with the two girls, while Mrs Marsden did her weekly baking.

On Sunday mornings, the whole family went to morning mass, except for Raymond. The Marsdens may not have been the most ardent Catholics, but they attended their local church every Sunday. He'd been conscripted to the Church of England at an early age, so he was dispatched to another nearby church. Instead of going to service alone, however, he spent the time sitting in the cleft of trunk and branch at the top of a tree in a nearby wood. He couldn't say why he never made it to church; his feet just refused to take him there. His lofty seat amongst the rustling branches was the loneliest place in the world and yet he was drawn to it. The hour he had to waste pretending to be at the morning service gave him time to reflect on the suffocating circle in which he was trapped.

Mr Marsden favoured his son above his own daughters, never mind him, and Roger used this to his own advantage. The smirks on Roger's face when Mr Marsden made ever-more frequent barbed remarks about his silence only made Raymond clam up more. Good-hearted though she was, Mrs Marsden was a schoolteacher, relying on instruction rather than compassion, while Janet and Mary couldn't help treating him like a rescued bird with a broken wing.

The top of a tree, with the weathered steeple of the church – where he should be singing and praying – poking above the woodland canopy, wasn't such a bad place to be really.

*

One evening, Mr Marsden came home with a pair of boxing gloves for Raymond. While Raymond mumbled his thanks, Mr Marsden explained his reason for the unexpected gift.

'Roger's been boxing for years. Before he started he was a scrawny thing and too quiet by half. He started coming to the TA with me and getting lessons. It taught him how to stand up for himself. He's pretty good now. You can box together in the evening in the hallway. It'll do you more good than sitting with your books in the dining room every night. Roger will teach you.'

He said all this with genuine enthusiasm and a beaming smile on his broad face, as if it was the answer to everything, while Raymond's attention was transfixed by the gleam in Roger's eye. Mr Marsden turned to his son.

'Now then, Roger,' he said, 'go easy on him. You've got to teach him properly, just like you've been taught.'

'Sure, Dad,' Roger said, his too-handsome face a picture of righteousness.

That evening, Raymond was reading *Great Expectations* on his bed. He'd read it many times, but sometimes he picked random passages to browse through or he would just stare at the inscription inside the cover and wonder. Roger entered the bedroom and ripped the book from his hands.

'What's this?' he asked. 'Oh, we did that at school. It's crap. What's all this about? *Miracle Boy has been saved for something special?* Don't tell me you think that's you. What a joke. I'll show you what you've been saved for. Get your PE kit on and your boxing gloves. It's time for your first lesson.'

In shorts, vests and pumps, they boxed in the narrow hallway while the rest of the family watched television in the front room. Raymond knew from the off that Roger intended to use these character-building sessions to legitimately inflict pain on him, the family interloper. Roger could box, but Raymond had been brought up in a dog-eat-dog institutional world and knew how to hold his ground. He could have attacked, but instead he concentrated on defence. He warded off Roger's most vicious blows, but inevitably some got through. When they did, Raymond tried not to flinch and put his head down and his gloves up again.

As the contest was becoming more intense, Mr Marsden came lumbering down the hall on his way to the toilet.

'How's he doing, Roger?' he asked his son. 'Is he learning all right?'

'Oh, yeah,' Roger said, panting. 'He's definitely learning.'

'Smashing,' his father said, heaving himself up the stairs.

Taking advantage of Raymond's distraction, Roger hit him full in the mouth behind his father's back. Raymond's head rocked back and he tasted the salty flavour of blood on his lips. He curbed his instinct to retaliate and raised his gloves in front of his face to take guard.

*

Still under the dull spell of a Latin lesson, Raymond and Titch trudged homewards along the school drive through a carpet of burnished leaves like two weary legionnaires.

'I hope you don't mind me asking, Rom,' Titch ventured. 'Do you live in a children's home?'

'No,' Raymond said.

'I just thought, with those tokens you have to use.'

'I live in a foster home.'

'Well, that's not bad, then,' Titch said.

At that moment, Rollo and Poggy ran past.

'Hey, Rom,' Poggy called out. 'Is your sister still modelling for Hammer Horror films?'

'Of course she is,' Raymond retorted. 'Is your mother still seeing Boris Karloff?'

The two boys ran off laughing.

Without warning, a heavy hand smacked against the back of Raymond's head, while at the same time a voice hissed, 'Shut it, dickhead.'

Raymond snapped. He went for his attacker with such unrestrained fury, arms flailing like demented windmills, that his assailant was beaten into submission before he even knew what hit him. It didn't matter that the other boy was older and bigger. Raymond's wrath knew no bounds and he was frustrated that the other boy capitulated so easily. What he really wanted at that moment was a fight to the death.

With his antagonist beaten and crumpled on the ground, the fire within Raymond died. He turned away, joined a dumfounded Titch and proceeded up the hill to the village. None of the older boy's friends followed him or tried to take issue with him.

Throughout his journey home Raymond walked in this

world but marched through another. If anyone spoke to him, he didn't hear them. He didn't even bother to conceal his plastic tokens on the bus and looked around to challenge anyone to make a smart remark, but no one drew attention to it.

*

Raymond wasn't surprised to find himself in the narrow corridor outside the headmaster's study on the morning after the one-sided fight. He waited, nerveless, until bespectacled Miss Senior, the school secretary, stuck her prim head out of the door of her office and told him to go in. He entered the gloomy, low-ceilinged room, which was crammed with dusty books, and stood before the desk. The headmaster, known to all as The Gaffer, looked up.

'I am aware of your circumstances, Rawnsley,' The Gaffer said, looking grim, 'but at this great school we have welcomed students from all walks of life and we expect of them the same high standards of conduct. There are no exceptions. Whatever reasons might prevail, there is no excuse for brawling and fighting.'

Raymond set his jaw.

The Gaffer's eyes narrowed beneath his shaggy brows.

'Rawnsley, I suspect you were provoked, but a Slevin boy has to practise forbearance regardless. This may be a lesson that you have to learn the hard way and it is my painful duty to ensure that you do.'

Raymond didn't flinch as The Gaffer stood up. He opened one side of his black gown and selected the middle one of three bamboo canes poking from the long pockets within. Holding it by one end, the Gaffer tapped the other end against the palm of his hand. This was the sort of forbearance Raymond was used to.

'Bend over, boy, and brace yourself against the desk,' The Gaffer ordered.

Raymond fixed his gaze on the untidy collection of volumes in the bookcase in front of him and tried to read their titles, as three swishing whacks of the cane smacked against his raised buttocks. For once he was grateful for his thick flannel trousers, but each explosive blow still sent shooting pains down his legs.

After his punishment The Gaffer dismissed him. Despite the spasms in his legs, Raymond held his head high as he walked down the long corridor flanked by classroom windows, through which the furtive eyes of fellow students followed him. He turned into the toilets at the end of the corridor and, once inside a cubicle, he pulled his trousers down and lowered himself onto the bowl, letting the cool porcelain soothe his inflamed skin.

'Great school my arse,' he muttered.

Good on the Outside

'Folks down south think it's grim up north,' Mr Marsden said, 'but them's the ones that's choking in smog in London. We've got good air and clear skies. Mind you, Seth at work says snow's coming and he's never wrong. We might have a white Christmas.'

Raymond was reading a school library book, *The Outsider* by Albert Camus, in the dining room while Mr Marsden was talking to his wife in the kitchen. He sympathised with those people suffocating in London. The air around him often felt dense and ready to do him harm, particularly during the hours he spent trapped in the bedroom with Roger each night, and not just because of Roger's noxious bodily odours. His foster-brother smelled like his father, especially after sweating and grunting over their so-called boxing lessons. Still, he'd survived autumn and into winter and now the Christmas holidays were about to begin.

He'd already noticed a change in the mood of the household and recognised that it was down to Mrs Marsden, who had the same extended holiday as the children. She was the family moderator, the one who tried to make Raymond's life at least tolerable, and her permanent presence made a difference, especially when her husband was at work.

Mr Marsden's workmate was right. Soft snow began to fall until it was thick and deep and the world around them became a picture postcard. Raymond helped the girls decorate the house with paper-chains and baubles until every room downstairs glittered under the electric lights. Meanwhile, Roger adopted the air of a young man who needed to save himself for greater endeavours and didn't get involved in such childish things. Nonetheless, the Christmas spirit seemed to affect him, because, although he acted the domineering older brother to Raymond and his siblings, he was sometimes almost magnanimous.

A couple of days before Christmas, Mr Marsden arrived back from work, stamping the snow from his feet at the back door, with a Christmas tree so green and perfect that Janet and Mary clapped and squealed when he dragged it into the living room, leaving a trail of pine needles along the crimson carpet. When it was decorated by Janet, Mary and their mother, the tree stood twinkling in front of the snow-decorated front window.

'It's beautiful, isn't it, Raymond?' Mary said, her eyes sparkling.

Raymond agreed. Maybe it was a symbol of hope.

On Christmas Eve, the whole family bathed, before settling down to watch the BBC. In deference to the occasion, Mrs Marsden put a bar of Pears soap in the bathroom. Although they had to share the limited hot water, Raymond didn't mind following Roger in the bath, because the soap would have made bathing in a puddle of rainwater a luxury. He was glowing when he slipped on the clean pyjamas, which were kept warm in the airing cupboard, before going downstairs. Mrs Marsden insisted he join the family in the sitting room.

Drinking ginger beer in front of a glowing coal fire and watching television, Raymond began to float on a tentative cushion of anticipation. He went to bed early along with Janet and Mary, but not before they'd each drunk a drop of sherry, his first taste of alcohol, and eaten a delicious home-baked mince pie. On the landing, a bright-eyed Mary kissed him impulsively on the cheek as they bade each other goodnight.

'I bet you've never known a Christmas like this before, have you?' Janet said.

It was true. He hadn't.

*

Early on Christmas morning, Raymond was woken by the two girls bursting into the bedroom. Roger looked up, grunted and buried his head under his pillow. Undeterred, Janet and Mary sat on Raymond's bed and went through their presents of dolls, books, toys and games with him in breathless wonder, as the dawn broke and cast its steely light through the dormer window.

When the girls had exhausted their genial one-upmanship, they exhorted Raymond to explore the bulging stocking, which still lay unopened at the foot of his bed. He was apprehensive. What if there were only lumps of coal inside? He'd rather be alone if that was the case, but he had no choice other than to comply. It was a relief to discover that the stocking contained a surprising selection of gifts, including books, pens and handkerchiefs, some from members of the Marsden family that he'd never even met.

Finally, encouraged by the girls, he opened what was, without doubt, the star present, which had been placed on its own at the bottom of the bed. Mary became impatient with his careful removal of the gaudy wrapping paper and tore off a large strip to reveal a board game called Risk. Janet looked at the box open-mouthed.

'That's a new game,' she said, glancing towards Roger's bed. 'Roger usually gets that.'

Raymond saw Roger stir and begin to sit up in bed, his face as sour as Scrooge's before his enlightenment. The two girls gathered up their presents and left the room without another word. Roger threw back his covers and swung his legs out of bed, while Raymond sat with the box on his lap. In rumpled pyjamas, Roger approached, his narrowed eyes fixed on the shiny red box with 'Risk' emblazoned on the lid. Raymond waited to see what Roger would do, expecting him to snatch the box from him. Instead, Roger picked up the wrapping paper and stared at the gift label attached to it for what seemed a long time.

Raymond knew what it said.

Merry Christmas, Raymond. Love from Mum and Dad

Roger made a sound Raymond was all too familiar with, screwed the paper up into a ball, threw it against the wall and stormed out of the room. Raymond wasn't sure what to do. He placed the box on Roger's bed and walked to the partly opened door, where he stood and strained to hear. A fierce whispered argument was taking place downstairs.

'That should have been mine. It's always mine, every year.'

'Now then, Roger, we just wanted to make Raymond feel more at home. It doesn't matter. We all play it anyway.'

'I told you it was a daft idea, Hilda. You make too much of him. He's got to make his own way.'

Raymond closed the door and lay on his bed waiting for the inevitable confrontation with his foster-brother. Eventually, Roger returned, red-faced. Seeing the box on his bed, he picked it up and threw it at Raymond, who, although he caught it, still suffered a sharp dig to his chest from one of the corners.

'I couldn't care less about your stupid present,' Roger sneered. 'You can't play it on your own, can you?'

Raymond got dressed, while Roger lay back on his bed with his head to one side, ignoring the stocking and presents that lay unopened on the bottom of his bed. Instinct told Raymond that his foster-brother wouldn't open them in his presence and he hurried from the room. The delicious aroma of roasting turkey wafting up to meet him mocked him with the promise of unattainable Christmas joy.

When he entered the empty dining room, Mrs Marsden, with her hair unkempt and her pale blue dressing gown wrapped around her lumpy body, gave him a weak smile through the serving hatch and said, 'Merry Christmas, Raymond. Did you like your presents?'

'Yes, thank you,' Raymond replied, doing his best to return her smile, but probably failing as much as she had.

The Christmas spirit was reinstated by Mr Marsden's enforced joviality. He chided everyone for being glum and turned up the volume on the radio so they could all listen to a carol service while eating breakfast. At first the mood was strained, especially when a glowering Roger came down, but spirits were lifted by Mr Marsden, who picked up a Christmas card from the sideboard and opened it. Raymond saw that it was the card he'd placed there earlier.

'Merry Christmas to the Marsden family, from Raymond,' Mr Marsden intoned with mock solemnity.

For some reason Raymond couldn't quite fathom, this brought hoots of laughter from Roger and the two girls, while Mr Marsden chuckled. While Raymond wondered whether to smile and the others continued to splutter, Mrs Marsden declared, 'Thank you, Raymond. That's really nice.'

After that, Christmas was restored. The Marsden family hurried off to church as soon as breakfast was finished and, on this occasion, Raymond did the same. The snow was too deep and it was too cold to tramp through the wood and sit in a tree for an hour. The fact that he'd always been forced to go to church didn't make him immune to the uplifting ceremony performed against the glittering backdrop of candles brighter than light bulbs. Maybe, just maybe, he had something to be thankful for after all.

Later, the family was joined for Christmas dinner by Mr

Marsden's frail mother, his brother, who could have been a twin, and his sister-in-law; although it was a tight squeeze in the dining room, they enjoyed a noisy festive meal. Afterwards, they watched the Queen's Speech on the television and while the adults, including Roger, dozed in front of the glowing fire, Raymond played with the two girls and their new toys in the dining room.

That evening, after the guests had gone, Roger came downstairs holding the box with 'Risk' on it. His mother looked at him with narrowed eyes, but he ignored her and looked at Raymond.

'Do you mind if we all play, Raymond?' he asked with a disarming smile. 'We always play a new game at Christmas. Besides, you can't play it on your own, can you?'

It was a logic that Raymond was happy to concur with and he agreed.

They all gathered around the dining room table to play the game, whose object was world domination. Roger won handsomely by sweeping everyone's armies from his Russian base. A large tin of assorted chocolates and toffees, from which everyone could help themselves in moderation, had pride of place on the cabinet beneath the Sacred Heart. Raymond took moderation to its extremes until Mrs Marsden offered the tin to him.

It was Roger who carried the game of Risk back upstairs that night and placed it on top of his pile of games. Raymond didn't mind. It was a perfect solution as far as he was concerned. He fell asleep in a cocoon of warmth with his face to the wall and his bedclothes swaddled around him.

*

Boxing Day was a time for relaxation after the excesses of the day before. Throughout the day, everybody did what they wanted to do. Roger stayed in his bedroom, mostly in bed, and the girls played in theirs, while Mr and Mrs Marsden rested in the living room and Raymond read *Crime and Punishment* in the dining room. The house was so warm that the windows were steamed up and lights blazed in every room.

After a make-do tea of cold meats and Christmas cake, Roger suggested they all play Risk again and after clearing up, they gathered around the dining room table for an evening of family entertainment. Roger had conquered the whole of Asia by the time Mr Marsden, in sleeveless vest and leather braces, reached for the tin of sweets on the cabinet.

Raymond watched as his foster-father prised the lid from the tin, only to see his jaw drop.

'What the ...?' Mr Marsden exclaimed and turned the tin upside down. Two lonely sweets in lacklustre wrappers dropped onto the table.

In that instant, Raymond froze. It was as though the air had turned to ice and he could almost visualise the rivulets of condensation streaming down the window turning into icicles. The darkening look on Mr Marsden's face was a look Raymond knew only too well. Innocence didn't prevent a sick feeling of guilt from rising up in his stomach, as Mr Marsden's eyes fixed on the shifty look Raymond knew he was projecting. Although his foster-father pretended to widen his inquisition to include all the children, Raymond sensed, with growing discomfort, where his suspicions lay.

Roger was as ingenuous and helpful to the inquiry as it was possible to be.

'I know Raymond was in here by himself all afternoon, but it could've been anyone,' he said, looking like a saint. 'There must be empty wrappers. It's only fair to search everybody's things. You can start with my stuff in my bedroom if you want.'

Mr Marsden heeded his suggestion and disappeared from the room, while the others sat in awkward silence. Raymond

was conscious of the owl and the princess both glaring at
him, while Mrs Marsden chewed the corner of a fingernail.
Roger leaned back in his chair with his arms folded across
his chest and gazed at the ceiling with a blank expression.

Mr Marsden was only away a few minutes and when he re-
entered the room he had a pair of red boxing gloves in his
big hands.

'I found these under Raymond's bed,' he said looking at
Raymond with menace.

He held the boxing gloves over the table and shook
them. A kaleidoscope of multi-coloured sweet wrappers
tumbled out of them onto the polished veneer. The ice-cold
hand of fate gripped Raymond's heart, as the eyes of everyone but Mrs Marsden fixed him with looks of contempt.
Raymond saw the truth in Roger's smug face, but he still
reddened and lowered his head as if guilty.

Mr Marsden, his face mottled, didn't even bother to
obtain a confession.

'What have you got to say for yourself, lad?' he
demanded.

Raymond couldn't speak and fixed his eyes on a detached
Christmas paper-chain hanging down the side of the framed
piece of embroidery, into which was sown 'Home Sweet
Home' in coloured letters. He was trapped and he knew
that this was the way it was meant to be.

'When there's a rotten apple in the barrel,' Mr Marsden
intoned like a sermonising priest, 'it has to be removed as
quickly as possible. You, you greedy and ungrateful boy, are
a rotten apple. Good on the outside but bad on the inside.
You could have had whatever you wanted, but instead you
stole the lot like a thief in the night.'

There was a long painful silence while Raymond hung his
head and stared at the map of the world on the board game
on the table, wishing he was in some far-flung place rather
than this. He wasn't sure why he couldn't defend himself,

but he couldn't. Some things were just meant to be. Eventually, his foster-father told the rest of the family to go into the front room and watch television. When Mrs Marsden lingered and protested, he ushered her from the room also, saying, 'It's got to be done, love.'

Mr Marsden didn't waste time. He strode over to Raymond, pulled him from his seat and forced him over the table, scattering plastic armies to all corners of the earth. He laid into Raymond's backside and legs with his heavy work-worn mitt and, as his hand rose and fell, he said, 'Do not bring your wicked ways into this house ever again,' grunting between each word. His anger exhausted, he banished Raymond to bed.

In the dark, Raymond wrapped his pillow around his ears to shut out the mocking sound of laughter from the audience on the television downstairs and imagined himself suspended in purgatory. The pain in his legs was swamped by the searing sense of humiliation welling up inside him and burning his throat. It wasn't the first time he'd been wrongly accused in his life, but this was different. This time he'd been set up. He could have protested his innocence. He could speak up for himself if he wanted to, just as he could floor Roger in their boxing sessions if he felt inclined, but that wasn't the point. If he was a member of this family, someone else should have spoken up for him. That was the acid test. Enough was enough. If Roger gloated when he came to bed he would have to go for him.

He tensed and clenched his fists as he heard the bedroom door creak open.

'Good on the outside, bad on the inside,' the sibilant voices of the owl and the princess chorused.

The Demon in the Dining Room

Snow fell on snow after Christmas and the back of the Marsdens' bungalow was covered with huge icicles that hung from the gutters to the ground like gigantic crystal stalactites. The little house of frosty looks and icy stares was in the grip of winter's fist. Roger didn't gloat in front of Raymond. Instead, he adopted the same attitude of betrayal and disappointment as his father and sisters. His false sanctimony was like a knife twisting in Raymond's gut.

Mrs Marsden was different. She took the first opportunity to get Raymond alone and question him. Raymond could tell from her perplexed look and the uncertain tone of her voice that when she asked him *why* he'd done it, she really wanted to ask him *if* he'd done it. She sat close to him, with her hands clasped in front of her on the dining table; so close that her fingers were next to his.

'Everything in this house is as much yours as anybody else's,' she said. 'You don't have to steal. If you're not sure about helping yourself you only have to ask.'

He could sense that she wanted to touch him, but couldn't bring herself to bridge the final inch. He sat, rigid as a tailor's dummy, and said nothing. That inch was a mile, and not just a straight mile; it was a deep, impenetrable chasm. He was no longer using silence as a shield; he was using it as a weapon to slash at the injustice he felt. His heart was hard and impervious to the sadness in her voice and the fluttering reach of her hesitant fingers. Roger's treachery was bad enough, but the willingness, almost eagerness, of the others to believe in his guilt was worse.

The worst thing of all, though, was the knowledge that this was what they'd always expected of him. They all saw a stigma on him, even her, and that realisation made him contemptuous of her faltering failure to leap across the invisible divide. He withdrew his hands from the table and placed them in his lap. His foster-mother sighed and rose from the table.

*

The start of the school term was a welcome relief. Mr Marsden, in a brief speech during an uncomfortable meal the night before, talked about putting things behind them and making a fresh start, but this was the only start Raymond wanted: the opportunity to spend time away from the house.

He and Roger were wrapped in heavy coats and scarves as they left the house to trudge through the snow, with every breath hanging before them in the cold air. Still in sight of the house, Roger walked next to him.

'Raymond,' he began.

Raymond cut him short. 'When we're outside the house, you don't exist,' he said, 'and if you want to speak to me, you call me Rom.'

At first, Roger looked taken aback and stopped in his tracks, as Raymond marched on through the snow.

'I've got nowt to say to you, anyway, you pillock,' he eventually called out, regaining his composure. 'It's a stupid nickname, anyway.'

Their journey to school was the same as always, but this time, the barrier between them was mutual.

*

During the dinner break, pupils were allowed out into the frozen yard. Wrapped in scarves and with hands in trouser pockets, Rom, Titch, Rollo and Poggy mooched around by the tennis courts discussing what had become their favourite topic – girls; not that they had much experience between them to draw on and, even if they had, it would've been unlikely to live up to their lurid imaginings.

Out of the corner of his eye, Rom noticed a group of fourth-year boys coming towards them. His schoolboy antennae told him that they were approaching with menace and, without showing any outward sign, he stiffened. The group of four was headed by Starkey, a big, burly oaf and a well-known bully; at the back of the group, Rom saw Roger. Starkey stopped in front of Rom and his friends with his feet planted apart and his hands on his hips. His allies, including Roger, stood just behind him.

'Had a nice Christmas, Rawnsley,' Starkey sneered, 'or doesn't Santa bother with borstal boys?'

Without a word, Rom hit Starkey hard in the mouth. Stunned, the beefy bully put his hands to his face and slumped to his knees on the frozen ground.

Prefects came running across the quad like guards re-acting to trouble in a prison yard and Rom was marched into the school. Later that afternoon he was summoned to the headmaster's study, but it was worth the sizzling whacks of The Gaffer's favourite cane to have seen the look on Roger's face when he'd hit Starkey. For a split second, Roger thought the blow was for him and flinched and stepped back.

*

Arriving home, Raymond stamped his feet free from snow on the back steps before entering the steamy kitchen. Mrs Marsden was standing at the oven cooking something for tea.

'Hello, Raymond,' she said, half turning.

'Hello,' Raymond said, bending down to take off his shoes.

'Raymond, come in here now,' Mr Marsden's voice bellowed out.

Raymond made his way to the dining room, where his foster-father was sitting at the head of the table, with Roger on one side and Janet and Mary on the other. The almost comical looks of solemn disapproval on the two girls' faces, and Roger's faint smirk, told him he was in trouble.

'You've been fighting at school,' Mr Marsden growled. 'Roger hasn't been taking the trouble to teach you how to box for you to use it to attack other people. From now on, there'll be no more boxing lessons and I've confiscated your boxing gloves.'

Raymond glanced at Roger, who couldn't hold his gaze.

'You're walking a fine line, young man,' Mr Marsden continued. 'Go straight to your room and don't come down again tonight.'

Later that evening, while Raymond read by torchlight on his bed, hearing the sounds of the television filtering upwards from below, the bedroom door opened and Mrs Marsden crept in. She handed him some cold sausages wrapped in a napkin and sat down on the edge of his bed.

'You can't go without food, Raymond,' she said. 'Eat up quickly so I can take the napkin back downstairs.'

He bit on a sausage, relishing the taste of cold lard that coated it. His foster-mother looked on, her brown eyes soft with concern behind her spectacles.

'What's the matter, Raymond?' she asked. 'I know it's not easy for you, especially with what's happened recently, but don't take your troubles to school. You're a clever lad. The sky's the limit for you, it really is. Don't spoil it. I know things aren't easy at the moment, but we can get through it.

If you've got problems, just remember you can come and talk to me.'

Raymond wasn't ungrateful, but he wolfed down his sausages knowing that she would want to get back downstairs unobserved, although his real purpose was to get rid of her. Even her warmth could not melt the defensive shield around him, which was as cold and hard as the icicle curtain at the back of the house. Finally, he watched her tread across the room with a lightness that belied her heavy hips and disappear through the door.

He picked up his book, which was *The Pit and the Pendulum* by Edgar Allan Poe, and began to read again. By the time Roger came to bed, however, he'd long since closed his eyes and turned to the wall, although he wasn't asleep. Not a word passed between them.

*

Raymond, never talkative before, now remained mute at home, except for the occasional monosyllabic response. At the same time, he sensed that something unholy had manifested itself in that catholic household; a malevolent spirit had been brought out into the open that saw no reason to remain hidden anymore. Raymond imagined it hovering over the dining table during meals and inciting the members of a normal suburban family to cruelty. Now that the genie was out of the bottle, Mr Marsden and his offspring talked about him as if he wasn't there.

'Look at him,' one would say. 'He's like a Russian spy.'

'What's he hiding?' another would chime, picking up the thread.

'I wonder if he speaks English,' the next would ponder aloud.

'He can't speak at all,' Roger would say with naked malevolence. 'He's dumb.'

Sometimes, it was as if the callous cacodemon pinched

the faces of the girls, causing them to grimace, and exhorting them to whisper at Raymond when they saw him alone, 'Good on the outside, bad on the inside.'

Only when Mrs Marsden was in the room did Raymond sense the demon retreating to sulk in a shadowy corner between ceiling and walls, waiting for its next moment to strike.

Raymond bore his persecution in silence, but at Slevin Grammar, Rom compensated for his alter ego's stolen happiness by being increasingly rebellious and outspoken. He knew there was a line beyond which he could incur serious consequences, but he danced along it. He was fully aware, however, that every misdemeanour added to his store of indiscretions and brought the threat of ultimate sanction ever closer, but he flirted with consequence nonetheless.

In his home-life, the Pit of total despair, into whose desolate depths he might be forever flung, beckoned, and over his school-life swung the Pendulum of final retribution, ever closer. Each was an end in itself, but of the two he preferred the Pendulum. If he was careful, it might just cut his bonds and set him free from his torture.

Trespassing, lateness, rowdiness and outspokenness were the main causes of the impositions and detentions Rom incurred, sometimes with one or more of his friends, but mostly alone. He made no distinction between masters and prefects when sharing out his punishment tally.

Roger, of course, made sure that the Marsdens were made aware of Raymond's crimes. This only made the invisible demon lick his lips and breathe more righteous animosity into Mr Marsden and his offspring, while Mrs Marsden probed into the cause of his behaviour in desperation. Apart from polite responses, Raymond wore his silence like a second skin at all times.

*

Rom wandered back up the school lane with the Legion of the Disenchanted on a cold and clammy February afternoon. Their attitude to Slevin Grammar School was advertised in their dress. Ties hung at odd angles with the knot somewhere between chest and navel; one or more shirt buttons was left undone; and shirt tails hung outside mudspattered trousers.

Walking behind a group of first-year boys, they began to sing Cliff Richard's new number one, 'The Young Ones', laughing as the young boys broke into a trot and scampered up the hill. They were never bullies and were often champions, but the first-year boys weren't taking any chances.

'The look on Nero's face, Rom, when you said, "Who? Me, sir?"!' lanky Rollo, who'd started walking backwards in front of the others, exclaimed. 'Made me nearly wet meself. I thought he was gonna have a fit.'

Poggy laughed out loud. 'Me too,' he said. 'It was dead funny.'

'You wanna watch it,' Titch said, looking at Raymond sideways. 'You're pushing your luck.'

'Yeah, yeah,' Rom said, shrugging his shoulders. He was more concerned about delaying his journey home. 'Let's go to Woolies tonight.'

When they reached the town, they streamed off the bus amongst the herd of Slevin boys and headed towards Woolworths. The storefront was bright and gaudy as they entered and the display shelves were overflowing with a multitude of household wares. They made their way towards their favourite section of the store, gawping at the female shop assistants in passing; the most voluptuous of them causing them to nudge each other and snigger.

'I bet you daren't nick owt,' Poggy challenged the gang.

Whenever they went into Woolworths someone broached this idea. This had the consequence of making them look like shifty shoplifters, even though they'd never put the idea into practice.

As they browsed around the stationery shelves, Rom noticed a fastidious floorwalker watching them. Their ink-stained fingers drifted over shiny new pens, geometry sets, notebooks and pencil cases as the floorwalker began to move towards them. Rom saw him twitching with agitation as he tried to follow the butterfly fingers of the potential pilferers. Suddenly, the man advanced, calling out, 'That's enough. That's enough. If you're not buying then don't touch.'

Rollo, Poggy and Titch turned to face the floorwalker and, for an instant, obscured Rom from his view. Rom had, up until that moment, been admiring an attractive red leather bookmark embossed with gold filigree with a square-cut fringe at one end. Quick as a flash, Rom folded the bookmark into his fist and stuffed it into his trouser pocket.

The confrontation with the floorwalker, who was now fulminating on behalf of his precious emporium, became something of a melee. Having committed the crime in their minds, Rom's friends protested more than was necessary. The man became strident and commanded, 'C'mon. Let's have you out. You shouldn't be in here after school. I'll be ringing the school to let them know you've been causing trouble.' He herded them all out of the store like the commissionaire at the Ritz removing undesirables.

As the boys split up and Titch and Rom walked to their respective bus stops, which were in the same direction, Titch complained about the unjustified treatment they'd received. Just before they parted company in the light of an optician's window, Rom took his hand out of his pocket and opened it in front of Titch.

'Flippin' Nora,' Titch gasped, as he gazed at the fabulous bookmark, whose golden filigree glistened under the street-lights.

Rom jumped onto his bus just before it left the stop and found a seat at the rear. He examined the bookmark and, noting with satisfaction the price marked on a sticker on the back, he slipped it back into his pocket.

When the bus pulled up at the bottom of Coupland Road, Raymond alighted and walked up the road, past the long row of bungalows. The closer he got to the Marsden house, the more his spirits sank. When he reached the back door of the house, he focused his mind like a fakir about to walk over a bed of hot coals. Mrs Marsden was standing at the oven cooking something for tea.

'Hello, Raymond,' she said, half turning.

'Hello,' Raymond said, bending down to take off his shoes.

When he stood up, he could see the rest of the family reading magazines and comics at the dining table through the serving hatch. None of them looked up and he went upstairs to the bedroom he shared with Roger, after hanging his coat in the hallway. He pushed his satchel under the bed and slipped the bookmark under his pillow. Then, he went to the bathroom, used the toilet, washed his hands and went downstairs. When he entered the dining room and sat down in his place, no one looked up from his or her reading and no one spoke. The demon was dozing, but Raymond knew it would soon come to life.

*

During school assembly, Rom listened straight-faced as The Gaffer made an announcement. He'd received a report that some boys from the school, probably second or third year, had been acting suspiciously in one of the stores in town. Boys had no business to be wandering unaccompanied after school in the town shops, he reminded them. The honour of the school was in the hands of every boy who wore that noble badge and carried it abroad. His dark eyes, crowned with fierce bushy eyebrows, scanned the assembly as he finished by saying that he'd asked the store manager to detain any boy found in the store after school who couldn't justify his actions. Titch stole a glance at Rom along the solemn line of schoolboys.

That night, the boys went straight home, separating in the town to make their way to their own bus stops. The bus was waiting when Rom approached the stop. He could see Roger, glum-faced, hunched by one of the windows and, seeing that the bus was almost full, he decided to wait for the next one. The buses were frequent at that time of day and before long, Rom was gazing out of the window of the moving bus as it pulled out into the traffic with blazing headlights.

*

When Raymond entered the dining room on his return to the Marsdens', no one looked at him and no one spoke.

In the centre of the table was a red leather bookmark embossed with gold filigree.

Marsdens? 'Damners' more like.

Jackdaw

Raymond looked at the bookmark with resignation, while the family stared at him with stony faces. Roger leaned forward with a triumphant look on his face.

'We know where you got it,' he blurted out.

'Quiet,' Mr Marsden said. 'Leave it to me.'

After a short pause, Mr Marsden glared at Raymond and asked, 'Where did you get it?'

Raymond remained tight-lipped.

'Well?' Mr Marsden demanded after what seemed to Raymond like an age.

Raymond still stared straight ahead and said nothing. Mr Marsden reached out and turned the bookmark over. On the back was a price tag with the Woolworth name printed on it.

'It's from Woolworths',' Mr Marsden said. 'Now when were you last in Woolworths?'

Raymond's continued silence broke Roger's patience.

'It's just like I told you, Dad,' he said. 'The headmaster told us about it in assembly this morning. It was him and his mates hanging round Woolworths stealing and that's the proof.'

Mr Marsden looked at Raymond with an almost comical expression of hurt on his face. 'First you let *us* down and now the school,' he said, his big palms raised. 'You know the headmaster's going to have to be told, don't you? You'll be lucky to keep your place after this, and I'm not just talking about school.'

Raymond imagined the arc of the razor-sharp Pendulum as it swung so close to his body he could hear it hiss. Mr Marsden, as if reading his mind, swept his large hand through the air, just clearing the top of Raymond's head. Raymond didn't flinch.

'Get upstairs now,' Mr Marsden shouted, 'and don't come back down again today!'

Raymond left the room, catching a sad glance from Mrs Marsden through the serving hatch.

That evening, his solitary confinement was uninterrupted. Maybe she'd given up on him as well? It was wrong to steal, but he didn't have any conscience about it. Most inmates of children's homes steal from the enemy when they get the chance, which meant everyone but each other.

'You've done it now,' Roger sneered when he came to bed. 'You're gonna need a miracle to get out of this, Miracle Boy.'

Raymond turned his head from the wall and looked at his foster-brother without any trace of feeling. A flicker of uncertainty showed on Roger's face, before Raymond turned away again and pulled the bedcover over his head.

*

The next morning, during an otherwise silent and strained breakfast, Mr Marsden handed Raymond the beautiful, but damning, bookmark.

'When you get to school, take this to the headmaster and tell him what you've done,' he said. 'Maybe he'll be more lenient if you admit it, but you don't really deserve it.'

Raymond knew he had no choice. The glint in the eye of Roger, the school spy, told him that. So, after morning assembly, he made his way to the headmaster's study with a resigned tread. When he presented himself to the school secretary, she didn't need to ask his name, and when he said he had to see the headmaster, she assumed he'd been sent by a master for punishment.

He waited in the corridor until she called him and told him to enter the study. The Gaffer was sitting behind his desk looking at some papers in front of him and didn't look up until Rom was standing to attention before him. The Gaffer raised his head as if it was made of stone and lifted his shaggy eyebrows.

'Well, Rawnsley, what is it this time, boy?' he demanded.

Rom pulled the bookmark from his pocket and placed it on the desk in front of him.

'This, sir,' he said.

'This?' echoed The Gaffer, puzzled. 'What does it mean, boy? Explain yourself.'

'The boys who were in Woolworths, Sir,' Rom said, as if that was explanation enough.

The light of understanding began to dawn in The Gaffer's dark eyes. 'And you were one of them, Rawnsley?' he asked.

Rom nodded.

The Gaffer looked at the bookmark and Rom saw his bushy eyebrows begin to knit closer together.

'And you stole this,' he said, laying each word down before he picked up the next.

'I was going to pay for it, Sir,' Rom said, knowing it was a feeble offering, 'but he kicked us out.'

The Gaffer thought for a moment before asking, 'I suppose you had the money to pay for it?'

'I had the bookmark in my hand when the man in the store came up to us,' Rom said. 'I thought he might think I was stealing it so I put it in my pocket.'

'You thought he might think you were stealing it so you stole it,' the Gaffer said and sighed. 'Oh dear, Rawnsley. You'd better tell me who else was with you.'

Rom decided to fall back on his right to silence for the

rest of the interview, regardless of the consequences.

The Gaffer picked up the bookmark and ran his large thumb over the filigree pattern, like an archaeologist deciphering the secret history of an ancient artefact.

'Very well, Rawnsley,' he concluded, 'I am going to have to think about this. I don't have to tell you that this will have serious consequences. Go back to your class and keep this to yourself. I will call for you later when I've decided what to do.'

Rom went through the motions during the day, ignoring Roger's sidelong smirks when he saw him, and keeping his troubles from his friends. What they didn't know wouldn't harm them. Halfway through the afternoon Latin lesson, the school secretary entered the classroom. After a brief whispered conversation with the master, Nero, she looked at Rom and beckoned him with a crooked finger. He could feel the eyes of all his classmates on his back as he followed her through the door.

Back in the headmaster's study for the second time that day, he waited with head bowed for The Gaffer to pronounce his sentence, while the grimy faced clock on the wall ticked as if it was about to expire. Eventually, the ancient scholar spoke.

'Rawnsley,' he began, sounding as grave as a judge donning the black cap before pronouncing the death sentence, 'you have brought dishonour on this school and on yourself. Shoplifting is a criminal offence. It is not a schoolboy prank.' He heaved a sigh. 'There is only one sanction for committing a criminal offence while in that uniform. Have you any idea what that is?'

Rom nodded.

'Well, speak up, boy,' The Gaffer demanded. 'What is it?'

'To be expelled, sir,' Rom said, conscious of a strange thrill running through him as he spoke.

'That is correct, Rawnsley,' The Gaffer confirmed. 'It is the only possible outcome.'

He paused and looked Rom in the eye for what seemed like a long time. Finally, he drew a long breath and said, 'However.' He paused again. 'I have taken into account the fact that you came to see me, even though I suspect it was not of your own volition. Nonetheless, it is a mitigating factor and I have decided to keep this matter within these four walls.' He laboured to his feet and said, 'The fact that you have escaped the ultimate disgrace shouldn't be taken lightly; nor should you imagine that you are about to escape without any form of punishment.'

Rom knew what he was intimating and watched as he opened his black gown to reveal his selection of canes.

'You know the drill, Rawnsley,' he said. 'Assume the position with which you are so familiar.'

He administered six explosive whacks with the cane, the maximum punishment, before dismissing Rom with a warning not to talk about the incident and a reminder that he was only one more transgression away from final disgrace.

*

Despite a persistent, soaking drizzle, Raymond lingered at the back door of the Marsdens' house. There wasn't a door in his life he looked forward to opening, but this one least of all. As he dithered, he knocked over a line of empty glass milk bottles and gave himself away. No choice now. He entered the house.

'Raymond,' Mr Marsden called out from the dining room, 'get yourself in here now.'

Except for Mrs Marsden, who was labouring over steaming pans in the kitchen, the family was gathered round the table waiting to hear his account of the day. First the judge and now the jury, Raymond thought. In as few words as possible, he recounted what had happened in the head-master's study.

'I hope you realise how lucky you are,' Mr Marsden said

when he'd finished. 'I fully expected Slevin Grammar to expel a thief. You'd better be on your best behaviour from now on in. Anyway, this is not over yet, as you'll soon find out. Now go and get changed.'

As Raymond left the room, Mrs Marsden, who'd been listening at the serving hatch, gave him a weak smile, making it clear that she was the only one who was happy he'd escaped the ultimate sanction.

Later that evening, Raymond tried to concentrate on Latin grammar at the dining room table, but the text danced before his eyes. He was further distracted when he heard someone arrive and retire to the living room with Mr and Mrs Marsden. He couldn't hear what was being said, but somehow he sensed that it was to do with him. After a short while, Mrs Marsden came in and asked him to go into the living room.

When he entered the Marsden sanctuary, he found Mr Leather chatting with Mr Marsden.

'I see they've sentenced Hanratty to hang,' the ginger representative of the Welfare Department remarked to Raymond's foster-father.

'Aye,' Mr Marsden said, 'and not before time, either.'

They both looked up from their seats as if they'd just heard Raymond enter. Raymond looked down at the coffee table, on which were spread his most personal possessions, while both men scrutinised him.

'Sit down, Raymond,' Mr Leather ordered.

Raymond sat on the edge of the settee in front of the coffee table and waited, trying not to look at his collection of books and drawings on the table. It wasn't right to take someone's private things and display them as if they were for sale in a bazaar. The swan-necked woman with the limpid eyes in the picture above the glowing fire seemed to offer sympathy, but it made no difference to Raymond's feeling of violation.

The sharp-suited social worker, like an idling shopper, picked up his copy of *The Pit and the Pendulum* and opened it at the back page. Raymond held his breath. He knew what he'd written inside the back cover. Mr Leather read it out.

> *Take me from this place*
> *And put me into care.*
> *Give me rules and punishments*
> *And let me linger there.*

Mr Leather paused after his reading, while Mr Marsden looked on with a pained expression on his broad face.

'Well, Raymond,' Mr Leather said. 'This tells us a lot, doesn't it? It tells me you've not been prepared to make a real effort to adjust to family life.'

He dropped the book onto the coffee table and waved his hand over the paintings spread across it.

'These paintings indicate the same thing. You spend too much time daydreaming about an unrealistic world; somewhere that doesn't exist.'

He kept picking up pictures of mysterious temples and palaces with pink turrets and towers swathed in lilac mists while he spoke. He held them up by the corners with his thumb and forefinger, like a disinherited nobleman forced to scavenge through a rubbish tip.

'There's nothing wrong with imagination and some of these are quite good, but *this* is your world, here in this house, and that's what you should be concentrating on.'

His hand, which was like a woman's compared to the hams resting on Mr Marsden's knees, reached Raymond's most personal painting. It depicted a bookcase with a table in front of it, on which was a coiled rope, an open book with an image of a crossbow, a biscuit tin with a grinning skull on top of it and a box of matches. It summed up everything about Hillcrest and he'd spent many hours over it.

'This is the picture that really interests me,' Mr Leather

said, almost musing to himself. 'I think this tells us a great deal.'

Mr Marsden leaned forward and studied the painting then looked at Raymond and Mr Leather in turn with a perplexed look on his florid face. 'What does it mean?' he asked the ginger-haired sleuth.

'I think you'll find that Raymond has an unhealthy obsession with the past,' the self-deluded Sherlock Holmes informed his ingenuous Watson, while giving Raymond a look telling him that any interruption would be unwelcome. 'He dwells on things best forgotten.'

'What's that got to do with him stealing?' Mr Marsden asked, scratching his head.

'Who knows,' Mr Leather said, 'but I'm sure there's a connection. The jackdaw steals bright objects and takes them to its nest. It doesn't need them, but it can't resist. It's a compulsion. It can't do anything with the things it steals, but it hides them away anyway.'

'Ah, right,' Mr Marsden said, while looking as if he didn't understand.

Mr Leather explained further. 'It's obsessive behaviour,' he said. 'They can't help themselves. In Raymond's case, one obsession breeds another. It's part of a pattern based on living in a world that doesn't exist, in which case he has no moral conscience in the real world. It's also about keeping things to himself. That's what this secret hoard represents.' Mr Leather looked pleased with himself. 'You should check his belongings regularly,' he said. 'He can have no complaints if he's got nothing to hide. If you find anything that shouldn't be there then let me know.' He turned to Raymond. 'I'm going now,' he informed him. 'From now on, you're being watched. I don't want to be called back here again, because if I do it'll be to help you carry your bags. Just remember that Mr and Mrs Marsden are on your side. The rest is up to you.'

'I'll tell Mrs Marsden you're going,' Mr Marsden said and left the room.

As soon as he'd gone, Mr Leather picked up Raymond's copy of *Great Expectations* and opened it.

'Where did you get this from and what do you know about Miracle Boy?' he asked.

'I've always had it, but I don't know anything about it,' Raymond said, just about curbing the desire to show defiance to someone who, despite his badge of authority, was no more than a flagrant pickpocket.

'Well forget it, and anything else in the past for that matter. Make the most of what you've got here or you'll be on your way somewhere else.'

*

Any pretence that Raymond was an equal member of the family was completely abandoned by Mr Marsden and his children. Over the next few weeks, the demon in the dining room grew bigger and bolder on the rich pickings of malice and spite from around the table. Raymond could almost see it. Its hard, scaly skin was made of impregnable self-righteousness and it reeked of sweat and machine oil. Its malevolent face was twisted into a permanent sneer, sometimes triumphant, sometimes disdainful, and always ugly. One minute it barked like an angry dog and the next it whispered cruel remarks like a hissing snake.

Raymond knew that his only defence was stony silence. He knew it would take his words and twist them between its slimy fingers and thread sharp thorns and fragments of glass into them, before throwing them back in his face. His muscles ached with stiffness as he braced himself for whatever might be thrown at him.

The best times were in the evening when the family retired to the living room to watch the television, while he remained in the dining room with schoolbooks laid out on the table before him. The somnolent demon, gorged and sated from its evening meal, would slither into a corner of the room, too fat to hover anymore, leaving Raymond to daydream.

And the communication I have got to make is that he has great expectations.

He had no expectations of this world: the real world, as Mr Leather called it.

The Pin in the Candle

There was a piece of dialectic doggerel that Raymond had read somewhere and always remembered. He often repeated it inside his head.

> *Da Spring is sprung, Da grass is riz,*
> *I wonder where doze boidies is,*
> *Da boids is on da wing, but dat's absoid*
> *Surely da wings is on da boid.*

It always made him laugh, but he wasn't laughing now. The days were longer and the grass had certainly risen, judging by the Marsdens' unkempt back garden, but he didn't notice any birds on the wing. Within the house, an uneasy calm settled, as the daily routine of everyone's lives took over their thoughts and preoccupations, allowing Raymond to fade from the centre of the circle of disapproval and hide in the shadows. It was as if an unspoken agreement had been reached between the hostile members of the family and Raymond. They would allow him to be invisible as long as he didn't draw attention to himself or encroach on their familial territory.

*

It was a Sunday like any other, which meant the Marsdens absolved their sins in church, while Raymond sat at the top of his tree and worshipped the God of Solitude. In the afternoon, as it was a fine spring day, Mrs Marsden suggested that they all go for a stroll. During the walk, she insisted on walking by Raymond's side, while the others walked a few yards ahead. As she chatted, Raymond noted the frequent backward glances from the other members of the family, none of which were friendly.

When they returned, Raymond went upstairs to the bathroom. When he came out, Roger was standing at the top of the stairs. The thought crossed Raymond's mind that if he was in a children's home he would have heard Roger's approach and been prepared to face him.

'My mum, not yours,' Roger said, jabbing his finger at his own chest and then at Raymond's, before disappearing into his bedroom.

Later that night, Raymond was curled up in bed facing the wall, on the verge of sleep, when the bedroom light was snapped on and the bedclothes ripped off him. Mr Marsden, breath heaving, grabbed him by his pyjama jacket and hauled him from the bed.

'Come on! Downstairs!' he shouted and dragged Raymond to the head of the stairs. 'Get down!' he commanded, thrusting a confused Raymond down the blood-red steps.

The owl and the princess stumbled out of their bedroom, awakened by the noise and rubbing their eyes.

'Get back to bed,' Mr Marsden ordered, unable to take the anger out of his voice, which frightened the girls into scurrying back into their room.

He banged down the stairs after Raymond, shoving him along the hallway and into the dining room, where he hit the light switch and pushed him into a chair. Pacing the room in absurd-looking faded pink and white striped pyjamas, he revealed the cause of his rage.

Raymond listened, baffled, as Mr Marsden ranted.

'You put it there, didn't you?' he raved. 'Don't deny it. I

know it was you. You sneaked into our bedroom while we were watching television and put that drawing pin exactly where you knew I'd kneel down to say my prayers. To think I've prayed for you, when all the time you've been dying to get back at me for trying to keep you on the straight and narrow. You've got bad blood.'

The thought of Mr Marsden putting his full weight on a drawing pin when kneeling down to thank the Lord for the good life he led made Raymond wince. How could his foster-father believe he'd done it? He'd never even seen inside their bedroom. How could he know that his foster-father knelt in a particular spot to pray? He could only stare at the raving adult in disbelief.

'Stay there!' Mr Marsden yelled in an odd, high-pitched voice. 'You've been asking for this.'

As his foster-father crashed out of the room, Raymond glimpsed Roger through the partly open serving hatch holding an empty glass and sporting a milk-rimmed smirk. Roger drew his hand across his throat.

Mr Marsden returned with a broad leather belt in his hands and slammed the dining room door behind him. Grabbing Raymond by the collar and pulling him to his feet, he forced him face-down over the edge of the table. Raymond struggled as the shadow of the bloated demon, stinking of stale sweat, overwhelmed him. Using the leather belt, his foster-father thrashed him without mercy across the buttocks, and with each fearsome blow, he cried out, 'You evil demon! Don't ever do anything like that again!'

It wasn't just the electric blows that stung Raymond, even though they were made worse by the poor protection offered by his thin pyjamas. It was the crass stupidity and injustice of the charge.

As he squirmed in bed, he couldn't formulate a rational explanation. It was too bizarre even for his hated foster-brother to have done it to set him up again. Or was it? He dug his nails into his thighs and gritted his teeth, wishing he was mortally wounded.

His mad foster-father could explain that one to God.

*

One thing was clear to Raymond. The pin that pricked the catholic knee had also deflated any hope that Mrs Marsden might have entertained that the family situation would improve. This time, she had no doubt about his innocence and said so in private to him in the kitchen as soon as she could.

'I know you didn't do it,' she said, placing a light hand on his shoulder. 'I'm sorry, Raymond.'

From that moment, she started to defend Raymond openly. She admonished the girls if they showed any animosity towards him; she defended him in front of her husband; but she reserved the strength of her feelings for Roger. She took issue with him for being aloof; she scolded him for not doing enough to make Raymond part of the family; and she derided him for being spoilt and playing up to his dad all the time. It was clear that for Mrs Marsden, the penny had dropped, but to Raymond, it felt more like the pin had dropped from the candle.

He remembered a scene from one of his favourite books, *Moonfleet*, by J. Meade Faulkner. It was the passage where the fall of the pin inserted into a burning candle marked the moment of the craven villain's death.

The candle had burned down and the pin had fallen. Raymond was thrust into the centre of family conflict and, more than ever, he wanted to be somewhere else.

Rom to the Rescue

Raymond was late for everything because he never looked forward to arriving anywhere. He lingered in the in-between places, never taking the shortest route and always finding a detour or some bolt-hole where he could be alone and kill time. He spent more time sitting on toilet seats with his trousers up than with his trousers down.

One day, as Easter approached, he was late for a PE lesson. By the time he arrived at the changing room the other pupils had set off on the weekly cross-country run. While Rom changed into his vest and running shorts, Mr Ireland, the games master, castigated him.

'When are you going to realise, Rawnsley, that you can't get away with slack behaviour with me?' Paddy ranted, unconcerned about rules of privacy.

Paddy's voice and handclaps were still ringing in his ears as he hared across the sports field to the road. It was a perfect day and something inside him made him want to run hard. Just because Raymond was a bookworm didn't mean Rom had no athletic ability and he soon caught the usual stragglers.

'Hey, Rom,' Poggy called out as Rom ran past, 'your sister's not chasing you for nicking her lipstick, is she?'

'Nah,' Rom shouted over his shoulder, 'I'm chasing your brother for nicking her bra off the washing line.'

He felt a strange exhilaration and, with the wind in his face, began to gain on the front runners. He'd never felt so light and full of running before.

Roger, who took running seriously, was at the head of the field and gaped in astonishment as Rom pounded past. For a few moments, Roger managed to increase his pace and stay with him, but he was red in the face and gasping for breath. Rom's feet seemed to bounce on air above the tarmac as Roger struggled to stay with him.

Slowing his pace and high-stepping, Rom turned to Roger and taunted, 'Come on, Roger, your dad would be ever so disappointed in you.'

He didn't wait for an answer, breaking into an exuberant run and pulling away from his floundering foster-brother with ease.

'Bastard,' Roger shouted, gasping, as the wings on Rom's feet took flight and he rocketed away down the hill.

Paddy was astounded when Rom, looking fresh, ran into the changing room way ahead of the field.

'By heck, Rawnsley,' he gasped. 'If you haven't cheated you're a miracle. You're just what we need for Saturday.'

After questioning the other boys to make sure that Raymond had run the full course, he put him in the school team for the weekend race.

When Raymond informed the Marsdens that he was running for the school cross-country team that weekend, Mrs Marsden was pleased.

'Oh good,' she exclaimed. 'You'll be able to run with Roger.'

Mr Marsden glowered. He was proud of the fact that his precious son was in the school team, although he didn't know that it was regarded by most boys as no more than the masochistic refuge of the sad and lonely.

The night before the race, Raymond was reading *The Loneliness of the Long Distance Runner* by Alan Sillitoe, which he'd borrowed from the library for the sole purpose of winding Roger up. It worked. Roger clearly thought it was an instruction manual. He batted the book from Raymond's hands as he sat on his bed reading and hissed, 'Reading that's not gonna help you. There's no way you're gonna beat me tomorrow. You were just lucky the run this week wasn't a proper race. If it had been, you wouldn't have stood a prayer. Tomorrow's for real.'

*

It was the morning of the race. The two boys made their own way to school as they always did, separated by the length of a bus and their mutual hatred. The race promised to be well contested, because Slevin were up against Burham Manor, their main rivals for the undisputed crown of area champions. With the end of the season in sight, both teams remained unbeaten. Slevin had an enviable record for cross-country, mainly because the location of the school allowed for true cross-country running, while other schools were forced to use the urban streets, but Burham could boast a similar rural training ground.

The start was on the lower sports field. Slevin's top runner in the age group was a fair-haired boy called Richard Browning and Rom lined up next to him. All the runners crowded the tape, jostling for position, and amongst them Rom could see Roger leaning forward with an intense expression. Paddy blew his whistle with a shrill blast and the runners streaked away.

Rom decided to stick with the front runners and quick-ened his pace to get alongside Browning, but just as he did so, he was tripped from behind and stumbled, nearly bring-ing down another runner. The knuckles of his right hand and his right knee smacked into the tarmac, but he was able to glance up and see Roger running past him with his head turned towards him and a cruel smile on his face. Rom was so incensed that he leapt back into his stride as if his feet were on springs.

He pounded after the leaders as fast as he could, passing

Roger without even looking at him and keeping his eyes focused on Browning at the front of the pack. He soon found it was a test of pain and will to stay with Browning and the leaders, but he knew how to endure. He was a fakir.

Two thirds into the race, at a furious pace, Browning took a definite lead from his two main rivals from Burham, but Rom was still right beside him. As they pounded down the road towards the school, Rom edged past Browning, with the slap of the Burham duo's rubber soles right behind them. The school was in sight ahead of them, and the road junction before it, where they would have to turn left and head up a cruel hill for the last stretch, before turning into the lower sports field.

Rom and Browning, almost abreast, leaned into the bend and began to slog up the hill. This last piece of the course found Rom out. His lungs were bursting and his legs felt like jelly, as the strong-running Browning inched past him. When they reached the entrance to the sports field, Rom was staring at the soles of Browning's black pumps as they powered towards the finishing line. He could feel the Burham boys bearing down on him and hear the shouts from the spectators, as the finishing line loomed. As he collapsed over the line, the lead Burham runner was so close behind that he nearly tumbled over him. Lying on the grass, Rom sucked in lungfuls of air.

When he finally rolled over and sat up, a still strong-looking Browning sauntered over and clapped him on the back.

'Well done, Rawnsley,' he said with natural grace. 'I thought you had me there. You'd better get that knee seen to.'

'Wingborn' was a gracious champion.

Regaining his breath, Rom watched the other runners come in. Eventually, there was Roger, red in the face, not last, but not second either, staggering along the finishing straight. Raymond saw the look of hate on Roger's face as he ran up and veered to one side so that he almost ran into the post. He watched as his foster-brother stomped away, hands on hips, down the field towards the school.

*

At dinner in the Marsdens' dining room, Mrs Marsden asked Raymond about the race.

Roger jumped in and said, 'I got a real bad stitch, but I still finished. We won the race.'

'That's nice,' said Mrs Marsden. 'How did you get on Raymond?'

Roger cut in again.

'He was no match for Browning. Remember I told you, I beat him a few weeks back.'

'Yes,' Mrs Marsden said, 'but where did you both finish?'

Raymond saw Mr Marsden's face cloud over as Roger reddened.

'It's all about the team, Mum. Every place counts,' Roger blustered.

Mrs Marsden seemed determined to score points. She turned to Raymond and said, 'What position did you finish, Raymond?'

For the sake of harmony, Raymond would have preferred to agree with Roger's Corinthian-sounding ideals, but he could see she was hell-bent on an answer.

'Second,' Raymond said.

'That's excellent,' Mrs Marsden declared. 'It was only your first serious race as well, wasn't it? And, if I understand it correctly, it was against one of the top teams, wasn't it?'

Raymond didn't respond.

'Roger?' Mrs Marsden queried, raising her eyebrows above her spectacles and looking at her son.

Backed into a corner, Roger leapt to his feet, almost

spilling his chair behind him. 'What are you taking his side for?' he yelled. 'He doesn't even belong here.'

Tears of frustration sprang to his eyes, adding embarrassment to his confusion and anger. Arms flailing, he dashed from the room, knocking the clock from the cabinet in his haste. The thump of his feet shook the stairs, followed by the sound of his bedroom door being slammed.

Stern-faced, Mr Marsden rose to follow his son, almost hissing at his wife, 'Now look what you've done.'

Raymond was conscious of Janet and Mary's accusing stares and Mrs Marsden looked like someone who'd expected wine and tasted vinegar. He wanted to be somewhere else. As soon as he could escape, and despite the tiredness in his legs, he slipped through the back door.

Two teams of local boys were playing football in a field behind the back lane. Raymond climbed over the wall and asked if he could join the game. He'd played with them before and they knew he was a good footballer, so the two captains tossed a coin to decide which side he would play on. He was surprised when, sometime later, a wild-looking Roger joined the other side and took up a defensive position. Roger never played team games.

*

Raymond controlled the ball in the middle of the field, despite a bad bounce from a divot, and sidestepped the cowpat in front of him. With plenty of space ahead of him, he powered forward towards the opponents' goal, but, just when he seemed to be on for a shot, a flying leg came in from the side and hacked him down. Without any rancour, he raised himself to his knees to see who'd committed the foul. Roger stood over him and, with a sneer, kicked Raymond hard in the ribs. Raymond's breath was forced out of him and he slumped forward, as the players from both teams stopped in their tracks and stared in bewilderment.

'Not running so fast now, are you, Miracle Boy?' Roger said.

Raymond remembered that, in the legend, Romulus killed his brother Remus because he'd jeered at him. It was Rom who jumped up to face Roger and exact revenge for the humiliations he'd heaped on Raymond. The force of his attack bowled Roger to the ground and, pinned beneath the raging Rom, he was stunned and helpless to protect himself as Rom pummelled his head and body with his fists.

'You evil bastard!' Rom screeched. 'Don't you ever do that to Raymond again!'

Rom's fury was so out of control that the other boys, who would normally let a fight run its course, ran over and tried to pull him off the battered Roger. It took four bigger boys to drag him off his stricken, sobbing foster-brother. They pulled the still-cursing Rom to the other side of the make-shift football pitch as Roger, his face tear-streaked and nose bloodied, got to his feet and stumbled away with one hand to his head.

A Noble Cause

The drystone wall was an in-between place and Raymond perched on it for the rest of the day, staring across the farmer's field. He didn't go home for tea and nobody came to fetch him. It was dark when he dragged his reluctant feet home, steeling himself for the retribution he knew would come from his victim's father. He opened the back door as if peeling a plaster from a scab and entered the kitchen. Mrs Marsden was standing with her back to the kitchen cupboards, gripping the worktop behind her. She was about to speak when the living room door burst open and Mr Marsden appeared at the kitchen door with a face like a comic strip monster and his fists clenched at his sides.

'Right, you! Come here!' he roared.

Raymond was suddenly conscious of the dried blood spattered on his T-shirt and caked on his knuckles, and realised he was a red rag to a raging bull.

Mrs Marsden stepped in front of Raymond and faced her irate husband.

'No, Frank,' she shrilled.

'Get out of my way, Hilda,' he said with menace, stepping forward. 'He's got it coming and you know it.'

Raymond didn't want to hide behind his foster-mother's apron. He'd prepared himself for punishment, as he had many times before, but when he tried to step out from behind her, she put her arms out behind her to hold him back.

'Raymond, stay where you are,' she instructed. 'Frank, if you so much as touch this boy, I'm calling the police.'

Looking over Mrs Marsden's shoulder, Raymond saw the look of frustration suffusing his foster-father's broad red face.

'Hilda!' he spat through clenched teeth as he took another step forward.

Mrs Marsden closed her arms even tighter around Raymond and stood her ground.

'I mean it, Frank,' she said.

Her husband halted, shaking. Raymond was amazed to see the fury draining out of his would-be executioner as he stood before them, glaring. He'd never have imagined that Mrs Marsden would stand up to him like this, and subdue him.

'Right,' Mr Marsden barked. 'That's it. I'm taking Roger to my brother's. He's not staying in this house with him and neither am I. We won't be back until he's gone for good. It's been a mistake from the start. It was your idea, so you'll have to sort it out. You'd better keep him out of my way until we've gone.'

With that, he turned on his heels and stormed out of the kitchen. Mrs Marsden, still holding Raymond behind her, like a mother protecting her young in the wild, didn't move for a few minutes. Eventually, she stepped forward and turned to face him.

'Stay in here with me,' she said. 'I'll make you something to eat.'

Raymond watched her, a gentle woman with grey hair and spectacles, making beans on toast, and marvelled at the recent memory of her facing her large, brawny husband with fury in his heart. When she'd made the meal, he stood eating it at the worktop, while she stood by the door as if on guard. He was lifting his last forkful of beans to his mouth when the crash of the front door made the whole house shudder. Mrs Marsden didn't even blink.

'All right,' she said, 'we can relax now. Go into the dining room and I'll make a cup of tea.'

While he sat in the dining room waiting for the tea, Janet and Mary came out of the living room and went into the kitchen, from where Raymond could hear fierce whispering. Mrs Marsden raised her voice in exasperation.

'Look, I don't know, Janet,' she said. 'Just go back into the room and watch television. I'll talk to you both later.'

The girls disappeared back into the living room, but not before giving Raymond resentful looks as they passed the open dining room door. A couple of minutes later, Mrs Marsden bustled in with a cup of tea and a plate of biscuits, which she placed in front of him.

'I need to talk to the girls,' she said. 'Will you be all right on your own?'

Raymond nodded his assent and she left. He was tired. He looked around the tidy, familiar room and realised, with absolute certainty, that the Sacred Heart and the plaque with 'Home Sweet Home' on it would soon just be memories for him. The demon was dead and maybe now this room would return to what it was before he arrived: a simple room where a family gathered each day. That's what Mrs Marsden deserved, if not more. He couldn't take the place of her real son and he didn't want to. He felt no pride in what he'd done. Roger had asked for it and finally he'd got what he deserved.

*

Roger didn't turn up for school all week.

On Saturday, the beginning of the Easter weekend, Raymond's foster-mother told him to put on his Sunday-best clothes and wait in the dining room, as someone was coming to see him. Raymond sat at the table trying to read Joseph Conrad's *Nostromo* and wondering who could be coming to visit him. Maybe it was Mr Leather, who'd promised to carry his suitcases if things didn't work out.

While he waited, he could hear Mrs Marsden busying herself upstairs, while the girls stayed in their bedroom. When the doorbell rang, he heard Mrs Marsden hurry down the stairs and open the front door. He'd risen to answer the door himself and was standing in the hallway when she opened it. He was shocked to see the figure framed in the doorway.

It was Mrs Noble, his old Pictorial Auntie. He'd thought he would never see her again. She seemed business-like, as always, as she entered. She handed her lilac coat to Mrs Marsden and said, 'Hello Raymond. How are you?'

Still stunned, Raymond replied, 'I'm fine, thank you.'

Mrs Marsden hung Mrs Noble's coat in the hall and said, 'Raymond, Mrs Noble and I need to talk. Can you wait in the dining room?'

Seeing Mrs Noble sent a shiver of hope through him. Of all the adults he'd ever known, the 'Noble Lady' was the one who understood him best.

He waited and listened to the murmur of female voices in the next room, until finally his foster-mother came to him and said Mrs Noble wanted to talk to him on his own. His legs felt heavy as he made his way to the living room, feeling light-headed.

His Pictorial Auntie was standing by the fireplace with her hands by the sides of her pleated skirt when Raymond entered the room.

'Come here, Raymond,' she said, holding out her hands.

Raymond stepped forward and she grasped both his hands in hers.

'You're not happy here are you, Raymond?'

The touch of her hands and the sympathetic tone of her voice brought a lump to Raymond's throat and tears began to prick his eyes. He could withstand cruelty and pain, but kindness and sympathy broke his heart. Something inside him gave way and his tears began to flow.

'You don't have to say anything,' she soothed, releasing his hands. She cupped his face and wiped his tears with her thumbs. Her powdered face was close to his as she continued to speak. 'You don't have to say anything. I know you've had an awful time. I wish I'd known before. I thought this would be good for you. I didn't think I'd need to see you again.'

Raymond's shoulders shook and his tears flowed into her hands like the release of a long-dammed river. Mrs Noble's voice trembled.

'It's over now,' she promised. 'Mrs Marsden's told me everything. You're leaving today. Everything's arranged. Someone's coming to fetch you soon.'

She placed her tear-wet hands on his hair, stroking gently. Then she shocked him. She swore with feeling.

'I know it's been absolutely bloody, sodding awful, but I also know you're a brave lad.' She put her hands on his shoulders, guiding him to the settee and sitting him down. 'Wait here,' she said, composing herself and reverting back to her usual controlled self, 'I'm going to help Mrs Marsden with your things. Will you be all right?'

Raymond nodded, feeling numb.

When Mrs Noble left the room, Raymond sat, trembling, the tears still spilling down his face. He couldn't stop shaking. He rubbed his eyes with the back of his fists and looked around. He gazed at the olive-skinned woman in the painting above the fireplace. Her dark brown eyes seemed moist and her tumid lips seemed to twitch into an enigmatic smile. He rubbed his eyes again. Through the muffled roaring in his ears he could just hear the distant voices of the two women

When the doorbell rang, he jumped as if a gun had been fired next to his head. He heard the door open and then a man's voice in the hall, talking to the two women. Mrs Noble came into the room with his coat, her scented fragrance wafting into the room like a shaft of sunlight bursting into a deep woodland glade, and he stood up and took it from her. He didn't put it on, but held it so that it trailed on the floor. She put her hands on his shoulders and then clasped him to her silk-swathed breast so that her spectacle chain creased his cheek. He was a rag doll with a secret heart and soul. She pushed him back and held him by the shoulders again, a resolute look on her soft white face.

'You'll be all right, Raymond,' she reassured him. 'It's for the best. Come on.'

She placed her hand on his shoulder and led him to the door. Mr Pickup stood to attention by the front door with Raymond's suitcases at his feet and his hands behind his back. To Raymond's left, Mrs Marsden stood with her back to the wall. Her hands were clasped in front of her and her shoulders were slumped. The coloured reflections from the stained glass panel in the front door shone on her face and spectacles, behind which were glistening tears. Raymond lowered his eyes and shuffled past her, feeling her hand touch his trailing arm. Without a word, Mr Pickup opened the front door, while Mrs Noble squeezed Raymond's arm and pushed him forward.

Picking up the suitcases as if they were as light as a feather, Mr Pickup led Raymond towards his familiar black car parked by the roadside and nodded his head towards the back seat. Raymond climbed in, while Mr Pickup put the suitcases in the boot. Raymond felt drained. He didn't know where they were going and he didn't care. He glanced up at the house and saw two small faces peering from the dormer window, partly hidden by curtains. Mr Pickup started up the car and they began to roll down Coupland Road.

Mr Pickup didn't speak and Raymond didn't want him to.

Walking Back to Happiness

Mr Pickup parked the car in front of a white portico framing the entrance to a majestic-looking Georgian house. He switched off the engine and exited the car with purpose, opening the door next to Raymond as he headed for the rear of the vehicle. As Raymond climbed out, the silent chauffeur lifted his suitcases out of the boot and headed towards the entrance to the house, where he deposited Raymond in the care of a young woman with fine skin and a sympathetic face.

As the tyres of the departing car crunched on the gravel drive, she smiled and said, 'Welcome to Lawson Court, Raymond. Come on in. You'll have a room of your own for a while, until we find somewhere for you. I don't think you'll be here too long.'

She picked up one of Raymond's suitcases, which happened to be the lightest, and turned to enter the house. As she led him through a substantial hallway, his pre-occupation with the heavy suitcase didn't stop him from noticing the clean smell of scented soap that exuded from her. At the end of the hallway, she began to climb a broad flight of stairs.

'You've got plenty of time to unpack,' she said, looking back. 'Once I've shown you to your room, I'll leave you to it. Mrs Noble is on her way to see you to make sure you're settled. I'll come and get you when she gets here.'

At the top of the stairs, they walked down a long corridor

until she opened one of the many doors they passed. They entered and, lowering his suitcase to the floor, she announced, 'This is your room. Take your time. I'll be back soon.'

The room contained a comfortable-looking single bed with a pale green cover, a chest of drawers, a wardrobe and a table and chair. The lace-curtained window overlooking the front of the house made the room look homely, except for the ornate metal spikes on the other side of the glass. Were they there to keep people in or out? They wouldn't have kept Brian in. Raymond wondered how his old friend was getting on at home. Brian would have sorted out Roger a lot quicker than he had.

Raymond sighed and started to unpack, folding his clothes in the drawers and hanging his school uniform in the wardrobe. He felt like a robot from one of Brian's comics; even hiding his pictures at the back of the top drawer, behind his clothes, was automatic. When he'd finished, he pushed the suitcases under the bed, sat down on the chair and gazed out of the window, not at what lay below, but at the mocking blue sky. After a while, the nice-looking lady who'd shown him to his room came back.

'Come on, Raymond,' she chimed. 'Mrs Noble's arrived and she'd like to see you.'

His legs felt as though they belonged to somebody else as he followed her back downstairs. They went through a door on one side of the hallway and into a room with comfort-able chintz-covered armchairs grouped around. Mrs Noble was sitting in one of the chairs, her handbag resting on her knees. Raymond noticed for the first time that day that she looked pale and drawn, as if this momentous day had taken its toll on her too.

His Pictorial Auntie patted the chair next to her and he sat down. She inclined her head towards the young woman, who was now sitting opposite them, and said, 'This is Miss

Bellamy. She's going to tell you about Lawson Court and how long you'll be here. Don't worry. It'll be fine and it won't be for long, will it, Miss Bellamy?'

'Oh no,' assured the sweet-scented Miss Bellamy. 'Lawson Court is just a short-term home, while we find the best place for you to stay. You'll like it here. None of our children stay long and we try to make their stay as pleasant as possible. We'd like to understand you better, so we can make the best choice of home for you. Everybody has his or her own room, so you can be private. While you're here, you'll have some sessions with Dr Charlerousse. Don't worry about it. She understands children very well and is here to help them.'

While she was speaking, Mrs Noble nodded throughout until she decided to intervene.

'This is the right place for you at the moment, Raymond. You've had a tough time. The people here will help you and I'll come and visit you when I can. You'll be back at school soon and everything will be back to normal. I know you'll settle down and do well.'

Opening the clasp of her large black leather handbag, she reached in, saying, 'I brought something for you. You and I both know reading is the best medicine for you.'

She held out a hardback book and Raymond took it from her. He looked at the cover. It was *The Magic Mountain* by Thomas Mann.

'Thank you,' he mumbled, more grateful than he could say for seeing her that day, and thankful for her intervention.

'Well, I have to go,' she said, raising herself from her chair with some difficulty. 'I just wanted to see you safely into your new home.'

Raymond stood up as she took a step towards him. Holding him by the shoulders, she planted a cool, dry kiss on his forehead. Then she turned and shook hands with Miss Bellamy.

'Thank you,' she said, 'I'll be in touch to see how he's getting on.'

'You can wait here, Raymond, while I see Mrs Noble out,' Miss Bellamy said to him. 'I'll be back in a moment.

After a few minutes, Miss Bellamy returned and showed him around. Raymond was relieved that all the rooms they passed through were spacious and functional. This was more like what he was used to and he welcomed it after his claustrophobic ordeal at the Marsdens' house.

Finally, they entered a dining room. It was airy and pleasant, with clean tablecloths on the four tables, and a vase of flowers on a windowsill. The window looked out onto an elaborate garden at the back of the house.

'This is where we have our meals,' Miss Bellamy said. 'There are only seven children here, including you, so there's plenty of room. All the members of staff sit at the same tables as the children.'

Next to the window was a door that they proceeded through, which led into the garden. Although not huge, it had sunken walls, flowerbeds, lawns, shrubs and trees. In the lower part of the garden, Raymond could see a stone fountain, although no water spouted from the cherubic trumpeter heralding the sky. What also took Raymond's eye was an older girl sitting at the fountain's edge, looking in the opposite direction to where they were.

'That's Carol,' said Miss Bellamy. 'Come on, let's go and meet her.'

They walked down stone steps and across the lawn towards the fountain and, as they approached, Miss Bellamy called, 'Carol, I thought you were in your room. This is Raymond Rawnsley. He's just arrived. Can you look after him and bring him in for tea later?'

The girl turned her head and stared at them. Raymond guessed she was around sixteen, judging by the way her thin cotton dress strained against her breasts and hips. Her hair was fair, of medium length, and backcombed, revealing a lightly freckled face that squinted at the sun she now faced.

'Why me?' she complained.

'Because,' Miss Bellamy replied, heading back to the house.

'What's your book?' the girl asked, leaning forward and pushing her dress between her thighs with her arms.

Raymond had forgotten he was still carrying the book and looked at her, perplexed.

She ignored his confusion and said, 'Never read one. You haven't got any ciggies, have you?'

Raymond shook his head.

'I'm dying for a fag,' she complained. 'This place is all right, but they won't let you smoke. What are you standing there for? Sit down.'

She patted the flat stone lip of the fountain next to her. Raymond perched alongside her, his book in his lap.

'What are you in here for?' she continued, her blue eyes studying him as she turned to face him.

'Nothing,' Raymond said.

'You must have done summat,' she insisted. 'Don't you know what this place is?'

Raymond shifted. She was so close he could smell her disturbing natural scent.

'A children's home?' he suggested.

She gave a derisory chuckle.

'That's where you might end up, if you're lucky. This is an assessment centre. This is where they decide what to do with you. You might end up in an approved school or borstal, or summat like that. I'm here because me mum says I've gone wild. I haven't been to school for about two month, at least. Me boyfriend's twenty-two. I've been going round his place all the time. Do you know what we've been up to? How old are you?'

97

'Fourteen,' Raymond mumbled, spellbound by her candour.

'I'm nearly sixteen. I reckon I should be able to do what I like, but my boyfriend's right in it now. They won't let me see him. Do you know what I'm talking about?'

He nodded, comprehending. A life amongst girls had been an invaluable education. She grinned and then prattled on. 'They've put me in here to decide what to do with me. I've got to go to a new school near here after Easter. They can't do nowt. When I'm sixteen I'm off. You won't see me for dust. Me mum can get me a job in the mill. Once I'm making some brass, nobody can tell me owt. They can whistle. Have you heard that Helen Shapiro? I can sing like that. When I've got enough brass, I'm off to London and then I'll be walking back to happiness. Anyway, c'mon, tell me what you're here for 'cos you must have done summat.'

Her clear blue eyes and open face, with golden freckles sprinkled across each cheek, were so earnest and guileless he told her a faltering version of his story.

When he'd finished, she exclaimed, 'Well, you've done nowt wrong. I'd have brayed that Roger myself. In fact, he'd still be in hospital now. I reckon they'll just put you in a new home. They like to study you here first. There's more staff than kids and they're always watching you. They try and make friends with you and they're always asking you stuff. I get bored with it, me. Then there's Dr Charleyruss. She sounds like she's German. She makes you look at stupid pictures of nowt, like inkblots, and then asks you what you can see. She's always asking me sly questions about me dad, but I'm saying nowt, me. I think she thinks I've got some big secret, but I've nowt to hide. I am who I am, me.'

She chattered on in this vein for some time with a disarming lack of self-consciousness. Meanwhile, Raymond mulled over what she'd said about Lawson Court. He'd never heard of an assessment centre before and wasn't sure whether to believe her, although she seemed incapable of deceit. Although intimidating with her open sexuality, she was friendly and he needed friendship.

She continued, talking about her family. 'Me dad's always in trouble; me mum's always drunk; and me brother Darryl's in an approved school. Maybe I'm best out of it for a while, but I miss 'em as well. Do you know what me name is? Carol Farrell. Can you imagine me and me brother at school? Carol and Darryl Farrell. That's me stupid dad. When I was younger, me mum used to send me to school without knickers. All the lads used to be dropping their pencils under my desk, so eventually I used to give 'em a good look. I bet they wish they could have a look now. And me knockers have got really big. What do you think?'

She pulled apart the collar of her dress and leaned towards Raymond, revealing her ivory, freckle-free cleavage.

A voice rang out. 'Carol!'

Carol started, yanking the lapels of her cotton dress together, and then gave a sheepish grin. 'Oho! We'd better go in.'

Raymond rose and followed her into the house where they joined the gathering in the dining room.

A square-jawed, dark-haired man wearing a Fair Isle jumper and flanked by two young boys called him over to an empty place at his table.

'Hello,' he said as Raymond sat down. 'My name is Mr Makepeace. I'm one of the permanent staff here. These two young scamps are Graham and Peter Worden.'

The boys, with fair hair and short fringes, looked identical. They said nothing, but looked at Raymond with inquisitive blue eyes.

'That's right,' Mr Makepeace confirmed, 'they're identical twins, aren't you, lads? They don't say much, but we're working on it, aren't we, boys?'

He winked at them, but the two boys made no response to his bonhomie.

'This is Raymond Rawnsley,' he said to the twins. 'He's just arrived today. He goes to Slevin Grammar, don't you, Raymond?'

He didn't wait for confirmation, as the food was on the table: fish and chips with mushy peas.

'Tuck in,' Mr Makepeace instructed, and they began to eat.

The relaxed atmosphere during the meal struck Raymond. There was no grace said before the meal and everyone chatted throughout. Carol Farrell was right. This wasn't a children's home. Between mouthfuls of fish and chips, which he appeared to relish, Mr Makepeace continued to talk to him. He gave him a verbal tour of the room.

Indicating the table to their left, he said, 'That's Miss Bellamy, who you've met. She can be a bit barmy,' he said in a stage whisper.

The fragrant Miss Bellamy gave a mock frown.

'That's the irrepressible Carol Farrell, who lived in a barrel with her brother Darryl.'

Carol poked her tongue out at him, while he laughed.

Sitting next to Carol was a pale, mousy haired young girl in a grey cardigan, wearing pink spectacles.

'That's our resident genius, Pauline Pratt. No one can beat her at chess, can they Pauline?'

The girl responded with a faint and serious smile.

'Over here,' gestured Mr Makepeace towards the table on their right, 'we have Mr Witham. Mr Witham used to be a Rugby League player, so nobody messes with him.'

The large, muscular, tousle-haired man in question turned around and gave an infectious grin.

'Finally,' Mr Makepeace announced, having elevated his performance to one of a circus master, 'We have Noel Shaw, the demon dribbler.' He paused while the thin-faced, hollow-eyed young recipient of this accolade blinked in their direction. 'And last, but not least, the gorgeous Avril Whitely.'

The last-named, a plump girl of around fifteen with dark plaits and a navy blue cardigan stretched tight around her, simpered towards them, a piece of golden batter still protruding from her mouth.

'Everybody,' Mr Makepeace trumpeted, 'this is Raymond Rawnsley – serious student of literature and soon-to-be head boy of Slevin Grammar.'

It was a half-truth, but it still made Raymond blush.

Mr Makepeace chatted to him throughout the meal, mainly about school, all the time trying to involve the two silent twins, but to no avail. After a pleasant tea, of far more homely food than Raymond remembered from his previous sojourn under the care of the Welfare Authority, everybody carried their dishes to the kitchen to do the washing-up. Even this was different to what Raymond remembered, because on this occasion, the adults worked with them. The jocularity of the staff was much in evidence throughout, although he sensed that the response of the children to this was mostly guarded. After they'd finished their chores, and as he was standing around wondering what he should do next, Miss Bellamy came over to him.

'It's up to you what you do now, Raymond,' she said. 'You can spend some time in your room or watch television in the sitting room. I know it's been a long day for you, so there's no pressure to mix in straight away.'

'I'll go to my room, Miss,' he said.

'OK. Come down any time you like. We have supper at nine, so if you're not down, I'll pop up and see if you want any. By the way, there's a bathroom at the end of the upstairs corridor if you need it.'

With his book under his arm, Raymond found his way

back to his room. He lay on the bed and tried to read, but his mind wandered. If he wasn't going to stay long, why did he have to be there at all? Why did he have to see this Dr Charlerousse? There was nothing wrong with him. He was just a bit down at the moment, that's all. On the one hand, he felt a sense of relief at leaving the Marsden household forever. On the other hand, he felt empty and alone; he was a reject and a failure. What did life have in store for him now?

Carol Farrell's yearning for freedom and independence had struck a chord in him. He found himself thinking about the future, to a time when he'd be free, to an age when he'd no longer be under the control of the corporation's Welfare Department. Do this; do that; go here; go there. One day it would be different. Eventually, he closed his eyes and laid his head on the pillow.

The Liar, the Thief, the Arsonist, the Nymphomaniac and the Mute

Raymond woke to find he was still dressed in his day clothes, but someone had covered him with a blanket and closed the curtains. As he lay there taking stock, there was a tap on the door. He wasn't sure how to respond, but, after a moment, Miss Bellamy stepped into the room with a cheery greeting.

'Good morning. How are we today? I didn't bother waking you last night, as you were fast asleep. You must have needed that. Come on. Up you get.'

She threw open the curtains with a flourish as she said this, letting bright sunlight stream into the room. Raymond swung his feet onto the floor as she almost skipped back to the door.

'Come on, Raymond, let me show you where the bathrooms are. There are two and you can use either one. Carol Farrell usually keeps one to herself, so it's just as well there are two.'

She handed him a towel from a hook behind the door and led him along the corridor, pointing out not only the doors of inmates' bedrooms as they passed, but also those of the staff that were interspersed among them. When they reached the end of the corridor, she showed him the bathrooms.

'There's a new toothbrush for you in the locker,' she said, pushing him into one of the bathrooms. 'Get yourself washed and changed. Breakfast is in twenty minutes. You'll only need a T-shirt today. It's going to be a lovely day.' And with that she left him to his ablutions.

When he emerged from the bathroom, somewhat fresher and more awake, a bleary-eyed Carol Farrell, wearing a lopsided pale blue dressing gown, was stumbling along the corridor towards him in bare feet. Her backcombed hair was sticking up like she'd had an electric shock.

'Another day in Heartbreak Hotel,' she mumbled as she passed and locked herself in the bathroom.

*

The day seemed almost surreal to Raymond. In sunny weather, everybody played football and badminton in the garden. Members of the staff joined in the fun and games with gusto and encouraged anyone who sat on the sidelines to join in. Raymond was introduced to two new adults: Miss Priestley, who was dark, thin and earnest, and Mr Templeton, who was quite young, but bald. Both were as ebullient as the other members of staff he'd met the day before. The fun and games were infectious and his body began to feel like his own again.

Tea on the lawn, *Doctor Who* on television in grainy black and white pictures and a supper of digestive biscuits and hot cocoa rounded off the day and Raymond went to bed as tired and contented as he'd been for ages. When he went to the bathroom, Carol Farrell came out with her blouse half undone. Raymond couldn't help staring at its barely concealed contents. Carol grinned.

'I know what you're thinking,' she said. 'This place is like a Butlins Holiday Camp, the staff are Redcoats and I should be in the beauty pageant.'

She sauntered off down the corridor swinging her hips like a beauty queen.

'There's just one difference, Raymond,' she called out

without looking back. 'They won't let you go home when you want to.'

Raymond was sure he could detect a faint smell of cigarette smoke as he entered the bathroom.

Before drifting off to sleep in his room, he suddenly remembered something. It was Sunday. In fact, it was Easter Sunday, and they hadn't been to church once. He couldn't remember a Sunday when he'd not been to church, or at least pretended to.

There was still a week of holiday before school began, and every day went by in similar fashion. In between playing games, Raymond read his new book, often outside, sitting cross-legged on the lawn, or scribbled and painted in his room. His guardians were happy to let him do what he wanted, as long as he balanced the time he spent on his own with time with the rest of the inmates.

*

Raymond was reading on the lawn with the Worden twins sitting next to him when Miss Bellamy, demure in a white blouse and tennis skirt, called him into the house. Every time he read his book the twins sat next to him. The first time it happened, their silent presence unnerved him so much that he began to read aloud to them. From then on, they joined him every time he read, watching his face as if they were reading his lips. He'd no idea what they made of *The Magic Mountain,* which was deep and philosophical even for him, but they were listening with rapt attention when Miss Bellamy called. When he stood up to go into the house, they both stood up in unison and followed him.

'Not you two mites,' Miss Bellamy said and shooed them back into the garden. 'Come on, Raymond, today you're going to see Dr Charlerousse.'

She led him to part of the house he'd never been in before.

105

'These are Welfare Department offices during the day,' Miss Bellamy explained, as they passed doors with panes of dimpled glass on either side of a long dark corridor.

Eventually, she rapped on a dark oak door and a voice with a slight foreign accent called out, 'Come in.'

They entered a spacious room that looked like a doctor's surgery.

'Raymond Rawnsley, Dr Charlerousse,' Miss Bellamy announced, and without waiting for acknowledgement, turned with a swish of her skirt and left.

Dr Charlerousse was sitting at a large oak desk pushed up against the wall. She seemed old to Raymond. Her coarse, grey hair was tied back in a bun and she was wearing a cream blouse with ruffles at the collar and a purplish knitted skirt and jacket. As she turned to face him, he saw she had gold half-spectacles perched on the end of her nose and attached to a gold chain around her neck. She laid down her tortoiseshell fountain pen on a large blotting pad on the desk.

'Raymond,' she said, indicating a chair at the side of the desk, 'come and sit down here.'

Although her accent was not strong, he decided immediately from her clipped tones that she was Austrian.

'How are you enjoying your stay here?' she enquired as he sat down on the wooden chair.

'All right,' he answered, deciding that the grey eyes looking at him over the rim of her spectacles were not unkind.

'All right?' she said with a faint shrug. 'Only all right? Better than where you were before, no?'

Raymond nodded and folded his hands in his lap.

'Good,' she said, pursing her lips and studying him for a moment. 'Firstly, let me explain, Raymond. You will not be here for long. It was a difficult time for you in your foster home, no? We want to be sure we find the right home for

106

you. All the children here have had a difficult time and we
have to know what is best for them.' She paused but didn't
take her eyes off him. 'You are a very intelligent boy who
keeps things to himself. Therefore, I am going to tell you
about your new friends. This is a confidence, Raymond, *that*
I know you will respect.'

Raymond assumed a respectful and attentive look.

'The twin boys have lost their mother in tragic circumstances. Now they rarely speak, except to each other in
voices no one can hear. It will take a long time for them to
trust the world and not just themselves. Avril Whitely steals
because she has low self-esteem, because other children are
cruel to her, because even her own family made fun of her.
Noel Shaw likes fires. He likes them so much he starts them
whenever he feels frustrated or upset. Pauline Pratt is the
cleverest of girls, but she is very shy and lacks confidence.
This makes her tell lies all the time, often when she has no
need to. Carol Farrell is in denial. She cannot accept what
has happened to her so she acts as if it's normal, shall we
say, to be over-friendly. Children with difficulties, no?' She
paused, before adding, 'And Raymond Rawnsley?'

Raymond picked at a small piece of detached nail on his
little finger, sensing he was facing someone of infinite
patience. He was thinking of what she'd told him about
the other children. He'd met them all before in children's
homes. As far as he was concerned, there was nothing
remarkable about them. After a few moments of silence, she
leaned forward towards him, her bony hands resting on the
desk.

'We need to know you, Raymond, so we can do what is
best for you,' she said, and straightening up, she continued,
'and *you* need to know *yourself.*'

A further long silence ensued before she reached to the
far side of the desk to lift up a large black book, and placed
it in front of him.

'We are going to do a little exercise,' she informed him, 'and then you can go out and play with your new friends again. You are a smart boy and I also know you like to draw. Your imagination is good. I want you to look at the images in this book and tell me what you see. Don't hold back and don't be afraid to say what you think. We can all see something in everything.'

She opened the first page, which had an image of what looked like an inkblot, splattered and mirrored onto the page, as if it had been folded and pressed while the ink was still wet. He decided to open his mind to it and, looking at the first inkblot, he said immediately, 'A crossbow.'

Dr Charlerousse scribbled as she flipped through the pages and Raymond offered his suggestions for the images that were revealed.

'Very good, Raymond,' she praised when they'd finished. 'That's enough for today, I think. It has been very good to meet you. I would like to see you on Monday. I know you will be at school, but I will see you when you get home, no?'

Raymond rose to leave, but before he reached the door, she said, 'I've heard about your paintings. Do you think you could bring them with you next time, no?'

Raymond acquiesced and left her office, realising he was now a psychological study.

This might be 'No Laws Court', but the walls have eyes and ears.

When he got back to the garden, the Worden twins were sitting on the steps by the door. As he walked over to his book still lying on the lawn, the two dumbstruck boys walked behind him, and when he squatted down, they sat down beside him, watching his face intently as he picked up his book.

Football Fantasy

Raymond came down from his room in the evening while everyone else was watching television. The door to the garden was still open and the light was fading fast as he went through to breathe the evening air. Almost without a sound, Carol Farrell appeared next to him and grabbed his arm.

'Come on,' she said, dragging him towards the bottom of the garden and out of sight of the house.

She pulled him down behind a dense evergreen bush where the grass was overgrown, and knelt down in front of him. Leaning forward, she ran her tongue over her lips and placed her hand down the front of her dress, rummaging between breasts that shifted disconcertingly as she did so, and pulled out a crumpled pack of Woodbines and a box of matches.

'Wanna fag?' she asked with her face close to his.

He shook his head, trying to appear unconcerned.

She struck a match between cupped hands and lit the cigarette she held between her protruding lips. Taking a deep drag, she blew the smoke to one side, all the time studying him.

'You've been to see Charleyruss today, haven't you?' she said, picking a sliver of tobacco from her lower lip.

Raymond nodded.

'Did she say owt about me?' she asked, blowing a long stream of smoke towards his face.

'No,' he lied, turning his head away from the smoke. 'Why should she?'

Carol inched forward until she was almost on top of him, and clasped her strong thighs around his.

'No reason,' she murmured through a cloud of smoke. 'Just wondered, that's all.'

She continued to smoke her cigarette in silence, while Raymond tried not to squirm, having discovered that any movement made her tighten her grip on him. He'd recently found out that he could get an erection stroking a cat. With a final long drag, she stubbed her cigarette out in the ground beside her and threw the stub as far into the bushes as she could. She let the final wisps of smoke curl from her mouth, drawing them back between her lips, before exhaling again. As she did so, she squeezed his thighs hard between hers and leaned towards him so that her thin dress strained even more against her rounded breasts.

'Do you wanna snog me?' she breathed and puckered her lips in anticipation.

The smell of tobacco was mingled with her fragrant breath, but it wasn't unpleasant.

'No!' he cried, recoiling and thrusting his hands against her shoulders, then he jumped up so quickly that he nearly knocked her over. 'Let's get back.'

As he hurried towards the house in the evanescent light, feeling like an idiot, she called out, 'You're weird.'

Maybe he was. He'd wanted to kiss her though.

When he returned from the bathroom to his room later that night, and just as he was about to enter his room, she called softly from her door further down the corridor, 'Goodnight, Raymondo.'

As he turned around, she gave a coy wave and, with the other hand, lifted her pale blue dressing gown to reveal a milk-white thigh.

In bed in the dark, he wondered why he'd run away.

Maybe he'd read too many books and his idea of romance was too idealistic. He couldn't get the suggestive odour of sweet, cigarette-tainted breath out of his nostrils.

*

Raymond joined in a crazy game of football on the lawn on Saturday afternoon; crazy because they had to play around the fountain standing in the middle of their pitch. All the children played, except for Pauline, who stood on the lip of the fountain and acted as referee. The Worden twins were goalkeepers, one for each side. Carol Farrell was on Raymond's team, along with Mr Makepeace, while Noel Shaw, Avril Whitely and Mr Witham were on the other side.

Raymond was a decent player, but Noel was a wizard of the dribble. Once he got the ball he kept running round and round the fountain with it, so they had to gang up on him to get it back. Whenever there was a shot on goal and one of the Worden goalkeepers dived for the ball, his twin in the opposite goal dived as well. Carol was completely inept, but wildly enthusiastic and the effect of her exertions on her body held more interest for Raymond than her footwork. He was enjoying himself when Carol, eager to get the ball, clashed with Mr Witham. Laughing out loud, he wrestled her to the ground.

'Stop touching me!' Carol screamed.

Jumping to her feet, she ran towards the top of the garden, her legs kicking behind her, while she held the collar of her striped blouse to her throat. She threw herself into a garden chair, as the game came to a halt and Mr Witham and Mr Makepeace went up to her to calm her down. With Mr Makepeace holding her by her elbow, they took Carol inside, while the rest of them mooched around the fountain.

For a while Raymond heard Carol's raised voice being soothed by the calmer voices of the men, until finally, they came back out, Carol trailing in the rear. Further disarray was caused when Mr Makepeace declared the football game was at an end; Noel Shaw threw a tantrum, shouting in frustration, and thrashing the ground with his fists and feet until finally he had to be carried inside by Mr Witham. These events proved too much for the Worden twins, who hid behind the fountain and refused to move for a cajoling Mr Makepeace. Pauline sat cross-legged on the fountain above their heads and tried to help.

'Your mum's come to see you,' she cooed.

While this commotion was ensuing, Raymond retired to a chair at the top of the garden where he'd previously left his book and buried his head in the pages. Carol came up and slumped into the chair beside him, her legs splayed in front of her, and whispered, 'That dirty git's always gawping at me and trying to touch me.'

A moment later, a red-faced Avril flounced past, her arms folded across her chest, heading for the house. As she passed, she hissed at Carol, 'That's your fault, you tart,' inducing a fleck of spittle to escape from the corner of her mouth.

Carol made to follow her to remonstrate, but, in alarm, Raymond held her arm. She stopped and gave him a strange look, which made him let go, but she stayed where she was.

Calm was eventually restored. The twins crept from behind the fountain and came to stand on either side of Raymond while he read his book. Seeing this, he decided to sit on the lawn by the fountain so they could sit beside him. Mr Makepeace took Pauline off for a game of chess in the house, and Noel and Avril failed to reappear. Carol threw herself face-down on the lawn in front of Raymond and the two boys as he read out loud. As he read, the twins stared at him as usual, their lips moving silently with his, while Carol kicked her legs and destroyed innocent blades of grass.

Raymond became absorbed in the story of Hans Clastorp and his growing physical attraction to Madame Clavdia Chauchat, until, after a while, feeling uncomfortable with the subject, he glanced up. Carol was watching him just as intently as the Worden twins, her elbows planted on the ground and her head in her hands. She caught his glance and shifted, causing a button to open on her blouse so that her pendulous white breasts were exposed, and smiled.

Raymond reddened and concentrated on the book in front of him, divorcing himself from the words he read. He didn't look up again until Miss Priestley called them in for tea. As they stood up, Carol, brushing flecks of grass from her shorts, purred, 'That were dead nice.'

After the embarrassing aftermath to their game of football, tea was a little more subdued than usual, although all the staff tried their best to inject their typical joviality into the proceedings. Noel Shaw was still sulking over the premature curtailment of his favourite football game. Avril, her hair even more fiercely parted into ponytails than usual, was like a middle-aged woman at a whist drive who was being forced to suffer the presence of an unwanted member of the lower class; taking every opportunity to shoot daggers at Carol. Pauline was, in her serious way, aloof, and the twins were as impervious to efforts to draw them into conversation as ever.

When the meal was over, Raymond decided to escape to his room to read for a while and disappeared upstairs. After a couple of hours, during which he'd changed his mind and decided to do some drawing, he decided to miss supper and turn in.

Carol Farrell was playing football under a blazing hot sun. A film of sweat glistened on her heaving chest as she chased the ball around a pitch covered in a carpet of white daisies. Exhausted, she stopped and wiped her forehead with the back of her hand and squinted up at the sun. With a shrug, she began to unbutton her blouse and when it was open she slipped it back over her shoulders and let it fall to the ground. Her white bra could not hold all the flesh it was meant to contain. She smiled, reached round behind her and began to fumble with the fastener on her bra strap. Snap. Snap. The cups began to slip from her breasts and she shifted her hands to the straps on her shoulder.

A bell was ringing somewhere. It was getting louder and louder. Struggling through the fog of reluctant waking Raymond suddenly realised what it was.

It was the fire alarm.

Burning Desire

Mr Witham burst into Raymond's room and dragged the covers from his bed.

'Out! Out!' he shouted. 'Into the garden now! Go!'

Raymond swung his legs from the bed, slipped his feet into his slippers, and grabbed his dressing gown as he ran out of the bedroom. The upper half of the corridor was filled with grey smoke and staff and children alike were bursting from their rooms, pulling on dressing gowns and jumpers and running towards the stairs. The Worden twins were screaming and Miss Bellamy, pink candlewick dressing gown flying behind her, grabbed them both by the hand and clattered down the steps.

'Come on! Come on, everybody!' she cried, and the others followed.

They congregated at the top of the garden, clustering around while the questions flew.

'What's happening? What's going on?'

Miss Bellamy asserted order while she counted heads. Everyone was accounted for except Mr Witham and Noel Shaw.

'I'll go and find them,' Mr Makepeace offered, his dark hair unruly.

'No! No! Stay here!' Miss Bellamy ordered. 'The Fire Brigade is on its way.'

At that moment, Mr Witham came through the door, carrying Noel Shaw, whose head was buried in his chest.

'Is he all right?' a concerned Miss Bellamy implored.

'He's fine, aren't you, Noel?' Mr Witham grunted, just as they heard the sound of clanging fire engines arriving at the front of the house. Mr Witham put Noel down at Miss Bellamy's feet and assumed command.

'Watch him, Elizabeth. I'll go and direct the firemen. I managed to put the fire out, but we'll need them to check it. Keep everybody here until we get the all-clear.'

Then he was gone.

While all this was going on, Carol appeared next to Raymond as he stood at the back of the small crowd. She gripped his arm in hers and pressed herself close.

'Guess what,' she breathed in his ear.

Raymond was still disoriented and, unresisting of her grip, could only mutter, 'What?'

'I saw Mr Makepeace coming out of Miss Bellamy's room,' she whispered.

Raymond didn't quite comprehend.

'He was in her room,' she whispered. 'What do you reckon they were doing?'

'How do I know?' he mouthed. He couldn't help noticing that Carol was only wearing a pale blue cotton nightdress, which, the more it covered, the more it seemed to reveal. Even in the cool night air, a film of sweat began to prick his brow.

Her free hand crept round his waist and slipped inside his dressing gown to grip the jacket of his pyjamas.

'Carol!' Miss Bellamy's voice rang out.

Carol straightened and parted from him. 'I was frightened, Miss,' she said, fluttering her eyelashes.

'Let's all just wait here quietly,' Miss Bellamy said, narrowing her eyes at Carol. 'We'll be back inside before long.'

They waited. The air was cool as they stood around, during which time Carol edged closer to Raymond again and touched his hand with hers. After a while, Mr Witham appeared in the doorway. For the first time, Raymond noticed that he was dressed in slacks and a roll-neck jumper, while the rest of them were in nightclothes.

'We can go back in now,' he said to Miss Bellamy. 'We'll have to stay downstairs for a bit, while the air clears upstairs. It shouldn't take long. I suggest we give the kids a cup of cocoa.'

'Good idea,' Miss Bellamy agreed. 'Jim and Susan, could you make the cocoa?'

Her request was directed to Mr Makepeace and Miss Priestley. In orderly fashion they all trooped into the dining room, where Carol was ordered to put on a coat from the hallway, before Jim and Susan served them with hot chocolate. In the meantime, and after a quiet conversation between Mr Witham and Miss Bellamy, Noel Shaw was led off to the sitting room between them, his head bowed. Raymond noticed Mr Makepeace and Miss Priestley seemed impatient to join them as they hurried the rest of them through their hot drink.

'Come on, you lot,' Mr Makepeace cajoled, 'you should be in bed. It's very late.'

As soon as they'd finished drinking their chocolate, Mr Makepeace rushed to the sitting room, while Miss Priestley ushered them up the stairs.

The twins were reluctant to go and Miss Priestley asked Raymond to take charge of them.

'Their mum was killed in a house fire,' she whispered to Raymond behind her hand.

Raymond took the twins by the hand and they followed him meekly upstairs, where everything seemed none the worse for the fire. The inmates trooped down the corridor and each in turn disappeared into their rooms. Raymond opened the door of the twins' room to see them into bed. There were two single beds in the room, but they both scrambled into the same bed and snuggled down.

117

The corridor was quiet as he slipped into his room, shucked off his dressing gown and clambered into bed. He was wondering if it was possible to rejoin a broken dream, when he heard the click of a door, his door, and saw a soft spill of light enter his room.

'Raymond, are you still awake?' Carol asked in an urgent whisper.

He pretended to be asleep as she closed the door and sat on the side of his bed.

'Raymond,' she entreated, shaking him by the shoulder.

He fluttered his eyes open, pretending to wake. She was leaning over him in her cotton nightdress, smelling of soap and secrets. Her pale skin seemed to glow in the soft light filtering through the curtained window. Deep within the pit of Raymond's stomach, something began to swirl and bubble, like molten lead in a crucible.

'Carol, what are you doing in here?' he asked.

'Shush,' she soothed. 'They'll be ages. It was probably Noel that started the fire and they'll be questioning him. He's fire mad. I just wanted to ask you about that story today, about that Madam. That bloke loves her, doesn't he?'

'He likes her,' Raymond croaked as she took hold of his hand and began stroking the back of it.

'Do you like me?' she asked, lifting his hand and rubbing it against a cotton-sheathed breast.

He was entranced by the feel and smell of her and helpless to resist.

'Yeah,' he sighed, lost.

'You're a bit young, but you're really nice,' she murmured, spreading his fingers and increasing the pressure of his hand, 'and you read beautiful. When you were reading today on the lawn, I wanted you to touch me.'

She didn't speak for a while, breathing evenly and stroking his hand against the pulsing swell of her breast, so that the thin cotton of her nightdress was pushed aside and his fingers came into contact with the smoothest skin imaginable.

'Will you read some more tomorrow?' she asked in a tone that sounded odd. 'You can touch me again if you want.'

He could only nod. He was under her spell. Suddenly, she stood up from the bed and, with back arched, crossed her arms in front of her and gripped handfuls of the fabric of her nightdress at her thighs. She smiled at him in the half-light, a smile both gentle and lascivious at the same time. Slowly, a sight surpassing his most vivid dreams began to be revealed within touching distance, as his heart began to pound.

A distant voice from somewhere below broke the spell. The members of staff were on the stairs, making their way to bed. Carol was gone in a blur of ivory and pale blue, leaving Raymond to douse his own fire.

The Soulsearcher

Raymond woke up refreshed. The lyrics of 'Walking Back to Happiness' were going round and round in his head.

Said goodbye to loneliness
Whoop-pa, oh yeah

He threw open the curtains. Sultry clouds and rain couldn't dampen his mood. He almost skipped down to breakfast.

By lunchtime, the web of events leading to the fire was unravelled. Noel set light to a pile of clothes in his bedroom because the football match was abandoned. The matches he used were deliberately left in his room by Avril, who'd stolen them from the cigarette stash in Carol's room. Pauline's full and frank confession to the crime was not accepted.

The two main culprits, Avril and Noel, were sentenced to a day of one-to-one counselling, while Carol's cigarettes were confiscated. Compared to Hillcrest's draconian regime, which Raymond would never forget, this was lenient. Uncle Richard would have had a field day.

'That fat bitch Avril,' Carol muttered to Raymond when she returned from the sitting room. 'I'll have her.'

The poor weather, Carol's sulk and the general gloom in the house soon persuaded Raymond to retire to his room. For a while, he pottered about, tidying his things and making ready for school the next day, before lying down on his bed. He didn't realise that he'd fallen asleep until he woke up to discover it was time for tea.

Things were no brighter at tea, so after the washing-up he sat on a chair at the top of the garden. The air was still heavy and damp, although the rain of the day had stopped. After some time, and just as he was about to return to his room to read, Carol appeared, seemingly restored, with a sly grin on her face. His mood lifted in an instant.

Motioning for him to follow her, she headed down the garden and disappeared behind the fountain. Raymond followed and sat down next to her on the still-moist rim. Darkness was closing in under a lowering sky, as she pulled a packet of Woodbines and a box of matches from their usual secret nest.

'I thought you hadn't got any,' Raymond said.

She lit a cigarette in cupped hands and took a long drag.

'Brian gave them to me,' she said, looking at him sideways with smoke curling round her lips and nostrils.

'Brian?'

'Yeah, Mr Witham,' she expanded. 'He's not that bad, really.'

It just didn't seem right to Raymond.

'Carol,' he began, but she cut him short by placing her forefinger against his lips.

'Look,' she said, turning to face him, 'you're too young to understand. He's just a bloke. They're all the same. They want summat and I've got it. It's nowt. I still like you. We can go behind the bushes when I've finished this fag if you like.'

Raymond jerked to his feet, fighting the urge to smash his fists into the round cheeks of the stone cherub in the centre of the fountain. Carol reached out and gripped his arm, but he pulled away and stumbled towards the house.

'I haven't done nowt,' she called after him as he stormed into the house and headed for his room.

He felt betrayed. He was choked that a crass adult with a few cigarettes could destroy something he'd deluded

121

himself was special. He paced the room with clenched fists and a hard lump in his throat until, eventually, he threw himself face-down on the bed and screamed inwardly in frustration.

*

Raymond suffered a few friendly catcalls and comments, mainly from the staff, as he entered the dining room for breakfast in his school uniform. The Worden twins gazed wide-eyed at him and smiled, as he ate his sausages and beans and drank his sweet tea. Despite how he felt, their faces were so guileless he smiled back. Whenever Carol tried to catch his eye, he looked away. He finished his breakfast in a hurry and went to get his school jacket and satchel from his room. When he was ready, sweet-scented Miss Bellamy called him into the visiting room and inspected him.

'You look very smart, Raymond,' she said, making a slight adjustment to his tie, while he thought her skin was the most perfect he'd ever seen.

She handed him the hated plastic tokens he needed for his bus fare and said, 'Have a nice day, and don't be late back. You've got a meeting with Dr Charlerousse, remember.'

As he headed through the dining room Carol wolf-whistled and grinned at him, but he stared straight ahead, although he could still see her sudden frown out of the corner of his eye. Mr Witham rose from his seat and said, 'I'll show you where the bus stop is, Raymond.'

As they walked the short distance to the bus stop, Mr Witham tried to engage him in talk about school, but Raymond maintained a stony silence. When they arrived at the stop, the former rugby player turned to face him, hands in trouser pockets, causing his dark blazer to rise at the waist.

'Look,' he said, pulling one hand out of his pocket to scratch the side of his head with one finger, 'I know those tokens are embarrassing, use this instead.'

He opened his red-palmed hand to reveal a glinting silver shilling. Raymond looked at the coin nestling in Mr Witham's broad hand and didn't move.

'Go on,' Mr Witham cajoled, 'you'll have enough for some sweets as well.'

The bus arrived and the queue started to shorten.

'No. I'll be all right,' Raymond said, stepping onto the bus before Mr Witham could say anymore.

'Hamwit' could stick his money.

The school day was just like any other at Slevin: bell, book, pen and ink. The humdrum normality of it only emphasised the contradiction in Raymond's life. None of his friends knew he'd changed homes or that Roger Marsden was his ex-foster-brother, but then they'd never known of his association with him. He was treated to Roger's mean stare a couple of times during the day, but he looked straight through him. He remembered Roger telling him he didn't exist. Well, neither did Roger.

At the final bell of the day he headed home alone. As he walked up the driveway at Lawson Court, Carol was lounging against a column of the portico, waiting for him. She made her school clothes look as though she'd stolen them from a much younger girl.

'You look like Billy Bunter's best mate,' she said, laughing, as he approached, but he pushed past her, despite her half-hearted attempt to place her body in the way.

She followed and put a hand on his arm, but removed it when Miss Bellamy appeared in the hallway.

'Raymond, drop your things off in your room quickly and come back down,' Miss Bellamy said. 'Dr Charlerousse is waiting to see you.'

Raymond seized the excuse to escape from Carol and

dashed upstairs. In his room, he threw his blazer on the bed and dropped his satchel onto the floor. Seeing Carol and feeling her hand on his arm made him boil with a mixture of frustration and confusion.

He composed himself for a moment and remembered the pictures that Dr Charlerousse asked him to bring. He retrieved them from their hiding place and headed down to her office, where he knocked and entered at her command. She looked exactly the same as when he'd last seen her.

'Ah, today you are the student, no?' she said with a wry smile.

He nodded an abrupt assent and sat down in the chair at the side of the desk in response to a motion of her hand.

'And so,' she said, gazing at him with her intelligent eyes, 'how was school today?'

'All right,' he answered.

'Ah, Raymond,' she said with a glint in her eyes, 'this is an *all right* world we live in. What does it really mean? Does it mean 'so so'? Does it mean everything was good or just average?'

'Average,' he said.

She had an amusing way of talking that made him smile.

'So, how are you feeling after one week at Lawson Court?' she asked.

'Fine,' he replied.

'You have had an eventful weekend, no?' she said, continuing to look into his eyes. 'I think now you understand the others better, perhaps?'

Although she made a question out of nearly every statement, Raymond knew she didn't expect an answer. She inched her spectacles down her thin nose and looked at him over the top of them.

'I think, maybe, you are a good influence, Raymond. The Worden twins like you. I hear you have been reading to them. *The Magic Mountain* by Thomas Mann. It is set in

Switzerland, is it not? That is the country I came to England from. It is very deep reading for them, no? For you also, I think? But they are enjoying it? That is good, no? And Carol? You are friends also? She needs a true friend. Has she asked anything of you?'

She paused.

Raymond shook his head a little more firmly than he'd intended.

'No?' she asked, pursing her lips and studying him in a way that alerted him to be even more on his guard.

'No.' he replied, looking straight at her and holding her gaze as long as he could.

She changed tack again. 'I see you have brought your pictures. I can see them, no?'

He handed them over and she laid them out on the desk. She moved his special picture to one side and studied the rest.

'These are fantastical, no? Strange, mystic landscapes and faraway places. So interesting – the colours – pink, purple, blue. Like another planet. They are far away, no? In an unknown place? Is that what they are, Raymond?'

'Yes,' he answered, happy to be talking about something else.

'Of course, it is interesting there are no people in your pictures, is it not?' she continued to muse.

He interceded, as she made defence a natural reaction to almost every question. 'I'm no good at drawing people.'

She didn't look up. 'So interesting,' she mused. 'Your perspective. You are high up – on a hill? – up a tree? – in the air? Yes, maybe you are flying?'

Raymond shrugged as she looked up and smiled at him.

'No matter,' she said. 'From the imagination – this is what you paint. That is good – to imagine.'

She picked up his special picture and smoothed it out on the desk in front of her.

'This is the picture we must talk about,' she said. 'Do you know what *iconographic* means?'

Raymond wasn't sure, but he was smart enough to guess.

'A picture with a meaning,' he suggested.

'Yes, Raymond,' she said. 'We must talk about everything in this picture – the books, the rope, the skull, the tin, the crossbow, the matches, everything. Some things we must talk about more than others, no? But that is for next time, not for now.'

Relief flooded through Raymond.

She then put him at his ease by asking him mundane questions about school and the subjects he was taking, before she led him into a gentle interrogation about his time with the Marsdens. Her insightful questions, always obliquely framed, unerringly solicited answers she seemed to be seeking. Eventually, she brought the session to a close, asking him to come back to see her after school on Friday, then she handed him his pictures back; all but the special one.

'I will keep this for our next meeting,' she said, slipping his picture inside a green folder on the desk. 'Then we can talk about its meaning. It tells of your time at Hillcrest, no?'

He should have known that there were no secrets from her. After all, he'd already shifted her name and discovered he could make 'Soulsearcher' from it.

Dirty Cow

That evening, Raymond stayed in the dining room, poring over a difficult piece of Latin homework. Miss Priestley, seeing him working, told the other children not to trouble him and shepherded the Worden twins away when they sat down next to him at the table. Raymond agonised over convoluted declensions for quite a while before Carol slipped through the door. It was time for her secret smoke break.

'You coming?' she asked.

'No, I'm busy,' he said, pretending to be absorbed in his work.

'Liar, I've been peeping through the door. You've been staring into space and chewing your pen for ages.'

'I need to think,' he said, taking his pen out of his mouth and glancing at her, as if by accident.

'Why?' she questioned, catching his glance like a fish in a net and, walking behind him, she leaned over his shoulder, pressing her soft, electric body against him.

'Get off, Carol!' he cried, despising himself as he raised his arm and pushed her back.

She sprang back.

'You're just a stuck-up kid,' she said in a hurt tone. 'You think you're better than anybody else.'

'It's not that,' he protested, but when he looked round she'd disappeared into the garden.

He fought a fierce battle with himself, but just as he was about to surrender and follow her, Mr Witham appeared.

Seeing Raymond, he sauntered around behind him and leaned over his shoulder 'Amo, amas, amat,' he said, as if to himself. 'That's all I can remember of Latin.'

Raymond was overcome by a sense of loathing.

'I've finished,' he mumbled, picking up his books in a hurry and leaving the room.

In his bedroom, he threw his books onto the table and lay on the bed to think. His cheeks were burning. What had Dr Charlerousse said about Carol? She was in denial. She can't accept whatever it is that happened to her so she throws herself at people, something like that. He really liked her, but she didn't care about him. Compared to her he was a kid. Witham was a man. Should he tell someone what was going on?

He couldn't break the survival code he'd always lived by. Don't tell tales to adults, even if they are kind and well-meaning. Say nothing. Seek no favour. It was the best way, but he was in torment. He despised himself. He needed to talk to Carol.

When he went downstairs Carol was nowhere to be seen. All the other inmates were in the dining room drinking cocoa with Mr Templeton, Miss Priestley and Mr Makepeace. Mr Witham was standing at the doorway to the garden looking red-faced and uncomfortable.

'Cocoa, Raymond?' Miss Priestley asked, rising as he entered.

'Please,' he replied.

Mr Makepeace began talking to him about his homework, while Raymond kept one eye on Mr Witham.

'Latin, eh?' Mr Makepeace said. 'Never did it myself. Sounds a bit hard to me. Did you get it all done?'

'Yes,' Raymond lied.

'Good,' Mr Makepeace said. He addressed the twins, who sat watching Raymond. 'What do you think, boys? Fancy doing Latin some day?'

The twins nodded their heads in concert. While Mr Makepeace prattled on about school to the twins, Raymond watched Mr Witham out of the corner of his eye. The object of his scrutiny seemed decidedly uneasy as he stood, mug in hand, gazing out into the garden, and occasionally throwing furtive glances back into the room. Miss Priestley reappeared with Raymond's cup of cocoa and, placing it down on the table in front of him, asked no one in particular, 'Where's Carol?'

Raymond was certain Mr Witham flinched, before he said, without turning round, 'Gone up early.'

*

As Raymond was getting ready for school in his bedroom, he heard Miss Bellamy shout out Carol's name. He didn't take much notice at first because Carol's name was often in the air. A little later, as he stuffed his schoolbooks into his satchel, he became aware of a continuing commotion and peered out of his door to investigate. At the end of the corridor, just about to disappear down the stairs, he saw Miss Bellamy and Miss Priestley supporting a sobbing Carol between them. Just before they vanished, he noticed what seemed to be a towel wrapped round Carol's arms, which were held in front of her.

He threw the rest of his books into his satchel and rushed downstairs, but the women and girl were nowhere in sight. Mr Makepeace and Mr Templeton supervised breakfast with their usual manufactured good spirits, but Carol was conspicuous by her absence. Before leaving for school, Raymond accosted Mr Templeton in the kitchen and asked him what had happened to Carol.

'She's all right. Don't worry about it,' was all he would say.

Just before Raymond left for the school bus, Avril came up to him in the hallway and said with venom, 'Serves her right.'

'What do you mean?' he implored, but Avril turned on her heels with a shake of her pigtails and marched back to the dining room with her arms folded across her chest.

*

Carol was sitting in her usual place at tea. She wore a grey cardigan with long sleeves, but Raymond saw the white bandages peeping from under the cuffs. She looked like an unhappy schoolgirl and her usual banter with the staff was missing. Also, Raymond noticed, Mr Witham was not at his usual place at the table. Throughout the meal, the twins also looked glum and kept glancing at Carol.

After the meal, Carol disappeared with Miss Bellamy and Raymond stationed himself in the dining room with his homework and waited in hope. Eventually, Carol came into the room. Her shoulders were slumped and her hands were thrust deep in the pockets of her cardigan. Without a word, she sat down next to him at the table, her face pale and strained. Even her hair, which was normally backcombed, was brushed down around her ears. She looked down at the table in front of her.

'What happened?' Raymond asked.

'Cut myself,' she whispered.

'How?'

'Just did.'

'Why?'

'Because.'

'Because what?' he persisted.

A tear sprang to the corner of each of her blue eyes.

'Do you want to go for a smoke?' he suggested, regretting having pressed her.

'I've given up,' she stuttered, as big tears began to roll down her cheeks.

She dropped her head into her arms on the table and began to sob. Raymond leaned forward and put an awkward arm over her shoulders and began to pat her like a puppy, reiterating, 'It's all right. It's all right.'

'I didn't let him do it,' she cried between racking sobs. 'He called me all sorts and I deserve it. He said I egged him on. He was disgusting. I hate myself.' She lifted her head and her body seemed to convulse before she wailed, 'I'm a dirty cow.'

'No you're not,' Raymond said.

She drew a deep, tremulous breath, raised her head and wiped her cheeks with the palm of her hands. Her tear-stained face looked into his and her lips trembled.

'I'm sorry, Raymond,' she said in a quavering voice. 'I shouldn't have come to your room the other night.'

'I'm not sorry.'

She managed a lopsided half-smile and although her sobbing was subdued, the flow of tears down her cheeks was renewed.

'You're too nice for me,' she said, touching his hand with her fingers. 'Everybody likes you because you're clever and kind and you talk nice. Men only like me for one thing and women hate me because of it.'

'You're lovely,' he said. He'd never felt so much love for anybody before.

Hillcrest

Two people were missing from Lawson Court. Mr Witham was never seen again and the old Carol disappeared to be replaced by a shadow. For the rest of the week Raymond developed a routine. Each evening he spent an undisturbed hour on homework and then he read *The Magic Mountain* to Carol and the Worden twins until supper. The first night they started this, Miss Bellamy came into the dining room, where they were sitting at a table, and said they could use the visiting room, where they would be more comfortable.

Raymond sat on a small sofa, flanked by the attentive twins, while Carol curled up in an easy chair opposite, her head on one hand, resting on a cushion. Her grey cardigan was wrapped round her at all times, with the sleeves pulled down over her hands, and she said very little. One evening, Raymond decided the philosophical discussions between Hans and Herr Settembrini were just too incomprehensible and he stopped reading.

Carol blinked and said, 'Go on, Raymond.'

The twins nodded.

While he read, Friday's meeting with Dr Charlerousse preyed on his mind. It was always the same with things he wasn't looking forward to; they came in a rush.

*

Raymond made his way to Dr Charlerousse's office down the dark corridor and knocked on the door.

'Come in,' she called out.

When he entered, she was sitting, as always, at her desk, looking exactly the same as the times he'd seen her before.

'Sit down, Raymond,' she ordered, while finishing off some paperwork on her desk.

When she finally put down her tortoiseshell pen, she peered at him over her spectacles.

'Raymond,' she said and then paused, studying him for a moment. Her gaze was often more questioning than her words and he immediately felt on the defensive. 'You know what happened to Carol?'

He nodded and murmured an affirmative.

'It was something that had to happen,' she said, 'although it was unforgivable that it should have been brought about that way. You have been a comfort, no? You have a capacity for understanding the pain and sorrow of others. This is because you have felt those things yourself. However, it is you we must think about and we have things to discuss, no?'

'No,' Raymond said to himself, but he didn't move a muscle in his face.

In front of her was his special picture. She studied it, running her bony fingers over the composition while talking to herself.

'The books – perfect. And the table. What have we here? A box of matches and a tin – a biscuit tin, no? The skull on top of the tin – I don't think I like that. And the rope – it is coiled like a serpent. And here, the open book, with a fine picture of a crossbow.'

She looked up and locked her piercing eyes to his.

'Hillcrest, no?'

Raymond nodded. She was far too smart for him to deny it. What was worse was that she could probably decipher every hieroglyph in the picture.

'We must talk about everything in this picture, Raymond,' she said.

She was also a mind reader.

'Of course,' she mused, 'we can start with the obvious. The books, they are the mainstay of your life, no? They are your escape and maybe even sometimes your salvation. That is so, no?'

'Yes,' he said. That was the easy bit.

'The book with the picture of the crossbow,' she continued. 'It is beautifully drawn, Raymond. Will you tell me its meaning?'

'We made weapons to play in the woods with, like bows and arrows and spears,' he explained. 'One time we made a crossbow. I saw a picture of a crossbow in an encyclopaedia and Brian Walker wanted me to make it. We found wood and nails and other stuff in the outhouses.'

Again, not difficult.

'You didn't shoot anyone with it, I hope,' she said, smiling.

'No, we just played with it,' he said.

He didn't tell her about the time they'd used the crossbow to fire flaming bolts into the camp of a rival gang and razed it to the ground, or about the fiery retribution their enemies exacted on them by torching the summerhouse at Hillcrest and burning the lumber they'd collected for Bonfire Night. Nor did he tell her about Uncle Richard's growing anger as those events unfolded.

'Ah, boys,' she said. 'And Brian Walker, he was the leader of your gang, no?'

Brian was the one who'd started everything. Things were peaceful, if harsh, under Uncle Richard's regime before he arrived and led them into all sorts of scrapes. Brian was the leader, yes, but he, Raymond, was the brains.

'Yes,' he said.

'And the tin?' she said, continuing to probe. 'It is a biscuit tin, no?'

'Yes,' Raymond said, still feeling he was on safe ground.

'Uncle Richard used a tin like that to keep fines in. He called it the 'Owt, Nowt, Summat and Gorrit' tin. If we used any of those words we would have to forfeit some of our pocket money.'

Dr Charlerousse laughed, although Raymond could tell it was more in derision than amusement.

'And did it work?' she asked.

'Not really,' Raymond replied.

He decided not to mention that there was another reason he put a biscuit tin in the picture. The memory of how he and Brian climbed out of the dormitory window in the dead of so many freezing nights to shimmy down the side of the house and sneak in through the kitchen window to raid the pantry flashed into his mind. It was his idea to substitute the biscuits they stole with wooden dominoes and reseal the tin so it would still seem full. Uncle Richard's fury and revenge when he found out and they confessed was too painful to recount. Besides, Raymond didn't want to admit to her that he was a thief, although it didn't seem like that at the time.

'So many memories, Raymond,' she said.

Did she know he wasn't telling her everything?

'The skull on top of the biscuit tin,' she resumed. 'I believe that to be an affectation, although it has significance for what happened at Hillcrest, no? You draw very well. It is very realistic.'

Raymond nodded. She was right, although Uncle Richard's gaunt, thin-skinned face always reminded him of a skull.

'And last but not least, the rope,' she said in a level tone, although it seemed to Raymond like the knell of doom. 'The rope. Could anything be more symbolic of Hillcrest and the unhappy events that took place there? I wonder, Raymond, how those times might have affected you? It was a difficult time, no? First, to lose a friend in that way must have been devastating. Then, for your house-father to take his own life in the same way must have been shocking. I understand you and Brian Walker were the ones who found David Bleasedale on the swing in the wood. That is so, no?'

The memory of that day gripped Raymond in a cold fist and he only just managed to mutter, 'Yes. We found him. We thought he'd run away into the woods to hide because he didn't want to leave Hillcrest.'

'I need you to talk about it,' she said, looking at him over her spectacles. 'I don't believe anybody has talked to you about these things since they happened. That is true, no?'

'A policeman asked me questions,' he murmured.

'Ach!' she sighed. 'Interrogation only deals with the facts and I know the facts. Tell me about the day you found the boy in the woods. I want to know how you felt. Do not be afraid. There is only you and I here and nothing goes beyond this room.'

The sights and sound of that wild, wet night and the image of Squeaky Dave suspended from the rope-swing in the gloomy hollow of the yawning ditch swirled through Raymond's head.

'It started when Uncle Richard told David he was going to be moved to a home for older boys,' he began. 'He was very little for his age and he had a squeaky voice. He didn't want to go. He was scared he would be bullied. He'd been at Hillcrest longer than me. We all liked him. He was funny and kind.'

He shuddered. The room seemed to have turned cold. He couldn't tell her how Squeaky Dave had entreated him to intervene on his behalf. Raymond was their spokesman. Raymond was the boy who was good with words. Raymond was clever. Raymond was the boy who did nothing to help his friend.

'He ran away the day before he was due to leave. I knew

he'd gone to the woods because he told me he was going to hide there and asked if we would bring him food. It was a horrible night. The rain was lashing down. Uncle Richard got a search party of us boys together and we went into the wood. He split us up in twos, and me and Brian went off together. We went down to the ditch where the rope-swing was. We used to play there a lot, but David could never go on the swing because he had a problem with his arms popping out.'

He paused. Squeaky Dave's arms used to dislocate easily. He'd seen it happen once when Squeaky Dave was struggling into a coat. He could put them back himself. He remembered how he felt when Uncle Richard dragged Squeaky Dave up from the kitchen floor after he'd thrown a wailing fit of utter despair just before he was due to leave. Uncle Richard was oblivious to the fact Dave's arms had popped out and he was hanging like a broken doll while the rest of them looked on, appalled.

'Go on, Raymond,' Dr Charlerousse prompted.

'When we got to the ditch it was dark and pouring down so we couldn't see properly at first. Brian was the one who found him. He was ahead of me. I saw him stop at the edge of the ditch by the swing and I knew something was wrong. When I got there I saw what it was.'

He swallowed hard. 'David had hanged himself on the rope-swing,' he said in a cracked voice.

'How did you feel at that moment?' the doctor asked.

'I felt as though somebody had kicked me in the stomach. I fell backwards into a puddle.'

It was true, but he couldn't tell her about another stupid thought that came into his head immediately afterwards – it was the first time that Squeaky Dave had been on the swing. He always complained about not being able to do it because of his arms when they played there.

'We ran to find Uncle Richard and the others. I had to

take Uncle Richard back there while the others were sent back to the house to get help.'

'How was Uncle Richard?'

'He was shocked and then he was angry.'

Uncle Richard was always angry.

'We will speak of this no more today,' Dr Charlerousse said. 'But we must come back to it again. There is much we need to talk about, but it is enough for now. Thank you for telling me. Come with me and sit by the window.'

There was a window at the far end of the office, and in front of this were two dark wooden armchairs with red leather upholstery, which faced towards the window but were slightly turned towards each other. In front of the chairs was a low, polished table reflecting the light from the window. Dr Charlerousse got up and walked across to one of the chairs. Raymond followed her and sat in the other. When they were seated, she spoke.

'Sometimes in life one has to deal with pain in order to emerge as a more whole person. I think you understand this, but I am not talking about physical pain. I am talking about emotional pain. It is natural for us to want to avoid any kind of suffering, but a physical wound is difficult to ignore, so we have no choice but to endure it. Emotional pain is different; sometimes we can pretend it doesn't exist; sometimes we can delay it. However, it is always better to face it, so that it can be understood and then cured forever, just as poor Carol must now face her anguish to make her a whole person again. When we face our pain, we can begin to heal.' She had removed her spectacles and was waving them in front of her as she spoke. 'However, it is you that we must talk about.' She turned sideways on the edge of her seat so that she faced him fully. 'Why are you here, Raymond?' she asked.

'I was brought here,' he replied.

'No,' she said, her hands now resting in her lap, leaving

138

her spectacles to hang freely from the gold chain around her neck. 'You have been here, in care, all your life. Why?'

'I don't know,' he said, a feeling of dread beginning to rise in his stomach, as a cloud drifted across the sun and dimmed the light from the window.

'This is an important question, no?' she said. 'It is a question I know the answer to. Why don't you ask me?'

His mouth felt dry and he couldn't speak.

'You seek answers through books, but this is a question you have never asked,' she continued. 'The most important question of all is often the one most difficult to ask. Maybe it's better not to know the answer. Maybe it was better for Carol not to recognise the truth. I think not.'

She reached out her hand and lifted one of his hands from his lap and held it. He was hoping she would not speak, but she said. 'I have made arrangements. Tomorrow afternoon we are going to see your mother.'

The Truth Makes You Strong

Sitting next to Dr Charlerousse in the back of Miss Bellamy's Morris Minor, Raymond watched drystone walls and fields drift past and tried not to think ahead. Eventually, they turned in through open iron gates beneath a large stone archway and drove down a long driveway. Between the trees lining the drive, a sprawling ivy-covered building came into sight; they drove towards it and parked in front of the main entrance. Before they got out of the car, Dr Charlerousse patted the back of Raymond's hand and said, 'This will be difficult, Raymond, but you are brave, no?'

They got out of the car and walked up to the imposing entrance. As they passed through, Raymond saw a burnished brass plate to one side, on which was engraved 'Stokes Park Hospital'. They entered a large, high-ceilinged foyer with a long oak-panelled reception desk to one side, to which Miss Bellamy was dispatched by Dr Charlerousse to find out where they should go. Raymond waited with the doctor, filled with a deep sense of unease.

Miss Bellamy returned and led them down a long corridor with a black and white chessboard floor, which was lined with dark wooden benches beneath tall opaque windows. Every so often, there were double doors with small windows at head height. On the benches, and clustered around the doors, people sat like passengers in a railway station. They came to the point Miss Bellamy was looking for and found a bench with sufficient space to sit.

While they waited, Raymond's eyes took in the scene. For some reason he thought of Franz Kafka and *The Trial,* a book he'd borrowed from the school library some time ago. Beneath the high windows sat relatives in street clothes, some talking to patients, most of whom wore plaid dressing gowns over faded striped pyjamas and well-worn slippers. Some patients had blank looks; some fidgeted and looked nervous; some rocked back and forth; and others cried. An old woman stumbled down the corridor, her hands dancing, muttering profanities as she passed, and Raymond shrank back. A woman shrieked and he started. A man laughed and he trembled. He suddenly realised that Dr Charlerousse was talking to him.

'She cannot speak. She has not spoken since you were a baby. She will not know you. You will be brave. We cannot change the past, only the future.'

While she spoke, a stout matron appeared through the double doors outside which they sat. She looked around and motioned to them to come forward. They rose and followed her into an entrance area, which had light-green gloss-painted walls and more double doors at the far end. The matron pressed a bell next to these doors, which, following a metallic rattle, was opened by a male nurse dressed in white.

The matron was talking to Dr Charlerousse in a low voice as they entered a room with tables and chairs, beyond which were more solid-looking double doors. To their right, French windows opened onto a conservatory area with more tables and chairs occupied by visitors and patients. Standing to one side, watching everything, were two more male nurses dressed in white. Dr Charlerousse placed her hand under Raymond's elbow as they followed the matron into the conservatory. Furthest away from them, a woman in a plaid dressing gown was staring through the window across a rolling lawn into a ring of trees in the distance.

'It's a good day for her,' the matron said to Dr Charlerousse. 'Sometimes she gets nervous if there are too many people around, but today she is calm. There's no point in telling her who you are. We'll keep an eye on things in case she gets upset.'

Leading the way, she worked her way past the tables and chairs until they reached the seated woman. The matron leaned over her and said, 'Margaret, you've got visitors,' and left.

The woman didn't show any sign of having heard or seen anything to disturb her as she stared into the distance. As Miss Bellamy gathered an extra chair, so they could all sit at the table, Raymond looked at the blank-faced woman. Her body and face were heavy and her dark hair, streaked with grey, was cut in the same style as all the other patients: cropped around the nape of the neck to a single length. Just before they sat down, Dr Charlerousse whispered to him, 'We'll stay only as long as you want, Raymond.'

They sat at the table, Miss Bellamy on one side of the woman, Dr Charlerousse on the other side, and Raymond opposite. As they sat, he noticed a flicker of apprehension flit across the woman's dark eyes and a slight tremor start up in the little finger of her right hand, which rested on the table in front of her. Dr Charlerousse began to speak in her calm, accented voice.

'Hello, Margaret. We have come to see you today. I am Dr Charlerousse and this lady is Miss Bellamy. The boy is your son, Raymond. He is a fine boy, no? He is very clever – a grammar school boy now. You should be very proud. One day he will do great things.'

She spoke in a hypnotic voice, and all the while Raymond's mother never moved or turned her head. He knew she was his mother. Even in that distant, desolate face he could see something of himself. His breathing was suspended, as he watched the tremulous finger on his

142

mother's right hand slowly increase its beat. Dr Charlerousse continued to speak in temperate tones.

'We thought it was time for Raymond to see you – time for him to see his mother and to know himself.'

The finger began to beat faster, hardly touching the table, and Raymond's heart began to race alongside it. He could no longer hear what Dr Charlerousse was saying, although she continued to speak. The finger danced, faster and faster, until Miss Bellamy, out of sympathy and concern, laid her hand on his mother's right hand.

At the first touch of Miss Bellamy's hand, Raymond's mother exploded into frenzied panic, pushing the table back so that it tilted against him and spilling her chair as she jumped to her feet, She turned and ran, this way and that way, bumping into chairs and tables, and beating anything, patients and visitors alike, that stood in her way with wild hands, while emitting guttural grunts as she fought her way back to the ward. In shock, and concern for him, Miss Bellamy grabbed Raymond and held him close to her, enveloping him with her fragrance. Only Dr Charlerousse remained calm, turning her head to see his mother fly into the arms of the male nurses who had remained alert throughout.

They held his mother by each arm and calmed her, before leading her into the secret world beyond the doors to the ward. Raymond glimpsed bars on the windows within and, before his mother finally disappeared, he noticed that she was limping. He was numb with horror, his mind hurtling across a mystical landscape, an unknown land heavy with the scent of lavender.

Dr Charlerousse turned to face a still-trembling Miss Bellamy, as a man in a dressing gown at another table wailed. 'Maybe that was not wise,' she said.

'I'm sorry,' a contrite Miss Bellamy mumbled, releasing her grip on Raymond.

143

'It's understandable,' Dr Charlerousse said with an airy wave of her hand. 'I'll go and speak to the matron. Take Raymond into the corridor and wait, no?'

Raymond waited in the corridor with a tearful Miss Bellamy. She stroked the front of his hair as if he had an unruly calf-lick and wiped the tears from her eyes until Dr Charlerousse reappeared.

'She's calm now,' she informed them. 'And, Raymond, brave, remember?'

They walked back down the corridor and through the foyer to the car, leaving behind them the sounds of gibbering and wailing. A gentle breeze fanned Raymond's hot face as they walked across the car park. Miss Bellamy, still trembling, stalled the car the first time she tried to start it.

'Wait a moment,' advised Dr Charlerousse from the back seat alongside Raymond, and Miss Bellamy waited, her head inclined towards the steering wheel, before she tried again.

They drove home in silence until they scrunched their way into the driveway of Lawson Court. Entering the house, they stopped in the hallway, where Dr Charlerousse removed her gloves.

'Leave Raymond with me for a moment, no?' she said to Miss Bellamy.

Miss Bellamy headed towards the dining room and Dr Charlerousse turned to Raymond. 'Come, Raymond,' she said. 'We need to talk.'

In her office, she led him to the chairs by the window and told him to sit down. Still in a daze, Raymond stared at the sunlit patterns on the tabletop in front of them and allowed the odd, but strangely soothing, cadence of her voice to wash over him.

'That was very difficult time, no?' she said. 'I know it's hard for you to see the mother you have never seen before in those circumstances. Before you go, I want to tell you what I know about her. She was a very vulnerable young woman. Like you, she spent most of her childhood in homes, although these were special homes for children with severe difficulties. When she had you, she was living with her mother, your grandmother, who helped her look after you. Then your grandmother fell very ill and your mother couldn't cope. You had an accident – a fall. I don't know the details, but you were taken into care. Your grandmother died and your mother retreated into the world she now inhabits and has not spoken since. She had no one left. Your father, I'm afraid, is unknown.' She paused to give Raymond time to let this sink in and then she continued. 'One day you will learn more about that time and understand it better,' she said. 'For now, I want you to remember we cannot choose how we come into this world. It is a matter of circumstance beyond our control. We cannot choose our parents or the situation in which we live out our childhood. Many of the children you have met in your short life are better off in the care of the local authority than with their families.'

She shifted and turned more towards him.

'Like you, I have always been a great reader. I especially like English literature. It was one of the things that attracted me to come to this country to study. I love the works of Charles Dickens, which I read when I was young, but I am a psychologist. Salvation comes from within, not from without. The truth makes you strong.'

He looked at her and saw her eyes gleaming with the passion of her words.

'You are an unusual boy, Raymond. Many of the children I see have been damaged almost beyond repair. They have no means to protect themselves and too often they become the very thing that has harmed them. You are different, no? You have the means to rise above any situation. You have intelligence, compassion and humanity. I see it in you. I see

145

it in your behaviour with the other children here, and they see it in you.'

The hand she placed on his, although bony, felt cool and soft. She looked into his mind through his eyes and carried on talking.

'The truth makes you strong. Carol Farrell was a victim of terrible acts against her, but she couldn't accept she was the victim. Now she understands and the truth will make her strong. Do you realise the part you have played in that? Your friendship will help her and for that I am also grateful. You must think of your mother with the love she deserves. You can make her tragedy the beginning of something wonderful.' She patted his hand and rose from her chair. 'I will see you on Tuesday, Raymond. After school, no? Then we will talk some more and discuss your future. Now you can go to your room and spend as much time as you need there. Nobody will disturb you. You need time to think.'

*

Raymond lay on his bed and tried to digest what he'd seen and heard that day. It was official – the beautiful, romantic young couple, tragically killed in a car crash, leaving a mewling infant to survive the world alone, never existed. A mother who was a shambling mute in a mental hospital did. The truth makes you strong. He didn't feel strong. He felt paralysed and helpless. While his thoughts churned, one thing gnawed at him. There was more to this story than he'd been told.

Rising from the bed, he walked over to the window where his books were lined up on the sill, picked up *Great Expectations* and flipped open its blue cover. By the light of the window he studied the inscription on the first page, pondering over it for a few minutes before going back to lie on the bed with the book beside him.

The light was fading when Carol entered the room

without knocking and sat on the edge of the bed. She looked down at him without saying a word, before picking up his book and opening the cover. Her eyebrows knitted together in concentration as she read out in a low voice.

'*Miracle Boy has been saved for something special. And the communication I have got to make is that he has great expectations.*'

She continued to stare at the book, as if trying to make sense of the words. After a while, her eyebrows straightened and freckles returned to their normal position on her smooth brow.

'Is this yours?' she asked. 'Is it about you?'

'I've always had it,' Raymond said. 'I don't know where it came from. It's probably about somebody who had the book before me.'

'I don't think so, Raymond,' she said, tracing the copper-plate writing with her forefinger. 'It *feels* like it's about you. I bet somebody wrote that just for you and, even if they didn't, you can make it about you.'

She lay down on her back and wormed her arm under his head. After a long silence, she spoke. 'Miss Bellamy's really upset,' she said to the ceiling.

More Freckles

Raymond couldn't help noticing the cracks in Mrs Noble's normally immaculate face powder, around the corners of her mouth and eyes. It was the first time Raymond had seen them and, he also observed, she seemed pale and gaunt in her respectable tweed outfit as she settled into her chair in the visiting room. Maybe she, too, felt that the burden of life was sometimes too heavy. After saying hello, she didn't say anything for a while, but just looked at him with eyes that looked moist, but not with tears. Eventually she spoke.

'I can't stay long, Raymond,' she said. 'My daughter's given me a lift today and she's waiting for me in the car. It's probably just as well because I'm a terrible driver, or so she keeps telling me.' More fissures appeared in her make-up as she smiled. 'I asked Miss Bellamy to give me a ring if ever she thought you needed someone. She told me you saw your mother yesterday for the first time. It must have been a shock for you.'

'Yes,' Raymond said, unable to say more.

'Miss Bellamy told me all about it,' she said. 'It's a tragedy, but I know that if your mother knew you like I do she'd be so proud of you. There's nothing anyone can do for her, but you can be her hope in life. Through you, her life can mean something.'

Raymond swallowed hard. The topic was too new for him to talk about it, but he was grateful for her concern.

'Your future is what matters,' she insisted, 'not only to you, but also to me. I have great hopes for you. You owe it to your mother to be strong at all times.'

She began to fumble with the clasp of her handbag. 'I've brought something for you. I want it to symbolise this moment in your life.'

The bag opened with a snap; she reached inside and drew out a square black leather box and held it out to him, her hand shaking. He leaned forward, took the box from her and offered his thanks.

'Open it,' she urged when he sat back down and left the box in his lap.

He opened the hinged lid and stared in surprise. Nestling inside was a gleaming silver wristwatch on a bed of red satin.

'Go on,' she said, 'put it on.'

He lifted the watch from the box and clasped it round his left wrist, staring at it.

'Look,' she pointed out, 'it's got the date in the little window on the bottom of the dial. One day, that'll be the date you get your freedom. It will come quicker than you think.'

She looked pleased as he stared at the watch on his wrist. She began to rise from the chair with so much difficulty that he rose to help her, putting his hand under her arm. When she straightened up, she gripped his hand and looked again at the gleaming watch.

'Take care of it,' she said. 'When I see you again you'll be in another place. I know it will be the right place for you. I trust the people here to see to that.'

He saw her out to the front door. As they appeared on the front porch, a woman, who'd been sitting in a car, saw them. Slim and blonde, she dashed out of the car, her heels crunching on the gravel as she ran towards them.

'Come on, Mum,' she said, linking Mrs Noble by the arm and guiding her towards the car, 'let's get you home.'

As she said this, she darted a look of reproach over her shoulder at Raymond. His newfound spirit evaporated and he was consumed by guilt as the young woman helped her ailing mother into the car. She was about to climb into the driver's seat when she looked back at Raymond. She stopped and walked back towards him.

'Look,' she said, 'I'm sorry. I didn't mean to be rude. She shouldn't have been out today. She's not been well. She's always talking about you, though, and she'll be really happy she's been today.'

In recompense, she smiled and touched him on the arm, before bidding him farewell and heading back to the car.

Raymond's new watch sparkled in the sunlight as he waved goodbye to Mrs Noble and the car rolled down the driveway. He was still looking at his watch when he went back inside and met Carol in the hallway.

'Flipping heck, that's really nice,' she said, following his gaze.

Raymond looked at her. She was still enveloped in her cardigan and she looked pale and wan.

'Why don't you come and sit outside a bit,' he said, forgetting the watch.

They sat on the fountain in the sunlight and Raymond told her about his Pictorial Auntie.

'She sounds really nice,' Carol said. 'I didn't know there were people who cared about kids if they didn't have to. I mean, if they weren't their own or they weren't getting paid or summat. She must be flipping rich to buy you that watch, so you'd think she wouldn't bother about anybody else.'

'Not everybody thinks just about themselves, Carol,' Raymond said.

'Well I am from now on,' Carol said, lifting her feet from the ground and holding her legs out in front of her. 'I used to think I was worth nowt. Me dad used to think I was worth nowt.' She was staring down at her legs. 'It was him that started it all off.'

The silence hanging around them for the next few minutes was eloquent in its affirmation of their mutual understanding. Raymond put his hand on her shoulder. After a while, she looked up from her inspection of her knees and said, 'You don't have to tell me about yesterday, you know.'

Raymond told her everything, while she looked at him as if every word was as precious and delicate as a falling leaf. Her eyes scanned his face, alert to any change of expression she was ready to match with her own. When he'd finished, she turned her lips inwards and blinked, before reaching out and pulling him to her to hug him.

'When I said I was only going to think about myself, I didn't mean you,' she whispered.

*

Three weeks passed. Enough time for Raymond to finish reading *The Magic Mountain* to Carol and the twins. Enough time for Carol to stop wearing her cardigan like a shroud and for the criss-cross scars on her wrists to begin to fade. Enough time for Dr Charlerousse to continue to counsel him to come to terms with the past and look forward to the future. Enough time for her also to announce that a place in a new home run by a young couple called the Bests had been found for him and it was time for him to leave.

But there was never enough time for Raymond to say goodbye to Carol.

As they sat on the fountain for the last time in the crepuscular light of their final evening together, a light breeze made the branches of the shrubs around them sway and brush the lawn.

'I can't believe you're younger than me,' she said. 'Not long ago, I laughed at boys the same age as me. But, you,

you're the most grown-up person I've ever met. You like me for me, don't you, Raymond?'

'Of course,' Raymond said.

He wished he could tell her how much.

'Charleyruss is all right,' she said. 'I've promised her I won't do it again until it's right for me; until I know the other person cares for me and respects me as a person.' She grasped his hand in hers. 'You're the only one I'd break my promise for.'

'You've already given me enough,' he said. 'I don't know how I'd have got through these past few weeks without you. I was sick of everything when I came here. You were the first person I met. Remember? You were sitting here when Miss Bellamy brought me out on that first day. You chased my troubles away from the first minute. You're special and I'm really going to miss you.'

'Me mum always said freckles were tearstains,' she said, wiping her cheeks with her fingers. 'I used to be afraid to cry in case I got more. I'm going to get some new freckles now to always remember you by.'

*

Mr Pickup waited by his car on the driveway while Raymond said his farewells on his last day at Lawson Court. All the staff came to wish him well and the fragrant Miss Bellamy gave him a long hug. He would have liked to have told her that he'd made 'Maybell' out of her name. It suited her. The Worden twins refused to leave his side, each clutching one of Raymond's exotic paintings, a gift from him, until Miss Bellamy took hold of each of them by the hand and held them back while Carol said her final goodbye. This was a long embrace filled with whispers only Raymond could hear. Her last words were, 'Don't ever forget you're Miracle Boy.'

Everyone came out onto the driveway to wave him off, as

Mr Pickup started up the engine and began to pull away. From the backseat, Raymond's last memory of Lawson Court was of Carol, waving his gift to her, *The Magic Mountain*, wildly above her head.

A Normal Home

Raymond stared at the back of Mr Pickup's head. He'd never noticed the wispy white hairs on the back of his neck before, which were in sharp contrast to the jet-black hair on his head. He realised that he'd never looked at Mr Pickup closely before. He was a shadow. What was the name of the ferryman who carried the souls of the dead across the river Styx that they'd learned about in school? Charon, that's who he was. Raymond might as well be dead for all the notice Mr Pickup took of him.

He turned his attention to the passing scenery, as the driver steered the car along the main street of the picturesque village of Slevin, before spinning the wheel to begin the descent of a steep hill flanked by corporation houses. At the bottom of this road, the driver turned right and after a short distance, guided the car to the side of the road. The rasping sound of the handbrake being engaged brought a discordant end to their smooth journey.

Raymond looked at the house they'd stopped by. It was a utilitarian dwelling with cream-coloured plaster walls besmirched with the ravages of weather and industrial pollution. Apart from the fact that it was bigger, it was almost indistinguishable from the other houses on the street. The signs of segregation that characterised his previous children's homes were missing and the only barrier between the house and the outside world was a low privet hedge a small dog could have jumped over.

Mr Pickup climbed out of the car and began to lift Raymond's suitcases from the boot, while Raymond stepped out and waited on the pavement. The sombre chauffeur, carrying both suitcases, led the way up the garden path, which was littered with plastic toys, and knocked on the blue front door. A tall, slim woman wearing fashionable spectacles, which looked capable of independent flight, opened the door.

'Come in, come in,' she welcomed, pulling the door wide open and standing to one side.

Mr Pickup entered only far enough to deposit the suitcases on the dark linoleum floor of the hallway and then retreated, nodding at the woman before heading back to his car. With an encouraging smile, the woman placed an arm across the back of Raymond's shoulders and ushered him into the house. The smell that assailed Raymond's nostrils when he entered reminded him of the tantalising bakery in Slevin, which only the well-off boys could afford to patronise.

'Gordon, he's here,' the woman called out to someone in the house as she closed the door behind them.

Raymond heard the sound of heavy footfalls, which he could only think of as bounding, descending the stairs to the hallway from the upper storey. A pair of very long legs in black trousers came into view, followed by a tall, dark-haired man, who strode up to Raymond with a gleaming smile on his dark, angular face and gave him a firm handshake.

'Raymond, good to meet you,' the man said in an accent that wasn't local. 'I'm Uncle Gordon and this is Auntie Dawn. Welcome to Manorholme. Let's go into the sitting room.'

He led the way through the nearest door into an airy room, which extended from the front to the back of the house. The decor of the room, along with the furniture it contained, was modern and practical. Maroon, foam-filled easy chairs were grouped around an electric fire with a wooden surround. A television with a blank screen stood in one corner and a bookcase, which seemed to contain only illustrated children's books, occupied an alcove.

What struck Raymond most about the room was that it seemed to be divided in its purpose: part living room, part playroom. The playroom part of the room looked out onto the back garden and contained a table surrounded by wooden chairs. The Formica top of the table showed signs that one of its uses was for painting, while on the white wall by it was a gallery of childish paintings and drawings.

'Take a seat, Raymond,' Uncle Gordon said, indicating one of the easy chairs.

Raymond sat down in the nearest soft chair, noting that when Uncle Gordon sank into his, his knees stuck up in the air like twin black peaks. Nonetheless, his rangy figure didn't hide the fact that his new house-father was strong and well-coordinated. Raymond also detected genuine goodwill in Uncle Gordon's swarthy face, which made him feel at ease.

Glancing at Auntie Dawn, who'd seated herself with her slim legs pressed together at an angle, Raymond thought her graceful poise complemented her husband's rugged looks perfectly. The Bests were the youngest house-parents he'd ever come across.

At that moment, a small, dark-haired boy of around four years old burst into the room. When he saw Raymond he stopped, put his finger in his mouth and sidled up to Auntie Dawn, where he lolled back against her slender legs and stared at the newcomer.

'This is our son, David,' Uncle Gordon announced. 'Say hello to Raymond, David.'

'Hello, Raymond,' the little boy said and gave him a shy grin.

'Hello,' Raymond replied and smiled back.

'Are you coming to live with us?' David asked, twisting his right foot around at an oblique angle to his body.

'He is, David,' Auntie Dawn said, 'but you run along now and leave us to talk. I thought you were playing with Frances and Lesley.'

'I am,' David trilled, twisting away from his mother and shooting out of the room. 'We're playing Doctors and Nurses.'

The warm laughter that followed dispelled any remaining fears that Raymond had about his new home.

'Now then, Raymond,' Uncle Gordon said, 'before I show you around, let me tell you about Manorholme. You'll find our way of running a home is to try to create a family atmosphere. Unlike some of the bigger homes I know you've been in, we think we can achieve that in a home this size. In fact, Dawn and I wouldn't want anything bigger than this, would we, pet?'

He glanced at his wife, who smiled back.

'I'll tell you now,' Uncle Gordon continued, 'we're pretty new to this lark, but we reckon that's a good thing. At least we haven't got stuck in our ways and bored with the job. We know your background and we think you'll suit us and we'll suit you. You'll be the oldest child here and, as far as we're concerned, you're a young man, which means you'll have privileges the others don't have, but they also come with responsibilities. We hear you're good with younger children and we're sure you'll find the ones here are a nice bunch. Anyway, you'll meet them soon and find out for yourself. We have rules here, mind, but the main aim is for everyone to be happy. Now, I know Auntie Dawn has things to do in the kitchen, so I'll show you around.'

Uncle Gordon confirmed Raymond's earlier impression of his agility by springing to his feet with one bound.

While Auntie Dawn excused herself, her husband gave

Raymond a tour of the ground floor, which, besides the sitting room, contained a kitchen and dining room, as well as a washroom and toilet. There was one other room, which Uncle Gordon told him he and Auntie Dawn used as an office. Adjoining the hallway was a corridor, along which were coats hanging on hooks and shoes lined up against the skirting boards.

Long-striding Uncle Gordon led Raymond through a side door at the end of this corridor and onto a paved path at the side of the house, which ended at the back garden. Here, there was a spacious, patchy lawn surrounded by a wooden fence. Children were playing around the metal frame of a swing in the far corner.

'Come on, you lot,' Uncle Gordon called out to them. 'Come and meet the new member of the family.'

The children ran over and congregated around them, and Uncle Gordon went through the introductions, after first calming his boisterous son, who was boasting to everyone that he'd been the first to meet the new boy.

'Right, everyone,' Uncle Gordon announced, 'this is Raymond.'

Raymond bestowed what he hoped was a benign smile on the upturned faces in front of him.

'Right, first off,' Uncle Gordon said, 'this is Frances.'

He put his hand on the coal-black, frizzy hair of an Afro-Caribbean girl with big brown eyes and a dazzling wide smile. She was the first black child Raymond had seen in a children's home.

'How old are you, Frances?' Uncle Gordon asked her.

'Eight,' she replied and then puffed out her cheeks like balloons.

Uncle Gordon then put his hand on the head of a fair-haired little girl with pigtails and a Milky Way of freckles cascading down each cheek.

'This is Lesley,' he said.

'Seven,' she announced without being asked.

This set the pattern for the introductions of Paul, five; Bernard, seven; and Stephen, nine: three boys in baggy khaki shorts and grey shirts who would have blended unremarkably into any schoolyard. With formalities completed, the children were sent back to play, which they did without demur.

Next, his new house-father took Raymond upstairs and showed him the five compact bedrooms and two bathrooms, before leading him to a small bedroom with two single beds.

'This is your room,' he said. 'You'll be on your own, so you can have your choice of beds. I'll bring your suitcases up later and you can unpack then. For now, I reckon we deserve a cup of tea.'

When they went down to the kitchen, which was filled with delicious aromas, Raymond was introduced to Mrs Hanson, who helped with the housekeeping and cooking. She was a stout, middle-aged woman with ruddy cheeks and she welcomed Raymond with a fond smile. When Uncle Gordon mentioned they'd come down for a cup of tea, she laughed and said, 'Gerraway with you. You'll drown in tea one of these days, Gordon. Besides, it's nearly dinnertime. Ah, go on, then. The lad's probably parched. Go and sit in the sitting room and I'll bring it to you.' She looked at Raymond. 'I suppose it'll be nice and sweet, will it, young sir?' she said, wringing her hands in a parody of a menial servant.

Raymond nodded, warming to her.

Over hot sweet tea in the sitting room, Uncle Gordon told him that he and his wife came from the north-east of England, near Middlesbrough somewhere, although he was at pains to point out that they weren't Geordies. Raymond didn't really understand this distinction, but it enabled him to put a place to their engaging way of speaking. Uncle

Gordon was a civil engineer by trade and Auntie Dawn had worked in a nursery school in their hometown. They liked children and had wanted to try something different for some time.

'It was Auntie Dawn who saw the posts advertised for house-parents in this area and applied,' Uncle Gordon explained. 'We were flabbergasted when we got the job. It was a lot easier than we thought it would be, but we're not complaining because it's what we wanted. Anyways, tell me a bit about you and what you're interested in.'

Feeling at ease, Raymond conversed openly about school, football and books until he heard what sounded like the banging of a spoon against a pan.

'Dinnertime,' Uncle Gordon said. 'Come on.'

The children ran about, changing their shoes and washing their hands in the downstairs washroom, as Raymond and his new house-father made their way to the dining room. In no time at all everyone was seated around the one large polished table, while Mrs Hanson served the crusty meat pie, peas and potatoes that constituted the main course of the meal. After Uncle Gordon murmured a perfunctory grace, they all tucked in with a relish Raymond soon found was justified.

'Hey, pet,' Uncle Gordon said to his wife, while chomping a mouthful of food. 'You're going to like this. Raymond's a big reader. One of his suitcases is full of books.'

He turned to Raymond. 'Auntie Dawn's a big reader as well. She loves books. I reckon you two are going to have a lot to talk about.'

'I'd like to look at them later, if you don't mind, Raymond,' Auntie Dawn said. 'Will that be all right?'

'Yes, of course,' Raymond said, pleased by her interest.

'Can I look at them too?' David, whose chin barely reached above the table top, piped up.

'Now you know, pet,' his mother said, wiping a crumb

from the corner of her son's mouth with her thumb, 'books are important and you've got your own.'

*

Raymond couldn't help glowing as Auntie Dawn looked through his book collection.

'These are all classics, Raymond,' she said. 'Boys of your age are usually reading *Biggles* or comic books. Except for the Dickens, which I love, I haven't read any of these. Where did you get them all from?'

'Some were school prizes,' Raymond replied, affecting a modest tone. 'A lot of them came from my Pictorial Auntie, though.'

'Ah, yes, Mrs Noble,' Auntie Dawn said, giving him a dimpled smile. 'We were told about her. Sadly, she's ill at the moment and can't come to see you. I hope you'll have enough to read until she brings you more supplies.'

'I can get books from the school library,' Raymond said, although he hoped that Mrs Noble would soon be well enough to visit him.

'I am sure she'll be up and about soon,' Auntie Dawn said. She continued looking at his books while stacking them on the chest of drawers in his new bedroom. 'You could do me a favour,' she mused. 'I enjoy reading, but I don't have your knowledge of literature. If you select books for me, we could talk about them when I read them. I promise I'll take great care of them.'

Raymond was flattered and agreed. She told him to take his time over his first selection and left him on his own for a while, telling him he could come down when he felt like it. When she'd gone, Raymond gazed at his precious library, suddenly feeling the burden of responsibility.

What would she like?

Many of his books might be heavy-going for the non-serious reader, he thought, chewing his lip and casting his

eye over titles like *War and Peace* and *Crime and Punishment.*
Some might be a bit dark, he pondered, tapping his finger
on his Edgar Allen Poe collection. Maybe something light
and humorous, he considered, picking up his copy of *Three
Men in a Boat* and studying the cover, before slotting it back
in its place. Would she like *Moonfleet,* or was it too much of
a boys' adventure? She might have liked *The Magic Mountain,* but of course he'd given that to Carol Farrell, and *Great
Expectations* was one book he couldn't lend out.

He just couldn't decide until his eyes lit on *The History of
Mr. Polly* by H.G. Wells. He couldn't explain why he liked
the book so much, but it had lifted his spirits for a while at
a time when he needed it. He picked up the book and put
it under his arm.

Downstairs, he wandered into the empty sitting room and
placed the book on a low table by the fireplace. The picture
gallery on the wall by the window caught his eye and he
moved over to explore. Smiling faces on matchstick figures,
holding hands beneath a big yellow sun, seemed to be a
predominant feature of the haphazard collection. He was
just thinking that one of the things that made Manorholme
seem friendly was its casual untidiness, when Auntie Dawn
entered the room. He looked round just as she spotted
the book on the table, saying, 'Ah, you picked one out for
me.'

As she looked at the cover, he saw the slightest frown
cloud her fine features and his heart sank.

'Oh,' she said, 'H.G. Wells? He's all about time machines
and stuff, isn't he?'

'This is different,' Raymond said. 'I can change it if you
don't like it, though.'

'Oh no,' she said, brightening again. 'I trust you. I'll look
forward to reading it.'

'I think you'll enjoy it,' Raymond said, glancing at his
shoes rather than her.

Placing the book on the mantelpiece, she said. 'Now, Raymond, you've got three choices. You can stay in here. You can go outside and get to know the other children, or you can go for a walk and explore your new neighbourhood.'

Raymond's only concern was to do what she wanted and he quickly surmised what her favoured option was. The opportunity to see the neighbourhood was an unusual privilege for a children's home, but he opted to go out into the garden with the other children.

When he reached the back garden, David came running up to him.

'Push me on the swing,' the little boy cried. 'They won't do it. They said they're fed up of it.'

While Raymond propelled David on the swing, the other three boys concentrated on an idle game of Pog with coloured marbles on a threadbare patch of lawn. The two girls, Frances and Lesley, were far more curious about the newcomer and came to stand by the frame of the swing. While David screeched with each upward surge of the swing, the giggling girls asked Raymond questions about where he'd come from. Adopting the role of an amiable adult, Raymond entertained them with fanciful explanations, while they twirled around laughing, with grey skirts flying, at his responses, before conferring in whispers about their next question. Frances's big brown eyes seemed permanently startled throughout.

After a time, the boys gathered round and, as the afternoon wore on, Raymond fabricated a colourful past chequered with secret connections with royalty, emergency call-ups for the England football team as a schoolboy wonder, and missions to save the world. He pushed each child in turn on the swing after David became both bored and dizzy. By the time they were called in for tea, Raymond felt like everyone's big brother. He could see Auntie Dawn, who must have been keeping an eye on them, was content when they congregated for tea.

*

The sitting room became a cosy library once the children were tucked up in bed; one where it was perfectly acceptable to talk from time to time. Uncle Gordon pored over a book about civil engineering; Auntie Dawn soon became engrossed in *The History of Mr. Polly*; and Raymond began to reread *Three Men in a Boat*. He was sure his new house-parents would have let him stay up longer, but he excused himself when he became tired. Auntie Dawn, curled up in an armchair with her face obscured by the auburn tresses of her soft hair, raised her head and beamed when she wished him goodnight.

In his new bed beneath the window, overlooking the back garden, Raymond mulled over his initial impressions of his first day at Manorholme. His new house-parents were natural and friendly. There was no pressure on him to fit in, nor was there any competition with children of his age group. He would even be able to walk to school from here, which meant no more plastic tokens, not that he cared much anymore what others thought.

Something else occurred to him. Manorholme was a children's home, which, after his foster home experience, was a comfort, but it was like no other children's home he'd known. Manorholme was a 'Normal Home'.

No Miss Havisham

'That's not what I expected at all,' Auntie Dawn declared, snapping *The History of Mr. Polly* shut. 'To be honest, I wouldn't have touched H.G. Wells with a bargepole if it wasn't for you, Raymond. I really enjoyed that. Tell me what *you* like about it.'

'Well, it's about someone who's unhappy with his life,' Raymond said, uncertain about his credentials as a literary critic. 'Nobody takes Mr Polly seriously, but then he gets the chance to make a new life and he takes it. He finds what he's looking for, but it isn't fame and fortune or anything like that. It's just being happy with his life.'

'That's spot on, Raymond,' Auntie Dawn said, nodding. 'Being content is worth more than gold. What I like is that he's not really a hero. He's just an ordinary man, sometimes even a bit of a clown. He's like a fish out of water until he finds the right pond to swim in.'

Raymond liked that analogy. Looking at her gazing at him through her flyaway spectacles, with the book clasped to her chest and her legs tucked under her, he decided she was refined without being haughty. He liked that too.

'So,' she said, 'what surprise have you got in store for me next? It doesn't have to be happy ever after, mind. I don't mind being challenged.'

*

165

Auntie Dawn was reading Dostoyevsky's *Crime and Punishment* a few days later, when Uncle Gordon returned from a trip somewhere with Manorholme's latest family member. He astounded everybody by announcing that the new, sandy-haired member of the household had the remarkable name of Poppleton of Cilldara. The new arrival was unabashed by everyone's stares and she began to nosey around the sitting room on unsteady legs.

The whole household was smitten by the little golden retriever puppy as it tail-wagged around the room. The children didn't want to go to bed when the time came, and David lay on his back, letting the little puppy stumble around and over him, and refused to budge. Uncle Gordon picked up his son as if he was as light as a feather and the excited puppy jumped up at his long legs while he carried the giggling boy from the room.

Later, when all the children were in bed, Uncle Gordon said, 'We need to find a name for her. Poppleton of Cilldara is a pedigree name, but we need an everyday name. I'm not calling that name out on the street.'

'She's a girl, so maybe we should call her Poppy,' his wife suggested.

'Nay, pet,' Uncle Gordon said, winking at Raymond, 'Poppy's too soppy. What about Pepé?'

'Isn't Pepé a Mexican male name?' Raymond asked.

'Aye, that's as mebbe, but only somebody as smart as you would know that,' Uncle Gordon said with a grin. 'I think Pepé suits her. What do you think, pet?'

'Aye,' Auntie Dawn nodded, 'I like it.'

'That's it, then,' Uncle Gordon declared. 'Pepé it is. Now then, Raymond, she's going to need training and I reckon you're the man for the job. That means taking her out for regular walks, especially in the evening, and making sure she does her business in the right places. You've also got to train her to come when she's called and sit when she's told. You can take her across to Bentley's Fields, but don't let her off her lead until she's completely used to you. When you cross the road, make her sit first and wait on the curb until you're ready to cross. So, what do you think?'

'Yes,' Raymond agreed. 'I can start tonight.'

'Nay, leave her for tonight,' Uncle Gordon said, looking at Pepé curled up in a basket in front of the fireplace. 'She's had a big day and she's fast asleep already. We'll leave her in the hall with some newspapers down and make sure all the doors are closed before we go to bed. She's bound to make a mess for a while anyway.'

*

Manorholme was on the edge of a large housing estate close to rolling meadows, known as Bentley's Fields. Raymond took Pepé there every day, and, once she'd learned the obedience that seemed second nature to her, he began to let her off her lead to gambol. Sometimes he was accompanied by the children of Manorholme, but he preferred it when he was on his own with Pepé on their evening walks. He liked being alone and he enjoyed the new freedom he had to wander. Besides, on his own he could talk to Pepé, which she seemed to like, cocking her soft ears and looking at him with her intelligent brown eyes, as if she understood every word. New to Manorholme, they were starting the same journey together.

One evening, Raymond was heading home when he saw two girls of around his own age in his path. One was blonde and petite and the other was dark and plump. Raymond's natural instinct was to wrap himself in a cloak of indifference, but Pepé, unleashed, ambled up to them, wagging her tail and bobbing her head. The fair-headed girl squatted down on her haunches and began to stroke the willing puppy and tickle behind her ears. As Raymond approached, the girl looked up.

'What's its name?' she asked, squinting up at him. Her voice was light, maybe even thin, but to Raymond it sounded musical.

'Pepé,' he replied. 'It's a girl,' he added, just in case she was familiar with Mexican names.

The blonde girl's friend, who was dressed in a pale-blue cotton summer frock with a frayed white collar, stood with her robust legs planted apart and her arms folded beneath her substantial bust.

'You're from that kids' home, aren't you?' she challenged.

'What's it got to do with you?' he replied, matching her tone.

'She doesn't mean owt by it,' the fair-haired girl said in a conciliatory voice and straightened to stand before him. 'You go to Slevin Grammar, don't you? I've seen you walking to school. It's a bit stuck-up there, isn't it?'

'You've got room to talk,' the stout girl said and, turning back to Raymond, she added, 'She goes to that private school, Milford Hall.'

Raymond studied the fair-haired girl, as the two girls began to exchange banter as if he wasn't there. Her medium-length golden hair, held in place by a blue headband, was wavy and brushed behind delicate ears. Her skin seemed translucent and her eyelashes were long and almost white. She was dressed in a summer frock, like her friend, but the effect was far more elegant. The dark-haired girl caught his stare.

'Everybody gawps at her like that,' she said with a hint of acrimony, 'and *she* always pretends she doesn't notice.'

'I don't,' the other girl protested, but she smiled at Raymond and made him blush.

168

'Come on, Pepé,' he said, kneeling down, both to hide his embarrassment and to fasten the lead to the puppy's collar, 'we'd better get home.'

*

Raymond wasn't sure how it came about, but the awkward meeting with the two girls led to them becoming his regular walking companions. They always seemed to meet by accident and parted with no more than a 'see you around', but he began to take more trouble over his appearance, particularly his dark, wavy hair, which he tried to tame with copious amounts of water before going out.

During their walks, he learned that the pretty girl was called Penny Smith and her buxom friend was called Veronica Halsall. They were lifelong friends who lived next door to each other and loved to chatter about minor events in their everyday lives and often bickered. When they weren't arguing or dissecting some other girl's morals, they sang pop songs with such harmony it belied their fractious relationship. They both liked watching *Juke Box Jury* and were well up on current hits.

They often sang a song together called 'Come Outside'. This was a song performed by a male and female singer in cockney accents, which consisted mainly of the male singer inviting the female singer to 'Come outside' and her replying 'Get lost'. Raymond, who spent a lot of time surreptitiously comparing the girls' breasts, was amused that busty Veronica took the male part.

'You haven't told us your name yet,' Veronica button-holed him one balmy evening.

'It's Raymond,' he said, cursing the fact that she made him feel diffident.

'Ha!' Veronica snorted, for reasons that Raymond couldn't comprehend.

'Ooh, I like it,' Penny gushed. 'I'm going to call you Ray. It sounds so American.'

'American,' Veronica said, folding her arms under her chest. 'Ha!'

Raymond thought to himself that when it came to females he preferred dogs, except, of course, for Carol Farrell.

*

Weeks of sunny weather passed by without a cloud to mar Raymond's horizon. Then one afternoon, as he returned from a walk with Pepé and was unfastening her lead, Auntie Dawn came out of the kitchen followed by tantalising aromas.

'Hello, Raymond,' she said. 'I need to have a word with you in the office. Come in when you're ready.'

When he entered the office, Auntie Dawn was sitting behind a desk and picking at the loose wrapping of a parcel in front of her. Her face, with her spectacles illuminated by the light from the window behind her, had a look of concern.

'Sit down, Raymond,' she said.

Raymond sat down on one of the wooden chairs in front of the desk, wondering why she seemed so sombre.

'How was your walk?' she asked.

'It was fine,' Raymond answered and, able to distinguish preamble from subject matter, waited for the real purpose of his summons.

'I've got something for you,' she informed him. 'It arrived at the Welfare Department and they've asked us to pass it on to you. It's a gift, but it also contains some bad news, I'm afraid. You'd better open it.'

She handed him the parcel with its partly detached brown paper wrapping. Puzzled, he unfurled the paper around it and found that it contained a black oblong box, which, when he opened it, revealed a set of elegant black and silver drawing pens. The parcel also contained a letter in a torn envelope. He withdrew the letter, knowing this must be the bad news, and began to read.

Dear Raymond,

I am writing to you with sad news about my mother, who you knew as Mrs Noble. Unfortunately, she became very ill and sadly passed away two weeks ago. We will all miss her deeply, as I'm sure you will. I am so sorry that in our grief we didn't contact you earlier, but a photograph she kept of you reminded us of how much she cared for you. She spoke of you often and I'm sure you would like something to remember her by, which is why I've sent you the pens. My mother said you were artistic, so perhaps they will help you in that respect.

I'm sorry to be the bearer of bad news. Please think of her fondly sometimes and strive to achieve the future she always said you were capable of.

Yours Sincerely
Patricia Noble

Raymond read the letter three times and each time the stark message refused to change.

'I'm so sorry, Raymond,' Auntie Dawn said with feeling. 'Go up to your room if you want some time on your own. I'll call you when tea's ready. We can talk about this later, but only if you want to.'

Raymond carried his letter and parcel up to his room and sat on his bed. He couldn't work out why he felt empty of feeling, and yet that emptiness weighed down on him like a stone. His thoughts and feelings always came wrapped up in words, so he could unpick them and subject them to internal debate, but not this time. This time there was nothing. Did that make him a bad person?

The clang of spoon on pan startled him. He put the pens

in his top drawer, slipped the letter inside the front cover of *Great Expectations* and went down to tea.

After the post-meal chores, he told his house-parents that he was taking Pepé for a walk.

'Are you sure?' Uncle Gordon asked. 'I can take her if you want.'

'No, it's all right,' Raymond said, noting at the same time the look Auntie Dawn gave her husband, which signalled that he should agree.

When Raymond was ready, with Pepé on her lead, he made towards the door with Auntie Dawn close behind him.

'Raymond,' she whispered.

He turned to face her and she placed her hands on his shoulders and pressed a cool cheek to his. It was only a fleeting embrace, but he was surprised by it and felt awkward.

He didn't get far into Bentley's Fields before he decided to sit on a wall beneath the pink blush of the evening sky and keep Pepé on her lead. He knew she wanted to explore, but she seemed to sense his mood and sat patiently on her haunches beside him. He stroked the velvet fur on the top of her head.

'I don't know how to feel, Pepé,' he said. 'When Mrs Noble first started visiting me I thought she was something to do with the book, that she was the key to *my* great expectations, but I soon realised she was no Miss Havisham.'

Pepé cocked one ear and put her head to one side.

'I never even went to her house and lots of times when I was with her she preferred to talk to adults, but she was the only person who's ever visited me and the more I got to know her, the more I got to like her. She pretended to be a stuck-up lady, but she wasn't really. She knew a lot about life and about books. And she turned up at the right times. I'm not saying I needed her, but I'm glad she was there. I don't think she'd mind me not crying now. I bet she knows how I feel. I'm going to miss her. It's just you and me now, girl.'

'Hello, Ray.'

Startled, Raymond looked up to see Penny Smith standing to one side of him wearing skin-tight blue jeans and a figure-hugging white sweater. He was grateful she was on her own and tried to put the image of her sitting in a bath of cold water from his mind, which he knew was the preferred method of shrinking denim jeans.

'I'm sorry,' she said, twisting the fingers of one hand around a finger of her other hand, as if she was turning a ring.

'What for?' he asked, noticing the sun-streaks in her hair and the light golden tone of her skin beneath the roseate sky.

'For disturbing you,' she said, shrugging her shoulders. 'You seemed to be miles away.'

He squinted at her as she hovered, caught in the rays of the dying, blood-red sun.

'Don't worry about it,' he said, trying to sound nonchalant. 'I was just thinking.'

'And talking,' she said.

Her smile was dazzling and the imaginary ring seemed to dissolve, as she dropped her hands to her sides and swung them backwards and forwards.

'My auntie's died,' he said.

Her smile crumpled into a look of sympathy.

'She was my Pictorial Auntie,' he said by way of further explanation.

'What kind of auntie is that?' she asked, raising her fine eyebrows.

'A special one,' Raymond said, easing himself off the wall. 'Come for a walk and I'll tell you about her.'

Outrageous Fortune

'She's growing fast, Raymond,' Uncle Gordon observed, squatting down in front of Pepé, who stared at him with limpid eyes. 'She's had a good summer and you've trained her well. She's as fit as a butcher's dog and as meek as a lamb. She'll miss you now you're going back to school, but I'll take her out during the day. Now, you'd better get a move on or you'll be late.'

Raymond stroked Pepé's nuzzling head, hitched his satchel up on his shoulder and headed off.

Walking to school in the face of a fresh breeze to begin the new term, he spotted Penny Smith at the bus stop on the opposite side of the road. She looked so pretty in her grey school uniform and straw boater with purple ribbons, and the fact that her coy wave was just for him put an extra spring in his step.

Cresting the hill onto the main street of Slevin, he saw the school bus pass by, the windows crammed with animated Slevinites and wide-eyed new boys. Raymond was a fourth-year boy now, but his sympathy was still with those pale young faces staring out of the windows, unaware that the caps they wore would soon be flying off their heads.

He reached the bus stop in time to see Titch, Rollo and Poggy alight.

'Rom, me old mate,' Poggy cried out. 'Has your sister found out who the father is yet?'

'Yeah,' Raymond replied. 'Turns out it was your dad.'

Titch and Rollo fell about laughing, while Poggy was lost for words. After a bout of backslapping, the Legion of the Disenchanted sauntered towards school amidst a flurry of airborne school caps.

The first day was relaxed, consisting mainly of receiving new timetables and hand-me-down textbooks, and Raymond and his friends remained light-hearted throughout the day. It wasn't the time for dwelling on the grey days they knew lay ahead, but for reminiscing on what they'd got up to during the summer holidays. Raymond listened while Titch, Rollo and Poggy recounted their adventures and family excursions, without revealing much himself.

His summer break had floated through a haze of sunshine, laughter and dog walking. During that time, he'd enjoyed a holiday in a hostel in the Lake District with the Manorholme family. Yes, they were like a family; even more so when they were away; long walks through gorse and heather; laughter and games; storytelling and reading; surely just a happy, if somewhat motley, family in anybody's eyes. Even though Raymond said nothing about it to his friends, this time it wasn't because he felt at any disadvantage. It was just that old habits die hard and, besides, in this world you never know when things might change and make you look foolish.

The only blot on the day was seeing Roger Marsden between lessons. It appeared at first that his former foster-brother was either blind or Raymond was invisible, but then Roger's lip curled just enough to scotch both theories. Raymond was unmoved. None of the boys milling about the corridor knew Raymond was supposed to have been Roger's brother for a time. Whose fault was that?

At the end of the day, Angus asked Raymond to stay behind after an English Literature lesson.

'I've got something I want you to do for me, laddie,' Angus said, 'and when I tell you what it is, I want you to bear in mind I've chosen you out of the whole school.' Angus paused and pulled on his long nose, which Raymond recognised as a habit of his when he wanted to say something important to the class. 'It's Founder's Day in a few weeks,' Angus said. 'You know what that means: pomp and ceremony in the Town Hall in front of an audience of families and local dignitaries. The headmaster will deliver his annual speech. Mr Dyson will have the choir primed to deliver some choice pieces and one or two selected boys will give appropriate readings. This year I want you and me to do something together.'

He pulled his nose again before continuing.

'This school was founded during the reign of King James the First of England, aye, and the Sixth of Scotland, let's not forget, when art and literature flourished. That is something I'm going to give a talk about, to remind our audience of the spirit of the age when the school was founded. There is no better exemplar of that spirit than William Shakespeare, who was at the peak of his powers at the time, and that is where you come in. I want you to follow my discourse with a reading of one of Shakespeare's finest passages: Hamlet's famous soliloquy.'

'Me, sir?' Raymond said, flattered and apprehensive at the same time. 'Are you sure I'm the right person, sir?'

'You are *my* candidate, laddie, and there is no better one in this whole school,' Angus insisted. 'You have a natural feel for literature and the written word that I couldn't impart to most of these boys if I was locked in a classroom with them for a hundred years.'

The thought of that ordeal seemed to make Angus shudder.

'You have the diction, and with practice we'll make it perfect. We have weeks to work on it, although it will mean you giving up some of your dinner breaks. What do you say, laddie?'

'Yes, sir, if you really want me to,' Raymond said, persuaded more by obligation to Angus than duty to the school.

'I surely do,' Angus said. 'Now you'd better run along home. We'll make a start during the dinner break to-morrow.'

Raymond made towards the classroom door and was just about to exit when Angus called out, 'Rawnsley!'

'Yes, sir?'

'Do you know what Hamlet's soliloquy is?'

'Yes, sir. "To be or not to be", sir.'

'Aye, laddie.'

*

When Raymond told his house-parents about the reading, they were delighted.

'That's excellent, Raymond,' Auntie Dawn said. 'You can practise in the evenings. I'll help you if you like.'

'What's a soliquilly?' Uncle Gordon asked.

'It's like a speech where someone's talking to themselves,' Raymond said, ignoring his house-father's mispronunciation, as he suspected it was deliberate.

'So you'll be talking to yourself?' Uncle Gordon said.

'Stop teasing him, Gordon,' Auntie Dawn said. 'This is a big honour.'

'Aye, it sure is,' Uncle Gordon said, adopting a serious tone. 'We'll help you all we can, lad.'

Over the next few weeks, Raymond worked hard to perfect the reading, not just with Angus and his ever-willing house-mother, but also with Pepé on their walks, which he never neglected. Somehow, during that time, he and Penny Smith began *going out* together. What the distinction between that and walking a dog together was, or what determined when one became the other, was a mystery to Raymond.

Girls understood these things better than boys.

'If you're going out together, why don't you hold hands?' Veronica asked one mild, tawny autumn evening as he roamed Bentley's Fields with Pepé and the two girls.

Raymond's response to this exasperated query from Veronica was to look straight ahead, but then something bumped against his hand, as if by accident, and an instant later he felt cool fingers slip between his. He looked at Penny and she smiled with her bottom lip curled behind teeth as white as snow in the dusk.

From then on, he was going out with Penny, even though Veronica was always with them. Raymond didn't mind her presence, even though he often thought the friendship between the two girls strange, especially as Veronica sometimes found it hard to disguise her resentment. If it wasn't for her, he reasoned, he would never have realised he had a girlfriend.

*

Raymond was calm. He knew the speech off by heart and Angus was fulsome in praise of his final reading. The evening before Founder's Day he went through it one final time with Auntie Dawn and when he finished she clapped her hands together in delight.

'To pee or not to pee, that is the question,' Uncle Gordon said, rising to his feet and heading for the door, where he turned round. 'By the way, Raymond, we're coming to see you tomorrow night. Mrs H is going to stay late so we can give you our support.'

After that, Raymond was nervous. He'd never been represented at any school event before. No one had ever talked to his teachers about his progress on open nights, or sat in an audience on his behalf, or cheered him home on sports days. He was going to fail. His voice was going to turn into Squeaky Dave's and the whole school and all their mums and dads, brothers, sisters, aunties and uncles were going laugh at him.

His sleep was fitful that night, but it didn't stop him dreaming.

Raymond stood at the lectern in front of the massed audience. Two sheets of paper with Hamlet's soliloquy written on them in large neat letters, with words to be emphasised in capitals, were laid out before him. In the audience, he spotted Mr and Mrs Marsden staring at him. Next to them, Janet and Mary were mouthing something.

'Good on the inside, bad on the outside.'

The lump in his throat grew larger.

'Get on with it,' a voice from the tiered ranks of the school behind him cried out.

It was Roger.

Raymond opened his mouth and uttered 'To be or not to be' as loud as he could. His voice sounded like a girl's; a big soft girl who was being squeezed by the throat. People in the audience began to titter.

'That is the question,' he squawked.

'The question is – why are you wearing your pyjamas?' Roger called out.

At that, the audience fell about laughing.

The worst thing, the worst thing of all, was that Auntie Dawn and Uncle Gordon were laughing as loud as anybody.

*

Founder's Day was an important date in the Slevin Grammar School calendar: a chance to remind the town of the school's history and tradition. The boys sat before the audience in the Town Hall on steep wooden tiers in ascending years, while the school choir, conducted by Dimwiddy, occupied centre stage in front of the soaring pipes of a fabulous organ. On either side of the choir, masters sat in rows.

Raymond wished he was sitting on one of the higher tiers

with his year group, but, instead, he sat, feeling uncomfortable, behind the row of masters to one side of the choir. Gazing around the opulent hall, with its ornate columns and balconies, he regretted agreeing to what he was about to do. The benefit of the countless hours he'd sacrificed to perfect the reading of the soliloquy was about to be put to the test and his confidence was ebbing.

The choir was coming to the end of a song Raymond didn't know, or at least didn't recognise at that moment. The noise was scrambling his brain and the demented antics of baton-waving Dimwiddy weren't helping either. He knew Angus would soon be getting to his feet next to talk about the age when the school had been founded, before introducing Raymond to the lectern for his performance. Time was refusing to stand still.

Raymond knew Angus's speech. The master had gone through it with him so he knew exactly when he would have to take the stage. It was a brief lecture, but interesting and informative, and it put into context the founding of the school in an age of art, education and discovery. Angus delivered it well, his accent giving emphasis and drive to his words, and the audience was attentive. Raymond despised it. It was far too short.

He heard his name and got to his feet. It was difficult putting one foot in front of the other, never mind the prospect of having to get a string of words in the right order. Angus beckoned him to the lectern with an outstretched arm and an encouraging smile, which only made him look like a ghoul summoning Raymond to the execution block. The soliloquy was already laid out on the lectern, hidden from the audience, and Raymond stepped up to it. Angus had thought of everything. Now it was up to him.

Time, which had galloped up to now, stood still, as Raymond scrutinised the faces looking up at him. Up to

now, sitting behind the row of masters, he'd avoided looking at the audience. Now it seemed vast. Directly ahead of
him, among the sea of faces, he saw four souls he would
rather not have in his eye line. Mr and Mrs Marsden, with
their daughters, Mary and Janet, were sitting rigid in their
seats and staring straight at him. They didn't look encouraging and he swallowed. He had to begin.

'To be or not to be: that is the question.'

It didn't feel right. He was going to stumble. His eyes,
which probably looked panic-stricken to the audience,
swept the hall, before coming to rest on what he'd hoped to
see. Auntie Dawn and Uncle Gordon were sitting three rows
from the back. She smiled and Uncle Gordon gave a small
thumbs-up sign. Auntie Dawn pressed her hands together
in front of her chest and lifted them slightly towards him.

'Whether 'tis nobler in the mind to suffer the slings and
arrows of outrageous fortune ...'

He read the whole soliloquy to Auntie Dawn, no one else.
The emotions portrayed in her sympathetic face were his
guide and the more her eyes shone the more his voice grew
in strength, and the words came out just as they'd done in
the best of his practice sessions. When he finished, the
applause in front of him and behind him seemed deafen-
ing. He couldn't help grinning, because that's what Auntie
Dawn and Uncle Gordon were doing. He also noticed Mrs
Marsden clapping with enthusiasm, while her husband and
daughters were open-mouthed, as if in shock at hearing
him say so much in one go.

Forbidden Ale

Christmas came to Manorholme in a flurry of snowflakes that painted embroidered lace curtains on the cold window panes. Little David was in raptures when he saw it on Christmas Day morning and ran around all the bedrooms to tell everyone about it. As the house warmed up, the curtains parted to reveal a crystal pageant and throughout a morning of unwrapping presents and playing with new toys, all the children kept going to the windows to marvel at it.

The presents came from unknown well-wishers, but for the first time in Raymond's experience, his house-parents also gave every child a present from them. Raymond's personal gift was a book. His house-mother was watching him as he removed the wrapping paper to reveal the cover of *Billy Liar* by Keith Waterhouse.

'I thought you might like something contemporary to add to your collection,' she said. 'I've heard it's very good. I hope you like it.'

Raymond had never read a book he didn't like. He even read his school textbooks in one go; well, at least the ones for history, English Literature and geography. He was certain, though, that he would like this more than most.

Inch by inch, the blanket of snow thickened, while Frances's brown eyes grew ever bigger. Mrs Hanson brought her husband, a jovial man wearing the most flamboyant cardigan Raymond had ever seen, to share their Christmas dinner and he spent the day making everyone, adults and children alike, laugh out loud with his jokes. Christmas dinner, the finest example of Mrs Hanson's culinary skill in Raymond experience so far, was enjoyed by the liveliest group of diners with whom he'd ever shared a table.

In the afternoon, Mr Hanson helped the children build a snowman with a carrot for a nose and pieces of coal for its eyes and mouth, and Raymond donated his school scarf for the final touch.

'It's snow teacher,' Mr Hanson cried. 'Let's knock its silly head off with snowballs.'

The ensuing barrage of snowballs sent Pepé into a frenzy until she eventually coughed up the tasty tidbits that Mrs Hanson had fed her from the Christmas dinner. That was a signal for them all to calm down and they trooped indoors ready for warmth and rest.

In the evening, Mr Hanson continued to entertain everybody. He knew more tricks with a pack of cards than a professional conjurer and even Raymond and the adults were baffled. Eventually, the children went to bed content and the adults and Raymond settled down to watch television, until 'God Save the Queen' brought the day to a close. Mr and Mrs Hanson set off on their short walk home laughing into the teeth of a blizzard and Raymond went to bed.

While waiting for his body to warm the sheets, he slipped his hand under his pillow and pulled out an envelope. There was enough light from the window for him to see the letters 'SWALK' written across it. He didn't open it, but he knew what it said in the greeting card inside.

I will think of you every day until I see you again,
Love Penny, xxxxxxx

He hadn't even thought to give Penny a card and hers suggested that there was much more to their relationship than had been so far demonstrated. Still, there was nothing wrong with dreaming, was there?

*

The cold weather refused to release its grip and by the time Raymond returned to school for the start of the new term, the pavements were buried beneath thick packed ice. Every morning and afternoon he saw Penny at her bus stop and held her gloved hand, while she bemoaned the fact that her father wouldn't let her out at night for some time to come. Raymond's own evenings with Pepé were curtailed by the freezing cold and pitch-black nights and he was confined to brisk walks on the road alongside Bentley's Fields.

'I can't wait for spring,' Penny often purred with her breath hanging in the air.

Spring took its time to break the icy stranglehold that bound the lives of everyone at Manorholme to hearth and fire, but it was a cosy time nonetheless. A freezing bedroom made the bed seem warmer and Mrs Hanson's hot food was never more delicious.

Raymond couldn't remember a time in his life when he'd actually looked forward to getting home from school. He recalled all those times he'd dragged his feet and kicked stones as he was drawn back by reluctant obedience to wherever it was he called home.

Now it was different. The house was always bright as he approached. The smell of Mrs Hanson's homely cooking made his stomach growl when he opened the door, and Pepé greeted him like a beloved friend she'd thought she'd never see again. The other children chorused their happy greetings when he poked his head around the sitting room door, and Uncle Gordon often greeted him with a teasing remark.

His house-father loved a topical joke and still hadn't tired of declaring 'To pee or not to pee', before going to the toilet and, ever since Lesley had embarrassed Raymond at the dinner table by revealing he had a girlfriend called Penny, Uncle Gordon was fond of singing 'Pennies from Heaven'.

One day Raymond arrived home from school and immediately sensed a change in the atmosphere. Uncle Gordon gave him only the faintest smile before disappearing into the office and Auntie Dawn was nowhere to be seen. Even Pepé seemed subdued as she sidled up to him as he removed his coat, scarf and shoes in the corridor. Puzzled, Raymond was about to go up to his room to get changed when Mrs Hanson called out to him as he passed the kitchen door.

'Raymond, do me a favour, love, and lay the table for tea, will you?'

Raymond didn't mind helping Mrs Hanson. She was a benign and interesting gossip and often allowed him to taste the delectable food she prepared for their meals. As soon as he entered the steamy kitchen he could tell she was bursting to tell him something, especially as she waved to him to close the door behind him.

'There's trouble,' Mrs Hanson said to him in a low, urgent voice.

'What trouble?' Raymond asked, perturbed. He'd begun to think that trouble was a thing of the past and he didn't relish its return.

'Do you remember what a lovely time we had at Christmas?' Mrs Hanson said, as she scooped a spoonful of stew from a simmering pan.

'Yes, it was great,' Raymond said.

'Well,' Mrs Hanson said and then paused to offer him the spoonful of stew to taste. 'Do you remember Stan, my husband, bringing some of his homemade ale and us adults had some with dinner and some in the evening?'

'Yes,' Raymond said, letting the savoury soup slip down his throat and warm his insides.

He remembered the beer because Mr Hanson gave him a sip and he hadn't liked it.

'That's what the trouble's about,' Mrs Hanson said. 'The Welfare Authority found out about it. It's strictly against the rules to drink on duty. Uncle Gordon and Auntie Dawn have been given a severe warning. They're not happy.'

'How did the Welfare find out?' Raymond asked.

'Doris Wrigley,' Mrs Hanson pronounced, her voice filled with distaste. 'She used to work here before me. Trouble is, half the food used to find its way back to her house. God knows what she did with it. She's as thin as a bar of soap after a long day's washing. It was a dead giveaway when she had fruit laid out on the sideboard even though nobody was ill. No wonder she got found out and got the sack. She probably thinks she's having a go at me, but I wasn't officially working on Christmas Day. It's not right those two should cop it. I'll bet these kids have never had such a good Christmas.'

For the first time in his life, Raymond was overcome by a feeling of sympathy and protectiveness towards his guardians.

'The thing is, Raymond,' Mrs Hanson said, biting her thumbnail. 'I think it was me. I told a few people what a good time we had. Me and my big mouth. We did have a good time, though, didn't we? Where's the harm in that?'

There was always harm, somewhere, just waiting to happen, Raymond thought later in bed with his blankets wrapped tightly around him. Things couldn't go right forever, could they? There was always a rule to be broken if you weren't careful. Uncle Gordon and Auntie Dawn were new to his world. They didn't understand that the ground they walked on was made of thin ice that could crack at any moment.

Don't Go

The dark world outside was still locked in snow and ice as Raymond read in front of the glowing electric fire. At his feet, Pepé lay sleeping on her side on the rug, her paws twitching as she romped somewhere in her dreams. Auntie Dawn was curled up in her armchair reading her latest book and Uncle Gordon sat at the table with a construction magazine open in front of him. Raymond watched his house-parents, waiting for the moment he could do something for them.

He'd been trying to be helpful to them in every way he could since they'd been reprimanded. He looked after the children and told them stories to make them laugh. He made supper for his house-parents during the evenings when they were alone together and attempted to distract them from their troubles by talking about books. If there was anything at all he could do to lift the mood of depression hanging over them, he did it.

When Uncle Gordon stirred and closed his magazine Raymond was on his feet in a flash.

'Anybody want a cup of tea?' he asked, injecting as much nonchalance into his voice as he could.

Uncle Gordon looked up at him with his dark eyebrows arched and then suddenly grinned. His teeth were white against his chiselled, swarthy face.

'Christ sakes, Raymond man, you're driving us potty,' he said. 'We're not leaving Manorholme, so you can relax.'

Pepé woke up and, seeing Raymond on his feet, began to circle him with her tail wagging to a crazy canine beat.

'I guessed Mrs Hanson must've told you, because you've been trying so hard to cheer us up all the time,' Uncle Gordon continued. 'You already know why, so I'll tell you the rest. We got hauled up in front of Miss Meakin, the Head of Welfare. We didn't mind so much, because rules are rules, even though we didn't do anything wrong. What's worse is we got reprimanded for being too soft. Some of the other house-parents complained that we're making life too easy for you lot. I've no idea how they get to know such things and, besides, it's ridiculous.'

'I told you, pet,' Auntie Dawn said, looking up at her husband. 'You're too outspoken at meetings. We can do things our way, but it doesn't do to preach to others. They resent it. That woman from Backville Manor said we've got it easy. We don't have to deal with the teenage tearaways she says she's got in her care.'

'Aye, well, that's as mebbe,' Uncle Gordon said, 'but I don't like her attitude in any case. Still, let's put it behind us. About that cup of tea, Raymond – forget it. Gan and get that bottle of whiskey hidden in the cupboard under the sink.'

Auntie Dawn laughed so much at this that she drew up her slim legs up and hugged her knees, while Raymond beamed.

After that, all was well in their little world again. On cue, the big thaw arrived and the walls of compacted snow at the roadsides began to melt. Better still, Penny told Raymond at the bus stop on the way to school that her dad was going to let her out again. The improved weather meant that he could take Pepé for longer walks in Bentley's Fields again and now Penny could come with him, even if it did mean having Veronica in tow.

*

188

Raymond met the two girls at the gate to Bentley's Fields on a dank and gloomy March evening for their first walk of the year. It was wet underfoot and there were still pockets of crystalline snow lying in the fields, so they stuck to the pathways, which were rutted with puddles. Penny gripped his hand, saying the ground was slippery and dangerous. Veronica had no one to stop her slipping, but she'd had the foresight to wear Wellington boots and advertised her practicality by splashing through every puddle.

Eventually, they turned back and as they walked they began singing a new Beatles' song, called 'Please Please Me', at the tops of their voices. As they neared the gate, Penny told Veronica to go on ahead while, suddenly oblivious to underfoot conditions, she pulled Raymond behind a gnarled tree.

Raymond expected their first chaste kiss, but Penny's hot and hungry lips soon disabused him of that notion. Judging by the press of her body, the sensual movement of her mouth against his and the grasping of her fingers at the hair at the back of his head, she'd taken a few imaginary steps forward in the game of love since they'd last been together. He was almost gasping for air by the time she let him go, but it was only to whisper endearments before she plunged back onto his lips again.

Raymond was reeling, but his physical self responded to her urging of its own accord. She opened her coat and pulled his hands inside, where they became independent agents of his growing desire. Her breasts, to which she moulded his hands, were round and firm and felt alive, even though they were covered by her thick pullover.

Raymond knew they'd crossed the Rubicon together, but he was no Julius Caesar and his heart pounded with the fear of being caught. Veronica's loud coughing was almost a godsend, but at the same time it was difficult to pull away from Penny. When he did, he saw her face was flushed and her lips looked as though they'd been stung by bees. She smiled, once again demure and innocent.

From then on, Raymond looked forward to their walks with fear and excitement, knowing each one would culminate in more lustful abandonment behind the tree. Over the next few weeks, Raymond's eager finger soldiers, guided by Penny, broke through her button defences and lifted the portcullis to plunder the most perfect treasures lying within. At the same time, he couldn't help thinking that everybody knew what he was up to; in particular, his house-parents and his masters at school, and every strange look and every odd remark filled him with the dread of discovery.

Trapped by Penny's entreaties and his own lust, the length of time Raymond spent behind the blasted oak increased and Veronica's coughing, despite the fairer weather, grew more pronounced. But Raymond was always careful never to break the nine o'clock curfew insisted on by his house-parents. He'd always thought it was generous, considering he'd never enjoyed such freedom before. It wasn't enough for Penny, though, and she ensured he began arriving home late, first by a few minutes, which went unremarked upon by his house-parents, but then by longer.

One evening, Raymond slipped through the door of Manorholme with Pepé more than half an hour late. Uncle Gordon was waiting for him.

'What time do you call this?' Uncle Gordon asked, standing tall with his hands on his hips in the frame of the sitting room door.

'I'm sorry,' Raymond said. 'I didn't realise what the time was.'

'You've got a watch,' Uncle Gordon pointed out, 'and, besides, I reckon you had another reason for being distracted. You know we try to be fair, Raymond, but you're abusing our trust. If you want to help us run a happy home it's a two way street. Go straight to bed and think about it.'

Without another word, Uncle Gordon stepped back, letting Pepé trot into the sitting room, before closing the door. Alone, Raymond was crestfallen. He'd let his house-parents down. He knew, since the Christmas drink incident, that they'd been under pressure to conform to the rigid regime that was the norm in children's homes. He'd heard snatches of conversation and oblique references between the adults, which told him that they were still being sniped at in the meetings they attended every so often.

He reached the bottom of the stairs and hesitated before making a decision and turning towards the sitting room door. Gripping the handle, he pushed the door ajar and poked his head around it.

'I'm sorry,' he said, feeling the dagger of his house-mother's disappointed frown pierce his heart. 'It won't happen again. Goodnight.'

*

Raymond stuck to his promise, despite Penny's unabated appetite for petting. She didn't like it when he glanced at his watch and pulled away, and often sulked, but he was insistent.

'Don't go,' she pleaded.

'I have to,' he replied.

At least Veronica's coughing seemed to improve.

Pouting, he began to comprehend, was second nature to Penny and it began to irk him. He knew that other boys would envy the liberties such a pretty girl allowed him, but reality was not the same as dreams. He could spend the evening locked in Penny's embrace, but it was Carol Farrell who came to him in the dead of night. His tree time with Penny began to feel like being blindfolded and fed morsels of sponge cake.

When it came to love, which Penny laid claim to like a

Girl Guide's badge she'd earned, the closest he came to the purity of emotion, described with such eloquence in books, was in his feelings for Auntie Dawn. Often, when he was alone with his house-parents in the evenings, he would steal a glance at her while she read one of his books. Her profile, with her high cheekbones, fine skin and lustrous hair, was perfection. His feelings were pure and yet, somehow, it was her looks that embodied everything he liked about her; her intelligence; her refinement; and most of all, her compassion.

Raymond came to view weekends, when Penny and Veronica seemed to be wrapped up with their families, as almost a relief. He could take Pepé out alone for the whole afternoon if he liked, or he could take the Manorholme children with him, which he often did.

Visiting days were a time he was especially inclined to solitude, especially now that no one came to visit him since the loss of his Pictorial Auntie. On one such day, good weather, and the imminent arrival of visitors for the other children, prompted Raymond to set off with Pepé. When he said he was going, Auntie Dawn's fond look made him suspect she understood his reasons. Attaching Pepé's lead, he was pondering this when he heard a knock on the front door. It must have been the first visitor. It was time to clear off.

He was about to exit by the side door, as Auntie Dawn went to answer the front door, when he heard snuffling. Intrigued, he followed the sound and found Frances standing at the bottom of the stairs dressed in her best coat. Seeing Raymond, she rubbed her eyes with the backs of her hands and tried to smile, but Raymond noticed her ebony cheeks somehow retained the tracks of recent tears, like finger marks in the condensation on a window at night.

'What's the matter?' he asked her in his kindest voice.

'I don't want to go,' she whispered.

Her brown eyes were full of entreaty and Raymond understood. He knew Frances's visitor was her aunt, who was obviously very religious, because on each visit she took Frances to a chapel for some kind of service. Raymond, wise in the ways of childhood unhappiness, had noticed before that Frances was often subdued on her return and so unlike her usual self.

'Then don't go,' Raymond said. 'Leave it to me.'

At that moment, Auntie Dawn returned to the hallway with Frances's aunt. She was a large black woman with a sour face and a ridiculous hat. Raymond didn't even need to think.

'She doesn't want to go,' he announced, standing as tall as he could with Pepé at his heel like a guard dog.

Frances's aunt looked shocked and, for an instant, so did Auntie Dawn, but then her face softened.

'Is that so, Frances?' she asked the forlorn figure on the stairs.

Frances nodded and huge tears began to roll down her cheeks.

'Don't you be silly, girl,' her aunt burst out. 'Get those feet moving right now or we're going to be late.'

The aunt stepped forward, but Auntie Dawn stretched her arm backwards with her hand upraised. The glowering aunt stopped in her tracks.

'Frances, do you want to go?' Auntie Dawn asked, emphasising every word.

'Nooo!' Frances wailed and clattered back upstairs in her patent leather shoes.

The argument between the belligerent aunt and Auntie Dawn brought Uncle Gordon into the hallway. Pepé whimpered as heated words were exchanged, but Raymond's house-parents held their ground and finally the disgruntled aunt left without Frances.

When she'd gone, Auntie Dawn put her hand on

Raymond's shoulder and gave him a troubled smile.

'Well done, pet,' she said. 'You did the right thing. Now off you go and don't worry about this. It'll sort itself out.'

Raymond headed for Bentley's Fields with Pepé, lost in thought. He didn't just read books; he absorbed them into his view of life. He'd got into the habit of finding an author in the school library he liked and reading everything he could find by them. He'd recently read George Orwell's *Animal Farm* and *Nineteen Eighty-Four*. They only confirmed his understanding of the ways of overriding authority and he feared that there might be trouble.

Who Said That?

Mrs Hanson inveigled Raymond into her cosy kitchen with the promise of a taste of her pie crust.

'They're in trouble again, Raymond,' she informed him when he'd closed the door. 'They've been up before Miss Meakin and put on a final warning for not letting Frances go with her horrible auntie. Ooh, that Miss Meakin is so hard-faced you could straighten nails on her. Now poor little Frances has got to go with her auntie whenever she calls for her and Uncle Gordon is fuming.'

It was no more than Raymond expected. He almost regretted the part he'd played in it. Sometimes, though, there was no choice, even if it was a path that always ended in the same place; just like when he and his old mate Brian kicked at the traces of injustice at Hillcrest.

This time his house-parents talked about their frustrations openly in the evenings when all the other children were in bed. Even more disturbing, Uncle Gordon began to read newspapers and journals, often commenting about jobs advertised in his field of civil engineering. Raymond felt a compulsion to watch over them at all times and couldn't wait to get back home from his evening walks.

Penny, on the other hand, was as keen as ever to consummate their 'true love', but she sensed his distraction, proving to Raymond his lips and hands were not as decoupled from his mind as he'd thought they were.

'What's wrong, Ray?' she asked one evening, beneath the

boughs of the oak tree. 'Don't you fancy me anymore?'

'Yeah, course,' Raymond assured her.

'Well, then,' Penny murmured and placed his hand on her cool thigh just above the hemline of her skirt.

This was unchartered territory for Raymond, but he wasn't in the mood for more blind exploration.

'I've got to go,' he said, pulling his hand away and moving out from behind the tree to where Veronica was holding Pepé by her lead.

Veronica gave him an odd smile when he took the lead from her and he began to hurry home, lost in thought. Penny might be the most attractive girl on the estate, but, somehow, something was missing. He liked her, but if she was a book she'd be a slim volume; a kind of 'Dear Diary' of inconsequential events that some girls deemed to be essential to their lives. Now, if Carol Farrell was a book, what a page-turner that would be.

Later that evening, Uncle Gordon looked up at his wife from the magazine he was reading.

'There's a major hydro-electric engineering project in Australia called the Snowy Mountains Scheme,' he said. 'It's a huge project and they're advertising for engineers and offering very favourable conditions like assisted passage and housing. This is right up my street. I'm more than qualified, pet.'

'I'm going to bed,' Raymond announced. 'Goodnight.'

'Night, pet,' Auntie Dawn said, giving him a strange look.

'Night, Raymond,' Uncle Gordon said without looking at him. 'Now then, pet, like I was saying, this is just perfect. Think about it.'

Raymond closed the door behind him and went upstairs. As he made his way to his room, after brushing his teeth in the bathroom, Auntie Dawn appeared at the top of the stairs.

'Don't worry about it, Raymond,' she said to him, peering

over her bird-in-flight spectacles. 'Uncle Gordon's feeling a bit down at the moment. I think Australia's a bit of a pipe dream, don't you? We've never even talked about emigrating. He just needs something else to think about right now. Sleep well.'

Raymond didn't go straight to sleep. He felt uneasy. He was sure that Uncle Gordon would apply for the job in Australia. Why wouldn't he? His house-father was clearly excited about it and seemed to be getting more frustrated about the shackles imposed on them by the Welfare Department.

*

Exams became more serious with each passing year for Slevin Grammar pupils. This year, the year before the most important exams, the O levels, which would determine whether students stayed on to pursue an academic career or left to join the local textile workforce, the exams were arduous.

The other members of the Legion of the Disenchanted were complaining as Raymond accompanied them up the hill from school after a Latin exam, the last of the series.

'What a stinker,' Poggy exclaimed. 'It'd have been bad enough if I'd managed stay awake in Nero's lessons. I've only got two hopes of getting a decent mark in that exam. No hope and Bob Hope.'

'Same for me,' Rollo sighed, 'and I prefer Bing Crosby, so I've got even less chance than you.'

'How did *you* get on, Rom,' Poggy asked turning to Raymond.

'All right,' Raymond said.

'He's skated it,' Poggy cried. 'He's been swotting all year.'

'There's a difference between Rom and us,' Titch stated before Raymond could respond, 'He can do it with his eyes shut.'

Raymond protested, but the truth was that he'd had a good year at Slevin. Not that he curried favour with any of the masters or prefects, but the loss of the 'new boy' tag, the acceptance of his welfare status, and the fact that there were more boys who were younger, rather than older, than him in the school, helped him settle down. Even more so, a contented home life with house-parents who took a real interest in him made all the difference to his academic performance.

He mulled things over as he continued the rest of his journey alone. Home life was the key. Thankfully, things seemed to have settled back to normality at Manorholme since Uncle Gordon's flirtation with ideas of a new career. The sun was shining; the days were longer; and his house-father was cracking jokes and singing silly songs again.

When Raymond arrived home after his Latin exam, he felt light-hearted. The exams were over and he'd be able to go out after tea with Pepé. The aromas wafting from the kitchen smelled good and Pepé was as pleased as ever to see him. She was almost full-sized now, so he was glad she'd stopped jumping up at him. He stroked and patted her as her long tail made wild patterns in the air.

'Raymond, can you pop in for a minute?'

The voice was Auntie Dawn's and when he looked up, Raymond saw her head poking out of the office door. Giving Pepé a final pat, he obeyed her request.

'Ah, Raymond,' Uncle Gordon said when he entered the office. 'Come in and shut the door behind you.'

Raymond closed the door and approached. Uncle Gordon was sitting behind the desk and Auntie Dawn was perched on a chair to one side. They looked normal enough, but Raymond was apprehensive. He didn't have good memories of being summoned into offices.

'Sit down, Raymond,' Auntie Dawn said. 'It's nothing to worry about.'

She looked at her husband, as if to say with her eyes, 'Shall you tell him or shall I?'

Raymond interpreted the look and didn't feel anymore at ease as he sat on the chair in front of the desk.

'We've got some news for you,' Uncle Gordon began, accepting the mantle of messenger. 'Do you remember me talking about the job in Australia?'

Raymond's heart sank as he nodded his head.

'Well,' Uncle Gordon said and then paused before he continued, 'I applied.'

He stalled again and Raymond noticed Auntie Dawn give him an anxious look.

'The thing is,' his house-father said and glanced at his wife, 'I got the job. We talked about it, didn't we, pet? We decided it was too good an opportunity to miss. If we're ever going to do anything like this, now's the time. David's the right age to start a new life.'

Raymond was seeing much more than what was in front of him and none of it was good.

'We don't want to leave you and the other children here,' Auntie Dawn said, 'but this is too good a chance to miss. Everything's fixed.'

'I'm really pleased for you,' Raymond heard himself say.

He remembered the time when he and Brian found Squeaky Dave hanging in Millacre Ditch, so long ago. From the moment he saw that ghastly sight it felt as though he was lost in a deep tunnel. For some time afterwards it seemed that the voices around him were coming from somewhere distant. Nothing seemed real.

That's how it felt now. His ears were stuffed with cotton wool. His eyes were glazed with film.

'How would you like to come with us?'

Who said that? Did somebody say that? A veil lifted from Raymond's eyes. His house-parents were beaming.

'I said,' Uncle Gordon repeated. 'Do you want to come with us?'

Do fish swim? Do dogs bark? Do birds fly? Raymond knew there were exceptions to most things, but in this case there wasn't. There was only one answer and he gave it.

Australia versus England

Raymond said nothing to anyone about his potential departure for new shores, even though golden possibilities tumbled through his mind. In the meantime, his houseparents did their homework. They knew he had no other known relatives apart from his mother and they knew her situation. They would have to apply for adoption, but surely it would be a formality.

It would, wouldn't it?

Mrs Hanson knew his secret, just as she knew everything, and she put her arm around his shoulders when they were alone in the kitchen, covering him with flour.

'I couldn't be more happy, Raymond,' she said. 'If ever people deserved each other it's you and them. I'm giving up when you're gone. This'll be a grand way to finish and Mr Hanson is hankering after me spending more time cooking for him. I can read him like big print.'

She began to brush the flour from Raymond's black school jumper with her hands, but only succeeded it making it worse.

'I'm taking Pepé as well,' she said, abandoning the attempt to clean him up. 'That way you'll know exactly where she is. My Stan can't wait. He's dog mad. Now, get that table laid for tea. You're going to like my fish pie. Fanny Craddock would die if she tasted it and knew the ingredients I'd got to work with.'

Raymond would miss Pepé, so it was reassuring to know

that she would be going to a good home. He started to think of people and things he'd miss when he was in Australia, but he had no one to miss really. The image of his mother was lodged in the back of his mind ever since he'd visited Stokes Park Hospital, but the fact was she'd never actually been his mother. He'd always been alone; never connected to anyone around him.

He knew he should include Penny in his mental list and felt guilty, but he couldn't. He didn't see much of her as the school year drew to a close, because her father insisted she stay in and revise for exams, and Raymond was grateful for such paternal devotion. He felt like a fraud in her company.

Even in the stolen moments they managed to snatch together Raymond didn't know how Penny put up with him. Unaware of his feelings, her ardour hadn't dimmed at all, despite the fact that his hands beneath her blouse were like those of a baker who kneaded dough every day of his life. He knew he should end it with her, but he didn't know how, especially when she adopted the latest Beatles song, 'From Me to You', as their love song.

Uncle Gordon threw himself into the Australia project as if he'd been pining for something to get his teeth into. Like Raymond, football was his sporting passion and he followed the fortunes of his hometown team avidly. Cricket, though, was Australia's number one team sport, he informed Raymond, and so it was time to swot up on it. He brought home a book on the Ashes series and regaled Raymond with facts and figures about the great clashes between England and Australia.

'Just think, Raymond,' he said, 'we'll be over there for an Ashes series. The next isn't 'til 1966 and that's three years away, but by then we'll be fair-dinkum Aussies. It won't stop me supporting England, though. I'll never stop doing that.'

Raymond wasn't sure he would ever like cricket. He was a good football player, but his enforced attempts at playing cricket at school only highlighted his incompetence. He'd just have to get used to it, but there was another concern. He tried to find books in the school library by Australian authors, but without success. Eventually, he asked Angus whether there were any famous Australian authors he could read.

'Hmm,' Angus said, musing. 'There's not that many, but that's not surprising because it's still a young country. The ones that spring to mind are Ruth Park and Patrick White. Why do you ask, laddie?'

'Just interested, that's all,' Raymond said.

'You're a strange one, Rawnsley,' Angus said, bestowing on Raymond one of his rare smiles. 'I'll see what I can find for you.'

A week later, after an English Literature class, Angus gave Raymond a book called *The Harp in the South* by Ruth Park.

'That took some finding, laddie,' the master said. 'A friend of mine lent it to me, so be sure to bring it back when you've read it.'

Raymond thanked him and took it home. He read it over the next two evenings. It was a story of an Irish immigrant family and their life in a Sydney slum after the Second World War. Poverty, despair and violence were its main themes and even though the main character makes something of her life, it left Raymond with mixed feelings about the immigrant experience.

'The thing that worries me,' he told Pepé on one of their walks, 'apart from missing you, that is, is the town we're going to live in outside Melbourne is only small. What if there's no football and no books? How am I going to survive?'

Pepé pushed her wet nose into his hand and looked up at him with her wise animal eyes that seemed to say, 'Just like you always have, Raymond.'

*

Raymond left school on the last day of the school year clutching his report book, which was sealed in a brown envelope. As soon as he and his friends were outside the school gates, Poggy ripped open his envelope and withdrew his report book from inside.

'You're not supposed to open that,' Titch said. 'It's for your mum and dad.'

'Me mum and dad don't give a toss,' Poggy said, opening his book and glancing at the first page.

'Bugger!' he breathed.

He turned the page.

'Double bugger!' he said and sighed.

Raymond knew this might be his last day at Slevin Grammar School, but he wouldn't miss it. As for his friends, they would all have parted when their school years ended anyway. He slipped his own envelope into his satchel, wondering what Slevin Grammar School's last word on him would be.

*

'Brilliant.' That's what Auntie Dawn said as she perused his report later.

'Really?' Raymond said, surprised. He'd had a decent academic year, but …

'That's what it says,' she said in wonder. 'Your English master's comment – "Brilliant". That's it. That's all it says – "Brilliant". I couldn't agree more. Besides that, you're third overall in your year. Well done.'

Her delight was genuine and Raymond's eyes took in the picture that always personified his feelings for her. Her brown eyes were wide behind the lens of her spectacles. Her skin was perfect. Her auburn hair was soft, falling in waves onto her shoulders as she bent her head over his report book.

'Good onya, sport,' Uncle Gordon said, clapping

Raymond on the shoulder and making him jump. 'That's a bonzer report.'

They were all chuckling when David ran into the office, stopped in his tracks and then started laughing too, for the sheer fun of it.

After David left to play with the other children, Auntie Dawn's face became serious.

'We've had news about our application to adopt you,' she informed Raymond. 'There's a meeting next Friday. We'll know straight after that. The waiting's nearly over and I expect nothing but good news.'

'Aye,' Uncle Gordon said. 'Then we can really start taking our new life seriously.'

'What do you mean *seriously*?' Auntie Dawn said. 'You're practically an Australian already.'

*

Raymond forced himself to feel confident. It was the day that the most important decision of his life would be made by unknown people in an unknown office. There was no room for doubt. This was his day. Soon he'd be living on the other side of the world. He might never know who'd given him *Great Expectations*. He might never know if he was Miracle Boy and why, but what did his past matter? Why shouldn't he have great expectations like everybody else?

He spent the morning helping with household chores and in the early afternoon, he set off for Bentley's Fields with Pepé. It was a hot day and he was dressed in blue jeans and a white T-shirt. He imagined he looked like James Dean, even if he couldn't manage sideburns like the ones his school friend, Rollo, sported. He'd brushed back his dark hair and used water to flatten the waves and, being slim and athletic, the effect of pushing one hand inside the pocket of his jeans and adopting a slight swagger ought to mean that no one should have to squint too much to get the picture.

Penny and Veronica were sitting on the wall by the entrance to Bentley's Fields, waiting for him. Both girls were dressed in fresh cotton summer frocks with narrow waists and buttoned bodices, and each of them had a piece of bright red chiffon wound into her hair.

'What's with the hairdos?' Raymond asked as he approached.

'We're just having a laugh,' Veronica said. 'We're celebrating no more school.'

The girls fell into step with him as he entered their rambling playground. The sun was never brighter and the fields never greener.

'Yippee!' Penny shouted, clapping her hands. 'Come on, let's race.'

Raymond released Pepé from her lead and broke into an energetic trot. Veronica, despite not being as light as Penny, ran faster than her friend and jogged alongside Raymond. Eventually, Raymond stopped, not just to wait for Penny, but because Veronica's bouncing chest was just too distracting. Penny came running up like the pretty high school girl she was; arms and legs going in all directions, but mainly at the expense of forward motion. Veronica looked at Raymond and raised her brown eyes to the heavens.

They meandered down to the brook that ran through one of the furthest fields, where they sat down the grassy bank. Before long, Penny and Veronica began an argument over whether the popular singer, Frank Ifield, was from Australia or England. Raymond listened without much interest while watching Pepé dipping her paws at the water's edge.

Veronica was adamant that Frank Ifield had been born in Coventry, but Penny was equally unshakeable that he was Australian through and through. Raymond thought it was an odd argument to be listening to in the circumstances he was in. He decided Veronica must be right because she seemed so certain of her facts and, in any case, there must be lots of Australians who'd been born in England. He'd soon be one of them.

It wasn't unusual for a disagreement between the two girls to become heated and Raymond saw Penny's cheeks beginning to redden. She turned to him.

'Right, Ray, you've got to decide,' she ordered, while at the same time her eyes told him the answer she wanted. 'What's it to be – Australia or England?'

'It must be England,' Raymond found himself saying with ill-disguised impatience.

'Ray!' Penny cried out in exasperation and hit him on the shoulders with her fists.

Raymond's gaze strayed towards Veronica, who raised her eyes to the heavens, just as she'd done earlier, only this time Penny saw her.

'Well,' Penny exclaimed, getting to her feet.

Turning on her heels, she began to hurry homewards, walking stiff-legged while waving one hand in the air and muttering something indistinct.

'You'd better go after her,' Veronica said, as Penny disappeared over the brow of the hill.

'No,' Raymond said and snapped a tall blade of grass from the ground and put it between his lips.

It was better this way. Today was the day to end it. Soon he'd be leaving forever and he didn't want any theatrical farewells.

He looked at Veronica, who was leaning back on her hands with her legs straight out in front of her and who, for the third time that afternoon, raised her brown eyes to the sky and gave him a sympathetic smile. He smiled in return, but then realised that he was staring at her breasts, which jutted forward from her arched figure. Veronica smiled.

'I've seen you looking loads of times,' she said.

Raymond could have protested as she unbuttoned the bodice of her frock. He could have got to his feet and walked away as she fumbled behind her back and then lifted her cotton bra to reveal two swollen snowy globes capped by dark mushrooms, but the cake was on the table and it had his name on it and, even though it wasn't his birthday, he shuffled forward on his knees.

*

When Raymond entered Manorholme, he knew something was wrong. Auntie Dawn was waiting in the hall with an unmistakable look of distress on her face. Pepé bounded in and pawed at her, hoping to be petted.

'Down, Pepé!' she snapped, causing Pepé to slink to her basket in unhappy confusion, her tail low between her legs.

'You'd better come into the office, Raymond,' Auntie Dawn said in a resigned tone of voice, while avoiding looking into his eyes.

Raymond knew for certain it was bad news. The dark look on Uncle Gordon's face when Raymond entered the office was unwanted confirmation.

'I'm sorry,' his house-father said with a gesture of helplessness as soon as he saw Raymond. 'It's bad news.'

'It seems your mother has a relative,' Auntie Dawn said. 'This relative, who doesn't wish to be known, has blocked the idea of adoption on behalf of your mother.'

'It gets worse,' Uncle Gordon said. 'In fact it couldn't *be* any worse. You've got to leave tomorrow morning. You're going to Backville Manor.'

Raymond felt ice-cold liquid rushing through his veins. While Uncle Gordon raged about injustice, every emotional treasure Raymond had hoarded since coming to Manorholme crumbled to nothingness.

It was like the aftermath of an accident. After the initial

shock, his mind started to cope with the new reality in an almost clinical way. It was as if he was a soldier trained to deal with this type of eventuality. He had to leave in the morning. Well, at least he wouldn't have time to mull over it and let it torture him like poor little Squeaky Dave had.

'It's all right,' he said, barely opening his mouth in case the burning bile in his throat spilled out. 'I'll sort my things out.'

He left the room and climbed the stairs. His house-parents didn't follow him. They probably understood that he wanted to be alone. He pulled his suitcase out from under his bed, opened it and began to pack his books into it. All but one, that is.

He left *The History of Mr. Polly* on top of the chest of drawers.

The Screaming Abdabs

Raymond woke early. The gloom and despair of the previous evening seemed incongruous in the light of the morning sun streaming through his bedroom window. In a way, he just wanted it to be over now. He didn't want to be the cause of unhappiness in this home, and the distress in Auntie Dawn's eyes was too much to bear.

He rose and went through his morning routine. He didn't feel like James Dean today and made no effort to look like him. The closest he'd come to being a rebel was suckling like a baby at the plump breast of a cooing girl in a field and worrying that someone might come over the hill at any minute. Now things were back to the way they always were and there was no point in looking anything but nondescript.

When he went downstairs into the kitchen, Mrs Hanson was preparing breakfast alone. As soon as she saw him she clasped him to her oven-warm apron in a big hug.

'I just don't know what to say, Raymond,' she breathed, pressing his head into her bosom. 'It's enough to give you the screaming abdabs. I just can't believe it. The rotten buggers!'

She held him at arms' length by the shoulders and studied him. Her thick coarse hair, the colour of ash, flowed back from an unusually florid face and her eyes seemed to search for something in his.

'They've broken Auntie Dawn's heart,' she said. 'You're

210

going to have to be strong, but I know you are. Miracle Boy's survived before and he'll do so again.'

'Why do you call me that?' Raymond asked.

She seemed to hesitate, as if on the verge of telling him something, before she said, 'It's not my place to say. Come on, we'd better get on.'

Her subsequent preparations for breakfast threatened grievous bodily harm on every utensil within her grasp, while Raymond did his best to focus on counting cutlery and laying the table in the dining room.

Breakfast was a subdued ritual of forced normality and Raymond couldn't bear to look at the sad faces around him. Afterwards, he waited in the sitting room and watched the other children, who'd been sent out to play in the back garden.

He started at the sound of a loud knock at the front door, followed by the unmistakable, long-striding footsteps of Uncle Gordon. Keys rattled and the door groaned, followed by the voice of his house-father who issued a curt, 'Wait there', to whoever stood there. The door to the sitting room opened and Uncle Gordon announced in a sombre tone, 'It's time, Raymond.'

Raymond braced himself and walked out of the sitting room. Everybody was lining up in the hall, except for Mrs Hanson, who could be heard butchering something in the kitchen.

'I'd better put Pepé on her lead,' Uncle Gordon said, holding the straining dog by the collar.

Raymond said goodbye to all the children in turn. Frances chewed her bottom lip and her big brown eyes glistened. David lunged forward and hugged Raymond's legs until his mother picked him up and clasped him to her in one arm. With her other arm she gave Raymond a fierce hug and whispered into his ear, 'We'll never forget you, Raymond. Take care, pet.'

Next, Uncle Gordon gripped his hand and ruffled his hair. His strong, tall nearly-father seemed lost for words and just shook his head. Pepé was pulling hard on a tight rein and Raymond reached down and stroked her soft, velvety ears, while she whimpered, as if her instinct told her that he was leaving for good.

Raymond turned towards the front door and Uncle Gordon reached out to open it. When the door opened, Raymond saw smug-faced, ginger-haired Mr Leather standing there with his feet apart and his hands clasped in front of him. Behind him, at the end of the garden path, dark-suited Mr Pickup stood in front of his gleaming black car.

The sight of his carrot-topped nemesis exuding unmistakable relish in his duty made Raymond step backwards, at which Mr Leather stepped forward and grasped his arm. The claw-like fingers digging into him made Raymond's resolve to be calm and resigned dissolve. He tried to pull his arm away, but Mr Leather tightened his grip.

'Leave me alone,' Raymond cried and ripped his arm away.

Mr Leather at first recoiled against this desperate cry, but then threw his arms around Raymond's waist and shouted to Mr Pickup to help him. The other man didn't move, so Mr Leather exerted more force and began to drag Raymond down the path, while everybody, adults and children alike, began to shout in protest. Instinct made Raymond dig his heels into the path, but Mr Leather was too strong; he hauled him towards the car and flung open the rear door.

'What are you doing to him? Leave him alone.'

Raymond was shocked to discover that the voice behind this entreaty was Veronica's. There she was, standing on the pavement in a pale green dress with her mouth wide open. What was she doing there?

212

'Don't interfere, Miss,' Mr Leather grunted, shoving Raymond onto the back seat where he pinned him against the far door by the throat.

Gagging from the throttle-hold, Raymond saw Mr Pickup stride up the garden path and pick up his suitcases from the hallway. Uncle Gordon watched with disdain, while holding back Mrs Hanson, who looked as war-like as Queen Boudicca with a frying pan in her hand. Stony-faced, Mr Pickup returned to the car and put the cases into the boot, which he closed with a shuddering slam. Raymond could feel Mr Leather's heaving breath on his face, as Mr Pickup leaned into the door through which Raymond had been forced. The corporation driver's chiselled face was impassive and his eyes glinted.

'Let go of the lad – *now*,' he hissed. 'How would you like it if someone came and dragged you out of *your* home, you pillock?'

Mr Leather seemed as stunned as Raymond and released his grip, while Raymond, locked in the older man's unblinking stare, shrank into the corner of the seat. Mr Pickup retreated and closed the door, before climbing into the driver's seat and starting up the engine.

Raymond's last sight of Manorholme was accompanied by the jumble of raised voices whose words were indistinct except for his name. Over the top of this cacophony, Pepé barked like never before. As the car pulled away, Veronica ran round to his window and placed her hand against it. He couldn't hear what she said, but he could read her lips.

'I always wanted to be your girlfriend.'

Was that lipstick she was wearing?

*

Backville Manor was a traditional children's home. Raymond recognised that as soon as the car turned into the long driveway. The grounds they entered were enclosed by a high stone wall, which not even someone as tall as Uncle Gordon would have been able see over. The house in front of them was a substantial, two-storey, mid-Victorian edifice of grey, weathered stone with a wide frontage, boasting two impressive full-length bays and topped by cross gables with ornate finials and steep, grey-slated roofs. In front of the house was a sweeping lawn with tall trees dotted around the perimeter within the boundary wall.

Mr Pickup parked alongside some wide stone steps in front of an imposing blood-red door with burnished brass furniture. As they got out of the car, the door of the house opened and Raymond looked up to see a tall, well-dressed, handsome woman standing in the entrance. She had a flush of colour high on her cheeks and thick, fair, well-groomed hair swept back under a white Alice band. Her gaze towards Raymond was intense.

While Mr Pickup retrieved the cases from the boot of his car, Mr Leather placed a hand on Raymond's back and pushed him forward. The woman stood aside to let them enter a dark hallway, but said nothing. Raymond stood in shadow, while Mr Leather, suddenly toadying, turned to the woman and said, 'We had a bit of bother.'

'Well, we won't have any more of it, Mr Leather,' the woman said, glancing at Raymond, who in turn was noting her straight-backed posture and the shape of her breasts, which seemed unnaturally lifted and pointed beneath her pale-green cardigan. He noticed something else: a faint smell. It was coming from her. It was as if perfume had been unsuccessfully used to mask something unpleasant. At that moment Mr Pickup appeared with Raymond's two suitcases and dropped them onto the floor inside the door. The woman arched her well-plucked eyebrows.

'Two?' she queried.

Mr Pickup shrugged.

'Well?' she asked, looking at Raymond.

'That one's got my books in,' Raymond said, pointing to one of the cases.

'Well, you'll just have to put them in the bookcase in the playroom along with the rest,' she said in a tone that brooked no argument. 'We've no room here for you to keep your own personal library. Put the case in the play-room if you would, please, Mr Pickup.'

Mr Pickup gave Raymond a glance, but Raymond couldn't interpret its meaning. The corporation driver picked up the heavy suitcase and disappeared down a corridor at right angles to the hallway. He returned within a minute, just as a dark-haired youth passed by along the corridor.

'Derek Bickersdyke,' the woman called out and the youth stopped and turned towards her. 'Take this new lad up to your dormitory and get him sorted out. You know which bed he's having.'

'Yes, Auntie Sheila,' the lad, who was about sixteen, dark and good-looking, assented.

'Go on, then,' she ordered Raymond. 'Get your case and follow Derek.'

Raymond picked up his suitcase and Derek motioned him to follow up a stairway to the left of the entrance hall. Raymond left his abductors without a backward glance, although he could hear Mr Leather attempting to initiate what promised to be an ingratiating conversation with Auntie Sheila.

Leading the way, Derek turned left at the top of the stairs and doubled back towards a landing and then turned right into a long, shadowy corridor. Raymond didn't see much of this corridor because they entered the first room on the left they came to. This was a dormitory with seven beds with their heads against the walls. Not even bright light from the windows at the far end could make this room seem anything but dull and brown.

Raymond didn't need anyone to draw him pictures to recognise a typical dormitory. Beside each bed was a companion chest of drawers. Three of the beds were against the wall to the right of the door they entered and the end one of these was alongside a window. This was the bed Derek led Raymond to and indicated, with a nod of his head, that it was to be his.

'You've been in homes before, haven't you?' he asked Raymond, as if expecting confirmation.

'Yes,' Raymond replied, not in the least bit offended that the answer was expected by the other boy. Welfare boys could see the stigmata on each other.

'Not like this one, you haven't,' Derek said. 'Anyway, you know the routine.'

Butter Wouldn't Melt in Your Mouth

'That's not a bad bed, that,' Derek said, sitting down on the next bed, while Raymond unpacked and stowed his clothes away in the bedside chest of drawers. 'By the window, see? It was Peter Mellor's. He left about a week ago. I hope you have more luck than him.'

He then pointed to the bed in the adjacent corner of the room beneath another window. 'That's my bed there. If you lean out of that window and look to the right, you can see straight into the girls' dorm. Some of them might even give you a peek of their bits, especially Monica or Elsie. They both like showing what they've got.'

Raymond glanced at the window by his bed, outside of which was what looked like the top platform of a metal fire escape. He could also see that the dormitory overlooked an area at the back of the main building. There was a door with a clear glass pane to the right of the metal platform and he worked out that this was along the corridor on which they'd started out. He could also see that it was possible to climb out onto the fire escape from his window. Derek seemed to read his mind as he worked all this out.

'You could try it,' he said, 'but you'd better find out what happened to Peter Mellor first.'

Raymond looked at his new companion, who clearly favoured nonchalance over amiability, and took in his dark eyebrows, his heavy-lidded brown eyes and the beginnings

of reasonable sideburns. He didn't bother asking Derek
what happened to Peter Mellor. He knew he'd find out
soon enough and, besides, he wanted to finish his unpack-
ing and get to his unattended books. He'd already noted
the plain wooden wardrobe standing against the wall opposite the windows.

'Can I hang my stuff in there?' he asked Derek, nodding
towards the wardrobe.

'Sure,' Derek's said. 'It's for us all to share.'

Raymond lifted his black school blazer with its gold badge
from his suitcase and turned towards the wardrobe.

'Whoa!' Derek cried, jumping to his feet and grabbing
the lapel of the blazer so he could study the badge on the
breast pocket. 'What's this, then? Slevin Grammar? Please
don't tell me you go there.'

'I'm afraid so,' Raymond said, shrugging his shoulders
and trying not to sound too apologetic.

'Jesus!' Derek exclaimed. 'I hate them bastards. What're
you doing there? I thought they were all toffee-nosed gits
from posh families.'

'Not all of them, obviously,' Raymond sighed.

'You poor sod,' Derek said, standing aside so Raymond
could make his way to the wardrobe. 'I almost feel sorry for
you. You're gonna get the piss taken out of you summat
rotten. You can't go to a stuck-up school like Slevin and live
here.'

Clearly you can, Raymond thought to himself as he began
hanging his clothes in the wardrobe. While he did so, Derek
stood in the middle of the room and talked to him in a low
voice.

'I'm gonna do you a favour,' he said, 'so listen up. A lad
like you'll get eaten for breakfast here if you don't know the
rules straight off.'

He raised one finger.

'Rule Number One: stay out of Auntie Sheila's bad books,

if that's possible. She's an evil witch who likes to mess with your head.'

He raised a second finger.

'Rule Number Two: don't trust any of the lasses. They'll do owt to get into Auntie Sheila's good books.'

He raised finger number three.

'Rule Number Three: don't give Uncle Andrew any excuse to batter you. There's only one thing he likes better than touching the lasses up and that's beating the hell out of one of us lads. Peter Mellor knew that better than anybody.'

A fourth finger went up.

'Rule Number Four: find some way to get out of here. That's what I'm working on.'

He wiped his nose with the back of his hand.

'Now come on. Let's get back down.'

*

Derek led the way along the passage at right angles to the entrance hall and, Raymond guessed, parallel to the corridor upstairs. Coats hung on hooks along the right-hand wall and assorted footwear threatened to spill out of shoe lockers beneath them. Derek entered a room on the right that Raymond immediately recognised as a playroom.

The familiar lockers, bookcase, table and chairs were all there. In fact, it was almost an exact match for the playroom at Hillcrest, even down to the bay window overlooking the front lawn. There were unlikely to be any toys played with in here, though, or any small children to play with them for that matter.

The one person who was already in the room when they entered was a young woman with curly blonde hair, who was looking out of the window with her hands resting on the knee-high sill, so that her shapely rump was her most prominent feature. She turned around.

'Raymond – flipping – Rawnsley,' Shirley Spencer exclaimed.

Raymond stared at a round-faced, full-figured young woman, whose big, blue, distended eyes and blonde curls were the only remaining clues to the skinny, pop-eyed young girl Raymond once knew at Hillcrest.

All he could manage to say was, 'Shirley'.

'Don't tell me you've come to live here,' she said, looking serious.

'Course he has,' Derek interceded. 'D'you think he's chosen this dump for a holiday? That's his suitcase over there – full of books, would you believe? He's got to empty it and sort his locker out.'

He adopted a wheedling tone.

'So you know each other, eh? Do us a favour, Shirley, will you? Look after him 'til dinner.'

Shirley's exasperated cry of 'Derek' was left hanging in the air as the door closed. She rolled her big eyes upwards and planted her hands on rounded hips, from which her grey pleated skirt hung just above her knees.

'Did he tell you which locker you're supposed to have?' she asked.

'Yes,' Raymond said, feeling like an unwanted guest. 'He said it belonged to some lad who's just left.'

'Peter Mellor,' she said. 'Those are shoes you definitely don't want to be stepping into. I suppose you've got his old bed as well. Come on, let's get you sorted.'

She walked down the row of pale-green wooden lockers, whose slapdash paint job testified that they weren't designed to be an attractive piece of furniture. Shirley opened a locker door near the end of the row.

'This is it,' she said. 'Now I know it's you. I'm not surprised that case is full of books. Raymond the reader – reading owt and learning nowt.'

'I know where everything is now, so you can get lost if you

want,' Raymond snapped, mostly from exasperation at the size of the locker compared to the number of books he owned, rather than the reminder of how irritating she could be.

'All right,' she said, holding up her hands, 'I'm sorry. Don't get your knickers in a twist. I know you're not a kid anymore. Let's not fall out.'

Raymond placed his case flat on the floor and opened it. Then, kneeling down, he began the attempt to cram his personal possessions and as many of his books into the locker as possible. Shirley leaned on the lockers next to him with her chin resting on one hand.

'I need to ask you summat,' she said in a low voice. 'Promise me you'll say nowt to anybody about what happened at Hillcrest.'

Raymond looked up at her. The sweater she was wearing had pink and purple horizontal stripes that accentuated her full upper figure. She was a different person to the scrawny, wan-faced girl from Hillcrest he remembered and she looked earnest.

'Do you mean what happened to Uncle Richard?' he asked.

'You know what I mean,' she said, looking over her shoulder as if she feared they might be overheard.

'Don't worry about it,' he said and she looked relieved.

There was a time that Raymond wouldn't have known what she was talking about, but he was old enough to appreciate now that he and Brian probably weren't Uncle Richard's only victims.

'Thanks, Raymond,' she said. 'I'll leave you alone for a bit.'

She left the room, leaving Raymond to the realisation that he could only fit one or two of his most precious books into his locker, which in any case wouldn't lock. He'd no choice but to put most of his books on the bookcase, as instructed by his stern-looking new house-mother. When he'd finished stacking the books on the bottom shelf, in the hope that no one would bother to squat down to see them, he went to the bay window where he slumped down in a lumpy armchair with his head in his hands and closed his eyes.

It could have been a moment for contemplation, a time to take stock of his situation, but instead all he felt was a bleak despair centred on a crude wooden locker that was too small and insecure to provide a proper home for his most precious possessions. It seemed like a metaphor for his existence.

*

Raymond stood before the desk in his house-parents' office facing his house-mother. Reclining on a chair next to her, a large white cat studied him with baleful yellow eyes. Raymond looked at Auntie Sheila. Every aspect of her seemed to be the product of excessive grooming and the hands she placed on the desk in front of her didn't look as if they'd ever been subjected to housework. He could tell by her demeanour that he was about to receive a lecture.

'Welcome to the real world,' she said with a cruel smile on her painted lips. 'I've heard so much about you and the special treatment you've been getting. Don't worry. We'll soon put you back on the right track. I know everything there is to know about you. Trouble's followed you around, but you thought you'd wheedled your way into a cushy number. What you didn't know is, your soft house-parents knew nothing about the system.'

She smiled to herself and reached out to stroke the cat, which purred like a machine as she trailed her long nails through its fur.

'I knew Uncle Richard at Hillcrest,' she said, boring through him with her eyes. 'I don't believe the lies that have been told about him. I've never met a man more dedicated to his work. I was devastated when I heard what happened to him. Don't give me that butter-wouldn't-melt-in-your-mouth look. You played your part in that and since then you've showed your true colours in your foster home. They should have sent you here straight away. I know just how devious you are. No wonder your mother tried to kill you. Now get out of my sight until you're called for dinner.'

Blackevil Manor

'How'd you get on with Torpedo Tits?' Derek asked.

He was sitting opposite Raymond on the windowsill in the playroom with a faint smile on his lips. To his right stood a tall, large-boned youth with incongruous jet-black curls on top of a big head with cropped temples. This young giant was staring down at Raymond with a curious look on his pimpled face. To Raymond's left, sitting in an adjacent armchair, was a figure Raymond couldn't comprehend. Was it a middle-aged man with the face of a child, or a child with the body of a man?

The man-child was thickset with a solid neck and severe short-back-and-sides, which was plastered across the top of his head with Brylcreem and parted at the side, although some tufts on the crown of his head refused to lie down. He had a sad and quizzical look on a face that could have belonged to a woman, except for the dark stubble on his chin that was at odds with the soft blond lashes fluttering over the most intense blue eyes.

'That's Bernard,' Derek said, which caused the man-child to smile in a way somehow beatific. 'Before you ask, nobody knows why he's here. You're happy though, aren't you, Bernard? He's backward. I bet he's not more than five up top. He goes to a special school. I bet there's some fit birds there, aren't there, Bernard? He's harmless, but you've got to watch out for one thing. He likes taking stuff apart. Problem is, he doesn't know how to put them back together again – do you, Bernard? You know what he's got his eyes on? That swanky watch on your wrist – haven't you, Bernard? You'd better keep that with you at all times. If Bernard gets hold of it, it'll be in pieces in no time. Won't it, Bernard?'

Throughout this cross-talk, Bernard smiled like an immaculate saint.

'He's dismantled all sorts,' Derek said. 'He's done clocks, watches, radios. He's fascinated by what's inside things.

'The big feller here,' he tapped the thigh of the young giant next to him with the back of his hand, 'is Callum McFadden. He's come all the way from Ireland. Isn't that right, boyo?'

Callum grinned down at Raymond, exposing a mouthful of crooked teeth.

'Callum,' Derek said with a wicked grin, 'is famous for being a bedtime artist.'

Raymond knitted his brow and, seeing it, Derek explained further.

'You know, he paints his sheets every night. He's in love with the five-fingered widow.'

'That's not fair, Derek,' Callum complained in a thick Irish accent. 'There's no need to tell him things like that.'

'You're right,' Derek agreed, 'he'll find out soon enough. He's in the next bed to you. Any road, how did you get on with Auntie Sheila?'

'All right,' Raymond said, still trying to come to terms with the recent meeting with his new house-mother.

No wonder your mother tried to kill you.

'Nobody gets on well with Auntie Sheila,' Derek said. 'She'll give you a hard time to start out with. She likes to make her mark early.'

No wonder your mother tried to kill you.

Raymond started at what sounded like a bell being rung.

'Dinner,' Derek said, getting to his feet.

Raymond brought up the rear as they made their way back along the corridor and through a door on the right into the dining room. There were three tables in the room; Derek led Raymond to the one nearest the window and indicated where he should sit.

'Peter Mellor's old place,' Derek whispered.

Callum and Bernard sat down at the same table. At the next table, there was a collection of females, all of whom were eying him with interest. Apart from Shirley Spencer, there was a buxom young woman with straw hair and red cheeks, which looked like they'd been painted on; another girl who was dark-haired and petite; another, wearing spectacles, who was slim and angular; and, finally, there was Veronica Halsall.

Raymond blinked. No, it wasn't Veronica. This young woman was considerably more buxom than the ample Veronica. She caught his eye and the look on her face was one of sexual challenge. Raymond averted his gaze.

There were four people seated at staff table. Facing Raymond was Auntie Sheila, looking immaculate and omnipotent. To her right was a man who Raymond took to be her husband, Uncle Andrew. Thickset and shorter than his wife, with coarse, dark hair, he was an interesting contrast to the elegant Auntie Sheila. He was as dark and swarthy as a farm labourer, with a face somehow handsome and ugly, ingenuous and cruel, all at the same time.

To Auntie Sheila's left was a young girl of around six or seven years of age. She was, without a doubt, Auntie Sheila's daughter. She was pretty with blue eyes and blonde hair in ringlets and was, Raymond guessed, fond of party dresses like the one she had on.

The fourth member of the staff table was a young woman with her back to Raymond. She had a long, slim neck and dark, wavy hair. Somehow, Raymond knew she wasn't a member of staff, but he guessed that she must have special privileges to be sitting at the staff table.

Next to the staff table, Raymond could see a middle-aged woman with ruddy cheeks stacking wooden trays on the other side of a wide serving hatch. He surmised that she was standing in a kitchen and the trays had been used to serve the plates of food in front of each diner, which were decorated with some sort of meat pie, mashed potatoes and cabbage. His nose told him that she was no Mrs Hanson. School dinners would be a luxury from now on.

Everyone appeared to be waiting for a signal and it was no surprise to Raymond when Auntie Sheila, not her husband, provided it.

'Before we begin dinner,' she announced, 'we must welcome a new boy. His name is Raymond Rawnsley and he's a pupil of Slevin Grammar School. Now, he may well think there's nothing we can teach him, but I'd like to assure him he's wrong. You all know how much I relish the challenge of educating new arrivals. For what we are about to receive, may the Lord make us truly thankful. Amen.'

Thus began Raymond's first silent meal at Backville Manor. The only conversation was led by Auntie Sheila at the staff table. Her husband seemed taciturn and almost monosyllabic, preferring instead to concentrate on his food. Whereas she maintained an erect carriage and held her head high so that she had to lift her fork a long way from her plate, he adopted the opposite posture, so his fork had only to move a minimal distance to his mouth.

*

When Raymond entered the playroom after post-meal chores all the girls were gathered in the bay window, either sitting in chairs or on the sill. Beyond them, he could see through the tall windows to where Derek and Callum were playing football on the lawn outside. He hesitated in the open doorway and was about to retreat when the girl he'd initially thought looked like Veronica Halsall cajoled, 'Come on in. Don't be bashful.'

Even though he bridled at the way she spoke, as if she was coaxing a child, Raymond entered. He closed the door behind him and was about to head for the bookcase, when the same girl said, 'Come over here, then. Don't be shy. We might as well get to know each other if you're going to live here.'

Feeling self-conscious under the gaze of so many female eyes, Raymond walked over to the window and perched on the corner of the sill, trying to look at ease.

'Right,' the girl who'd invited him over said, leaning towards him in her armchair. 'I'm Monica and you're right – I've got the biggest jugs in here.'

All the girls laughed out loud at this outrageous introduction.

'If you're lucky,' Monica continued, pulling her shoulders back and expanding her impossible chest even more, 'you might get a proper look at them one day.'

'It's a dead thert!' the straw-haired girl with the red cheeks lisped. 'It doethn't take much for Monica to get them out.'

Monica's tone hardened just a fraction.

'That's Elsie,' she said. 'She shags for fags. She prefers Capstan Full Strength, but she'll toss anybody off for a couple of Woodbines.'

'I like Woodbines,' the straw-haired girl protested. 'They're a thmoother thmoke.'

After the laughter died down Monica continued her introductions.

'I've heard you already know Shirley,' she said, pointing to Shirley Spencer, whose face was impassive.

Raymond nodded.

'This is Wendy,' Monica said, indicating a lissom, brown-haired girl, who gave him a shy smile.

'And finally, this is Theresa, who hasn't actually got any knockers at all.'

The tall, bespectacled girl blushed, while the other girls chortled.

'Get lost, Monica,' Theresa stammered. 'Just 'cos you've got ginormous knockers doesn't mean I've got nowt.'

'Yeah, sure,' Monica retorted, 'I've seen them and they're just bee stings.'

While they squabbled, Raymond dithered over whether to try to slide out of the room. Suddenly, Elsie, who had watery blue eyes to match her straw hair and red cheeks, pointed out of the window and called out, 'Hey up. Look, they're off.'

At first, Raymond wasn't sure what she was pointing at, until their house-parents' young daughter, accompanied by the young woman who'd been sitting at the staff table, came into his view as they walked down the drive towards the gate.

'She's taking her to the park, the thtuck-up cow,' Elsie announced.

'That's Mary McCluskey,' Monica explained to Raymond. 'She's Auntie Sheila's favourite because she sucks up to her and looks after her daughter, Sarah. Mind you, she's not daft because she gets out of this place more than we do. Sarah's a nasty little piece of work, though. She looks down on everybody and she's always running to her mum with tales. I really would like to throttle her sometimes.'

'All the time,' Elsie said with feeling.

'Any road, ignore them,' Monica advised Elsie. 'I'm more interested in finding out from Raymond here what it's like to be a homo.'

'I'm not,' Raymond protested, taken by surprise.

'Course you are,' Monica stated. 'They're all queers at Slevin-chuffing-Grammar. I've seen them in their stupid uniforms holding hands and skipping through the town centre. I bet you've never had hold of a proper lass, have you?'

She squeezed her breasts together so they inflated like balloons in front of him. At that moment there was a knock at the window and he was relieved to see Derek gesturing to him to join them outside.

'That's it, go and play with the boys,' Monica called out, as Raymond left the room to a collective cackle from the girls.

*

The dormitory was full. Apart from the boys he'd met earlier, there were two other lads who appeared at tea-time. They were Stuart Collins and Nigel Normanton, both workers. Stuart worked on a chicken farm, which Raymond thought was funny when he learned of it, because with his long neck and protruding Adam's apple, Stuart looked a bit like one of his charges. Nigel, who was tall, with mousy, crinkled hair, worked in a textile mill, where he was training to be a finisher.

Raymond tried to ignore the rhythmic grunting coming from the next bed, and as the groaning turned to settled breathing, he turned onto his side to face the window.

How quickly things changed. One minute he was lying in a sun-drenched field with a girl who wanted him to kiss her, but not necessarily on her lips, the next he was lying in a strange dormitory in a gloomy house under the control of a hostile house-mother. It was like being back at Hillcrest: a house of dark corners, deep shadows and repression.

He'd always thought of Hillcrest as 'Chillrest'. Could this be 'Blackevil' Manor?

He wasn't going to be passive anymore. He was going to stand up for himself and he was going to find things out, like the mystery of *Great Expectations* and Miracle Boy.

No wonder your mother tried to kill you.

Most important of all, he was going to find out if what Auntie Sheila said was true and, if so, why?

Visiting Day

Raymond sat on a wooden stool in the yard, beneath a red and orange sky, with a long line of shoes in front of him. The yard was at the side of the house and was obscured from the front by a wall and a solid gate, wide enough to let delivery wagons through. The area was enclosed by high walls and along the back was a row of unkempt single-storey outbuildings. Raymond had entered the yard by a door from an annex next to the kitchen, which acted as a washroom, with a boiler, an industrial-looking washer and a wooden drying frame suspended from the ceiling.

The shoes were lined up for cleaning, which was Raymond's main daily chore. Auntie Sheila kept everyone busy through the summer holidays with all kinds of menial tasks, but this job was reserved especially for him. At the end of every day, when the workers returned and when those who were at home finished whatever they'd been doing, their shoes were left in the washroom for Raymond. It didn't matter whether they needed cleaning, they had to be polished and Auntie Sheila was alert to the slightest imperfection.

In some ways, Raymond didn't mind this chore. He even made it last as long as he could. The evenings were pleasant and the job in hand took his mind off things. He also discovered that he wasn't just a shoe cleaner; he was also a lookout for the secret smokers who came out singly or in pairs for a few drags of their cigarettes. The washroom protruded from the side of the main building and the area behind the extension was hidden from the house. It provided a perfect refuge for the clandestine smokers, and all the inmates, except for the guileless man-child, Bernard, smoked.

While smokers smoked, they talked.

'That's something else you've got from Peter Mellor,' Shirley said to Raymond from the shadows. 'He used to hate that job.'

'So, what happened to him?' Raymond asked, although he'd already heard snippets of information about the lad who always seemed to be in trouble. 'Everybody talks about him like he's dead.'

'He fell foul of Uncle Andrew,' Shirley said. 'He was always walloping Peter. Mind you, Peter kept asking for it as well. He wouldn't do owt he was told. Then, one day, Uncle Andrew beat the living daylights out of him. I don't know what for, but he went berserk. You don't want to give Uncle Andrew any excuse to have a go at you, Raymond. He uses his fists like you're a punchbag. Anyhow, it's a wonder he didn't put Peter in hospital. I'm surprised the poor bugger could even walk, but somehow he climbed out of the bedroom window and ran away. He went to the police to show them what Uncle Andrew had done to him.'

'Good for him. What did the police do?'

'They didn't do owt,' Shirley snorted, sending a stream of smoke into the air. 'The bobbies brought him straight back here. That's when Auntie Sheila took over. She made his life hell. He didn't see the light of day for ages. Finally, he managed to run away again. This time he broke into the scout hut just down the road from here and set it on fire. When the police and fire brigade came, he was sitting on the wall waiting for them, calm as you like. They *had* to take him then. Now he's in an approved school and you've got his rotten job.'

Raymond remained silent and pensive while he buffed up the toecap of one of the worker's shoes.

'Makes you think, doesn't it?' Shirley said as she slipped back through the washroom door into the house.

Raymond had plenty of food for thought. Like the unfortunate Peter Mellor, he'd not seen the light of day much either in his first few weeks at Backville Manor. Liberty was a precious commodity all the inmates would sell their souls for, but it was most freely available on Sundays. Raymond soon learned that Sunday night was the highlight of the week, for then the inmates were allowed to go to a local youth club after church. There they could listen to pop music, sip fizzy drinks, fraternise with the opposite sex and pretend, at least for a few hours, that they lived free lives.

Raymond remembered his first Sunday in his new home. He'd noticed an unmistakable frisson in the air, despite the tedious compulsory trip to the morning service at the local church. As the day wore on, he could sense the anticipation and, by teatime, the clatter of cutlery punctuating the silence seemed to have an urgent beat. Every chore was completed in double-quick time and before long everybody was gathered in the playroom in their Sunday-best clothes.

They were eager to depart, not to the evening church service they had to attend, but to the youth club afterwards, where they could stay until ten o'clock.

Auntie Sheila appeared in the doorway and told them that they could leave and, as they filed past, she scrutinised everyone. Raymond was at the rear, just behind Bernard, and he kept his eyes downcast as he passed his housemother, trying not to notice her strange musk, which was like some sort of secret effluvium she couldn't suppress no matter how much effort she put into her meticulous appearance. He heaved an inward sigh of relief as he entered the corridor and followed the group towards the front door.

'Raymond Rawnsley, where do you think you're going?'

His heart sank as he turned around to face his house-mother's triumphant face.

'Privileges have to be earned,' she said 'and you have a long way to go. I think you'll find that there are shoes in need of an extra polish. Have fun.'

When Raymond turned around, the corridor was empty. He imagined the others running headlong down the driveway and through the gate before they could be caught.

Weeks had passed and he still hadn't been to the youth club.

'Hey up, Raymond, don't look so cheesed off. You've nearly done. Only two more pairs. Mind you, one of them's mine so make sure you do a good job.'

The voice that dragged Raymond back from his reverie was Derek's, the latest visitor to Smoker's Corner.

'Flipping heck, look at that sky,' Derek continued. 'Red sky at night, shepherd's delight. It's gonna be a good day tomorrow. Especially good, in fact – it's visiting day.'

'It's not much good to me,' Raymond said. 'I haven't got any visitors.'

'You lucky bugger,' Derek exclaimed through a cloud of smoke.

'What's lucky about that?' Raymond asked, perplexed.

'Anybody who hasn't got visitors gets kicked out for the afternoon,' Derek explained. 'A whole Saturday afternoon of freedom every month. I keep begging me gran not to visit, but she won't listen, silly old bat.'

*

Derek was right. Auntie Sheila's view appeared to be that those who didn't have visitors, the forgotten, were best forgotten on visiting days and they were banished after dinner. Maybe she thought that their listless figures detracted from the homely atmosphere she wanted to project to outsiders.

Raymond didn't mind. He had other plans. He intended to be a visitor himself.

As soon as the unwelcome group was outside the gates, Monica crossed the road in a hurry.

'Right, I'm off,' she called back. 'Meet here at four-thirty so we can all go back in together.'

'Me too,' Nigel said and turned down a side street. 'See you later.'

'They always do it,' Shirley said to Raymond. 'Come on. We're supposed to go to the park.'

'Sorry,' Raymond said. 'I've got to go.'

'What?' Shirley said. 'You're going to leave me and Wendy to look after Bernard on our own?'

''Fraid so,' Raymond said and turned to run towards a bus stop on the corner, where a bus was already waiting.

'Where are you going?' Shirley called after him.

'Visiting,' Raymond shouted back and jumped on the bus.

His heart was pounding as he climbed the stairs and sat on the back seat. An irrational fear that Auntie Sheila would change her mind and come sprinting through the gate after him made him drum his fingers against the window with impatience.

It was a relief when the engine started up with a rumble and the bus began to pull away. Raymond kept his head bowed until they were well out of sight, fearing he could be seen from the house. He was the only upstairs passenger on the bus, but that didn't seem to offend the happy-go-lucky conductor, who clambered up the stairs singing 'Sweets for my Sweet' and tapping his ticket machine in time. When Raymond paid his fare to the town centre, he asked the thin-faced conductor which bus he needed to catch for Stokes Park Hospital.

'That's the loony bin, isn't it?' the conductor said, pushing the peak of his cap back and scratching the top of his forehead. 'They don't come out once they end up in there. One of the patients there killed another one a while back. They've got workshops there. They make all sorts of stuff, even furniture. One loony put a chisel straight through another loony's eye just because he looked at him funny. That's a laugh; they all look funny. It's always happening, but they don't put it in the papers. I know because me sister-in-law's a cleaner there. You'll need the number thirty-six. Every thirty minutes on the hour and half-hour from the bus station. Good luck, mate. Rather you than me.'

Having imparted this information, he clattered downstairs promising sweets for his sweet and sugar for his honey, leaving Raymond grateful that there'd been no one else on the upper deck to overhear their conversation.

In town, Raymond waited ten minutes in the bus station for the number thirty-six, which, by the time it left the stop, was almost full. The journey to Stokes Park Hospital took almost thirty minutes, during which time Raymond kept checking his watch. Time was his enemy. He didn't dare to think of the consequences if he was late home for tea.

When the bus arrived at the hospital, Raymond immersed himself in the general throng heading for the entrance. He felt like he was on a secret mission, which, in a way, he was. He remembered the way to his mother's ward and headed down the unnerving corridor, but when he reached the forbidding locked doors he lost his nerve and, instead of ringing the bell, he sat down on a bench to compose himself and work out exactly what his plan was.

It occurred to him, having got to this point, that he didn't really have one. His only thought was to get to his mother. If he was going to find out anything about himself it was his only starting point. Maybe, if it was just him, she would talk. Now it seemed like a stupid idea. He probably wasn't even old enough to go on the ward on his own. The matron would laugh at him. And even if he did get to see his mother, she wouldn't be able to say anything. And even if, just imagine, she could talk, what would he say to her?

Er, I hope you don't mind me asking, but I hear you tried to kill me when I was a nipper and I was just wondering why?

'Excuse me, are you all right?'

Startled, Raymond looked up, conscious that he'd been muttering to himself and probably looked like he'd escaped from one of the wards. A plump nurse, maybe in her early-thirties and with a kind, appealing face was looking down at him. She was standing in front of the ward doors as if she was about to enter.

'Yes,' Raymond said, searching her sympathetic face for signs to give him the confidence to tell her why he was there.

It was now or never.

'I've come to visit my mother, but I don't think they'll let me see her,' he said in a rush.

'What's your mother's name?' the nurse asked.

'Margaret Rawnsley,' Raymond said.

'Margaret?' the nurse said with a note of recognition. 'Have you come on your own?'

'Yes,' Raymond said.

She surprised him by sitting down next to him on the bench.

'What's your name?' she asked.

'Raymond.'

'Well, Raymond,' she said. 'I'm really sorry, but it's just not possible. You can't just turn up here. We have to know beforehand and you have to be approved. Why don't you come with your mother's sister? That'll be your auntie, won't it?'

Although Raymond gave her a blank look, his heart skipped a beat. At the same time, she seemed to comprehend that what she'd just said was news to him. She appeared flustered and said, almost to herself, 'You don't know, do you?'

Raymond explained his circumstances in a few short words.

'Wait here a minute,' she said when he'd finished.

She stood up and rang the bell next to the ward doors and disappeared inside when they were opened. After a few minutes, she came out again and sat down next to him.

'We keep a record of all visitors,' she explained. 'Mrs Eaton comes to visit Margaret every month. I've met her and I'm certain she said she was her sister, although she doesn't look like her. You do, mind. She comes the first Saturday of every month and always brings a big bag of grapes. Margaret loves them. She always comes at three o'clock, which is the official visiting time. That's all I can tell you. Please don't say where you got this information from, will you?'

Raymond assured the compassionate nurse that he wouldn't say anything to anyone and thanked her. When she'd gone back on the ward, he wandered back down the corridor towards the main entrance, oblivious to the distressing sights and sounds around him. He couldn't believe it. He had a lead. He'd be back on the first Saturday of next month.

*

Without any religious or philosophical training, Raymond learned to live like a stoic. If he needed to, he was able to adopt an almost ascetic state of mind, where he could practise indifference to everything external, so that his victimisation by his sadistic house-mother and the deprivations he suffered were unimportant. It didn't matter to him how he spent his time, as long as time passed. He had only one fixed point in time etched on his mind.

'You should look a bit more miserable sometimes,

Raymond,' Shirley said when she was having a sly smoke one evening and he was cleaning shoes. 'Auntie Sheila's narked she's not getting to you. She keeps asking everyone what you like and don't like. That's what she does. She likes to find out the best ways of hurting people. All she knows is you like reading so far, so she's making sure you don't get much time with your books.'

'Don't worry, Shirley,' Raymond said, 'I don't care what she does. I can close my eyes and make her disappear any time I like. I can be who I want and go where I want and she can't stop me.'

Shirley rolled her big blue eyes and shook her head in wonderment, saying, 'Raymond, I haven't got a clue what you're talking about half the time. You're in a dream world. Any road, I've been meaning to ask you something ever since you came here. What do you really think happened at Hillcrest? We never saw you after you and Brian were taken to hospital.'

'I heard about Uncle Richard when we were in hospital,' Raymond said after thinking for a moment or two. 'It was a shock, especially after the way we'd wound him up. I reckon after he'd beaten us, and what with Squeaky Dave doing what he did, he was in so much trouble he took that way out. Maybe we pushed him too far.'

Shirley stubbed out her half-smoked cigarette against the wall before slipping the remainder, which all the smokers referred to as a docker, into the pocket of her cardigan and crouching down on her haunches so she was on Raymond's eye level.

'Kids' games,' she hissed. 'Do you really think that's why Uncle Richard did what he did? I'm going to tell you what really happened and then you'd better keep your trap shut about it. At the end, Brian used you. All your games did get under Uncle Richard's skin because he didn't like anyone going against him. Squeaky Dave killing himself probably put him under pressure as well, but Brian deliberately tried to push Uncle Richard over the edge. There was a reason. Brian knew something I'd told him.'

She stopped talking, pulled the docker out of her pocket again and relit it.

'Bloody hell,' she said after a long, hard drag on her cigarette. 'Brian knew Uncle Richard was interfering with some of us girls because I told him. You can't imagine what it was like. What's worse is that cow, Auntie Sheila, either doesn't believe it or thinks we egged him on. Brian wasn't just trying to push Uncle Richard over the edge. Well, he was, but it was only to get to Auntie Alice. She knew, you see. That's what I can never forgive her for. It worked. When her husband put you and Brian in hospital, it was the final straw for her and she snitched on him for what he'd been doing to us. And that's what Uncle Perfect couldn't face up to. That's why he hanged himself in Millacre Ditch, the bloody coward!'

She stood up with legs slightly apart, breathing so hard that her chest rose and fell beneath her cardigan. Her big blue eyes were blazing in the twilight. Raymond was dumbstruck. Uncle Richard's demise had been a source of suppressed guilt with him for so long. He'd even felt guilty about not telling Brian in hospital about Uncle Richard's death. Now he'd just discovered that he was the one in the dark.

In the gathering gloom, light dawned for Raymond. He'd guessed Uncle Richard had been up to no good with the girls from the questions the police sergeant put to him in hospital, but it was only now, seeing Shirley's distress, that he really understood what it meant. He'd been stupid enough to think that their boyish pranks were the cause of such momentous consequences, but a far more sinister play was being acted out. He'd taken a beating, but what had Shirley suffered?

'I'm sorry, Shirley,' he said. 'I didn't know.'

'I know you didn't,' she said, stubbing her cigarette butt against the washroom wall before flicking it as far away as possible. 'I'm not getting at you, Raymond. As it turned out, what you did helped. Come to think of it, it must have hurt as well. I'd better go.'

'Just one thing,' Raymond called out as she made to go back inside. 'I've always wondered. What happened to Strawberry Paul and Itchy Alan?'

Shirley turned to face Raymond with the closest thing to a smile he'd seen from her yet. 'That was the only good thing to happen at Hillcrest,' she said. 'Their mum came back from London. They went home.'

After she'd gone, Raymond put brush to leather like a man trying to scrub away an insult daubed on his front door. He was still polishing when Monica appeared for her evening smoke. She gave him a knowing look.

'Has Shirley just been out?' Monica asked, and when Raymond nodded she quickly followed up with, 'You're quite cosy you two, aren't you? Mind you, you're made for each other really. You're a queer and she hates blokes.'

There was no rancour in the way she said it and she prattled on for the rest of her smoke break in blithe fashion. Raymond pretended to listen, but his mind was on what he'd heard from Shirley. It all made perfect sense now. Even Dr Charlerousse had said that there were other factors which contributed to Uncle Richard's demise.

'You're not listening, are you?' he became aware of Monica saying, as she ground the remains of her cigarette under her heel. 'You're somewhere else. I don't think we've had one like you here before. If you're not dreaming, you're either reading books or staring at the girls' tits. Yeah, I've seen you. That's how I know you're not really queer. Mind you, when it comes to me, I can't blame you.'

Raymond had learned so much from books, but there

were many things about life he never really understood: girls in particular, even though he'd grown up alongside them. The thing they seemed to flaunt the most, their sexuality, was also the thing that seemed most precious to them. The girls at Backville Manor might give it away casually, maybe even desperately, but if it was taken against their will, they would be destroyed. Raymond sensed that there was a fine line somewhere with these girls, but he had no idea where it was.

The same thing didn't apply to Shirley's experience, though, did it? That was like having the flesh stripped from your bones and being powerless to do anything about it. That was just evil.

Bad to Me

A thin brew of excitement simmered in the Backville Manor inmates' secret pot, waiting to be brought to the boil. The bleak summer under Auntie Sheila's yoke was about to be broken, thanks to their house-parents' one-week holiday, when they would be returning to their hometown somewhere in North Yorkshire.

On the day of their departure, everyone gathered in the bay window of the playroom to watch Auntie Sheila, Uncle Andrew and Sarah leave in their grey Morris Oxford. As the car rolled down the drive, some of the girls, with Monica and Elsie to the fore, actually waved and smiled.

'Have a nice trip to North Yorkshire,' Monica cooed through a fixed smile. 'I hope your car crashes and you die on those lonely moors.'

'Monica!' Wendy cried. 'You can't wish that on a little girl.'

'You're right,' Monica said. 'I hope Sarah survives, and then gets eaten by wolves.'

'There are no wolves on the moors,' Raymond pointed out.

'Bloody badgers then,' Monica spat and everybody laughed.

At the moment the car turned into the road and disappeared from sight a spontaneous cheer rippled round the group and Monica jumped up and down, her large breasts bouncing in opposite time to her feet. Bernard stared at them with wide eyes and a serene smile on his face. Seeing this, hysterical Monica juggled her breasts in Bernard's face, which caused him to blush like a girl and her to cackle even more. The holiday was under way.

The relief house-parents were an old couple called Uncle Stanley and Auntie Maude and the happy inmates knew them and liked them. The collective sense of relief was evident a short time later, when all the smokers, except for Mary McCluskey, the unofficial child-minder for their absent guardians, were lined up at the back of the wash-room puffing on cigarettes. Raymond, although he didn't smoke, stood amongst them and sucked in the atmosphere of freedom. No one spoke and all that could be heard was the satisfied inhaling and exhaling of breath.

The following afternoon, Raymond was reading Jack London's *The Call of the Wild* in the playroom when Shirley Spencer came in and sat down on the windowsill next to him.

'Aren't you excited, Raymond?' she asked.

Nonplussed, he replied, 'What about?'

'The youth club, stupid.'

It hadn't occurred to Raymond that he'd be allowed to go to the youth club in Auntie Sheila's absence. Rather than live on false hopes, he decided that the simplest thing to do was go and ask, so he made his way to the kitchen where he found portly Auntie Maude mixing something in a bowl.

'Am I going to the youth club tonight?' he asked her.

'Why do you ask?' she responded with a look of puzzlement on her rosy face.

'Because Auntie Sheila doesn't normally let me go,' Raymond said.

'Why not?' she asked.

Mary McCluskey, who was slicing a large block of corned beef, interceded.

'There's no reason,' she said. 'It's just because he's new here. He can go with me if you like.'

*

Raymond's hair was combed back and lightly held in place by a dab of Brylcreem and his shoes had an extra polish. He walked at the back of the group with Mary on the way to church, not because he needed the support she'd offered, but because he sympathised with her for the silent treatment she got from the other girls. He knew that all the girls would take her place as Auntie Sheila's favourite in a trice.

On the way, they came to a coffee bar.

'It's only just opened,' Mary told him, as they all gazed through the window at the cane furniture, rubber plants and jukebox.

Beneath a pall of smoke, young men with exaggerated sideburns and elaborate quiffs, and young women with backcombed beehive hairstyles, were drinking frothy coffee from glass cups and tapping their fingers to the loud beat. The faces around Raymond staring in through the window looked hungry, but he knew it wasn't for food.

'Rockers,' Monica snorted and turned to go.

'You'd be in there like a shot if you'd got enough brass,' Theresa said. 'Any of us would. Never mind; we've got the youth club.'

Throughout the remaining walk to church, along up-and-down streets, past weathered stone terrace houses, the girls, arms linked, sang Beatles' songs at the tops of their voices, as if to bolster the belief that they'd got the better choice of the evening's entertainment.

Church was church; to be endured; the minutes willed away until the final hymn and prayer before escape to freedom. None of them hung around to chat with the vicar afterwards. As if any of them would. The Backville Manor group was first out of the door.

When they arrived outside the youth club, it looked to Raymond like what it was: a disused chapel in need of repair. The girls led the way up dark and dusty wooden stairs to the upper floor, which was where the youth club was held. As soon as they arrived, Monica and Elsie disappeared into the toilet, before re-emerging after a few minutes with their hair backcombed, eyes dark as coal, lips almost as pale as their skin and skirts much shorter than when they'd arrived.

Raymond wandered through the two rooms of the youth club. The first was laid out like a coffee bar with tables and chairs and a crude wooden bar where soft drinks, crisps and sweets were on sale. Behind the bar, which was decorated with bright holiday posters, there was a turntable, from which loud pop music was being played through speakers on the walls. The lighting was rudimentary, although some attempt to create atmosphere had been made by stringing coloured light bulbs around the bar. An adjoining room, where the lighting wasn't much better, contained a snooker table, as well as a table tennis table that was already being put to use by Nigel Normanton and Stuart Collins, who both gave the impression of being no mean players.

A friendly vicar, whose attempts to appear trendy were undermined by a bald patch, which made him like a monk, introduced himself to Raymond and then ushered him over to meet his buck-toothed wife who, along with their attractive, dark-haired daughter, ran the snack bar and put records on the turntable. There were already plenty of young people there, among them some pretty, local girls who all passed Raymond's rapid inspection of their most notable attributes.

Amongst the youths, who were also eying the girls, there were three males who looked to be in their twenties. Raymond couldn't decide if, with their greased hair, long jackets, drainpipe trousers and winklepicker boots, they were Teddy Boys or Rockers. Monica and Elsie, both sporting new tops with spectacular cleavages, joined this older group. The other Backville girls soon began dancing in a small circle by the bar, watched by some local boys who were standing close by.

Raymond stood in shadow by the bar and observed everything. He saw Derek approach one of the older men and whisper in his ear. Both of them left the room, only to return a couple of minutes later. Then Derek joined a mop-haired girl, who'd arrived while he'd been out of the room, and they went to sit at a table furthest away from the bar. The music seemed to affect everyone and feet were tapping on the dusty floorboards everywhere. Doing the same made Raymond feel less wooden, as he watched Monica leave the room with the same man Derek had spoken to, closely followed by Elsie and another man.

'There they go,' a disdainful voice uttered.

Raymond hadn't noticed Mary approach him. She hadn't changed her appearance like the other girls since arriving at the club, although she was attractive enough anyway, except for the glum look on her face.

'They've gone down to the basement,' she said. 'It's deserted down there and there are no lights. I don't have to tell you what they're up to. Sometimes they get so many cigarettes they end up selling some to the other girls. Anyway, they're not worth thinking about. Do you want a Pepsi?'

'Yes, please,' Raymond said.

'Give us some money, then,' she said, holding out her hand.

For the rest of the night, Raymond sat at a table with Mary, who kept up a bitter running commentary of the comings and goings of various couples, while the music blared. At the same time, she kept stealing glances at Derek and the girl he was talking to, which seemed to make her even more bitter. Raymond thought she was a good-looking girl with nice breasts and if she wasn't so miserable it would have been good for a young man to be seen with her. When the current number one song, 'Bad To Me' by Billy J. Kramer, was played, everybody sang along to it, except Mary, who just stared at Derek's back.

Just before ten o'clock, Monica and Elsie reappeared and by the time they all met downstairs to go home, they'd removed their makeup, changed their clothes and rearranged their hair. Although they walked home in a group, Mary resumed her position at the rear and Raymond felt duty-bound to walk with her. Monica kept glancing back at Mary as she boasted of her night's exploits.

'I'm flipping knackered,' Monica complained. 'That Tommy Carter's a right bloke.'

'Yeah,' Mary muttered to Raymond, 'so what's he doing at a youth club then?'

'I heard that, Contrary Mary,' Monica said. 'He knows where he can get a good shag, that's why.'

'He knows where he can get an easy shag, you mean,' Mary retorted.

'Right,' Monica shouted, spinning round on her stout legs to face Mary, with her chest heaving. 'Do you want braying, or what? Don't forget, Uncle Andrew's not here to protect you.'

Mary linked her arm with Raymond's and clung on and he was relieved when Derek stepped in front of Monica and put his hands on her shoulders.

'Knock it off, both of you,' he said. 'We've got a whole week off from Uncle Andrew and Auntie Sheila. Let's not spoil it.'

'All right then,' Monica said, pacified, 'but that scrubber's got no room to talk. She forgets now she's wormed her way into Auntie Sheila's good books.'

Only Raymond saw the wink Derek gave Mary.

*

Their house-parents' holiday was over too soon for the inmates of Backville Manor, but to Raymond it meant that there were only days to go to the first Saturday in September. He needed a plan. He wouldn't be able to use visiting day, as that was the last Saturday in every month.

Preparing the contents of his satchel in the dormitory for the start of the new school term, he thought things through. He wasn't looking forward to the stick he was going to get when he appeared at breakfast in his uniform. Nor did he relish having to explain to the members of the Legion why, once again, he was travelling from a different direction to school. The return to school, though, was part of his plan. Football was the key.

He played for the school football team for his year. Although they played on Saturday mornings he was sure Auntie Sheila wouldn't know that it wasn't an all-day activity, nor, he imagined, would she care.

The following morning, he put up with the taunts of his fellow inmates about his school uniform. He ignored Monica's half-hearted remarks about his sexuality and he was blind to Auntie Sheila's sneers. He even fended off the questions from his schoolmates about the change in his route to school with vague excuses about moving house.

Raymond was oblivious to anything that didn't have a direct bearing on his mission to visit Stokes Park Hospital and it was a relief when he saw his name on the team-sheet on the noticeboard for the first game of the season on Saturday. He was always a first pick, but it was good to know that he was in the team. A lie was better if it was only half a lie.

That evening, he did his best to portray an air of insouciance when he approached Auntie Sheila in the kitchen after tea and told her he was in the school football team on Saturday. Her sculpted eyebrows arched like silky caterpillars.

'The football team?' she queried. 'Can't they do without you?'

'I've been picked,' Raymond stated, trying not to sound desperate and hoping he was giving the impression of someone being press-ganged.

She made him stand by the table, waiting, while she cogitated with a finger to her lips. Raymond saw Sarah, her daughter, copying her mother and he wanted to laugh, but didn't flinch.

'I'll need a note from whoever's responsible,' Auntie Sheila said eventually. 'Otherwise, you're going nowhere.'

Sarah grinned as Raymond suppressed a groan. He'd just been asked by the nemesis of his home-life to ask a favour of Paddy, the schoolmaster who'd always demonstrated the most naked animosity towards him. The cruel smile playing on Auntie Sheila's delineated lips made him suspect that, through some form of evil telepathy, she knew this.

The next day, he was full of determination as he made his way to the gymnasium during the morning break to find Paddy, who was pushing a wooden vault into position for the next lesson. When Raymond told him he needed a note so he could play football at the weekend, Paddy, gruff as ever, was intrigued.

'You've never needed one before,' he said. 'Why do you need one now?'

'Because I've got a new home,' Raymond said, not knowing how else to put it.

'A new home, Rawnsley?' Paddy snorted. 'Is there nobody who can put up with you for long, boy? What makes you think we need you so badly to be writing letters to all and sundry? You can see I'm busy. Go away and let me think about it.'

If Raymond's two enemies had colluded, they couldn't have arranged things better to keep him in an agony of suspense for the rest of the day. He'd accepted defeat by the time he set off home with shoulders slumped. He felt like an uncomfortable misfit. His shirt collar was too small and the sleeves of his blazer no longer covered his wrists properly. He was growing, but not that fast. Normally, his house-parents would have seen to it that he'd got everything he needed for the new school year, but now there was no one who cared about these things and he didn't feel inclined to ask.

He'd managed to drag his scuffed shoes halfway across the schoolyard, when he heard his name called out and turned to see Paddy standing in the school entrance. Raymond turned back and walked towards the burly games master, who held out a piece of paper towards him.

'I don't know what we're going to do with you, Rawnsley,' Paddy said, placing the paper in Raymond's hand. 'Take this before I change my mind.'

Before Raymond could thank him, he turned and disappeared into the gloomy interior. Raymond waited until he was outside the school gates before he sneaked a look at the note. He was amazed to discover that, in the politest of terms, Paddy, or, as he'd signed himself, Mr Ireland, requested that Raymond join the team on Saturday morning, as he was essential to their success. Raymond couldn't believe what he was reading.

As soon as he got home, Raymond took the note to Auntie Sheila, who glanced at it and said, 'Well, if you're not back for dinner, then you'll have to do without.'

The days crawled by, but finally Raymond was sitting in a blissful English Literature class, the last lesson on Friday afternoon. The subject matter was *The Song of Hiawatha* by Henry Wadsworth Longfellow and the boys were taking turns, in seating order, to read verses. From pupil to pupil, the reading of the lilting poem became seamless and soon Raymond was floating above the shores of Gitche Gumee, by the shining Big-Sea-Water, smiling down on the orphaned Hiawatha as he was being tended by the wrinkled old Nokomis until he came to land, feeling light as a feather, at the end of the school week on the eve of the sixth of September 1963.

Miracle Boy

Raymond was so distracted that he didn't play well in the football match and he received a tongue-lashing from Paddy afterwards, even though they'd scraped a narrow win.

'I can't believe I had to write a begging letter to get you, Rawnsley,' he snapped. 'Play like that again and you're out.'

Raymond took the criticism in his stride and endured the after-match formalities until he could rush off.

He arrived at Stokes Park Hospital in plenty of time. Through turbulent clouds, the sun kept spotlighting him, as he sat on a bench near the entrance and waited. From there, he could watch visitors arriving. He knew what he was looking for: a middle-aged woman carrying a large bag of grapes.

He tried to avoid negative thoughts, but couldn't help them creeping into his head. It was a hospital. There'd probably be loads of middle-aged women carrying grapes. She might not even turn up. If she did and he recognised her, she might not want to speak to him. After all, she'd never visited him in all these years.

As the time got closer to three o'clock, the influx of visitors increased. Among them was more than one middle-aged woman carrying a shopping bag. What if the grapes were concealed in there? Suddenly, his eyes lighted on a dark-haired woman who was approaching from the car park. She wore a brown coat buttoned up to the neck and was carrying an open shopping bag with a bulging brown paper bag poking out of the top. Did she look like his mother, or what he remembered of her? Not really, but the nurse said that she didn't.

This woman was thinner than his mother and her face was sharper, but the dark hair and skin complexion were similar. He decided to follow her, falling in behind her amongst the crowd of new arrivals. She took the correct corridor for his mother's ward, but the crowd of visitors thinned, so he dropped well back. It wouldn't do for her to think he was stalking her, especially if it wasn't the right woman. When she stopped at the doors to his mother's ward and rang the bell he almost whooped with triumph. He sat on a bench to wait. His plan was to accost her when she came out.

Raymond kept his eyes downcast and stared at the chess-board floor, anxious not to catch anybody's eye in this place. Every time he heard footsteps approaching, his heart-beat increased, but no one sat down next to him.

Whenever somebody left the ward Raymond jumped to his feet, only to sit down again when he saw it wasn't her. Eventually, the doors opened and the woman walked out into the corridor. As she approached, Raymond said nothing, hoping that somehow she would recognise him and be the first to speak, but she walked past him with no more than a bemused glance in his direction.

'Mrs Eaton,' he blurted out, turning to follow her.

She stopped in her tracks, turned around and said, 'Yes?'

'I'm Raymond,' he said.

Her face seemed to drain of colour.

'Raymond Rawnsley,' he expanded.

'I know who you are,' she said, regaining her composure. 'What are you doing here?'

'I came to see you,' he said.

'Well, don't just stand there drawing attention to your-self,' she said. 'Let's walk to the entrance. We can talk along the way. Now, what do you want to see me about?'

Raymond fell in beside her as she began to walk down the corridor in a determined fashion, although she flinched when an unshaven, toothless old man in a plaid dressing gown made as if to dart towards her, but then veered away cackling to himself.

'It's about my mother,' Raymond said. Feeling that this was inadequate, he blurted out, 'Someone said she tried to kill me.'

Mrs Eaton stopped in her tracks and turned to face him with shock registered in her dark eyes.

'Who told you that?' she asked in a voice that seemed to have risen in pitch.

'Somebody,' Raymond mumbled, suddenly feeling foolish.

She started walking again and said nothing until they reached the entrance hall, where she stopped and faced him again.

'We can't talk here,' she said. 'My husband's waiting in the car and he won't be happy if he sees me with you. My mother lives in Slevin village, near your school. It's Number Five, Fernlea Walk. It's just past the church. Can you remember that?'

Raymond nodded.

'Come and see me there straight after school on Monday,' she instructed. 'I'll be waiting for you.'

*

'You've got no chance of catching the milkman with your mum, Rom,' Poggy called out as Raymond rushed up the hill to the village straight after school.

For once, Raymond didn't have time for a smart reply. He was in too much of a hurry. Instead of continuing on to the bus stop at the top of the hill, he turned left up another hill past a long terrace of old cottages. When he reached the village church, he turned left again onto a narrow lane flanked by ivy-covered cottages. This was Fernlea Walk. He found Number Five and knocked on the plain wooden door. It was opened immediately by Mrs Eaton, looking very prim in a conservative dark-blue dress. She stared at him for a moment, as if there might be some doubt about his identity, before inviting him in.

He followed her into a small living room with a low ceiling and an open fire with glowing coals, despite the fact that the weather wasn't cold. A small, grey-haired old woman with dark, twinkling eyes was sitting in a wing-backed chair by the fire, and when she saw him she cried out.

'Here he is – Miracle Boy!'

Raymond thought the old girl must be senile. Nonetheless, she seemed spry enough as she got to her feet and ushered him into the room, saying, 'Come on, lad. Don't be shy. Let's have a proper look at you. Well, you've survived pretty well, haven't you? Miracle Boy has become grammar school boy, eh. He's got nice eyes, Elizabeth, and an intelligent face. He'll be a catch for someone one day.'

'Stop fussing over him, mother,' Mrs Eaton said, earning Raymond's gratitude. 'Sit down and give him some room.'

She turned to Raymond. 'I've got tea and biscuits ready, Raymond. Sit on the settee and I'll bring the tray in.'

She disappeared, while Raymond sat opposite the old woman, who was studying him with shrewd eyes. Fortunately, her uncomfortable scrutiny lasted no time at all, as Mrs Eaton reappeared with a tray of tea and biscuits, which she placed on a low table before sitting down next to Raymond. She then proceeded to pour and distribute cups of tea with the minimum of fuss.

'Right,' she said when the tea had been dispensed, 'I don't suppose you've got much time, Raymond, so let's get on with it.' She took a sip from her cup and then placed it on the table in front of her. 'I never expected to have to tell you these things, but you've found your own way here, so I've got no choice.'

'You had the choice a long time ago,' her mother muttered into her teacup.

'Mother,' Mrs Eaton scolded, 'that doesn't help.' She turned back to face Raymond. 'As I was saying, I have no choice. If you come looking, then you've a right to know.' She sighed. 'I was twenty-one when I met your mother. My dad had just died.'

So, she wasn't his mother's sister.

She cast a soft glance at her mother before continuing.

'She came to the funeral with her mother – your grand-mother. There were ructions and it all came out. My dad was also your mum's dad. Your mother was two years younger than me.'

What does that mean?

'She should never have come to the funeral,' the old woman snapped, rocking backwards and forwards. 'She should have let sleeping dogs lie. It had all been done and dusted many years before. Fred had nowt to do with her after the bairn was born. He'd have turned in his grave if he'd known she'd turned up as brussen as she did.'

'All right, mother,' Mrs Eaton said. 'I know it's not easy bringing these things up, but it's not Raymond's fault, is it? Anyway, it happened and I found out I had a half-sister. I went to see her afterwards. I couldn't ignore her.'

'You were like a bull at a gate in them days,' her mother said.

'I had to see her,' Mrs Eaton insisted. 'She was my sister.'

'Half-sister,' the old woman retorted. 'There's a big differ-ence.'

'Mother,' Mrs Eaton sighed, 'I know how you feel, but just let me get on with it. You agreed this boy has a right to know the truth.'

She turned yet again to Raymond.

'I felt sorry for your mother, Raymond. She'd had a hard time. She'd been brought up by her mother on her own and they had very little.'

Again the mother intervened. 'Them as has nowt, is nowt,' she spluttered into her raised teacup. 'She'd had an affair with a married man and she'd had a baby by him. My husband! No wonder her family disowned her.'

'That's history, mother,' Mrs Eaton said with a shrug. 'The fact is she brought up the child on her own. Margaret, your mother, Raymond, had a rough time. There was something wrong with her and for a long time she was in a special home in Liverpool. Your grandma moved there so she could be close by her. Your mother had severe mental problems.'

'You know why that was?' the old woman asked. 'It was because she was one of twins and the other one died at birth and she only just survived, but her brain was damaged. It would've been better if ...'

'Mother,' Mrs Eaton almost barked, causing Raymond to jump and catch his foot under the table, making the pots rattle. 'That's enough now. That poor woman brought up a sick child on her own. That must've been really hard. And Margaret had to do without a father. I had the father she should have had.'

'When I went to see her, Raymond, your grandmother was really kind to me. She had no bitterness at all. All she cared about was Margaret. They'd come back from Liverpool and were renting a house on the bottom side of town. Margaret's mother got her a job working alongside her in a mill. Margaret was really pretty and really shy. The only person she would speak to was her mother, but I got to know her and she got to trust me. She never went out and it was difficult for her to do things on her own. She couldn't read or write, so even things like shopping were difficult. I started taking her out with me and we got on well together. She liked to laugh.

'Anyway, it was near Christmas and there was a big dance in town. The place is pulled down now. I asked Margaret's mother if I could take her with me and she said yes, as long as I looked after her. I did Margaret's hair for her and she was really excited. The place was packed.'

Mrs Eaton paused and took a long drink from her teacup.

'I lost her,' she moaned, as if it had only just happened.

'It wasn't your fault, Elizabeth,' her mother said, showing sympathy for the first time.

'I lost her,' Mrs Eaton said in a more composed voice. 'I was too busy enjoying myself. We were dancing with two lads who'd just got out of the army. There were so many people on the dance floor we got split up. When I looked for her later, I couldn't find her. I should have done something, but I just told myself she would have gone home. It wasn't far for her to walk. I found out afterwards she didn't get home until late the next day. Her mother was worried sick. Margaret wouldn't tell her what had happened and she was angry with me for leaving her. To cut a long story short, Margaret got pregnant.'

While Raymond listened he'd been staring down at his hands. When Mrs Eaton stopped, he looked up and saw her dab a tear from the corner of her eye with her finger. He looked back at his hands again.

'I didn't see Margaret for a long time,' she went on.

'That's because her mother blamed you for what happened,' her mother crowed.

'I know,' Mrs Eaton said, 'and I didn't blame her. I blamed myself. Anyway, your mother had you, Raymond, which was the good thing to come out of all this.'

'Then you became Miracle Boy,' the old woman said.

Raymond stared at her.

'What she means is this,' Mrs Eaton said. 'When you were

260

about four months old your grandma fell seriously ill. She'd been having treatment for pernicious anaemia, I think it was. I imagine all the worry and looking after a baby, as well as your mother, didn't help. The fact is she became so ill she couldn't do anything. A lot of this is guesswork. Your mother couldn't cope with you without your grandma. As I've told you, they lived at the bottom end of town. There's a street called Alderley Street with a row of terraced houses right on the pavement. The neighbours knew the situation with your mum and they were used to seeing your grandma out with the baby. When they hadn't seen them for days and couldn't get an answer at the door, they became worried and called the police. The police came and started banging at the door and your mum appeared at an upstairs window with you in her arms.'

Raymond was getting used to the fact that when Mrs Eaton paused without being interrupted by her mother, it meant that something unpleasant was coming. He felt his heart beating fast.

'I don't know what your mum was thinking,' Mrs Eaton said eventually, almost as if she was talking to herself, 'but she threw you out of the window. You landed on top of the police car and bounced into the road. Then your mother jumped after you.'

'That's how you became Miracle Boy,' the old woman shrilled. 'You bounced off the roof of the police car into the path of a car driving past. You went straight through the windscreen of that car and landed on the front passenger seat. The driver was so shocked he drove off the road into a lamp-post. It killed him. It was headline news on the front page of the Chronicle – 'Miracle Boy!' That's how we first found out about it.

'Every day after that, there was a piece in the paper about how you were doing in hospital. Everybody was talk-ing about it and following your progress. At first you were critical. They said prayers for you in our church. Then you started to get better. It was Christmas time and it was like a miracle had happened in the town. You were famous without knowing it – 'Miracle Boy fighting for life' – 'Miracle Boy improving'. There were so many flowers delivered to the hospital they had to send them to old folk's homes. I know because I used to work in one. When the *Chronicle* was delivered in the afternoon, all the old folk would be asking about Miracle Boy.'

'It's true, Raymond,' Mrs Eaton confirmed. 'I couldn't bear to look at the paper. Your grandma and your mum were also in hospital. Your grandma died of some kind of blood disease shortly afterwards. Your mum was in a coma for weeks. I went to visit her regularly. Even when she opened her eyes it was like she was still in a coma. She was in trouble, of course, for what she'd done to you, but they didn't prosecute her. I think she did what she did out of love because she knew she couldn't keep you without her mother and she didn't want anyone else to have you.

'When she was fit enough to be moved, they committed her to Stokes Park. She's been there ever since. I visit her every month and nothing's changed in fifteen years. I'm her next of kin, so I've always kept an eye on what's happening with you. I ring up the Welfare Department every now and then and they tell me where you are and how you're doing. I know all the homes you've been in and the schools you've been to. I talk to your mum about you when I visit her.'

She paused and looked a little uncomfortable.

'You've got a right to ask me why I didn't do more for you. I'll be honest. The fact is, I was young and single when you went into care from hospital and I wasn't ready for that kind of responsibility. I'm married with two daughters now. My husband has very strict ideas about family and honour. He barely tolerates my visits to your mother. He'd go spare if he knew I'd met you. I know it's not been easy for you, but I always thought it was best for you not to know any of this. I still think that. I think they were wrong to take you to see your mother in the first place. That's it, Raymond, there isn't anything more I can tell you. Is there anything you want to ask me?'

Raymond was drowning in information, but he had questions.

'Why didn't you let me be adopted?' he asked.

'Two reasons,' Mrs Eaton said, looking him in the eye. 'Firstly, your mum's had nothing in this life; no father; no childhood; no life. I couldn't allow her own son to be taken away from her, even if she never understands. I'm sorry. Secondly, I was consulted about you being fostered and that didn't work out very well, did it?'

'What was the name of my grandma?' Raymond asked.

The old woman butted in. 'You know, I can't remember. After her baby was born, she started calling herself Rawnsley, which was my husband's name. You couldn't stop her, which seems wrong to me. Her first name was Vera and she came from a family that lived out Newhouses' way. They were a bit stuck up, which was why they dropped her when she disgraced herself.'

'She had a right to call her daughter Rawnsley, anyway,' Mrs Eaton said, 'and that's the name Raymond's got. Have you got any more questions, Raymond?'

'Yes,' Raymond said. 'What do they tell you when you ring up the Welfare? Do they tell you what it's like in children's homes? Do they tell you how some of the people treat us? Did they tell you when I was in hospital and why? Did they tell you why the foster home didn't work out?'

Not being of a cruel nature, he didn't ask any of these questions out loud. They merely flashed through his mind. What he actually said was, 'No.'

'So,' said Mrs Eaton, 'where do we go from here, Raymond?'

'Home,' he said, getting to his feet.

'Is there anything I can do for you?' she asked, rising also.

'Yes,' Raymond said. 'I want to you to visit me, and when you do I want you to take me to see my mum.'

'She doesn't say anything,' Mrs Eaton stuttered.

'I know,' he said. 'It doesn't matter.'

As he headed for the door, he heard the old woman say to her daughter, 'It looks like Miracle Boy is as stubborn as you, Elizabeth.'

What Books?

The way Raymond was feeling, all he needed was an opportunity to act on impulse. One minute he was polishing shoes and the next minute he was sitting on the roof of Backville Manor; not the tall, gabled roof of the main building, but the flat roof of the extension housing the kitchen and dining room. A cool breeze danced around him, as he sat with his back against the stone parapet and his knees almost under his chin. He was thinking. He was thinking how he wished he could stop thinking.

He'd climbed onto the roof by way of the washroom annex. It was easy to climb up onto the metal dustbins lined up against the wall in Smoker's Corner and from there scramble up onto the washroom roof. Once there, he climbed up onto the apex of that roof from where he could lever himself up onto the flat roof. It took less than a minute.

The possibility occurred to him weeks before, while cleaning shoes, but only now had he acted on it. If he was caught and asked to explain why he'd done it, he wouldn't bother to explain it was a 'Nobody Knows I'm Here' place, like the church avoidance tree he'd used at the Marsdens'. Who would understand that? Not Auntie Sheila, that's for sure.

He didn't stay long on this occasion because his thoughts couldn't find any place to be comfortable, but now at least he knew he'd got somewhere he could be alone.

Later that evening, Raymond entered the dormitory and

came upon a startled and flustered Bernard, who was sitting on his, Raymond's, bed with Raymond's mystery painting in his hands. The rest of Raymond's private pictures, which he'd secreted in his bedside chest of drawers, were scattered on the bed. Bernard jumped as if he'd been stung by a hornet and dropped the picture onto the floor, where it rolled itself up again like a parchment. His eyes filled with tears in an instant and he flapped his hands as if trying to shake off flypaper.

If Bernard's smile was a thing of joy and wonder, his tearful look of confusion and remorse was heartrending. The fact that he was only half-dressed in a striped shirt and underpants, which were too big for him despite his solid frame, might have made him look ludicrous, but it only increased the pathos. Raymond was touched and any initial anger he might have felt melted. While the tears rolled down Bernard's face, he kept muttering, 'Sorry, Raymond,' in a plaintive, lip-trembling chant. Raymond walked over to him and put an arm around his shoulders.

'It's all right, Bernard,' he soothed. 'There's no harm done.'

He continued to console the man-child until, eventually, Bernard's tears stopped flowing and a small smile, like the watery sun after a shower, began to radiate from his wet face. Raymond sat him on the bed, picked up his 'parchment' from the floor and cajoled, 'Come on Bernard, you can look at my picture if you want.'

He unfurled the painting on his knees. Bernard smiled and rocked backwards and forwards as he studied the picture, pointing and muttering with excitement, like a child in a fairground. Raymond explained the objects on the table in the picture and Bernard repeated the words and touched each object with his forefinger.

'That's a tin, you know, for biscuits,' Raymond said. 'That's a skull, but I wish I hadn't put it in now. That's a rope. You can use it for lots of things. That's a book with a picture of a crossbow. You can fire bolts with a crossbow. They're a bit like arrows. That's a bookmark, so you don't lose your place in the book. That's a drawing pin – careful you don't prick yourself.'

Bernard withdrew his finger in a hurry and put it in his mouth, making Raymond laugh.

'You daft devil, Bernard,' he said.

Bernard was as happy as the proverbial sand boy and kept sucking on his finger. Raymond began to roll up the picture and adopted a gentle, but serious, tone.

'Now, Bernard, you can look at this picture and the others whenever you want, but you must ask me first. OK?'

Bernard, eyes blinking and soft blond eyelashes fluttering, nodded.

From that day on, Bernard, who was always ready for bed first, often walked across to Raymond's bed in his striped pyjamas and asked, smiling, 'Picture, Raymond, please.'

Raymond always gave him the picture and, until lights out, Bernard sat up in his bed, staring at the images in front of him and smiling the sweetest smile. Before they went to sleep, Raymond eased the picture from his hands and put it back in its now not-so-secret hiding place.

What Raymond did keep secret from everybody was the Miracle Boy story. That was for no one else to pore over. He hadn't even come to terms with it himself yet. It was too bizarre and the fact that someone died as well chilled him. He wondered if Auntie Sheila knew the story, as other adults in his life seemed to have done. If so, did she think he was indestructible? If she did, it didn't stop her trying to break him.

*

Returning home from school on a day like any other, Raymond went about his usual routine; hanging his jacket on his hook in the corridor and leaving his shoes in the washroom at the end of a long line of other pairs for the daily shoe-cleaner, who was a close personal friend. Routine and the low-level ennui that accompanied it continued to fool Raymond that everything was normal, as he changed from his school uniform into his everyday wear of grey shirt and denim jeans. It wasn't until he entered the playroom to await the call for tea that he knew in an instant the day was anything but ordinary.

Every time Raymond entered the playroom, his first glance was always towards his books on the bottom shelf of the bookcase. This time he looked twice before it registered. The shelf was empty. In fact, the bookcase was almost totally denuded. Dumfounded, he almost staggered to the barren shelves and began to run his hands along them as if expecting to discover the books were somehow invisible.

'What? Where are the books?' he stammered, aware that there were others in the room, but unable to tear his eyes away from the barren shelves.

'Dunno,' was the first response, which was made by an uninterested Monica, who was staring out of the window across the lawn, as if she was waiting for her prince to come and rescue her.

'Dunno?' Raymond cried out. 'What kind of an answer is that? Books can't just disappear. Where are they? Who's taken them?'

He swung round to stare at what he now saw were two of the girls, Monica and Shirley, and Bernard, who was smiling as always, but with fear in his eyes.

'Calm down, Raymond,' Shirley said. 'We don't know. We hadn't even noticed.'

'Hadn't noticed?' Raymond ranted. 'How can you not notice? One minute there are rows of books, the next minute there's nothing but fresh air. They were *my* books.'

The light of comprehension illuminated Shirley's big,

blue eyes, as they swept the empty shelves.

'Oh, I'm sorry, Raymond,' she said, 'I didn't realise you meant *your* books. I've honestly no idea where they are. Have you any idea, Monica?'

'Not a clue,' Monica intoned, still not interested and not bothering to turn around.

At that moment, they heard the summons for tea, but Raymond was scouring the room, although there was no place where the books could have been hidden unless they were distributed in all the lockers. This didn't stop Raymond looking behind curtains and chairs while the others left the room, although Shirley lingered long enough to exhort him to hurry up and not be late for tea.

Raymond was late. He was the last to enter the dining room, where everyone was seated in front of their already cooling meal, waiting for permission from Auntie Sheila to begin eating. Raymond's face burned as he entered the room and turned to face the staff table, planting his feet on the linoleum.

'Where are my books?' he demanded.

The walls of the silent room seemed to contract in time with the collective intake of breath. Auntie Sheila's supercilious half-smile and narrowed eyes caused only the slightest furrow to dissect her high forehead.

'What books?' she asked, without her hard mask slipping.

'You know what books,' Raymond said in desperation. '*My* books.'

'Raymond Rawnsley,' she said in a voice of ice, 'you're late and your tone is insolent. If you have something you want to discuss, see me after tea. Now, everybody's tea is going cold. Either sit down this instant or leave the room and do without.'

'But,' Raymond said, flustered.

'Leave the room now,' she ordered, 'unless you'd like Uncle Andrew to escort you.'

The glowering look on Uncle Andrew's face, no doubt caused by his impatience to tuck into the food on the plate in front of him, warned Raymond that he'd better retire from the scene with haste. He turned on his heels and left the room with a stiffness he hoped looked like dignity. Back in the playroom, he slumped in a seat by the window and mourned his lost books, for he was now certain they were lost. He'd seen the gleam in Auntie Sheila's eyes.

After a while, Shirley appeared.

'She wants you now,' she said, looking sympathetic and placing a hand on his shoulder. 'I did warn you, didn't I, Raymond?'

Raymond followed Shirley back to the dining room. He was determined to exercise as much self-control as possible in the face of what, he realised, was a planned public humiliation. The meal was over and everybody was waiting to be excused when he entered and stood before the staff table. Auntie Sheila seemed serene.

'Well, Raymond Rawnsley,' she said, 'you had a question you wanted to ask.'

'I asked where my books were,' Raymond said, hoping the quaver in his voice was sensory rather than audible.

'Are you referring to the fact that the old books have been cleared from the bookshelves to make way for a new batch?' she asked while placing a manicured fingernail against her cheek. 'Are you suggesting some of those books were yours?'

'Yes,' Raymond said, trying not to grind his teeth.

'Oh dear,' she said with mock concern. 'Don't you think it was a bit careless of you to leave them there if you wanted to keep them, especially as we recycle our books periodically?'

'But you told me to put them there,' Raymond said, feeling his composure slipping.

'Excuse me,' she said, her face hardening. 'I think you'll

find I told you you couldn't keep them in the dormitory. Everybody knows the books on those shelves are corporation property. It is no good bleating about your mistake now. The books have been collected and are gone for good. Feel free, however, to read the new ones when they arrive.'

Raymond knew it was futile to argue, although he sensed she would welcome it. There was no point because there was no arbitration. She was judge, jury and executioner. His loss scorched his insides and she knew it, but her face remained impassive as he held her look and said nothing.

Eventually, she said with a wave of her hand, 'Well, that's settled, then. You may all leave the table and get on with your chores.'

*

Still mourning his books, Raymond was taking his woe out on the line of shoes in the yard when Shirley sneaked out for her smoke. Remaining hidden from the house, she spoke to Raymond almost in whispers.

'I warned you, Raymond. You've been too cocky. You should have at least pretended all the work and grounding was getting you down. She'll always find a way to get at you. It's better to make her think she already has. Even I learned that pretty fast. You're not as smart as you think you are.'

The last comment made Raymond look up in anger.

'Hey, don't take it out on me,' she said. 'I'm really, really sorry you've lost your books. All the lasses are. We've been talking about it and we think it's really cruel. I know how much you loved your books. I was telling the others I remember you reading to us at Hillcrest when you were just a little tot. It was amazing. You could read better then than most of us can now. Nobody's bothered about books here, but we know they meant a lot to you and we all hate Auntie Sheila for getting rid of them.'

Between then and bedtime, just about all the inmates

271

managed to express some sort of sympathy. Nigel Normanton, the textile worker who was always serious about everything, came up with a surprisingly profound perspective.

'You've read all those books, haven't you?' he asked
Raymond.

'Of course,' Raymond replied.

'Well, think about it,' Nigel said. 'She can't take that away
from you, can she? A book is just part of a tree. All the
stories inside those books are inside you now.'

*

Raymond's wounds were still raw a couple of days later, as
he moped in the playroom while the others were at the
youth club. He still had one book left in his locker, which
was *Great Expectations*. It was the book he'd chosen to
protect above all others. He looked at the inscription inside
the cover, as he'd done many times over the years.

*Miracle Boy has been saved for something special. And the
communication I have got to make is that he has great
expectations.*
  A Well-wisher

The well-wisher was wrong. Raymond might once have
been Miracle Boy, but there was nothing special on his horizon. His only expectations were to endure as best he could
until he could get a job and a place in the working boys'
hostel. He snapped the book shut and placed it on the
barren bookshelf. Maybe some other boy like him would
pick it up and read it one day.

The moment the book left his hands he felt free; free of
fear, doubt and expectation. He was no longer a boy with
books. He was much more than that.

Batman

It was cold and dark on the roof of Backville Manor. Bonfire Night was imminent. The only significance this very English November the fifth celebration had for Raymond was that it was the only time of year that boys could buy fireworks; in particular, penny bangers, some of which were hidden in his trouser pockets. These vicious little explosive squibs, which most boys, at least once in their lifetime, had to hold in the hand when lit until the last moment before throwing, had been specially prepared by Raymond.

The sequence of events that led him to the roof this night began with one of the many chores Auntie Sheila heaped on him. While working on the outhouse clearance, intended to fuel the bonfire Uncle Andrew was building in the yard, Raymond was reminded of Hillcrest. There, his reputation for ingenuity was founded on making use of anything he could find to fashion into weapons for use in woodland games. The ball of thin string he'd salvaged from the clearance was a case in point.

A penny banger can be given a much longer fuse by unwinding the blue touch paper and inserting a length of string before winding it back again. Raymond had devised and used this method in the past as a prank, but this time there was a special reason. He'd overheard a conversation between Auntie Sheila and Mary McCluskey in the kitchen, while he was in the washroom, in which his house-mother revealed that she was terrified of explosive fireworks.

Raymond smiled to himself in grim satisfaction, as he suspended the bangers on long pieces of string from blocks of wood lodged in the gutter, so they were level with the top of the kitchen window. When everything was in place, he withdrew a box of matches from his pocket, pulled the bangers back up and lit the extended fuses, before lowering them again.

A minute or two later he was in the washroom, which was his winter shoe cleaning station, where he breathed in the ever-present smell of boiled cabbage. He could hear Auntie Sheila in the kitchen instructing Mary and Shirley on how much treacle to use as they made parkin for Bonfire Night. Raymond made sure he could be heard as he went about his chore, but his ears were cocked.

'Shirley, you're not doing that right,' he heard his house-mother say in exasperation. 'Give it here.'

From the sounds that followed, Raymond could picture Auntie Sheila beating the mixture for the dark, sticky cake in a bowl with a wooden spoon. Raymond's brush was poised in the air above a shoe as he listened to the radio play unfolding. The beating of the spoon was interrupted by the first of the bangers outside the kitchen window exploding with a loud crack, immediately followed by another. Then there was a scream and a crash, which Raymond knew was the bowl shattering on the floor. The rest of the bangers went off with loud staccato reports, which seemed to be amplified by the window pane. More screams and cries of alarm rang out, followed by the scrape of chair legs on the linoleum and then the slam of a door.

Raymond composed his face into a mask of innocence and strolled into the kitchen to see Mary on her knees trying to rescue shards of pottery with dark cake mixture still stuck to them, while Shirley leaned on the table with her mouth open and her big eyes popping. There was no sign of Auntie Sheila.

'What was all that about?' Raymond asked with his arms spread.

'Must be lads throwing bangers at the house,' Shirley said, as her look of shock dissolved. 'They did it last year.'

'Did you see her?' Mary asked in wonder. 'She just ran amok.'

Before anyone could respond, an infuriated Uncle Andrew appeared in the doorway.

'Mary, go and see to Sarah,' he ordered. 'She's crying her eyes out. If I get hold of those lads they'll wish they'd never been born. Raymond, clear this mess up and, Shirley, bring your Auntie Sheila a cup of tea. Make it sweet.'

Raymond was happy to clear up the mess. He was laughing inside and congratulating himself. That couldn't have gone better. He began to sweep up the broken pottery with a brush and dustpan with gusto, while Shirley put the kettle on the hob.

When Shirley returned from carrying freshly made tea through to the staffroom, she gave Raymond a strange look.

'Why are you grinning like a Cheshire cat?' she asked him.

'You've got to admit it was funny,' Raymond said. 'Who'd have thought she'd be so scared?'

'She's nearly in tears in there,' Shirley said. 'She's shaking like a leaf. I reckon we owe those lads, whoever they are.'

Raymond knew it was unwise to say anything, but he felt too good to keep it to himself.

'I'm the one who's owed,' he said in a low voice.

'What are you on about, Raymond?' Shirley scoffed. 'You were in the washroom cleaning shoes. I could hear you.'

Five minutes later, after Raymond's careful and convincing explanation, Shirley was looking at him with newfound respect. It made a satisfying change from her usual scorn.

*

Feeling satisfied with himself, Raymond retired to the play-room to take advantage of the new batch of recently arrived books. As he browsed the shelves, he was sure he got one or two knowing looks from the girls, who were gathered around the table playing cards.

He was reading Alistair Maclean's *The Guns of Navarone* when he was approached by a delegation of the girls led by Monica.

'Well, I never thought you had it in you, Raymond Rawns-ley,' Monica said, poking his right shoulder with a chubby forefinger. 'I always thought if you fell in a barrel of tits you'd come out sucking your thumb.'

'What?' Raymond protested, although he knew what she was referring to by the guilty look on Shirley's face as she stood at the back of the group.

Monica put her hands on her powerful hips and pushed her large chest out.

'Come off it, Raymond, you crafty bugger,' she said. 'We know it was you and we know how you did it. Don't worry, we won't say owt. We just want you to do summat for us.'

'What?' Raymond parroted.

'Sarah,' Monica said, grimfaced. 'We want you to string bangers up outside her bedroom window. We want you to scare her to death.'

'You're joking,' Raymond said in desperation. 'Sarah's room is at the top of the house at the front. I'm not Batman.'

'Elsie'll give you ten minutes in the downstairs girls' toilet,' Monica said with a leer.

'Be there in two minute-th' Elsie said, setting off.

Raymond couldn't even look at her.

'There's no need,' he blurted out. 'I'll do it. I'll do it.'

All the girls, except Elsie, laughed.

'Maybe you'd prefer one of the lads,' Monica suggested. 'Where's Bernard?'

'I've said I'll do it,' Raymond said, 'but I haven't got any more money left for bangers.'

'We'll get the money together, don't worry about that,' Monica assured him. 'You just get your Batman outfit sorted out.'

The girls withdrew to another part of the playroom, where they huddled together and whispered. Eventually, Monica came over and crouched by his chair while he pretended to read, but the force of her presence made him look up. Was she deliberately showing as much cleavage as possible? He couldn't help thinking that if Monica had been farm-reared it would've been for meat rather than dairy; she smelled of lard not butter. Oblivious to his thoughts, she held out a handful of copper coins, obscuring the open pages of his book with her chunky red palm.

'Get some bangers on your way home from school to-morrow,' Monica instructed. 'Do it tomorrow night and do a good job. We want the little cow scared out of her wits.'

*

There was a bitter breeze when Raymond clambered onto the flat roof with a pocketful of the long-fuse bangers he'd prepared. Now he'd have to venture further than he'd been before. He studied the tiled incline to the apex of the main roof of the house. It looked steep and glistened in the dark. He decided the best method was to sit back and propel himself upwards with his hands and feet. When he tried it, he was relieved to find that it worked, although the tiles were cold against his buttocks. When he neared the top, he turned and gripped the ridge tiles and pulled himself up.

He was in full view of the houses across the road, but even though the lights were on in some of the houses, the curtains were closed. He would just have to take his chance. Just to his right was the pitch of the roof of one of the bays at the front of the house. He inched his way across and straddled it. Keeping as low as possible to avoid being seen by any passersby from the dimly lit street, he inched his way towards the front of the house until he reached the ornate finial capping the gable. Sarah's bedroom window was directly below. The breeze buffeted his face as he removed his prepared bangers from his pocket, tied each one to the finial with string and lowered it down.

He paused for a moment. He didn't really like frightening children. The memory of young boys crying in the dark on their first few nights in a children's home would never leave him. Still, if any young girl deserved a scare it was horrible Sarah.

He pulled the fireworks back up and lit the long fuse of each with the glowing end of a smouldering piece of string he carried in his mouth. The bangers were primed. Pushing himself backwards along the ridge, he reached the main roof, from where he slid down to the flat roof on his backside. Checking the coast was clear, he clambered down to the ground and entered the house with the nonchalant look of someone who was not feeling, as he was, the ache in his crotch caused by bumping along the ridge tiles of the roof.

In the playroom, he buried his head in *Guns of Navarone* and ignored the meaningful glances of the girls. Before long, he heard muffled detonations going off at short intervals at the front of the house, accompanied by smiles and twitching eyebrows all round, and then shortly afterwards, a commotion from within the house. Library rules had never been so well observed in this playroom, as nobody spoke or moved.

Eventually, the door opened and Shirley entered the room. Her big blue eyes were shining with excitement and she had the palm of one hand pressed to her throat above her heaving chest, as if she was having difficulty breathing. She sat down in a chair next to Raymond and the other girls edged closer. At first, she waved her hand in front of her mouth like Raymond sometimes saw her do to get rid of the smell of tobacco after a cigarette, but a hard stare from Monica put paid to her histrionics.

'It was brilliant,' Shirley gasped in a half-whisper. 'Sarah came flying downstairs screaming like a banshee. She's still crying her eyes out and saying bad men are trying to kill her. Auntie Sheila looks just as scared. They're clinging to each other like they're on a shipwreck. Uncle Andrew has searched the grounds and told them whoever threw the fireworks has run off, but Sarah won't go to bed. Uncle Andrew has promised her she can sleep in their bed, but he doesn't look happy.'

'He was probably hoping for a jump tonight,' Monica said. 'God, can you imagine them two at it,' she added with an exaggerated shudder.

She turned to Raymond. 'As for you, you can have a jump any time you like.'

Raymond buried his head in his book and ignored the cackles. Later, he went to the downstairs toilet and when he opened the door to leave, Elsie barred his way and pushed her way in. Closing the door behind her, she put her back to it and lost no time in opening her blouse and pulling up her bra to expose her large soft breasts.

'All yourth, Raymond,' she breathed.

'I don't want to,' Raymond said, taken aback by the speed of events.

'Courth you do,' Elsie said, pushing her chest out and reaching down to stroke his crotch.

'Hmm, you really do,' she murmured.

God help him, he did.

*

He'd always known he'd get caught. Juicy gossip was a precious commodity that could be traded for favours at

Backville Manor and all the inmates knew about his crime. It was only a matter of time and it was no surprise when a raging Uncle Andrew cornered him in the washroom. The first-hand experience of his house-father's violent temperament lived up to everything whispered about it, but somehow it was bearable. It was, however, inadequate. It couldn't change the fact that he'd made a fool of the book bandit.

When Raymond limped into the dining room, all the inmates were accompanying Jerry and the Pacemakers on television in a rendition of their current number one record, 'You'll Never Walk Alone'. He wondered if they were singing so loud to drown out what they must have heard, but when they saw him they stopped singing.

From Russia with Love

Rom was as prickly as a bear with a thorn in its paw. It was depressing February and the mock O level exams were imminent. However, the daily grind of persecution at Backville Manor was sapping Raymond's motivation to do well at school. Besides, if ever a place was designed to be unsuitable for him to concentrate on revision, it was Backville Manor. Auntie Sheila made no concessions to the fact he needed peace and quiet to work in, as well as ensuring that he got limited time. He struggled through as best he could in the playroom against noise and interruptions from the inmates, but his heart wasn't in it.

The three months since his firework escapade had contained nothing but dreariness. The only events of note were the assassination of President John F. Kennedy in America, which caused a great stir, even though it took place in another world, and Raymond's visits to his mother in hospital. Auntie Sheila couldn't stop his visits, but Raymond knew she would if she could. There was nothing she could do, though. Mrs Eaton was his relative, even if Raymond couldn't bring himself to think of her as his aunt.

The visits to Stokes Park Hospital with Mrs Eaton were all as surreal as the first one.

*

They sat at a table by the conservatory doors amongst other patients and visitors. His mother looked straight ahead and gave no sign of acknowledgement. Her dark, grey-streaked hair was lank and her brown eyes were unblinking. Her cheeks looked swollen, as if they were bruised under the skin. Mrs Eaton lifted a full brown-paper bag out of her handbag and tore it down the side to reveal a bunch of luscious, green grapes. She flattened out the bag and began to detach grapes from the bunch, making sure to remove any traces of the stem. When she'd completed a handful, she placed them in front of Raymond's mother. Raymond watched, fascinated, as his mother began to eat the grapes, one by one.

'Go on,' Mrs Eaton said to him while preparing more grapes. 'You're here now. Talk to her.'

Raymond felt uncomfortable. It seemed strange talking to someone who didn't even seem to see or hear him. Then it occurred to him that it didn't matter what he said, so he could just tell her the truth.

'Hello, I'm Raymond,' he said in a soft voice. 'I came to see you a long while ago, but you probably don't remember. I was with a woman doctor and a lady smelling of flowers. You got a bit upset, but I know you're going to be all right today. If I'd known you were here I'd have come to see you a long time ago. Mrs Eaton doesn't think it's a good idea, but then again, she can see her mother whenever she likes.'

Mrs Eaton raised her eyebrows, but he kept his tone light.

'Anyway, I'm glad I'm here now. I don't know what you've been told about me, but I go to a school I don't like much and I live in a home I hate. Apart from that, everything's fine. I can't wait until I leave both of them. I'll get a job and then I'll be free. Nobody will be able to make me do what I don't want to do. I'll come and visit you more often then.

'I like reading. I used to have lots of books of my own, but someone gave them away. I don't mind. I'm never going to keep a book again. When I've read a book I'll give it away. The only good library is a public one.'

282

Mrs Eaton kept destalking grapes, but she was staring at him. He ignored her and carried on talking to his mother.

'I don't know why the wrong people seem to end up in jobs where they can make other people's life a misery. Still, seeing you here I can't complain. I'll be free one day. I just wanted to say, I know what happened and it doesn't matter. I know you had your reasons.'

'I'll take over a bit now,' Mrs Eaton said.

She talked to her half-sister about everything from the weather to Lee Harvey Oswald and passed grapes to her for the rest of the visit, while Raymond listened and watched. His mother consumed all the grapes like a watchful squirrel eating nuts, but never once gave any indication that she understood what was being said to her. When it came to leaving, it was just a matter of Raymond and Mrs Eaton standing up and walking out, while his mother continued to stare straight ahead. Halfway down the corridor, Mrs Eaton stopped in her tracks and began rummaging in her handbag.

'You'd better get a move on for the bus,' she said, not looking at him. 'My husband's coming to pick me up. Off you go, Raymond, and take this with you.'

She pressed a ten shilling note into his hand.

Every visit was the same.

*

The money Mrs Eaton gave Raymond bought pasties and sweets for the Legion of the Disenchanted, but it couldn't take the permanent sour taste out of Raymond's mouth. He knew he'd not done well in the mock exams and he needed something to alleviate his melancholy. With the exams over, he decided to make a request to Auntie Sheila. He'd got nothing to lose.

Raymond's schoolmate, Poggy, lived close to Backville Manor and he suggested that they should go to see the latest James Bond film, *From Russia With Love,* at the local cinema, but even Bob Hope wouldn't have given Raymond a chance when he knocked at the door to his house-parents' room. He entered in response to Auntie Sheila's command and found her watching television with Sarah. When Raymond opened his mouth to speak, she held her hand up to stop him and continued watching the television. He waited while the news that Barbie the doll had a boyfriend called Ken was relayed to Sarah and her mother. Eventually, Auntie Sheila gave him permission to speak.

'The exams have finished and I wondered if I could go to the pictures tonight with a mate from school,' Raymond said, conscious of Sarah's hate-filled eyes boring into him.

To Raymond's surprise, Auntie Sheila laughed, and not in her usual sardonic way.

'Full marks for cheek,' she exclaimed.

She turned to Sarah, who was still staring at Raymond.

'What do you think, Sarah? Should we let Raymond go to the pictures tonight?'

'No,' Sarah said.

'What if he says sorry for frightening you with those fireworks last year?'

'No.'

'What if he says he's really, really sorry?'

'Maybe.'

'Well, Raymond?' Auntie Sheila said.

'I'm really, really sorry, Sarah,' Raymond said, crossing his fingers behind his back.

Sarah sniggered.

'You can go,' his house-mother said.

Raymond couldn't believe it. Maybe she had a heart after all beneath those pointed breasts.

She scotched that notion just as he was about to leave the house to meet Poggy at the cinema for seven o'clock. Raymond thought he was making a discreet exit, but she must have been waiting, because she appeared behind him as soon as his hand touched the handle of the front door.

'You haven't asked me what time you're supposed to be back,' she said.

Raymond's heart sank. He knew her tricks.

'Nine o'clock,' she said. 'Now run along and have a nice time.'

He stepped out into the cold air and closed the door behind him. Standing on the steps, he pulled his coat collar around his neck and wondered whether it was even worth going. She'd probably rung the cinema to find out what time the film finished and then lopped an hour off that. She would be enjoying her moment.

He met up with Poggy at the cinema and they bought tickets at the booth in the well-lit foyer from a young woman with thick make-up, who was trying to read a magazine at the same time as serving customers. Then they were shown to their seats by an ancient usherette just as the B film was starting. Stretching their legs out under the seats in front of them, they settled down as low as possible.

Raymond never intended rebellion. He'd resigned himself to going home at the correct time. Maybe it was the immaculate Sean Connery as James Bond or the alluring Daniela Bianchi as Tatiana Romanova, who made Poggy groan every time she appeared on screen, that held him in his seat. Whatever it was, he stayed to the end of the film, way beyond the time he should have gone home. Only the character of Rosa Klebb, who could get a job at Backville Manor if ever she tired of working for SPECTRE, reminded Raymond that he would have to suffer retribution for his tardiness.

Raymond dragged his feet and even stopped to buy some chips on his way home. He might as well be hung for a sheep as a lamb. He daren't look at his watch, but the streets were dark and deserted as he approached Backville

Manor. All the lights in the house were off except for the one in the hallway. He might need a Miracle Boy moment.

The brass doorknob on the front door was as cold as ice. He took a deep breath and opened the door.

Uncle Andrew stood in the dimly lit hallway facing the door with legs apart and his brawny arms, with sleeves rolled up, hanging by his sides. His face was in shadow, but he exuded an air of menace.

'I had a nosebleed,' Raymond blurted out like a pathetic schoolboy making an excuse for being late.

'You will have,' Uncle Andrew rasped, raising clenched fists and striding towards him.

It was a one-round, one-sided fight. It didn't just take place in the hallway, but also crashed around the kitchen, toppling chairs in its wake. All Raymond could do was try to fend off the welter of vicious, heavy blows raining on his head and body.

Uncle Andrew only stopped his assault at the bottom of the stairs, leaving Raymond to crawl up to bed.

Raymond slept fitfully, finding it difficult to stay in one position. He knew he must have looked a sight when Callum stared at him in shock as he tried to roll out of bed in the morning.

'Good Lord Almighty,' the big-hearted lump of a lad exclaimed. 'You've surely been in an accident with a car or a train, Raymond. You should be in the hospital.'

Raymond tried to speak but could only mumble through cracked and swollen lips. Bernard, in crumpled pyjamas, looked across at Raymond and immediately began to cry and flap his hands. Nigel Normanton approached Raymond's bed and winced as he studied him.

'Yeah, you know what train ran into Raymond, don't you?' he said to Callum. 'It was the Flying Yorkshireman. This is Peter Mellor all over again. Come on; let's give him a hand to get dressed.'

Even with help, Raymond discovered that dressing was a painful process. In the bathroom he found it impossible to clean his teeth and he could only dab at his face with a wet flannel. Through half-closed eyes he saw in the mirror that his bloated face looked twice its normal size. He made his way to the stairs, where it seemed to take an age for him to work his way down, as every step tugged at his aching ribs. At the bottom of the stairs he came face to face with Auntie Sheila. In the slits he was peering through she looked like a plaster model.

'Raymond Rawnsley, you look as though you've been in the wars,' she said. 'I knew it was a mistake to let you out. I suppose it was local youths, was it?'

He knew she was trying to put words into his mouth.

'Uncle Andrew,' he mumbled with difficulty.

She placed her face close to his and he saw her jaw stiffen.

'I beg your pardon?' she said through clenched teeth.

His tongue felt too big for his mouth and he could feel spittle dribbling from the corner of his mouth.

'Uncle Andrew,' he spluttered into her face.

His eyes were so fixed on her immaculate, merciless mask that he didn't see the swinging, open hand coming before it smashed into the side of his swollen face. It felt to Raymond as though his eyes were filling with blood. He just managed to catch a fleeting look of regret clouding his house-mother's face, like someone who realises a split second too late that they've made a false move.

She turned and headed for the kitchen, saying in mock exasperation to nobody in particular, 'I'll swing for that lad one day.'

A Hero's Return

After a breakfast Raymond could barely eat, during which the silent disgust of the inmates was as palpable as the unpleasant odour of the food, Raymond stood in front of Auntie Sheila in the office.

'You got what you deserved last night, but Uncle Andrew might have been a bit heavy-handed,' she said, shifting her eyes towards her cat, Lady, whose eyes gleamed. 'He was tired and he's still seething over what you did to Sarah. You might have ended up with a few bruises, but Sarah could still be having nightmares in years to come. You can take a few days off school until you look presentable. I'll let them know you've had a fall.'

She turned her gaze away from the cat and back to him.

'You are supposed to be intelligent,' she said. 'I'm sure you can understand what's in your best interest.'

Raymond looked at her porcelain mask. At that moment it felt as though the two of them were cocooned in their own separate world. She was trying to appear confident, but he could see something lurking in a small yellow facet of her grey-green eyes: it was fear. He could smell it in the strange, unpleasant musk that her perfume could never hide. He said nothing and hobbled out of the room without leave.

He was grateful for the sympathy of the other inmates, expressed in words by some and doleful looks by others.

Shirley helped him into a chair in the playroom and asked him which book he would like her to bring him, but he wasn't in the mood for reading.

Later, when everyone was either out or engaged in some other business around the house, Elsie came in and pulled up a chair next to him as if she was visiting a patient in hospital.

'We can thpend thome time together again if you want,' she said, touching his hand. 'Nobody's around.'

'No, it's all right, Elsie,' he said.

'Maybe when you're feeling better,' she said.

'We'll see,' he said.

When she'd gone, he smiled inside in a way that his cracked lips wouldn't allow. That was some bunch of grapes.

*

The visible signs of Raymond's 'accident' took more than a week to disappear sufficiently for Auntie Sheila to allow him to go back to school. Paddy, the games master, was eagle-eyed enough to spot something, though, as Raymond laboured to breathe, struggling through the devilish obstacles devised for circuit training.

'Let me look at that nose, Rawnsley,' Paddy said, putting a hand under Raymond's chin and tilting his head back. 'Hmm! How did this happen?'

'Fight, sir,' Raymond mumbled.

'Thought so,' Paddy snorted. 'Well, Rawnsley, you're going to hospital. I've seen enough boxing injuries to know the bone in your nose is broken and displaced. This should've been seen to at the time. Now I reckon they'll have to break it again and reset it. Go and get changed and wait in the changing room. When the lesson's over I'll run you to hospital myself.'

Later, Paddy drove Raymond to hospital in a car reeking of dank dog. He even went to the desk with Raymond and made sure that he was checked in before leaving. Sometime later, Raymond saw a doctor.

'How did you manage this?' the doctor asked while examining Raymond's nose.

'Football,' Raymond mumbled with tears in his eyes.

'You wouldn't believe how many people come here as a result of chasing a ball about,' the doctor observed. 'Now close your eyes and grit your teeth. This is for your own good.'

After the doctor realigned his nose by painful manipulation, he left Raymond lying on a trolley bed with his eyes closed and an icepack over the bridge of his nose.

'Raymond.'

The sound of his name made Raymond open his eyes to see a familiar face looking down at him. It was Nurse Goode, although her uniform told him that she should now be called Sister Goode.

'What have you been up to now?' she asked with concern.

'I ran into a tree in the dark,' Raymond said, losing confidence in his previous excuse.

Sister Goode covered his hand with hers and gently lifted the icepack. She winced.

'You look more like you've run into a bus,' she mused. 'Are you sure that's how you got this? I remember what happened to you the last time I saw you. Where are you living now?'

'Backville Manor,' Raymond informed her.

'I've heard of it. Is everything all right there?' she asked.

'Yes,' he replied.

She surprised him by sitting down on the edge of the bed.

'Look, Raymond,' she said, 'I'd find it hard to believe you got this if you'd been fighting Cassius Clay for the heavyweight championship of the world. Is there is anything you want to tell me?'

Raymond looked at her. Her dark hair was tied back beneath her starched cap and her hazel eyes gazed at him from a kind oval face. He couldn't imagine her without her uniform. It complemented her like a crown suited the Queen. He knew if he said something she would take up the cause with vigour, but, as always, he preferred to keep his troubles to himself. It was either a matter of pride or shame and he didn't know which, but he didn't want to be anyone's cause.

'It's all right,' he lied. 'I was just unlucky. I wasn't watching where I was going.'

She frowned as if reluctant to believe him.

'I'll tell you what I'm going to do, Raymond,' she said, rising. 'I'm going to ring Backville Manor and tell them to keep an eye on that injury and take good care of you.'

*

'Why did you go to hospital?' Auntie Sheila asked Raymond.

'The games master took me,' Raymond said.

'Who's this sister and what right has she to interfere in our business? I said you'd been in a fight and she said you'd told her you'd run into a tree. I had to tell her you were always making things up. In future, you say nothing to anybody about what goes on inside these four walls. Do you understand?'

Raymond didn't reply.

'Well?' she said.

'We're not supposed to lie,' Raymond said.

'Don't get smart with me, Raymond Rawnsley,' she said with a hint of exasperation. 'I'm the one who can decide whether or not your life is worth living – no one else. Don't you forget that.'

It was a game of cat and mouse. She was clever, but so was he. She'd been easy on him since the incident; excusing him from shoe cleaning and other chores and letting him read in the playroom, and he took advantage of it. He thought of Peter Mellor as he read a book from the new crop, *The Road to En-Dor*, by E.H. Jones, which was an extraordinary escape story. He didn't intend to try the same escape as Peter, but Raymond knew that his house-mother's worry was that *he* might be believed if he decided to confide in anyone outside the home.

One source of satisfaction to Raymond was the tension between his house-parents. It wasn't overt, but it wasn't subtle either and Raymond was sensitive to the nuances of human behaviour. Auntie Sheila's disdain for her husband was as clear to Raymond as the smell clinging to her, although he guessed that most of the other inmates were oblivious to both. Shirley was different and she concurred with Raymond on both counts in an outdoor conversation when he resumed his shoe cleaning duties.

'She can't stand him,' Shirley agreed when Raymond mentioned it to her. 'You can tell by the way she looks down her nose at him. I reckon that's what makes him the way he is – belting the lads and pawing the lasses. He knows better than to come near me though. I'd kick him straight in the goolies and he knows it.'

'I reckon that's what makes her the way she is as well,' Raymond said. 'She's bitter, but she has to keep up appearances, so she takes it out on us.'

'You can smell the bitterness on her,' Shirley said. 'She tries to cover it up, but she can't hide it.'

'You've noticed it too?' Raymond said. 'I thought I was the only one. Nobody else mentions it.'

'Hillcrest gave us the nose for it,' Shirley said, as the butt of her cigarette flew in an arc over a small hedge near the corner of the yard. 'We can smell that sort a mile off.'

Sometimes Shirley could be all right. It was just a pity that she was so sarcastic most of the time.

*

Raymond's mock exam results were below par, especially compared to the standards he'd set the previous year. That was the reason he found himself in Slimy Hanson's office.

'What's going on, Rawnsley?' the pompous deputy head said while holding up a sheet of paper. 'These results are nowhere near the standard expected of you.'

Raymond chose to use the stock answer schoolboys use to signify that they are going to reveal nothing.

'I don't know, sir.'

'Mm, Rawnsley,' Slimy said down his nose to the piece of paper, 'I know you've had your ups and downs at this school, but you might be surprised to know your academic ability is well regarded. Many of the masters expect you to do well in your O levels and be one of those to stay on for A levels. I have been of the same view, which is why these results are a surprise.'

This wasn't what Raymond expected and his look must have revealed as much to Slimy.

'Look, Rawnsley,' Slimy said in as close to a conciliatory tone as he could manage, which only accentuated his nasal whine. 'We are not unaware of your circumstances and we do appreciate that you may have encountered some difficulties. However, your ability is beyond question. Don't you want the opportunity to stay on at school and aim for a place at university?'

The light from a high window shone on Slimy's oiled hair, as he leaned back in his chair and awaited an answer.

Raymond hadn't even thought about the possibility of staying on at school. His future was mapped out – leave school at the end of this school year, get a job and hope for a place at the working boys' hostel.

'I haven't even considered it, sir,' he said.

'Well consider it now,' Slimy said and linked the fingers of his hands together in front of him.

'I can't do it, sir,' Raymond said after a minute. 'I've got to leave and get a job.'

Slimy looked as if Raymond had just refused the chance to play football for England. Raymond, though, was adamant. There was no other way.

*

Someone else, an important person in Raymond's world, believed that there was another way. Raymond found it hard to believe the scrawny old woman straightening her fox stole around the shoulders of her oatmeal jacket was here at Backville Manor just to see him. He'd seen the black, chauffeur-driven car enter the drive from the playroom. He'd recognised Mr Pickup as the driver and he knew who this woman was. He'd seen her at Christmas parties hosted by charitable organisations to which children's homes were invited. She was Miss Meakin, the exalted head of the corporation's Welfare Department, and she'd arrived, un-announced, to see him.

Auntie Sheila was flustered. She dispatched Mary to bring tea and biscuits, shooed Lady from her regular place on the best chair in the office and brushed the cushion with her hands. She smiled at Miss Meakin and frowned at Raymond behind her back. When she was seated, Miss Meakin addressed Raymond.

'I've had a call from the headmaster of Slevin Grammar School,' she said. 'He was perturbed to hear that you had turned down a place for advanced education at the school, subject, of course, to your exam results. You do understand that Slevin is the best school in the area, do you not?'

'Yes,' Raymond replied, standing in front of her with his hands behind his back.

The eye of the dead fox strapped to Miss Meakin's thin chest glinted as she held up a bony hand.

'It is, therefore, a privilege that you have been offered this opportunity, is it not?'

'Yes,' Raymond agreed.

'Then why do I hear that you have refused it?'

Auntie Sheila looked alarmed, as if Raymond might say something that would damn her. Her cheeks, normally dusted with a hint of rouge, were red. Raymond took his time before answering.

'Because I want to leave and get a job,' he said finally.

Miss Meakin jerked her head back as if she'd been slapped. Auntie Sheila glowered and her eyes were sending all kinds of warnings to Raymond.

'By whose authority do you make decisions such as that?' Miss Meakin blustered. 'You are in our care until you reach the legal age of adulthood. It is our duty to make decisions that you may not be ready to make yourself. Sadly, many boys in care do not progress beyond the most menial occupations and some, regrettably, turn to crime. You have a better opportunity than most and it is one we have prepared you for in all the years you have been in our care. Do you imagine for a moment that I would allow you to snub it?'

Raymond reminded himself that her nickname throughout the homes was Minnie, but it wasn't her he was looking at; it was his house-mother. He had a choice to make. He could allow himself to be browbeaten by authority, the weight of which had suffocated him all his life, or he could stand up for himself.

'You can't pass my exams for me,' he said in the calmest voice he could muster.

Auntie Sheila's cheeks were as inflamed as a fishwife's chapped hands.

'Raymond!' she gasped.

It was the first time she'd called him by only his first name. She gathered herself and then her tone was so wheedling it was laughable.

'You should be grateful Miss Meakin's taken the trouble to come out here on your behalf. Do you think she's nothing better to do? She's here because she's concerned for your welfare, as we all are. That's what we're here for.'

Raymond remained steadfast as the argument went on and eventually he was dismissed with cold advice from Minnie to come to his senses before it was too late. By the time Miss Meakin left, tea was half an hour later than usual. When the collection of raging hormones that were the inmates of Backville Manor were seated in the dining room gazing at plates of sausage and mash, Auntie Sheila spoke.

'I realise you must be hungry,' she declared, 'especially those who've been working hard. You've got Raymond Rawnsley to thank for the delay.'

Raymond accepted the token reproving glances of his cohabitants, but he knew that they were more intrigued than put out.

Auntie Sheila said grace in one breath.

'For what we are about to receive, may the Lord make us truly thankful. Amen. Raymond Rawnsley, don't bother picking up your knife and fork. Leave the room and start your chores immediately.'

Raymond left the room with only one regret: he would miss having sausages. They were everybody's favourite food because they couldn't be spoiled by overcooking.

That evening, four people in turn brought Raymond a cold sausage. Nigel pulled his from out of his trouser pocket; Shirley produced hers from inside the sleeve of her cardigan; Wendy withdrew hers from inside one of her white ankle socks; and irrepressible Monica revealed her offering from deep within her cleavage and whispered, 'Oops! How did that get there?'

Raymond wanted to believe that their kindness was based on kinship, but he knew that they also wanted to know why Backville Manor was graced with a visit by Minnie Meakin.

When he told them, he got the impression that his status as a grammar school boy and an inmate of Backville Manor was less contradictory than it had been before.

They had news of their own: Auntie Sheila announced at tea that a new inmate was arriving the following day and he was reputed to be a bad boy.

*

Uncle Andrew led the 'bad boy' into the dining room when everyone was seated. The new arrival looked like a man rather than a boy. He had sandy hair, piercing blue eyes, a gap in his front teeth and a look of defiance. Raymond could see the girls' interest was immediately piqued, but so was his. He recognised him immediately; it was the one person, apart from the incisive Dr Charlerousse, who could decipher his mystery painting; it was Brian Walker, his companion-in-arms from Hillcrest.

The Chocolate Teapot

'This is Brian Walker,' Auntie Sheila announced when Brian was seated. 'He comes to us from a place of correction, which he will quickly return to if he steps out of line. For what we are about to receive, may the Lord make us truly thankful. Amen.'

Raymond wasn't allowed to speak, but he projected his welcome through raised eyebrows, which Brian must have seen, but instead of offering acknowledgement, Brian's gaze began to wander around the room. Maybe Brian didn't recognise him, although Raymond didn't think he'd changed that much. When Brian's blue eyes settled on Bernard, who was sitting next to him and staring ahead as if he didn't dare to look at the stranger, Brian curled his lip before shaking his head. Raymond was glad Bernard didn't see this because it would have brought tears to his eyes.

Without making it obvious, Raymond studied his old friend. Brian no longer had the same height advantage over Raymond he'd had when they were at Hillcrest, but his muscular physique and confident manner put years between them.

Brian seemed unaware of Raymond's scrutiny. In fact, throughout the silent meal, Raymond didn't once manage to catch Brian's eye, but he noticed that some of the girls did, especially Monica and Elsie. He returned the girls' stares with such a cocksure look that Raymond was amazed to see Monica blush and look away.

At the conclusion of the meal, Auntie Sheila swept from the room, calling out to Brian to follow her. Brian made for the door but Raymond put a hand on his arm. Brian's look was hostile.

'I just wanted to warn you,' Raymond whispered. 'She's an old friend of Uncle Richard's.'

'I couldn't give a toss,' Brian said and left the room.

Cleaning shoes later in the yard, Raymond pondered over Brian's coldness.

'He's not the same person, is he?' a voice said.

Shirley was standing in the lee of the washroom and withdrawing a cigarette from inside the sleeve of her cardigan.

'He looked straight through me when I said hello to him,' she said, lighting her cigarette with a match. 'He's in the playroom now with all the other lasses sucking up to him. It makes me sick.'

Raymond let her vent her spleen while he mused. A lot had happened to him since Hillcrest and the same was probably true for Brian. You couldn't expect people to stay the same and none of them could pretend they were kids anymore. He was prepared to take Brian at face value.

'He's changed a lot,' Shirley was saying. 'He looks mean and you can tell he's hard. Well, I don't need owt from him. If he wants to forget the past, that's OK by me.'

She sounded disappointed.

Raymond didn't get a chance to talk to Brian until later in the dormitory. Brian was allocated the spare bed by the door; he was putting clothes into the companion chest of drawers when Raymond went up to prepare for bed.

'Do you need a hand with anything?' Raymond asked.

'No,' Brian said without looking round.

'How are things?' Raymond asked.

'How do they look?' Brian said, still not looking round.

'How's things been, then?' Raymond persisted.

This time Brian looked round. He looked irritated.

'Just wonderful,' he sneered. 'I've been enjoying myself so much I decided to come here for a break. Don't start mooching around me like that cow-eyed Shirley. The past can stay in the past as far as I am concerned. I've got enough to cope with right here and now.'

'I just thought we were mates,' Raymond said and cursed himself for sounding lame.

Shaking his head, Brian turned back to stuffing clothes in drawers.

Raymond retired to the bathroom to wash and clean his teeth. When he returned to the dormitory all the other lads were preparing for bed. Brian was sitting on his bed hunched forward. Raymond walked over to his own bed to begin undressing, aware that Brian was looking over his shoulder and following him with his eyes. Brian got up and came across to him.

'Good bed you've got there,' Brian said, nodding approval.

Raymond looked up at him and said nothing. The gap in Brian's front teeth once made him look cheeky, but now it made him look menacing.

'The thing is,' Brian said, piercing Raymond with his eyes, 'I need it. I can't sleep near that loony over there and I have to sleep by a window.'

'We can't change beds just like that,' Raymond protested, conscious of all eyes in the room on him.

'I thought we were mates,' Brian said.

Raymond remembered when Brian was given a bed by a window at Hillcrest. He was through that window like a shot at the first opportunity. That was a time when they shared everything. Then, if Brian wanted anything from him, Raymond gave it without reservation.

'Go on, then,' Raymond said, seeing, beyond Brian's frame, a roomful of amazed faces.

Brian didn't even thank him. Instead, he strode over to

the bed by the door, picked up the chest of drawers in his arms as if it weighed nothing and carried it over to where Raymond was sitting. Then he picked up Raymond's chest of drawers and carried it across to the bed by the door.

'There you go,' he said, dusting his hands together. 'Now, get off my bed. I'm ready for a kip.'

Brian was the last to be ready for bed. Wearing only pyjama trousers and showing off his muscular torso, he took his time. From the top drawer of his bedside cabinet he withdrew a big silver alarm clock, which he wound up and placed on the windowsill by his pillow. Raymond wondered why he needed it. Early morning reveille was more reliable in children's homes than any alarm clock. Then again, Raymond knew the price individuals sometimes placed on the most innocuous personal possessions in these places.

When Brian finally climbed into bed, he threw his head down on the pillow and called out, 'Turn out the light.'

It was the rule that whoever's bed was nearest the door turned out the light. Raymond threw back his covers, rolled out of bed and stumbled across the linoleum to switch off the light. Back in bed, he lay on his back in the dark. The ticking of Brian's clock seemed to echo around the room.

*

Arriving home from school, Raymond went about his business as normal. If Brian wanted to rekindle an old friendship, that was fine. If he didn't, that was fine too.

Chores and a feeble attempt at homework took up Raymond's evening, during which he hadn't exchanged a word with Brian. Even at bedtime, in the dormitory, no words passed between them as they went about their routine. Raymond watched out of the corner of his eye as Brian reached for his alarm clock, which stood on the windowsill on short legs and had a big bell on top. The instant Brian's fingertips touched the clock, it collapsed in a heap. Raymond watched Brian stare in disbelief at the scattered components of his clock, some of which fell onto his bed, while the silver bell rolled slowly along the sill before wobbling over the edge and falling onto the floor with a metallic clang.

The sound of the bell hitting the floor hung in the air like the hum of a tuning fork and everybody in the room seemed frozen in time. Then Brian exploded into expletives. His face was twisted with fury, as he demanded to know who was responsible. Everybody knew who the culprit was, none more so than Bernard, who began to wail.

'It was Bernard, but he can't help it,' Callum blurted out.

With a snarl, Brian lunged towards the cringing manchild. Raymond was also moving and he flung himself between Bernard and his livid assailant so that, instead of Brian grabbing Bernard by the collar of his pyjamas, his hand collided with Raymond's face. The blow from Brian's hand was nothing to Raymond; it was the solid poke in the right eye by Brian's forefinger that really stung. Brian was taken aback. With his one good eye, Raymond could see Brian frozen in an attack posture with his muscular torso tensed. With tears already streaming down his cheek, Raymond spoke fast.

'I know you're upset, Brian,' he said, 'but you can't take it out on Bernard. He doesn't know what he's doing. You can see what he's like.'

Brian's chest was heaving, but he didn't move, which encouraged Raymond to carry on.

'It might not be as bad as it looks,' he said. 'Maybe I can fix it. I promise I'll have a go tomorrow.'

Nigel and Stuart both offered to help Raymond fix the clock. Nigel even began to retrieve all the pieces and lay them out on the windowsill. It was unlikely that they would have been able to overcome Brian by force, but they overcame him by collective goodwill. Brian's parting shot before he stormed off to the bathroom was, 'Don't let that loony come anywhere near me or my stuff again or nobody'll stop me knocking his block off.'

It was debatable who was shedding the most tears, Raymond or Bernard, but at least Bernard could turn his off once he'd been pacified. Raymond's pillow was soaked before he finally drifted off to sleep in the dark.

The next day, Nigel, who was the best of them with his hands, discovered that the alarm clock couldn't be fixed, even though when he put it all back together again it looked as good as new. Brian wasn't impressed.

'Well, it's not much bloody good then, is it,' he fumed. 'It might as well be a chocolate teapot.'

It still occupied a place on the windowsill by Brian's bed though.

Raymond understood how the pecking order worked in any institution, whether it was school or a children's home. The chocolate teapot was eloquent in its silence. Brian was owed; his wrath was only just in check and could be unleashed by anything. He was already top dog and none of the boys had the stomach to challenge him. Raymond could count himself among them, except he knew he would stand up for himself against his belligerent former friend if the time came to do so.

Owzat

Raymond didn't need any encouragement to join a Saturday afternoon game of football on the front lawn after he'd finished his chores. It was the first good day of spring and the sun shone as the boys played and the girls sat outside on the front steps watching them. In a game of 'Attack and Defence', Raymond found himself on the opposite side to Brian. His former friend was a solid defender, but Raymond was too tricky for him, and time and again he skipped past him and slotted the ball past Bernard, the hapless goalkeeper.

Raymond played for the sheer exhilaration of it, but dribbling past Brian, who swore in frustration at his team-mates, gave him an added sense of satisfaction. Brian couldn't dominate everything with the threat of brute force.

The girls began to cheer as Raymond approached Brian once more, taunting him with the ball tied to his foot by an invisible thread. Brian lunged for the ball, but Raymond dragged it away in a flash and knocked it past him. He was about to stroke the ball past Bernard, when his legs were whipped from beneath him by the sweeping arc of Brian's flailing leg. Raymond crashed to the ground in a heap, but leapt to his feet in an instant.

His fists were clenched, but he was not sure afterwards whether he'd intended to hit Brian. Even if he had, he never got the chance because Brian hit him first. Brian's fists were so fast and true that Raymond was laid out by half a dozen solid blows to the body before he could retaliate. Brian turned on his heels and walked away without a word.

Raymond never admitted defeat in a fight. His never-say-die spirit against all odds was what Rom's reputation was founded on at Slevin Grammar School, but he'd never faced anyone with the speed and skill of Brian. He'd been incapacitated in a flash. As he lay winded on the lawn and Bernard wailed, Raymond knew that by the time he got his breath back and could get back on his feet, it would be too late to retaliate. He'd been well beaten. He'd enjoyed humiliating Brian with his quick feet, but Brian had turned the tables on him with even faster hands.

It was embarrassment rather than pain that Raymond felt. He got to his feet and made his way across the lawn, waving away Nigel who tried to support him. The girls were gone from the steps, except for Wendy, who looked at him with sorrowful eyes.

'That wasn't fair,' she murmured. 'He's just a big bully.'

That night, before bed, Brian attempted to cut through the air of tension when they were alone in the dormitory.

'I didn't *want* to do that,' he said, while Raymond tried to ignore him by looking for some imaginary object in his top drawer. 'You of all people know you can't raise your fists to me and get away with it. I didn't hit you anymore than I had to, but I had to make sure you stayed down because I know you never give up.'

Brain stood over him as if waiting for a response, but Raymond continued to ignore him. Raymond wanted to turn around, but his pride wouldn't let him. At the same time, he recognised that this was the first acknowledgement by Brian of their previous history. He'd even made it sound like a compliment, but Raymond was still smarting from his defeat and wasn't ready to accept an olive branch yet.

'Please yourself,' Brian said and left the room.

Raymond wasn't appeased either when Shirley told him,

during her smoke break, that she'd seen Auntie Sheila watching his humiliation and smiling to herself. When his house-mother then allowed Brian to go to the youth club, a privilege Raymond hadn't managed to earn from her in months, Raymond's sense of injustice was complete. According to Shirley, Brian almost got into a fight with Tommy Carter over Monica at the club and, although it didn't come to blows, Brian won the right to take Monica down into the unlit bowels of the club for the evening.

*

Raymond steered clear of Brian for the next few weeks and made sure he always had a book to read if they were both in the same room. It didn't stop him observing, though, that Brian adopted a different attitude with the girls than he did with the boys. The youth with the simmering animosity disappeared to be replaced by a lad Raymond remembered from long ago. He was the lovable rogue to all the girls except Shirley, who seemed to have adopted the same stance as Raymond.

'I'm not sucking up to him like the rest of the lasses,' she told Raymond in the yard. 'He's going through them like a dose of salts at the club and they're lapping it up. And, have you noticed? He's even got Auntie Sheila at it. She acts like a big girl when he's around. It's enough to make you throw up.'

At that moment, Raymond was only half listening. Something else was on his mind. He'd been to see his mother that afternoon with Mrs Eaton and come away with something precious.

The visit itself was no different to the previous ones, but as they were leaving, Mrs Eaton surprised him by suggesting they should go to the hospital canteen for a cup of tea. In the canteen, she bought cups of sweet tea and crumbly scones and they sat at a small table. Raymond, eating his scone quickly before it collapsed in his hand, watched as she fumbled in her shopping bag.

'I've brought something for you,' she said, withdrawing a worn and ragged brown envelope and pushing it across the table towards him. 'I think these are rightfully yours. I don't know why I kept them. Guilt, I suppose. I liked your mother, Raymond, and your grandma. I'm sorry things turned out the way they did and I'm sorry your mum got hurt. Go on. Open it.'

Intrigued, Raymond opened the unsealed flap of the envelope and withdrew a sheaf of old and yellowed newspaper cuttings. Amongst them was a glossy black and white photograph that Mrs Eaton reached out for and tilted upright so they could both see it. It was a picture of two happy, smiling, young women on a seafront somewhere, wearing floral dresses and broad belts around their slim waists. The myriad cracks in the photograph couldn't hide their obvious happiness.

'Blackpool,' Mrs Eaton said in a faraway voice. 'That's me and your mum when we had some happy times. She loved that trip to Blackpool. We went on a charabanc for the day. I'd never seen her so happy and she was so pretty when she laughed and smiled.'

Raymond couldn't stop looking at the photo. His mother was pretty; open-mouthed and laughing; one foot half-turned in coquettish but natural fashion; eyes sparkling; almost irreconcilable with the lumpish, grape-eating robot he'd just seen; almost, but not quite. And it was the 'not quite' that fascinated him.

'The rest are newspaper cuttings,' Mrs Eaton said. 'I kept everything about you in the papers during that awful time. So many people were interested in you. You caused quite a stir. Maybe they'll remind you that you have so much to live for. In any case, they're your history and you should have them.'

Then she was in a hurry, gulping down her tea as if she'd a train to catch and slipping a ten shilling note across the table to him. Mumbling something about her husband and the next time, she rose and took her leave while Raymond continued to stare at the photograph. He was in no hurry. So, he'd be punished if he got home late. So what?

The remainder of his tea grew cold in the cup, as he studied the newspaper cuttings and was transported to the time of Miracle Boy. In all the cuttings, 'tragic' was the most over-used word; the incident was 'tragic'; his mother was 'tragic', although she was often also referred to as deranged; and, of course, he was 'tragic'. There was also speculation about the cause of the incident; interviews with neighbours; some sketchy background on his mother and grandmother; and brief reports on his progress. There was short article on the driver who'd died; an old man who'd died of a heart attack when a baby fell from the sky.

Something in one of the bulletins caught Raymond's eye. This was a photograph of a nurse surrounded by flowers. It was Sister Goode. Now he knew why she'd called him Miracle Boy so long ago and why she always took an interest in his welfare.

*

'He'll get his comeuppance,' Shirley was saying. 'He's too cocky by half, but I've seen the way Uncle Andrew looks at him.'

'What do you mean?' Raymond asked, interested enough to put his daydream to one side for a moment. He could look at his new treasures again later when he was on his own.

'Auntie Sheila was giggling like a schoolgirl at something Brian said,' Shirley explained. 'I saw the way Uncle Andrew was looking at Brian, like he had murder in mind or summat.'

'Brian wants to be careful, then,' Raymond observed, wincing at his own recent memory of his house-father's vengeance.

'It'll be his own fault,' Shirley said, nicking her cigarette out and stuffing the docker up the sleeve of her cardigan.

*

Uncle Andrew, in turns dour, violent and libidinous, was sometimes capable of surprising the inmates by being unnervingly playful, especially when it involved somehow getting his hands on the girls. The sun was shining outside, but Raymond was happy reading a book in the playroom. The other inmates were sitting around talking to each other in low voices and Elsie was sitting on the windowsill singing softly. Despite her lisp, she had a pleasant singing voice and her chosen song was 'A World Without Love' by Peter and Gordon, the current number one in the pop charts.

> *Pleath lock me away*
> *And don't allow the day*
> *Here inthide*
> *Where I'll hide*
> *With my lonelineth*

'Come on you lot,' Uncle Andrew cried, bursting into the room. 'You shouldn't be stuck inside on a day like today. Come on, everybody out onto the lawn. We're going to have a game of cricket.'

The new intake of books in the bookcase didn't have many gems, but Raymond's latest discovery, *The Grapes of Wrath* by John Steinbeck, was one of them and he was reluctant to put it down. Uncle Andrew's manic grin, however, didn't hide the fact that the summons to play was an order. Raymond had no choice but to join the group of unenthusiastic players as they trooped outside.

It soon became apparent to Raymond that the only reason Uncle Andrew wanted to play cricket was not for the health and well-being of his charges, but so he could get a bat in his hands. With willow in hand, he was hard to dislodge from the crease. Various people had a go at bowling at him, including one or two of the girls, but he stroked the ball around the lawn with accompanying cries of self-admiration, while the nearest inmate scampered after it.

Brian then picked up the ball to bowl. Raymond swapped places with Callum behind the wicket and got a perfect view of what happened next. Firstly, Brian walked back to measure out an exaggerated run-up, which meant crossing the driveway to the patch of lawn on the other side.

'Oho! We've got a Freddie Trueman,' Uncle Andrew cried. 'Come on, then, let's see what you can do.'

Brian started his run with stuttering steps before breaking into a fast stride. Approaching the bowler's wicket, he seemed to leap high in the air, while his ball-carrying arm swung over in a straight arc and released the ball, which thudded into the ground in front of Uncle Andrew's flailing bat before scattering his wickets.

'Owzat!' Brian yelled.

Monica clapped and squealed.

'I wasn't ready,' Uncle Andrew called out in embarrassment, giving Monica a hard stare. 'You are supposed to make sure I'm ready before you bowl.'

He turned and began to hammer the wickets back into the ground, as Brian stood staring at his back with his hands on his hips. Raymond retrieved the ball and rolled it back to Brian, who picked it up and turned to march back to the end of his run-up. Raymond crouched and watched as Brian held the red ball aloft and called out, 'Ready?'

'Get on with it!' Uncle Andrew snorted, while tensing himself and tapping the ground with his bat.

Raymond thought Brian's approach to the wicket was even faster than before. Although the ball was a blur, it was obvious that it was wide of the wicket as it thumped into the ground and Uncle Andrew stepped back to strike the ball with the full blade of his bat. It would've been a stylish shot, except the ball broke viciously on contact with the ground and veered into the wicket of the startled batsman.

'Owzat!' Brian roared.

This time nobody was foolish enough to applaud.

'You overstepped the crease,' a red-faced Uncle Andrew protested. 'That was a no-ball. If you are going to play, then play by the rules. Bowl again, and this time from the right length.'

The glances and raised eyebrows accompanying the unnatural silence were missed by the now not-so-playful patriarch of Backville Manor, as he prepared himself to face Brian. What happened next defied the laws of physics so far as Raymond was concerned. Brian seemed to run up even faster and everything suggested that the ball was going to be propelled at high speed, but somehow he managed to make it travel much slower than the previous two deliveries. Completely fooled, Uncle Andrew swept the bat so early it was almost over his shoulder by the time the ball hit the wicket. It was such an impossible trick that Raymond, who'd adjusted himself to try and stop a hurtling missile, was dumped on his backside.

'Owzat!' Brian cried.

Uncle Andrew reacted like a spoilt child by throwing his bat down on the ground and stomping into the house with his arms folded across his chest. The slam of the front door was still resounding as the girls gathered around Brian.

'Flipping heck, Brian,' Monica said. 'You've upset him now. How did you learn to bowl like that?'

'Me Uncle Tony was fast bowler for Nethersfield for

311

years,' Brian said. 'He says I could be better than him if I wanted, but I can't be bothered with it.'

Nobody had any interest in continuing the game once their house-father retired, so they all filtered back into the house. Raymond was more than happy to get back to his book and soon became absorbed in it, while around him the girls feted Brian for his prowess.

Later, in the kitchen, Raymond was helping with preparations for tea, while Monica regaled Shirley, who hadn't been at the cricket game, with the tale of Brian's hat-trick against their house-father. Brian clearly felt the need to issue a disclaimer.

'Uncle Andrew's not really that good,' he said. 'He's just a bighead who likes to pretend he's good with people who can't play. He's pretty rubbish really.'

Raymond was counting knives and forks to lay out for tea while this conversation went on and seemed to be the only one who saw the tense and brooding figure of Uncle Andrew in the doorway. What followed was familiar to Raymond. Uncle Andrew struck a heavy blow to the side of Brian's head.

Uncle Andrew may have had the element of surprise, but after that Brian did his best to retaliate. The other occupants of the room were scattered and chairs were overturned as the battle ensued, in which, despite Brian's youth and strength, the thickset and swarthy Uncle Andrew had a slight edge. Plates shattered, boys gasped and girls cried out before a kind of stalemate was reached with a snarling Uncle Andrew holding a bloodied Brian by the throat against the wall, while Brian gripped a twisted handful of his house-father's shirt in his fist. Who knows what might have happened were it not for the intervention of Auntie Sheila? Her cold voice rang out through the kitchen and it was impossible to know whether she was talking to her husband, Brian, or both.

'That's enough!' she ordered. 'Stop right now!'

Both man and boy looked sheepish as they let go of each other.

'Brian Walker, go and get cleaned up,' she commanded. 'The rest of you stop gawping and get on with your chores.'

She didn't say a word to Uncle Andrew, but Raymond was sure her eyes did, because he followed her meekly from the kitchen after Brian had gone. As things returned to some semblance of normality, Raymond couldn't help but reflect on the irony of Brian getting his bruises because of his superiority in sport, just as he had at Brian's hands. He didn't feel like gloating though. There was only ever one side he could be on.

*

Raymond was the first to find out that Uncle Andrew had seized on the first opportunity to vent any frustration he might still be feeling. Going to bed early, so he could read a while before the others came up, Raymond saw Derek lying face down on his bed fully clothed. He looked dead.

'Derek, are you all right, mate?' Raymond queried.

Derek rolled over onto his back. Raymond saw his bloodied, swollen face and knew it could only mean one thing.

'Uncle Andrew?'

'Yeah,' Derek said.

'Why?'

'He caught me and Mary McCluskey in the spare bed-room,' Derek said, wincing every time he moved his jaw.

The spare bedroom was at the end of the corridor and was sometimes used as a sick room. Even though Mary was regarded as the leper of the colony by most of the other inmates, especially the girls, Raymond wasn't surprised by this revelation. He remembered seeing Derek wink at Mary on the only night Raymond was allowed to go to the youth club.

'Do you need a hand getting ready for bed?' Raymond asked.

'No thanks, I'll manage,' Derek said.

Derek was in bed when the other boys came up to the dormitory. From their whispered conversation Raymond knew they'd heard about the beating. The word was that Mary took such fierce blows to the stomach that she couldn't stand or walk. The girls had put their animosity to one side and were helping her.

Bernard came up to him, as he often did, and held out his big hand.

'Picture, Raymond?' the man-child asked.

Raymond gave Bernard his mystery picture and went to the toilet. When he returned, Brian was studying the picture, while Bernard looked on, distressed.

'Every picture tells a story, eh, Raymond,' Brian said, handing the picture back to a relieved Bernard. 'We need to talk. Not here. Tomorrow in the yard.'

The House of Pain

'Who'd have thought it?' Shirley asked, as Raymond polished the shoes he was more familiar with than his own fingers and toes. 'They both kept that quiet, didn't they? I always wondered why Derek wouldn't look at the other girls when they all fancied him. He's a right dark horse, that one.'

Raymond was about to reply, when Brian appeared in the washroom doorway.

'I need to talk to Raymond in private,' he said to Shirley with a look in his eyes that said 'scarper'.

Shirley looked resentful, but she stubbed her cigarette out against the wall and went back inside with an exaggerated sway of her hips. Brian's eyes followed her, before he turned to Raymond and said, 'She hasn't changed much since Hillcrest.'

Raymond decided not to respond, as he watched Brian pull out a cigarette from the pocket of his jeans and tap the end against the back of his hand, before placing it between his lips. Then he withdrew a single match from the same pocket and struck it against the wall with a flourish and applied it to the cigarette.

'I've been hearing a lot since I got here,' he said, shaking the match until it went out, 'Monica told me what you did with those bangers. Nice trick.'

He flicked the match away, took a long drag of his cigarette, and leaned against the wall.

'That picture you let daft Bernard look at, it's about Hillcrest, isn't it?' he said.

'What of it?' Raymond replied, feeling wary.

'That lad who killed himself,' Brian said. 'What was his name again?'

'Squeaky Dave,' Raymond said, wondering where the conversation was going to lead.

'Yeah, that was it,' Brian said, pulling at his cigarette. 'Sad little bugger. Do you remember when we found him? You fell on your arse in a puddle.'

Why would you smile at such a terrible memory? Raymond knew it was in complete contrast to everything he felt about it and yet that is just what he did.

'We drove Uncle Richard crackers, didn't we?' Brian said, taking Raymond's smile and turning it into a grin. 'We paid the price, like, but we got him, didn't we?'

'Why didn't you tell me what was really going on?' Raymond asked, encouraged by Brian's levity. 'You know, about Uncle Richard and the girls.'

'Because they didn't want anybody to know,' Brian said. 'They thought people would blame them.'

'Why don't you talk to Shirley now, then?' Raymond pressed.

Brian studied him and dropped his cigarette butt between his feet. His jaw stiffened and Raymond feared he'd taken a step too far and spoiled this reunion.

'I don't paint pictures about the past,' Brian said after a pause. 'I'm not like you, Raymond, or Shirley. The past is summat I'd rather leave behind. You can see it in Shirley. She's dragging it around like a ball and chain. I'd rather not go there. All I'm interested in is the here and now, which is why I wanted to talk to you. To be honest, I thought you'd turned out as soft as the rest until I heard about how you'd put the wind up Auntie Sheila and Sarah. I should've known better. You always had guts.'

Raymond kept quiet.

'Look,' Brian said. 'I know I've been a bit of a twat, but I need you to help me out. What do you say?'

'What do you want *me* to do?' Raymond asked, intrigued and flattered.

At that moment, Monica slipped out through the washroom door and smiled at Brian.

'We're talking,' Brian said to her with narrowed eyes and Monica backed into the washroom with a frown.

Brian waited a moment until he was sure she was out of earshot and then said, 'This place is a shithole. Uncle Andrew is on the rampage with the lasses as well as the lads and that bitch, Auntie Sheila, has got everybody running scared and telling tales on each other. We've got to do summat about it.'

'In what way?' Raymond asked, feeling the thrill of a long-lost comradeship stirring.

'You were always the brains, Raymond,' Brian said, squatting down on his haunches. 'I need you to come up with some way we can sort Uncle Andrew and Auntie Sheila out for good. I know you can do it. If we don't do summat, somebody's gonna get seriously hurt.'

Brian fingered a swollen eyebrow and stared at Raymond.

'I might have an idea,' Raymond ventured.

'Great,' Brian said. 'What is it?'

'Give me time to think it through,' Raymond said.

'All right,' Brian said, rising to his feet, 'but make it good.'

That night, Raymond lay awake for a long time. He couldn't help reminiscing about the times he and Brian were just young lads at Hillcrest under the harsh regime of Uncle Richard. Raymond might have been the brains behind some of their escapades, but Brian was always the driving force. Their adventures seemed childlike now, but Raymond remembered his often-dry mouth and pounding

heart as they crept through the woodland shrub or clambered down a glistening drainpipe on a frosty winter's
night. Everything ended badly, but not for the reasons
Raymond once thought. Unbeknownst to him, they'd put a
stop to the crimes of their then house-father. Could they do
the same again?

The plan Raymond refined in his head over the next
few days owed everything to Miracle Boy and the battered
newspaper clippings that he kept close and pored over
whenever he was alone.

*

It was a Monday morning in mid-May and curtains were
being thrown open in the houses across the road from
Backville Manor. Raymond imagined sleepy eyes looking
across and being greeted with a strange sight. If they
looked, they would see, on the summit of each of the two
large bays flanking the main entrance to Backville Manor, a
figure sitting astride the apex of the roof just behind the
crowning ornate finial. Stretched between the two bays on
the canopy of the roof, and fastened by what were, in fact,
metal tent pegs hooked behind slate tiles, was a large white
banner on which was written in blood-red letters:

THIS IS A
HOUSE OF PAIN

'Do you think they know yet?' Brian called across to
Raymond from his perch above the girls' dormitory.

Raymond looked across at Brian from his own lofty seat
on the other bay. Brian's sandy hair was being lifted at the
front by a slight breeze and his blue eyes were shining. He
looked like he was riding on the prow of a ship into a sea of
adventure. Raymond couldn't let himself get carried away
by the thrill of what they were doing. He knew they were
sailing into the wind.

'It doesn't look like it,' Raymond called, 'but there'll be someone leaving for work before long. After that it'll be the school lot, so somebody will spot us soon.'

Just as the sun was beginning to peek from behind a pile of sleepy clouds, Raymond heard a sound below and, grasping the finial in front of him, he leaned over and looked down. It seemed a long way down to the top of Nigel Normanton's head. Nigel paused, as if distracted by something, before plunging his hands deep into his jacket pockets and setting off down the drive with hunched shoulders.

'Don't work too hard,' Brian called out.

Nigel stopped and looked around puzzled, but he didn't look up. Raymond began laughing in unison with Brian. This time Nigel, who was nearing the gate, did look up. There was no mistaking the look of shock on his face. Raymond waved at him and Nigel responded with a tentative wave of his hand. He seemed rooted to the spot, as if he didn't know whether to go or stay. Finally, with frequent looks over his shoulder, he headed through the gates and disappeared for an instant, before re-emerging from the shadow of the wall to cross the road to the bus stop, where a bus was already waiting.

A similar pattern followed for all those who emerged from the house, but it was telling that no one went back inside to inform their house-parents what was going on. Soon a crowd of schoolboys and girls congregated at the gate and began waving and cheering. Raymond and Brian waved back and hooted and hollered. Suddenly, the crowd fell silent and Uncle Andrew came into view, walking backwards down the lawn and staring upwards. Raymond could see the tendons in his house-father's neck tightening and his face growing redder.

Uncle Andrew turned to the gateway and strode towards it, shooing the young crowd away like a farmer scattering starlings. When the crowd dispersed, he strode back up the drive to the house without looking up. Before long, he reappeared with Auntie Sheila alongside him. Raymond saw the colour drain from her rouged cheeks as their banner came into her view.

'Get down from there at once,' she shouted, sounding almost hysterical. 'Are you trying to make us a laughing stock?'

'What do you think, Raymond?' Brian called out. 'Are we trying to make them a laughing stock?'

'I don't see anything to laugh about, do you?' Raymond called back.

'Get down now, the pair of you,' Uncle Andrew roared, but his voice echoed with impotence.

'What do you think, Raymond?' Brian called out again. 'Shall we get down?'

'No, I don't think so, Brian,' Raymond shouted back. 'I'm quite enjoying it up here.'

'Look, you've made your point,' Auntie Sheila shrilled, clearly struggling to keep the desperation out of her voice. 'If you get down now, it won't go any further. There'll be no punishments.'

'I'm trying to think of something,' Brian said, gripping his finial and leaning over the edge of the roof at a precarious angle. 'It just won't come to me. Oh, yes, here it is – Bugger off!'

'Right,' Auntie Sheila spluttered. 'You've had your chance. You're going to regret this.'

Their house-parents disappeared from view and for the next hour nothing happened, except for people stopping at the gateway to stare up at them. Occasionally, a small group would gather and point at them and talk amongst themselves. Raymond chatted to Brian and sometimes waved at spectators, but all the time he scanned the street for a particular spectator he was banking on arriving.

The morning sun had almost reached its zenith when Raymond's heart leapt. Two men in overcoats began to walk up the driveway. One carried a large flash camera and kept stopping to take photographs of them on the roof, to which Brian responded by waving his arms and kicking his legs. Uncle Andrew came running down the drive gesticulating.

'Stop! Stop!' Raymond heard him cry from his bosun's nest. 'You can't come in here. This is private property. Clear off or I'll call the police.'

As Uncle Andrew remonstrated, the photographer switched his attention to him. Raymond and Brian laughed and catcalled as this charade took place, but, eventually, Uncle Andrew ushered the two men back beyond the gateway and shut the metal gates with a long clang.

Raymond couldn't have been more satisfied. A key part of his plan was accomplished. That morning, someone at the Chronicle would have opened an envelope marked 'Important' and addressed to 'The Editor'. On opening the envelope, they would have found a letter and a newspaper clipping and they would have read the following:

Dear Sir or Madam,

You will see that the enclosed cutting from your newspaper from fifteen years ago is about a baby who miraculously survived being thrown from the upper storey of a house by his mother. At the time, you ran this story for a number of days and it gathered a lot of interest. You called the baby 'Miracle Boy' because of his escape from what could have been a fatal fall.

How would you like to find Miracle Boy again? Don't you think your readers would be interested to know how life turned out for him?

You can find Miracle Boy today on the roof of Backville Manor, which, as you probably know, is a children's home. The reason he is on the roof, along with a fellow inmate, is to protest against the appalling treatment meted out to the inmates of the home, which includes extreme physical violence and sexual harassment. I know you will not print unsubstantiated claims, but I suggest you send a reporter and a photographer to Backville Manor where you will at least get some good pictures to go with the story of Miracle Boy.

    Yours truly

    Miracle Boy

'What if Uncle Andrew tries to get up the back way by the flat roof?' Brian called out.

'What's he going to do?' Raymond called back. 'He can't carry us down. Besides, I don't think he's got a head for heights. We're better off keeping an eye on the front so we can see who arrives.'

'He might call the fire brigade,' Brian yelled.

'Same difference,' Raymond shouted. 'They can't force us down. It's too dangerous.'

He'd thought through most eventualities. Once they were up there, it was too dangerous for anyone to try to get them down against their will. The biggest danger, however, was time. He'd packed sandwiches, biscuits and a bottle of Irn Bru in his school satchel, which was strapped to him. The shopping bag strapped to Brian contained the same provisions. Raymond intended to stay there until at least the following day, which meant that they would have to stay overnight and maybe even snatch some sleep in this precarious position and that was why they were both secured by a rope around the waist fastened to the finial. The outhouses full of junk had provided everything they needed.

Apart from a constant audience by the closed gates, the next few hours passed without anyone coming out of the house. Raymond and Brian nibbled a few biscuits and called to each other from time to time. They were both aware that they were there for the long haul and they conserved their energy by leaning forward and resting their heads on their bags, which they used like pillows to cushion their heads from the ridge tiles. They were wearing layers of clothing to get them through the night-time vigil so, as the day warmed up, they took off their jackets and jumpers, which they added to their cushions. In the warm sun, Raymond dozed with one eye open.

In the middle of the afternoon, Uncle Andrew appeared below them.

'Comfy up there are you, lads?' he called up. 'I hope so, because you can stay up there as long as you like. It should be fun tonight. I hear it might rain. We're having sausages for tea. I hope you've got something to eat. Don't think anyone is going to take you seriously. You've already made fools of yourselves. Most people are stopping to laugh at you. See you later. I'm off in for a cup of tea.'

'Twat!' Brian said, staring towards Raymond with his head resting on his makeshift cushion.

When the time came for those at school to return, Uncle Andrew stationed himself by the gates so he could move on the laughing and jeering sightseers and usher the returning inmates up the drive into the house. All this activity made Raymond realise that his backside was aching and he began to shuffle backwards along the ridge of the bay roof.

'I'm going to have to stretch my legs,' he shouted to Brian. 'I'm stiff as a board.'

'Me too,' Brian replied. 'I'll keep watch here and go after you.'

When Raymond reached the ridge of the main roof he looked back over his shoulder. The flat roof below him was clear. He suddenly imagined it as an exercise yard in a prison. He slithered down and stretched his legs, before tiptoeing over to the edge of the roof and peering over. Below him he saw Monica, who had a crooked parting in her dark hair and a chest he could have eaten his tea off, smoking a cigarette.

'Psst!' he hissed down at her.

Monica looked up, startled.

'Raymond,' she whispered. 'What the heck are you doing there? I thought you were up on the front roof.'

'I'm just stretching my legs,' he said. 'I've got a sore bum from sitting up there all day. So, what did everyone think when they saw us up there?'

'Brilliant,' Monica said, 'but where's it gonna get you? You'll have to come down sometime and then you'll be dead meat.'

'Just wait and see,' Raymond whispered. 'If we can last until tomorrow then all hell is going to break loose.'

'I hope you're right, Raymond,' she said. 'Auntie Sheila is planning a fate worse than death for you and I can't see how you're going to get out of that.'

'What the heck!' Uncle Andrew cried, suddenly appearing around the side of the washroom.

Raymond jumped back and almost stumbled. He could hear the sound of his house-father's raised voice and what sounded like slaps, as he scurried back across the roof and scrambled up the tiles.

'All right?' Brian called out as Raymond appeared at the apex of the roof.

'Uncle Andrew saw me,' Raymond said as he shuffled back along the bay roof to the front of the house.

Brian began to crab his way back along the ridge of his bay.

'Don't you think you'd better wait a bit,' Raymond cautioned. 'He might climb up.'

'I'd like to see him try,' Brian laughed. 'In fact, I'd just love it.'

Brian disappeared over the ridge of the roof. It didn't seem too long before he was back. Instead of going to his own bay, he shuffled down the front of the roof until he was half-sitting just below Raymond with his feet in the gutter. It looked a precarious position to Raymond, but Brian seemed unconcerned. Twilight was drawing in and there was no longer an audience, except for the odd person who looked up in passing. Brian lit a cigarette and blew a plume of smoke over the edge of the roof.

'Are you sure about this, Raymond?' he asked, looking up.

Looking down, Raymond realised that, for the first time since Brian came to Backville Manor, their roles were reversed. Brian was looking up to him.

'This'll be all over the newspaper tomorrow,' Raymond reassured him, while praying he was right. 'Then the whole world will take notice.'

'Yeah,' Brian said, 'but will the whole world care?'

'The point is,' Raymond explained, not for the first time, 'the Welfare won't be able to sweep things under the carpet. They'll have to be seen to do something. That's the power of the press. They won't just leave things alone. There's a story and they'll have to give their readers an ending.'

'I hope you're right, Raymond,' Brian said. 'If we don't pull this off we'll be right in it. Still,' he said, flicking his cigarette far into the cooling evening air, 'we've been there before, haven't we?'

The World at the Gate

Raymond watched Brian climb back onto his perch and tie himself to the finial. The night was drawing in and lights were coming on in the windows of the houses spread out before them. Raymond was mentally preparing himself for an arduous night and neither of them spoke for a long time.

Out of the blue, Raymond heard the window below Brian being opened and when he leaned out and looked across, a head appeared. The tousled blonde curls were Shirley's and in the light spilling out of the window, her eyes were as blue as the Mediterranean sky in a painting Raymond had once seen.

'Can you hear me?' she called out.

'Yes,' Brian called back.

'Have you got a rope you can lower down?' Shirley asked. 'We've all saved you a sausage and we've got some bread for you.'

'Yeah, I've got a rope,' Brian said, untying the rope from around his waist. 'Hang on a mo.'

'Hi, Raymond,' Shirley called. 'Are you all right?'

'Yeah,' Raymond shouted in reply.

'Good,' she said, catching hold of the end of the rope Brian lowered down to her.

In no time at all, she tied the rope around the handle of a shiny beige handbag and called out to Brian to haul it up.

'Night,' she trilled and closed the window.

'I think you'd better come to mine this time if you want your supper,' Brian said and laughed.

Raymond crabbed his way over to Brian's bay roof and shuffled his way along so he was sitting behind him. In the gathering gloom they enjoyed a supper of cold sausage sandwiches, warmed by the support of the people below them. This raised their spirits so much that they sat like this for a long time picking out what they could see of the neighbourhood, like two tourists at the top of Blackpool Tower. Eventually, many of the lights in the windows of houses were turned off and Raymond said it was time for him to get home to bed, which made them both laugh out loud.

Was it hollow laughter? Raymond didn't think so, but he was nervous.

A few minutes after Raymond attached himself back to his station, Uncle Andrew appeared on the edge of the lawn down below them. He didn't look up, but in his hand he held a mug from which steam was rising into the night air. Still without looking up, he kept taking noisy slurps from his mug and releasing a large sigh every time he did so. Eventually, he threw the last hot dregs onto the grass and turned round to head back inside. Just before he disappeared from view, Raymond heard his voice float upwards.

'Goodnight, lads. Sleep well.'

'Get stuffed!' Brian shouted.

Raymond spent the longest night of his life on that roof. Sometimes he dozed, but always with one eye open. At one point, the breeze sprang up and their banner, which was really an old bed sheet, began to flap as the wind got underneath it. A couple of times, they had to scramble in the dark to reattach the metal pegs holding the sheet down to the tiles. Sometimes, Raymond climbed down to the flat roof and walked around and twice he urinated over the edge into the black void. He looked at his watch often as the hours crawled by.

What would Mrs Noble say if she could see him now? Would she be appalled or would she support him? He hoped it was the latter. What would Auntie Dawn and Uncle Gordon think if they knew? Thankfully, they were in faraway Australia and would never know. He could be there with them now if it wasn't for the curse that seemed to follow him around. Is this what Miracle Boy had been saved for?

Brian was equally restless throughout the night and sometimes they met on the flat roof, where Brian frequently speculated about whether they could climb down and find a way into the house for a cup of tea and a kip in an armchair in the playroom. It was a tempting thought, but Raymond convinced him that it would be far too dangerous.

Eventually, the dawn began to break and they clambered, stiff-limbed, back up to their perches to await the day that Raymond hoped would deliver everything he'd planned for.

The sun came up and an exhausted Raymond was dozing on his leather pillow when he heard an urgent voice from below. The bedroom window below Brian was open and Shirley was leaning out and looking up. Brian's head was down in front of him. Raymond called to him as loud as he dare without endangering Shirley and Brian's bleary-eyed face turned to him. Raymond gestured for him to look down.

'Pass the bag down on the rope,' Shirley hissed.

Brian fastened the handbag to his rope and lowered it down to Shirley, who drew it inside to fill it and then waved for Brian to raise it again, which he did. Shirley gave a final wave and disappeared. Raymond couldn't help thinking about Shirley's breasts. Seeing her leaning out in her nightie confirmed what Raymond had always thought; she had the most perfect breasts of all the girls.

It was a stupid thought. She didn't like boys and, besides, he might not live much longer anyway.

Brian opened the handbag and withdrew a tartan thermos flask, which he waved in the air. Raymond made his way across to sit behind him and enjoy a breakfast of hot, sweet tea and marmalade sandwiches. It was the most revitalising breakfast Raymond had ever tasted. He was ready for another day on the roof of Backville Manor.

Sometime later, Uncle Andrew herded the school contingent towards the gates, where a small crowd of boys and girls were already gathered. Uncle Andrew dispersed them and sent the Backville Manor group on their way. When he walked back up the drive, he kept looking up at Raymond and Brian and shaking his head. Brian called out to him.

'It didn't rain last night, then. It was fine up here. I slept like a log.'

Their glowering house-father ignored the jibes and disappeared.

Raymond knew they were burning their boats and hoped everything would work out. If they fell back into Uncle Andrew's hands, he would flay them alive before handing them over to Auntie Sheila's imaginative ministrations. Today had to be the day.

But for hours nothing happened, except the sun shone down on them and occasional passers-by stopped by the gates to look up at them. Brian began to get impatient.

'Flipping heck, Raymond,' he called out. 'Where's this world that's supposed to care?'

'Hang on,' Raymond said, crossing his fingers. 'They'll be here.'

Then, in a wonderful rush, the world woke up to their plight. It began with a black car pulling up to the gates and a man in a sombre suit getting out. As the man opened the gates, Raymond saw that it was Mr Pickup. The corporation driver got back in the car and drove up to the front of the house. Both Raymond and Brian grabbed their finials and leaned as far over the edge of the roof as possible. Mr

Pickup stepped out of the car, opened the rear door and Minnie Meakin stepped out and swept past him into the house.

Mr Pickup remained standing by the car and looked up. Raymond caught his eye, but the driver's face remained impassive. His movements seemed elaborate, as if he wanted them to keep their eyes on him, which they did, as he reached into the inside pocket of his dark suit jacket. Withdrawing a newspaper, he unfolded it and placed it on the roof of his car, as if he going to read it. From where he was, directly above the driver, Raymond could see that the front page had a picture of Backville Manor with two figures perched on the roof on each side of a large banner. The headline proclaimed, 'Miracle Boy and the House of Pain'.

'Front page news!' Raymond called out to Brian and his confederate whooped.

After that, a crowd began to gather at the gate, not of passers-by, but of people who seemed to have arrived with a purpose. Then, the reporter and cameraman, who'd been there the day before, appeared on the lawn. Raymond realised that they must have scaled the wall at the side of the house. Mr Pickup watched them without moving as they approached the house. While the cameraman took photographs, the reporter called up.

'Which one of you is Raymond Rawnsley?'

'It's him,' Brian shouted, pointing to Raymond.

'How are you, Raymond?' the reporter queried as the photographer snapped.

Before Raymond could reply, Uncle Andrew came into view and began to usher the two men away. As he pushed them out through the gate, a woman in a long dark coat forced her way in and began to stride up the drive. It was Mrs Eaton. Uncle Andrew ran after her and began to remonstrate with her, while Raymond could hear her insisting that she was a relative of his and had a right to see him.

His house-father tried to turn her around towards the gate, but she broke away again and shouted up to Raymond.

'Raymond, are you all right? I won't let them do anything to you. They'll have me to answer to.'

Uncle Andrew put an arm around her shoulder and steered her back down the drive.

'Who's that?' Brian asked.

'My Auntie Elizabeth,' Raymond replied.

Everything seemed to be happening at once. The reporter and cameraman, who'd been ejected, were working their way around to the side of the garden again. Another cameraman appeared on the pavement on the opposite side of the road and trained his camera onto the roof of Backville Manor. Brian raised himself up and began to wave his arms about and shout at the top of his voice.

Raymond was more interested in studying the gathering crowd. His aunt was still clinging to the bars of the gates and staring in earnest at him, while there seemed to be a lot of middle-aged women talking amongst themselves as if debating something. Many people were carrying newspapers and waving them about. People passing by were not just joining the crowd, but also joining the debate. Cars and vans were pulling up at the roadside. More cameramen appeared. Then two policemen arrived, but rather than move people on, they also seemed to join the discussion. Raymond was fascinated and Brian was exuberant.

'Woo hoo, Raymond!' Brian cried. 'The world is flocking here, boy. We're gonna be famous. They won't dare touch us now.'

After a while, a large red van drew up at the gates with its indicator blinking. The two bobbies cleared a way and the van sped up the drive and disappeared into the yard at the side of the house. Raymond made a mental note to check the back roof in a while. He was distracted, however, by the fact that boys and girls on their way from school began to be attracted to the crowd like moths to a flame. He noticed the Backville schoolgirls mingling with the crowd rather than entering the grounds. Monica, in particular, was enjoying holding court amongst a group of ladies, and two reporters and cameramen began to show an interest in what she was saying. Raymond smiled as Monica opened another button on her blouse and puffed out her chest.

'Raymond, look out!' Brian shouted in desperation.

Raymond turned around to see Mr Leather crouching on the ridge of the main roof.

'Raymond,' Mr Leather said, 'we meet again.'

As he spoke, he worked his way towards Raymond until he was balancing astride the ridge of the bay roof. He wasn't sitting, like Raymond, but half-standing with his hands on the ridge in front of him and his feet moulded to the tiled slopes on either side. The ginger-haired menace, dressed in dark trousers, braces, a grey open-necked shirt with rolled-up sleeves and soft black shoes, revealed that he possessed the aerial poise of a steeplejack.

'Don't be nervous,' he said to Raymond. 'I'm going to come and get you. Just stay exactly as you are.'

'Get away,' Raymond cried. 'Don't come near me or I'll jump.'

Raymond eased the rope down from his waist and over one leg, so he could spin around on his rump on the ridge and face his unwanted rescuer.

'No you won't,' Mr Leather said. 'Nobody ever does in your situation. I'm calling your bluff, Raymond.'

He leaned forward and gripped the ridge further on and then hopped forward like a frog. Raymond could see that with one more spring, Mr Leather would be close enough to grab hold of him. It called for desperate measures. He put one hand on the ridge in front of him and gripped the finial behind him with the other. Then he concentrated all his strength in his arms and pulled his feet up towards the ridge so he was crouching like the reptile in front of him. They must have looked like two animals poised to charge each other, he thought, as the clamour of the crowd below was stilled into silence.

'Now, don't be stupid, Raymond,' Mr Leather hissed between clenched teeth and without further warning launched himself forward.

Raymond rose up on his haunches to meet him, intending to parry his attempt to grab him. The collective, blood-curdling shriek from so many throats shocked him. What were they screaming for? Then he understood. He was falling backwards through the air.

No Words

'Hello, Raymond,' Sister Goode said. 'That's quite a dream you were having. Who's Barin?'

Raymond ignored her question. It would be too difficult to explain that Barin, a hero in the world of Raymond's imagination, was Brian. He blinked and tried to get his bearings.

'Do you know where you are?' she asked.

Raymond looked around. It was obvious that he was in hospital and he seemed to be in a small ward on his own.

'In hospital,' he said, licking his lips, which felt dry. 'How long have I been asleep?'

'On and off for quite a while,' Sister Goode said, lifting a plastic vessel with a spout to his lips without having to be asked.

Raymond took a long draught of cool water.

'Now just think,' Sister Goode admonished, 'if you'd told me how you got that broken nose the last time I saw you, you might not be back here today.'

'What happened?' he asked.

'Don't you remember?' she said, smoothing his pillow and overwhelming him with the smell of perfume and disinfectant. 'You fell off the roof of Backville Manor. Amazingly, you had a rope wrapped around your ankle that was fastened to the thingamajig on the roof, so you didn't fall all the way. Before you start congratulating yourself, you should know you've dislocated your ankle and torn ligaments in your leg. You've also got eleven stitches in the back of your head. You're in all the papers. It's Miracle Boy all over again. To be honest, Raymond, if I were you I'd try and find some other way to be well-known. If you try this stunt one more time it might be third time lucky for the Grim Reaper. Now, that's enough talk for the moment. Get some rest.'

She made sure he was comfortable and left the room, easing the door closed behind her.

Raymond gazed around him. The curtains at the window were closed and the room was peaceful in the half-darkness. There was a dull ache in his head, but not enough to stop him collecting his thoughts. Would you believe it? The rope he'd used to secure himself to the roof saved him from a much worse fate. He was glad he'd thought of that in his planning. The last thing he remembered was Mr Leather lunging at him. He could remember the falling part but not what happened after that. What happened to Brian? Was he still up on the roof? How long had he been here?

Over the next three days, he received enough visitors to fill in the gaps for him.

*

His first visitor was Mrs Eaton. Or should that be Auntie Elizabeth? Her excitability was out of character with the woman he'd visited his mother with.

'Oh, Raymond,' she twittered, 'when you were up on that roof, I had the jitters the whole time. I just knew you were going to fall. And when you did! Oh, my, I nearly had a heart attack. I hope I never see anything like that again. I've spoken to the Welfare and demanded to know what they intend to do with you. At first, they said they were thinking of moving you to another Authority, but I put my foot down. They're not moving you away and passing you onto somebody else. Oh, no! I gave them a piece of my mind. I told them. They've got to put their own house in order, not sweep things under the carpet.'

Even though she paused, Raymond decided not to interrupt.

'You know, after everything that's happened, I would have you come and live with me, but my husband, bless him, won't have it. He puts his own daughters first. Still, those awful people have been dismissed from Backville Manor. Gone! Just like that! At least the Welfare have got something right, although I suspect they were under pressure from everything being made public by the Chronicle. I wonder how the paper got to know you were their Miracle Boy. Still, it made a difference, didn't it? They're very clever these newspapers. Things will be better now at Backville Manor, you'll see, and I'll keep visiting you to make sure they are. You might even like it and not want to leave.'

She didn't say this all in one go, but it felt to Raymond as though she had. She left him with a bag of grapes, most of which she'd destalked while talking, and the last two days' copies of the *Chronicle*. Raymond found he didn't want to read about himself, at least not as Miracle Boy. Resurrecting Miracle Boy was just a device: a means to get all eyes focused on Backville Manor. It worked, but now he would prefer anonymity.

The next time Sister Goode called in to see him, she saw the papers and asked, 'Have you read these?'

'No,' he replied.

'Do you want to?' she pressed.

'No,' he affirmed.

'Good,' she said, 'I'll bin them, then.'

His next visitor was Minnie Meakin, the Head of the Welfare Department.

'You are a very resourceful young man, Raymond Rawnsley,' was her opening statement.

It was said, almost but not quite, as a compliment. She

displayed no rancour at the obvious embarrassment caused to her department, although she advised against talking to strangers about recent events. She stayed only a short while, during which she confirmed that after much deliberation it was decided that he would return to Backville Manor, where there were new house-parents. When he asked her about Brian, he was sure she seemed to wince when she confirmed that he would remain there as well. Raymond was pleased about that.

Apart from his first day visitors, Raymond received gifts of flowers and fruit from well-wishers, which arrived in such a steady stream that he asked Sister Goode to divert them to others who might benefit from them. It was embarrassing.

*

Raymond's visitor on the second day took him completely by surprise. It was Dr Charlerousse.

'I am not here in a professional capacity,' she declared, 'although I must admit to a certain curiosity not unconnected with my work. You can forgive me for that, no?'

She seemed to be wearing the same purple knitted suit and cream blouse with flounces at the front she'd always worn during their sessions at Lawson Court, and was as reassuring in her manner as he remembered so well. Of course he could forgive her. He expected it of her; he doubted whether there was any distinction between her private life and her work.

'Firstly,' she said, leaning forward in her chair. 'I have brought something for you. I remember you reading *The Magic Mountain*, which I'm still not sure I would recommend to any young man. However, if that is your cup of tea …' – She peered over her spectacles and added, 'Cup of tea, no?' as if questioning her English – 'I am sure you will like this.'

She handed Raymond a book. He looked at the cover. It

was entitled *Steppenwolf* and was by an author called Hermann Hesse.

'He is Swiss,' she said. 'Well, nearly; we don't talk about the German half. It is a book about the duality of nature. I think you will find it interesting, no? No matter – enjoy.'

'Thank you,' Raymond said.

'I came for a reason,' she admitted. 'I feel as though I failed you.'

'No, you didn't,' Raymond remonstrated. 'Manorholme was the best place and the people there were really good to me.'

'I know,' she said. 'I knew it would be, but it is not *that* I am referring to. I promised to tell you the truth and I kept an important part of it from you. I thought you weren't ready to learn about Miracle Boy. How did you find out? You must tell me everything, no? Well, at least what you want to tell me.'

Raymond gave her an accurate account of how he'd found out about Miracle Boy, starting with the bitter remark by Auntie Sheila through to his discovery of his aunt and her revelations about his past. Then, with subtle prompting, the astute doctor got from him a fair summation of the events at Backville Manor leading to their rooftop protest, which she interspersed with many exasperated cries.

'Ach, Raymond,' she said. 'You exposed a cancer. Unfortunately, it is a disease that can sometimes infect our institutions. It is foolish to imagine it cannot happen, but there are many who would prefer to ignore it. I apologise to you, Raymond. I made a bad judgement. I thought you were too young to know the full truth about your mother and what happened to you. I should have known that a boy who walks around with Thomas Mann under his arm is ready for anything.'

They both laughed.

'And so,' she said, 'if I were to look at your iconographic painting now, what new thing would I find?'

'Nothing,' Raymond said, grinning. 'I've done with that. The only thing I could add is a rope and that's already there.'

'Of course,' she said, rising. 'This time, though, it did good, didn't it?'

*

The third day brought the biggest surprise of all. The visitor who walked in brought a light into the room that couldn't be measured in watts. When she first entered, Raymond wasn't sure if it really was her. She was so much a woman and a very beautiful one in his eyes. Raymond was tongue-tied.

'Hello, Raymond,' Carol Farrell said. 'You look like Ali Baba with that bandage round your head.'

Her fragrance filled the room and her smile radiated unconditional happiness. She approached the bed and took hold of his hand, evoking the warmest memories. Her teasing breath against his cheek and the soft press of her lips made his heart flutter. In the finest circles, she would probably be regarded as tawdry, but to Raymond she was the most natural and appealing woman he'd ever seen.

'I've never read a paper in my life until I saw the picture of you in the paper on the news-stand on my way home from work,' she said, pulling her chair up close to the bed and resting her head on her hand so her face was close to his. 'I was gobsmacked – my reader standing up to the world. I read everything in the paper. I read about what happened to you when you were a baby. It made me cry and cry. Your poor mum. I'm sure she would be so proud of you now. I've told everybody at work you were me mate.'

Raymond interceded.

'I'm still your mate,' he said.

Carol's smile was beyond price.

'I know,' she continued. 'You'll always be my friend. Forever and ever. I'll never forget you reading that book to me. I've still got it, but I can't read it meself. I've tried, but it doesn't sound the same. When I was reading about you, about Miracle Boy, in the paper, it suddenly seemed like you were reading it; like you were reading your own story. Does that sound stupid?'

Raymond shook his head. Everything she'd ever said to him made sense.

'I'm working now,' she said, 'and I've got lodgings. Miss Bellamy helped me out a lot. I couldn't go back to me mum and dad's. I'm saving up and when I've got enough brass I'm going to London.'

'You told me that on the first day we met,' Raymond reminded her. 'Remember? You said you'd be walking back to happiness.'

'I don't know about that, Raymond,' she said, as a veil of seriousness fell over her lovely eyes. 'I've got a long way to go yet. I'm a bit frightened really, but Miss Bellamy's got a sister there and she says I can stay with her.'

'Carol,' Raymond said from a well of untapped love somewhere deep within him. 'You're the one person on this earth who deserves everything to work out for them. Wherever you go everybody will love you.'

A slight burst of breath escaped from her lips and she beamed.

'Raymond, you always talk so beautiful,' she gushed. 'One day you're going to write your own book and it's going to knock spots off that magic thingy. I'm so happy to see you. When you left Lawson Court I thought I'd never see you again. I'm going to keep the newspaper pictures, although I don't really like that one of you hanging upside down. Did it hurt?'

'I don't know,' Raymond said. 'I must have had a rush of blood to the head.'

Her laughter chimed around the room and Raymond imagined birds settling on the window ledge outside just to listen. She talked about her job as a mender in a textile mill and about her lodgings and he lay back on his pillow and looked at her. Gone was the fierce backcombing that was her trademark when he first met her. Her soft blonde hair was lustrous and brushed back behind her delicate ears. The freckles were still scattered across the bridge of her nose and high on her cheeks, but they looked as if they were freshly sprinkled every day. Her eyelashes were long and fair and her lips were sensuous without being too full. She didn't need airs and graces to be totally captivating.

'I've got a boyfriend,' she was saying. 'He works in the same mill. He's a nice lad and he treats me proper. I'm not sure what's going to happen when I go to London, though.'

Raymond wasn't in the least bit jealous at this news. In fact, he was glad she had someone to care for her. If ever he was going to write, as Carol suggested, he was going to have to find a way to express the love he felt for her. It wasn't a yearning love; it wasn't a can't-bear-to-be-apart love; it was a love waiting in every space they stepped into together; it was a love fused from memories they shared but never spoke about because they didn't need to. How could you write about that? There were just no words.

'I'm dead jealous,' he said.

The hug she gave him took the mock out of his seriousness.

'He'll never be able to read books and make me feel like you did,' she whispered in his ear.

'That's all right, then,' Raymond said. 'Just make sure he never reads any books. If I see him reading one, I'll poke his eyes out.'

Carol's visit seemed to last the blink of an eye. They

parted with a sweet kiss and a hug and with Carol telling him that, as they didn't know where each of them might be, he could always contact her through Miss Bellamy at Lawson Court.

All Wolf

Raymond practised a few steps around his bed on his crutches. He'd have preferred to do without them, but even though his leg was encased in a plaster cast with a metal heel, it was painful if he put any pressure on it. He was just thankful his head was no longer wrapped in a bandage. He didn't want to look like some kind of returning hero; he was apprehensive enough already about his return to Backville Manor, although he wasn't quite sure why.

'Right, Raymond,' Sister Goode said. 'You're all set. Let's get you to the ambulance. You'll be home in no time.'

She accompanied him to the ambulance bay and, before placing him in the care of the waiting driver, she gave him her special brand of hug: the one where his face was squashed between linen pillows. Then, while he got his breath back, she handed him a piece of paper.

'Promise me one thing, Raymond,' she said. 'If there's ever anything you're unhappy about then ring this number. Don't hesitate. Don't try to be a hero again. Just ring it. Promise?'

'I promise,' Raymond said.

He thought about his promise to Sister Goode in the ambulance, as it wended its way through the town's streets, which were slick with rain beneath a murky, swollen sky. He'd never made a promise to an adult. It was always expected that he would do as he was told. A promise implied choice and he'd never been given that luxury before. It made him feel grown up. After all, he'd be sixteen in a few months, by which time he'd have left school and found a job, or so he hoped.

The gates to Backville Manor were open; the ambulance swept up the drive unhindered and parked outside the front door. When Raymond hobbled out, he paused and looked up at the pinnacle of the cross gable above him. The finial, his anchor, was bent forward at a forty-five degree angle. The front door opened.

'Hopalong Rawnsley returns,' Shirley said with her usual sarcasm.

'Hiya, Shirley,' he grunted while levering himself up the steps on his crutches.

When he entered the hallway, the rotund figure of homely Auntie Maude appeared from the kitchen, wiping her hands on a tea-towel.

'Come into the kitchen, Raymond,' she invited. 'You look like you could do with a cup of tea.'

Raymond clumped his way across the floor and sank onto a chair at the kitchen table. Auntie Maude asked Elsie, who was buttering bread at the table, to turn off the transistor radio, which she did.

'Raymond, it'th tho nithe to thee you back,' Elsie spluttered, spreading more than margarine on the bread.

Others began to drift into the kitchen until everyone, except Brian, was crowded around. Bernard was beaming from ear to ear and kept touching Raymond on the shoulder, and all the girls questioned him at once. When he'd drunk his cup of tea and said all there was to say about his injuries and his stay in hospital, grey-haired Uncle Stanley, looking like someone's faithful old gardener, came in carrying a basket of deformed, overgrown carrots.

'Hello, Raymond,' he said with a passing nod, before addressing his wife. 'There you go, love. What did I tell you?

These were definitely worth salvaging. They're not too far gone. They just need a clean-up, that's all.'

'Right, you lot,' Auntie Maude declared. 'Clear off for a few minutes. Uncle Stanley and I have got to have a word with Raymond. We'll call you when we're done.'

Everyone filed out of the kitchen, while Raymond tried to second-guess what his new house-parents were going to tell him. His conjecture was that they would tell him there was no need for any more rooftop escapades; if he'd got any problems he could always talk to them; it was time to put the past behind him.

His well-meaning new guardians didn't disappoint him. They also told him they'd agreed with his school that he could return next week. Uncle Stanley would take him and fetch him in his car and Raymond would get special dispensation to stay in a classroom during breaks. They ended their chat by telling him that, although they were only temporary incumbents, they expected to be in the post for some time, as they didn't think the Welfare Department would rush trying to find permanent replacements. Raymond was pleased to hear it and was sure the other inmates would be too.

Later, Raymond was sitting by the playroom window with his crutches leaning against the arm of his chair. Everybody had made a fuss of him, but there was still no sign of Brian. Suddenly, he noticed everyone migrating to the other end of the room, as if there was some new attraction there. Surely it couldn't be the bookcase? He looked around as Brian sidled up to him and picked up one of his crutches.

'All right?' Brian growled.

'Yes,' Raymond replied, wondering why the moment felt like a high noon showdown. 'You?'

'So so,' Brian said, squinting along the length of the crutch as if he was looking down the barrel of a gun. 'Miracle Boy, eh? You kept that quiet, didn't you?'

'Well, yeah,' Raymond said, feeling defensive. 'I didn't know whether the paper would go for it.'

'Oh, they went for it all right,' Brian said. 'It's Miracle Boy this and Miracle Boy that. Miracle Boy saves the world. Miracle Boy and the Invisible bloody Man!'

He stopped looking through the imaginary sight of the crutch and held it in his hands like a rifle at the ready.

'We went into this together,' he said through clenched teeth. 'We took the same risks, but you kept things from me. You used me and I'm not happy. In fact, it's going to take a miracle for me not to beat your bloody brains out.'

Before Raymond could respond, Brian threw the crutch to the floor where it skittered across the linoleum and clattered against the skirting board. Turning on his heels, he stormed from the room and slammed the door behind him. Now Raymond understood why he'd been apprehensive about coming back.

The attraction at the other end of the room seemed to wane as quickly as it appeared and the others drifted back to the window area.

'He'll get over it,' Monica declared without conviction.

'Yeah, like President Kennedy got over being shot in the head,' Shirley muttered.

'Have you got nowt good to say about owt, you sour bitch,' Monica retorted.

Raymond left the girls to their typical fractious squabbling and sank into his thoughts. Why hadn't he told Brian everything beforehand? The simple fact was that he couldn't. He hadn't told anybody about Miracle Boy. He doubted whether it was a story he'd ever be able to tell. What if he'd bared his soul to Brian and told him the full extent of his plan? And then what if the Chronicle had shown no interest? He would have felt eternally stupid. Brian might resent the fact that he'd hogged the limelight, but he didn't understand the price Raymond had to pay.

Raymond didn't want to be Miracle Boy. He didn't want his past known to everyone.

*

Raymond didn't get the chance to make up with Brian, because Brian refused to speak to him. So, confined to home while the rest were at school or work, Raymond read the book Dr Charlerousse gave him and immersed himself in the world of *Steppenwolf*. One afternoon, he had Shirley, who'd been to a dental appointment and not gone back to school, for company. As usual, she was complaining.

'Brian's off his rocker,' she declared. 'You'd think we've got things just as we want them, but not him. You're not going to believe this, Raymond. He got out at night, the second night you were in hospital. He was dead angry about all the stuff in the paper about you. Nigel bought a copy on his way home from work. Anyway, that night, he robbed the off-licence down on Castle Street. You know, the one with all the writing over the windows. He must have got out of the bedroom window and gone down the fire escape. All the stuff he nicked – cigarettes, booze and stuff – is hidden in the outhouse. He only lets them he wants go in there.'

'The stupid idiot,' Raymond sighed. This wasn't the way it was supposed to be.

'Stupid is right,' Shirley said, gripping her knees and rocking backwards and forwards on the sill. 'He's gonna get caught. They might be soft, but Uncle Stanley and Auntie Maude are not stupid and neither are the police. Then there's the booze. It makes people do daft things. Monica and Elsie have been drunk every night and then they get jealous of each other. They'll give the game away. You know what'll happen then, don't you? We'll all cop it. We'll be back to square one. I can just hear somebody, probably in some office where all our names are written on pieces of paper, saying "I told you so." I just know it.'

Raymond could picture that office.

'What are we going to do?' he asked her.

'What do you mean?' she demanded, frozen in forward motion. 'What can we do?'

'We could get rid of the stuff,' he suggested, looking into her big blue eyes.

'How?' she mocked. 'In broad daylight and you with one leg!'

'Where there's a will, there's a way,' he said.

*

Shirley, dressed in jeans, blouse and Wellington boots, planted a spade into the soft earth, while Raymond leaned on his crutches. The hole she dug was close to a low privet hedge bordering the plot; next to Raymond was a wheelbarrow containing a dusty sack filled with Brian's contraband. She had gone to Auntie Maude, as Uncle Stanley was out on an errand somewhere, and suggested that, as an antidote to boredom, she would like to have a go at digging up more vegetables where Uncle Stanley had salvaged the overgrown carrots. Oh, and wouldn't it be a good idea if Raymond went with her, even if he couldn't be much help? It was a grand day and the fresh air would do him good.

'Come on, Shirley, put your back into it,' he urged.

'I'm putting my back and front into it, you twerp,' she snorted. 'Maybe you'd like to have a go.'

Finally, despite Shirley's ineptitude as a land girl, the hole was deep enough to bury the sack, which she then covered with soil. Under Raymond's direction, and despite complaining, Shirley tamped the earth down with the back of her spade to make the soil look as undisturbed as possible.

'Right, that's it,' Shirley said, straightening up. 'I deserve a fag.'

Raymond agreed, leaning against a dustbin in the shadow of the washroom while Shirley smoked. Stretching, she rubbed the small of her back and pushed her chest against her blouse. She caught Raymond's stare.

'Don't bother gawping at me like that, Raymond,' she warned. 'It's not going to get you anywhere. Why don't you try it on with Wendy? She fancies you, you know.'

Raymond felt himself blush.

'Ha,' she teased. 'Don't tell me you fancy her as well? I'm going to tell her then maybe one of you will make a move.'

'Don't you dare, Shirley,' he warned. 'Come on, anyway. We've still got to dig some of that plot up and see if we can find some vegetables.'

'Jesus, Raymond, you're a right slave driver,' she said, but she smiled.

They found a few worthless carrots for their efforts, at the sight of which Auntie Maude said, 'Never mind, the exercise will have done you good.'

After that, as if to distance themselves from the act they'd committed, they avoided each other for the rest of the afternoon. In the playroom by the window, Raymond continued reading his book and immersed himself in the world of Harry Haller – half man, half wolf of the Steppes. As the afternoon wore on, the rest of the inmates began to drift back to Backville Manor. Eventually, Raymond glanced up and saw Brian making his way up the drive. A thought struck him.

Brian was all wolf.

The Whispering Wall

Raymond's shoe cleaning days were behind him, not just because of his incapacity, but because Uncle Stanley declared that everyone should take care of their own shoes. Raymond wasn't disappointed about relinquishing the job, but he regretted losing his role as smokers' confessional. Some of the inmates must have valued it, because they still invited him to accompany them outside.

'Come with me while I have a smoke,' Shirley urged Raymond.

He was especially interested to talk to Shirley, his co-conspirator. He stumped through the washroom after her and waited while she put a match to her docker.

'Brian's completely baffled,' Shirley informed him, holding her cigarette aloft with her elbow resting in her other hand. 'Has he said owt to you?'

'No,' Raymond said. 'He's not speaking to me at all.'

'Well, he crossed you off the list from the word go,' Shirley said. 'You don't smoke and you're a cripple. Ha ha!'

She pulled a face at Raymond's scowl and blew smoke in his face.

'He doesn't think any of the girls would dare nick his stuff, especially me,' she continued. 'And none of the lads were around at the time. He's nervous. He thinks either Uncle Stanley or the police found it and now they're just waiting for him to make another move. He daren't do it again.'

'Good,' Raymond said.

'You know what, Raymond?' she said, studying him. 'You're a wonder. You read books. You talk well. You're as clever as I don't know what. You'd do anything for anybody, and yet underneath you're really crafty. And you've got guts. You've fooled a lot of people, including me. I should have known better after what you got up to at Hillcrest, but I always put that down to Brian. You're the one. You should be wearing your underpants outside your jeans and a vest with 'MB' on it.'

'Don't talk wet, Shirley,' Raymond said, feeling embarrassed.

'Oh, I'm not,' Shirley insisted. 'I see it all now. You had a go at Auntie Sheila long before Brian got here. While she was busy looking for your weaknesses you spotted hers and acted on it. You climbed the roof on your own, which no one else would have even dreamed of doing. And another thing, no one else would have dared come back from the pictures late like you did. Uncle Andrew did worse to you than he did to Peter Mellor, yet you just bided your time. Then, bingo! You got 'em. They're gone. Could Brian have done that alone? No way.'

'I couldn't have done it without Brian,' Raymond said.

'Don't make me laugh, Raymond,' Shirley said. 'You didn't need anybody. Brian was just useful company. Now you've got him tiptoeing along the straight and narrow without a clue that it's down to you. I'm impressed.'

'You're talking nonsense,' Raymond protested, although he was flattered.

Shirley put her face close to his and blasted him with a nicotine-filled, derisory laugh.

'You don't have to choke me, Shirley,' he said, waving his hand in front of his face. 'I'll admit it, but you of all people know what it's like. You've been in these places as long as I have. You're on your own. You've got to learn to stand up

351

for yourself and think for yourself. I'm not saying I'm a special case, but if you're me you really are in No Man's Land. I'm out on a limb here because I go to a different school and read books, and at school I have to use Mickey Mouse money and fight every lad who wants to put me in my place. Do you know what that means?'

'No,' Shirley said, looking at him as if she was seeing another Raymond.

'It means you really are on your own,' he said. 'When we were growing up at Hillcrest, I just kept my head down and did as I was told. I always liked reading and there were plenty of books for me to lose myself in. When I got older, everything started to change. I passed the eleven-plus and went to a different school to everyone else. That's when you lot started treating me different and that's when kids on the outside started calling me names.'

'I didn't treat you different, Raymond,' Shirley said, but her voice sounded apologetic.

'Yes, you did, Shirley, but so did everyone else. That's just the way it is. I'm not making a big deal out of it. It's just that I can't share anything. Being me is being alone, and being alone means I have to work everything out for myself. I have to use everything I've got. If I have to fight, I'll fight. If I have to use my brains, I'll use my brains. I'm not crafty. I'm just looking out for myself.'

'Not just yourself,' Shirley interceded, her cigarette now discarded, facing him with her arms folded across her chest. 'I remember you looking after the new kids at Hillcrest, reading to them and stuff. You haven't changed. Bernard follows you around like a lapdog. Face it, Raymond, you *are* different. Everybody's looking out for themselves but you. You were up on that roof for everybody.'

'She stole my books.'

'I know,' Shirley said with a big grin, 'and little did she know what she was letting herself in for. I'll tell you something, Raymond. You're not as much out on a limb as you think you are. We'd all like to be you, except the lasses, but then the lasses would all want somebody like you.'

'Does that include you?'

'Get lost, you crafty sod,' Shirley said and flounced back indoors, but in a way that told Raymond that she didn't really mean what she said.

*

Uncle Stanley dropped Raymond off at the school gates on his first day back at school. Making his way along the drive and across the yard on his crutches, Raymond saw many heads turn. If he caught someone's eye they either looked away or nodded in tentative acknowledgement. Being the focus of attention, overt or not, felt strange. It was a relief when Titch, Rollo and Poggy descended on him.

'Miracle Boy,' Poggy cried. 'You're like Clark Kent, disappearing and changing into Miracle Boy, except you're not a bit like Clark Kent. What's your special power?'

'The power to turn you into a gibbering wreck,' Raymond said. 'Look, don't call me that, all right? I mean, ever.'

'All right, Rom,' Poggy said, taking a step back. 'I just mean I'm proud of you, that's all. We all are.'

Titch and Rollo made their assent plain and the Legion of the Disenchanted placed themselves around him like a guard as they entered the school.

Later, Raymond wasn't surprised to be called in to see the headmaster. He knew The Gaffer would have some pronouncement to make about recent events. After all, he wasn't just a boy from a children's home who'd stood up for his rights, he was a Slevin boy. What surprised him was being invited by the craggy-faced old man to sit on a chair. He'd been to The Gaffer's study too many times and every time he'd stood to attention in front of the desk, before bending over it. It felt strange to be facing The Gaffer eye to eye.

353

The old scholar smoothed the lapels of his black gown and put his large hands together on the desk in front of him.

'Rawnsley,' he said in his rich timbre, 'It seems you have become the favourite of the fourth estate.'

Raymond's cognitive powers made up for his ignorance. Was The Gaffer being sarcastic about his appearance in the press?

'I appreciate that many may find your story interesting,' The Gaffer continued, 'but here at Slevin we prefer to maintain a modest profile. Fame is but fleeting, whilst the deeds we venerate are those to which a lifetime has been sacrificed, as you will observe from the Slevin Roll of Honour in the library. Miracles are not exalted here.'

He lifted a pair of spectacles from the desk as if he was going to put them on, but instead held them by one arm like a makeshift pointer.

'I appreciate you were in a difficult situation, Rawnsley,' he said, 'and the stand you took required a degree of nerve. I hope the injuries you sustained will not take long to heal. In the meantime, you will find the masters sympathetic to your disability. There is still a hope here that you will do well, but the examinations are fast approaching and you have some catching up to do. You would be wise to use your confinement for revision. If you have any problems, speak to your form master. There will be no need to camp out on the roof here to get attention.'

A faint suggestion of a smile flickered across his scholarly countenance, but before Raymond could respond to it in any way, he was dismissed.

*

Raymond made a decision. He wasn't sure why, but something compelled him. He was going to knuckle down and study hard. He told himself that, as he had the time because of his disability, he might as well, but, there was more to it than that. He just couldn't let himself be a deliberate failure.

While the everyday life of squabbles, taunts and laughter, sometimes cruel, often manic, swirled around him in at Backville Manor, Raymond kept his head inside his textbooks. His eyes were focused and his brain absorbed what he fed it like a sponge. He even stopped looking at breasts. Well, at least not with his usual dedication.

While Raymond kept his head down, life went on around him. Brian was still the surly dormitory bully and was still causing friction between Monica and Elsie, whom he rotated at random in his haphazard affections. His swag might have been swiped but, to compensate, he made the girls pay homage in the form of cigarettes and servitude. At the same time, he grumbled to all but Raymond about having to attend a bricklaying course and make regular visits to a probation officer.

The rest got on with their lives as best they could.

Mary McCluskey lived just beyond the pale, where Derek only occasionally joined her.

Shirley complained about everything.

Theresa twittered all week and stuffed socks down her bra each Sunday before going to the youth club, oblivious to the fact that everybody knew her secret.

Callum, his nocturnal activities curtailed by the presence of Brian in the next bed, seemed out of sorts a lot of the time.

The workers, Nigel and Stuart, were just biding their time until they could leave for good.

Bernard just smiled and studied Raymond's painting nightly, as if within it lay the secret of happiness.

Wendy, shy and winsome, stared – at him. Not when she thought he was looking, but he often saw her staring doe-eyed out of the corner of his eye. If they came into contact around the house, she was like a nervous heifer around him. It was unnerving.

Raymond set aside his crutches after a few days. He could get around on his pot leg well enough as the plaster only came up to below the knee. When Auntie Maude enquired whether he felt up to going to the youth club, he was happy to assure her that he was.

*

Arriving at the youth club, the girls disappeared into the toilets, leaving the lads to disperse to their chosen corners. Raymond was responding to the vicar's concerned query about his injuries when he saw Wendy enter the room a few minutes later. She looked at least four years older than ten minutes before and she was also taller. The soft lights and shadows of the club favoured girls who knew how to apply make-up, but Raymond was amazed at her transformation.

Over the vicar's shoulder, he took everything in; her backcombed hair swept upwards at the sides; her cheek-bones heightened by blusher beneath eyes accentuated by dark lashes and blue eye shadow; her lifted breasts and proud nipples beneath a pale blue top; her slim legs and smooth thighs beneath the raised hemline of her skirt; her raised heels that gave her an elevated poise. It was a meta-morphosis.

'Do you want a Pepsi, Raymond?' she asked.

'Er, please.'

Diplomacy wasn't the vicar's strong suit and he kept questioning Raymond, while Wendy bought two bottles of Pepsi and swayed across to a table at the far side of the room. Raymond saw that his weren't the only eyes following her. Finally, the vicar released him from his inquisition and Raymond limped across the room, less manfully than he would have wished. He sat down next to Wendy and she smiled and batted her eyelashes.

For a while, the two of them listened to music, while she threw him bashful smiles. After a few records, she leaned towards him and said something in his ear, but he couldn't hear what she said because, at that moment, everybody was stamping their feet on the wooden floorboards in time to a record called 'Glad All Over' by the Dave Clark Five.

'What?' he mouthed.

She leaned closer and he could smell her intoxicating scent and feel her lips brushing against his ear.

'Do you want to go downstairs?' she whisper-shouted.

He looked at her. Her cheeks were flushed and there was a hint of uncertainty in her pleading eyes. He nodded and they rose and crossed the dusty wooden floor together. As they passed the bar, Shirley caught his arm.

'She taking you to the Whispering Wall?' Shirley said with what looked like a leer.

'What's that?' Raymond mouthed, rather than said.

'You'll see,' Shirley said and tapped the tip of her nose.

In the basement of the disused chapel, Wendy took Raymond's hand and led him into the darkness. In the first room they entered, she guided him along the wall, like the blind leading the blind, until they came to an opening. Inside the next room, she continued to lead the way until they came to a corner and then she turned towards him with her back to the wall. Raymond was straining to see, but it was pitch-black. She bent forward and he realised that she was slipping off her shoes and then she stepped back and seemed to rise a few inches in the air.

Raymond felt around with his good foot and worked out that there was a wooden plinth at the base of the wall. It was probably there to cover water or gas pipes. Was this the Whispering Wall? And were those noises whispers or just sighs?

Suddenly, like a creature transformed by the night, Wendy pulled him towards her and fastened her wet lips to his. The taste of lipstick and saliva soon aroused him and he placed his hands on her slender waist as she began to turn her head this way and that to cover every part of his lips with hers. This was as far as he expected things to go, but his heart beat faster as she lifted his hands and clamped them to her bust, which seemed to expand beneath his fingers. Her kisses became even more inflamed, as she pulled her top and bra up over her breasts, so that nothing stood in the way of his hands and her naked skin.

Raymond wasn't sure how long they stayed there for, but he definitely heard the whispers. They seemed to get louder and louder, accompanied by groans, coughs and other strange sounds that he didn't want to interpret. During the time they were there, corresponding parts of his and Wendy's bodies made contact with each other, albeit mostly clothed, and danced to an ancient rhythm. He knew the frenzied vampire clinging to him was biting his neck and drinking his blood, but he didn't care. When they finally made their way out of the stygian chamber, the sound of loud whispering followed them.

Out of the Blue

'What did you make of Wendy and the Whispering Wall?' Shirley asked, stepping in front of Raymond as he headed to the bathroom before bed. Her big eyes were shining.

'Spooky,' Raymond replied. 'Are you sure she's not a vampire by night?'

'Maybe,' Shirley said. 'It certainly looks like you've been bitten.'

In the bathroom, Raymond was appalled to discover a vivid red love-bite on his neck just above the clavicle.

The following day, the subterranean siren who'd put her mark on him disappeared, to be replaced by a slight, plain girl who wore shyness like a well-worn cloak. Her coyness around him seemed even more extreme than normal.

For the next few weeks, Raymond worried and whispered. During the week he worried about everything and on Sunday nights he whispered about nothing. He didn't know why he was doing either.

The impending GCE O level exams were a source of strain on everybody in his year at school. Even those who were intending to leave at the end of the school year and get a job, and he included himself among them, were put under constant pressure to revise and achieve the best result they could. Raymond didn't need cajoling. Something inside him was determined to overachieve and then just walk away. He read textbooks until he was hollow-eyed and, in bed at night, he dreamed of a fading sunset and weeping masters.

It was the walking into the sunset part that worried him. He didn't know what he was going to do. The jobs on offer, the ones his friends in the Legion of the Disenchanted talked about, held no appeal for him, even though he didn't admit it to them. In a textile town, the opportunities for a grammar school early-leaver were mainly as a clerk in some office, or for the more adventurous, a trainee textile designer or colour-matcher with day release to attend the local technical college. What was he going to do? He'd told himself for a long time that it didn't matter as long as he got a job. Now it mattered.

As for the Sunday night whispering, he'd even less idea about that. He was attracted to it for obvious fleshly reasons, but there was more to it than that, though. The life he'd led drew him towards the secret and the clandestine. The dark bowels of the youth club and the dangerous, forbidden adventures taking place there were impossible to resist. The actual whispering was nonsense.

'Why so serious all the time, Raymond?' Shirley asked him during a smoke break one evening. 'You should be like a dog with two tails.'

'Why should I?' he retorted.

Whenever Shirley went for a smoke she gave him a signal to follow her and he did, even though it wasn't always a pleasure.

'Because you've got it made,' Shirley said. 'You're like, well, bullet-proof. Nobody dare give you a hard time now in case it ends up in the papers. Not that Auntie Maude or Uncle Stan would, but they're bending over backwards to give you all the time you need to do your schoolwork. Plus, you've got a girlfriend who's mad about you.'

'Do you mean Wallflower Wendy who barely speaks to me all week, or Wanton Wendy who lives in the youth club basement and drinks blood?' Raymond asked.

'She's just shy,' Shirley said with a laugh. 'Give her time.

It's easier to be someone different at the youth club. You're not complaining, are you?'

'Well, no,' he said.

'Good,' Shirley said, 'because Wendy's asked me to give you summat.'

Shirley put her hand up her cardigan sleeve and withdrew a small packet, which she palmed into Raymond's hand. Raymond stared at it.

'Johnnies,' Shirley said. 'Wendy bought a packet from Tommy Carter. Everyone gets them from him. You should be flattered. Now you're a boy scout. You're prepared.'

Raymond said nothing and slipped the packet into his pocket.

'Well?' Shirley queried with a mocking smile.

'Well what?' Raymond answered, feeling awkward.

'Do you know what to do with them?' she asked with a grin.

Raymond knew she was laughing at him and he couldn't stand it, so he left her. When he passed Wendy, who was mopping the kitchen floor, she blushed and cast her eyes down.

*

Raymond was hammering important dates and events into his subconscious from a history textbook in the playroom, while waiting for Mrs Eaton to come and collect him for their visit to Stokes Park Hospital. The exams were due to start on Monday and he was using every minute he could to cram. It was also a good excuse to shut everything out; especially the secret smiles cast his way by coy Wendy.

'Auntie Maude wants to see you in the office, Raymond,' Derek said, entering the room.

Raymond rose from his seat and placed his book on the windowsill. What did Auntie Maude want? Mrs Eaton should have been there by now. Maybe she'd rung to say she couldn't make it for some reason. If so, this was one occasion he wouldn't mind. He could do more revising.

He knocked on the door to the office and waited for permission to enter. He could hear voices from within. Maybe Mrs Eaton was there after all.

'Come in,' Auntie Maude called out.

Raymond opened the door and stepped into a parallel universe.

Mrs Eaton was there, along with Auntie Maude, but they were not alone. There were also three faces with varying degrees of suntan smiling at him. Uncle Gordon's tan was the deepest, making his teeth seem even whiter than Raymond remembered. Auntie Dawn's smooth cheeks glowed like honey in the light and her auburn hair was streaked with blonde strands. David, who'd grown a couple of inches since Raymond last saw him, sported a light tan on his face, except for round his eyes where the skin was still white, as if he'd been wearing goggles. Raymond was rooted to the spot and speechless. He was aware that his mouth was hanging open, but his jaw was oblivious to any commands.

It was David who broke the spell by running over to him and clasping his legs.

'Be careful, David,' Uncle Gordon said. 'Raymond looks as if he might fall down.'

His former house-father strode up to him and clasped Raymond's hand in both of his. Auntie Dawn also stepped forward and gave him a one-armed hug. Raymond had never been connected to so many people at one time.

'I know it's out of the blue,' Uncle Gordon said, 'but we've actually been back from Australia a couple of weeks. We wanted to check a couple of things out before we came to see you. We've got a lot to tell you.'

'Let's get organised first,' Auntie Maude suggested.

'Raymond, get a couple more chairs from the dining room and ask Mary to make tea for five. Oh, and tell her to bring a glass of milk for the boy.'

Raymond was glad to have something to do, which would give him time to clear his head. Nothing could have surprised him more, not even if Uncle Richard had come back to life and called for a visit with the noose still hanging around his neck. What were they doing here – and with Mrs Eaton? If she'd anything to do with it, he was going to start calling her Auntie Liz to her face.

With enough chairs, they all sat in a semi-circle in front of the desk with Auntie Maude behind it. Auntie Dawn took up the story.

'Australia didn't work out for us,' she began. 'Gordon was away working for weeks at a time. The town we lived in was quite small and there wasn't much going on there at all. At least the weather was wonderful and David could play out with the other children. The school we started him in wasn't too good, though – very basic. We missed each other while Gordon was away and then, when he was at home, we missed everything we'd left behind.'

'I couldn't get on with cricket, Raymond,' her husband said. 'Give me a proper game of football any day.'

'It's not all it's cracked up to be down under,' Mrs Eaton interjected. 'There's plenty that come back.'

'Anyways,' Auntie Dawn continued. 'We were already talking about coming home when we got a letter from Mrs Hanson. She was our help at Manorholme,' she explained to the other two ladies. 'The letter had some pages from the *Chronicle* with it. There you were, Raymond, up on the roof, then falling off it, and the whole story was laid out. We couldn't believe it, could we, pet?'

'Nay, pet,' Uncle Gordon said. 'But at the same time we weren't surprised. It took guts and brains to do what you did, Raymond.'

'There was no other way to get people to take notice,' Raymond said.

'Well, they certainly noticed, Raymond,' Auntie Dawn said with a smile. 'And we heard about it on the other side of the world. It was the final straw for us. We often talked about you. We made a hard decision not to write to you when we went away, because we didn't think it was fair on you, but we never stopped thinking about you. Once we got Mrs Hanson's letter, we decided to come home. We got back a couple of weeks ago, but we wanted to check some things out before we came to see you. We approached the Welfare and they put us in touch with Mrs Eaton.'

Raymond tried hard not to let his mind take him where it wanted to take him. Why was everybody smiling? He'd never seen Mrs Eaton smile like that before. Just listen! Don't jump ahead!

'We didn't want to get your hopes up after what happened last time,' Auntie Dawn said, 'but the way's now clear. We can either foster or adopt you. It's up to you.'

'That's right, Raymond,' Mrs Eaton said. 'Now I've got to know you, I can't stand in your way, especially as these good people have come all the way from the other side of the world for you.'

'We've rented a house, not far from Mrs Hanson, actually,' Auntie Dawn explained. 'We intend to stay in this area and look for a house to buy. Gordon's already got a surveying job on a new motorway project that's going to cut across the Pennines. If we foster you, it can be sorted in no time. We can sort out adoption later if that's what you want. You'll also be able to stay on at school if you want to. Maybe go on to university. You can do it. What do you think?'

'I can't believe it,' Raymond said, because that's exactly what he was feeling.

Things like this just didn't happen to him. He didn't get summoned to offices to hear good news. It was like, well, it was like a miracle. Everybody was staring at him and he couldn't speak.

David tugged at his sleeve and asked, 'Raymond, are you coming to live with us or not?'

'Yes, David, I am,' Raymond managed to say.

'Oh, goody,' David cried out.

There was a lot of hugging between everybody after that; more than Raymond had ever experienced in one place at one time.

The Pink Palace

Shirley had her back to the wall of the washroom and was smoking a cigarette. Raymond stood in front of her with his hands in the pockets of his jeans, while she blew smoke above his head.

'Have you any idea how gutted Wendy was?' Shirley asked. 'It was supposed to be a big night. Well, *the* big night.'

'I had to study for the exams, Shirley,' Raymond protested.

Shirley's big blue eyes narrowed.

'You're supposed to be leaving school and getting a job this summer,' she said and directed a stream of smoke into his face.

'Good results help even if you leave school early,' he said.

'Are you sure that's the reason?' Shirley pressed. 'How does one night studying instead of going to the club make a difference?'

'Because the exam was the next day,' Raymond said. 'That way it's still fresh.'

'Hmm!' Shirley said, giving every impression of being unconvinced. 'I still can't see it. There's summat you're not telling me. Don't tell me you're scared.'

To be accused of being frightened of anything was an affront to Raymond.

'All right,' he said. 'I might as well tell you, but you've got to promise to keep it to yourself.'

'Go on, then,' Shirley said, lighting up another cigarette.

'Promise?' Raymond insisted.

'Promise,' Shirley said. 'Now get on with it. You're costing me fags.'

'I might be staying on at school,' he said. 'That's why I've got to do well in the exams. In fact, I might be leaving here.'

'What?' Shirley exclaimed. 'You're kidding me.'

Raymond explained about his former house-parents and what transpired during their visit.

Shirley dispatched a long 'Phew!' on a stream of smoke.

'Lucky you,' she said. 'What happens next?'

'Auntie Maude's told me I've got to go to a meeting at the Welfare offices at Lawson Court straight after school tomorrow,' Raymond said. 'She says it's some kind of leaving committee and they're going to ask me questions.'

'What about?' Shirley asked.

'I don't really know,' Raymond admitted. 'Auntie Maude says they've got to be certain I'm doing the right thing.'

'Do you reckon I'll have to do that one day?' Shirley mused, as much to herself as Raymond.

'I don't know,' Raymond said.

'I don't think so, Raymond,' Shirley declared and paused to take a fierce drag of her cigarette. 'I reckon you're a special case, apart from being a nutcase, that is. Anyhow, good luck.'

*

The cloudless sky was azure blue and even at four-thirty the sun was still warm, but Raymond didn't remove his blazer as he walked the short distance from where he'd alighted his bus. When he reached the familiar gateway and turned into the driveway, the sight before him took his breath away. This wasn't the Lawson Court he remembered. The imposing building was pink, except for its white portico and uniform white windows, and the shale drive, which gleamed white in the glaring sun, was flanked by a riot of pink and lilac rhododendrons. He walked down the drive in a daze to be met by Miss Bellamy, who greeted him with the same fragrant warmth as on the day he'd first arrived there.

'Come in, Raymond,' she said with a broad smile.

'It's pink,' Raymond said, gazing up at the house.

'Oh, yes,' she said. 'It was a kind of beige when you were here, wasn't it? It's been repainted this year. It wouldn't be so bad if the garden wasn't already mad with pink and purple. If they made a jigsaw out of the whole thing, it would drive you crazy.'

She guided him into the hallway and led him into a small waiting room in the inner sanctum of the Welfare Department side of the house, and indicated for him to sit down. She sat on a chair next to him and told him that the committee hadn't arrived yet. Then she went on to explain that the committee was made up of people who were external to the Welfare Department. They were, in fact, members of the Board of Guardians, of which there needed to be three for this purpose. Today's panel would comprise of a magistrate, a clergyman and an eminent local business-man.

'They don't do this often, but it's partly because of your age,' she said. 'You've finally reached an age when your opinion matters. Between me and you, it's more likely because you've been in the limelight so much. They don't want to make any mistakes. They'll ask you questions, mainly about you and what you want to do. You shouldn't have any problems. Besides, they'll already have reports on you.

'When the committee have finished with you they'll send you away, but they'll make a decision today before they leave. That's only a recommendation to the Welfare Department, but they're unlikely to go against it. Whatever happens, you should know the outcome pretty soon after.'

After that explanation, they chatted for a while until a red-haired woman in a dark jacket appeared at the door and said, 'They're ready for you now.'

Miss Bellamy put a reassuring hand on Raymond's shoulder and smiled with encouragement.

'I can come in with you if you want,' she offered.

'Yes, please,' Raymond said.

The woman led them into a large room with tall windows at one end. The sight that greeted Raymond didn't fit in with what he'd imagined. He'd expected a courtroom with the committee sat at the bench, while he stood in the dock. Instead, the room was like a boardroom, with a large polished table dominating the room. On one side of the table sat three men in suits and Raymond and Miss Bellamy were invited to sit opposite them.

Raymond knew at a glance who each of the men were. The grey-haired, benign-looking clergyman on the right was easy because he was wearing a dog-collar. The sharp-faced magistrate in the centre was holding his hands clasped in front of him and looking stern, as if a heavy responsibility rested on his shoulders. The silver-haired businessman on the left, in the expensive worsted suit, was looking relaxed and leaning back in his chair. The magistrate led the proceedings, while the lady who'd shown them into the room took notes.

'Raymond,' the magistrate began, 'you do appreciate, do you not, that the corporation has a duty of care towards you until you reach the minimum age of eighteen, especially as in your case you have no other legal guardian who can take care of you?'

Raymond kept his head up and his eyes straight ahead as he said, 'Yes.'

'Good,' the magistrate said with a nod of his head. 'You will also appreciate that the corporation cannot abdicate its responsibility unless it is absolutely certain that your welfare is being protected.'

This time Raymond nodded and murmured his assent. It was clear that the magistrate was unable to divorce himself from his usual pedantic courtroom style, which would require only the minimum response from him, while the clergyman beamed at Raymond and the laconic business-man looked bemused and twiddled a silver fountain pen in his hands.

'In that case,' the magistrate continued, 'it follows that where a person of an earlier age than that at which the duty of care expires seeks to leave welfare accommodation, then the greatest diligence has to be exercised to ensure that the circumstances do not run contrary to the corporation's obligation. That is why we are here today. As members of the Board of Guardians it is our duty to ascertain that your welfare will continue to be protected. To this end, you should know that we have already satisfied ourselves that Mr and Mrs Best are of a fit and proper character. It therefore remains to us today to ensure that you yourself are ready to take this step.'

The businessman suddenly seemed to take a proper interest and leaned forward. Raymond stiffened and prepared himself for the interrogation he knew was about to begin.

'Do you think you're ready to leave the 'omes, lad?' the businessman interceded, to the obvious annoyance of the magistrate, who twitched.

'Yes,' Raymond replied.

'Well,' the businessman said while putting his pen back in his top pocket, 'explain why, and bear in mind I know from personal experience how tough it can be starting out in life.'

Raymond hesitated.

'If I stay in the home until I'm eighteen,' he began, 'I'll

be on my own when I leave. I'll have to have a job by then so I can look after myself. This way I'll have a home. I know Mr and Mrs Best, and I get on well with them.'

'That's all well and good, lad,' the businessman persisted, 'but you were fostered before, if I understand, and that didn't work out too well.'

'I was never asked before,' Raymond blurted out.

Miss Bellamy spoke up.

'I don't know of a more mature and capable person of Raymond's age,' she said. 'He spent some time at Lawson Court with us after a very difficult experience in an unsuitable foster home. He not only dealt with that extremely well, but the other children quickly looked up to him. Raymond is very bright. He's able to deal with difficult situations in a very rational way. I know he'll cope admirably and I would also say he has nothing to gain by remaining in his present circumstances, which may, in fact, hold back his progress as an intelligent adult.'

The look of admiration from the businessman towards Miss Bellamy was echoed in Raymond's mind.

'The recent and much-publicised escapade on the roof of Backville Manor; was that a rational response to a problem?' the magistrate cut in.

Raymond thought even the vicar looked afraid for him as he tried to gather his thoughts.

'There wasn't any other way,' Raymond stammered. 'We had to do something and we knew no one would believe us unless we made it really public. That's why we did what we did and told the newspaper.'

'In my opinion, that was very resourceful,' the businessman said. 'That's the kind of smart thinking you need in business sometimes.'

'Resourceful is a good word,' Miss Bellamy said, taking advantage of the passing bandwagon to aid Raymond further. 'If you look at it in that light, there aren't that many young men of Raymond's age who'd have thought up such an effective solution, never mind have the confidence to carry it out. Let's not forget either, that it was in response to a problem none of us would have wanted to go unresolved.'

Miss Bellamy's statement seemed to impose a silence over everybody and even the woman taking notes looked up. Then the mild-mannered vicar spoke up.

'Tell me, Raymond,' he stuttered, 'what have you learned from your time in the corporation's children's homes that you think will stand you in good stead in life?'

Raymond hadn't expected to be asked such a philosophical question. At first, he couldn't stop his mind coming up with facetious answers, such as 'never put a fox in charge of a henhouse', but he composed himself before he spoke.

'Being in children's homes teaches you that you've got responsibilities to others,' he said. 'You can't ignore it. You've got brothers and sisters whether you like it or not. There's always someone worse off than you and no matter what other people might think, it's not their fault.'

The vicar put his hands together as if in prayer.

'That's a very good answer, Raymond,' he said. 'I have no further questions.'

'Just one more from me,' the businessman said. 'What difference do you think living with the Bests will make to your future?'

'If I stayed at Backville Manor,' Raymond said, 'I would leave school in a few weeks and get a job and try for a place in the working boys' hostel.'

'Nowt wrong with that,' the businessman said. 'And the alternative?'

'With the Bests,' Raymond said, 'I'll try and stay on at school for my A levels. Then I'll try for a place at university.'

'Mmm!' the businessman said. 'I didn't have that luxury, but I'm glad my son has. Good luck, lad.'

No one had much more to say after that and Raymond was dismissed along with Miss Bellamy, while the committee stayed to deliberate. At the front door, he thanked his fragrant helper and she gave him a hug.

'Don't worry about a thing,' she said. 'Carol Farrell would have been proud of you.'

The fragrance of lavender lingered with him as he strolled down the drive between rows of vibrant blooms. At the gateway, he turned around and took one final look at the iridescent picture laid before him. He squinted until the vision was blurred, as if shrouded in mist. This was one of his mystical paintings.

*

Raymond didn't go straight back to Backville Manor. Instead, he stopped off in the town centre. There was something he had to do and it seemed like the right time to do it. He made his way towards what was known as the bottom end of town, asking directions along the way, until he found Alderley Street. It was an unprepossessing street with a row of terrace houses on one side and some small business yards on the other. He stared at the houses, which all looked the same: slightly dilapidated and grimy.

He picked one at random and imagined it was the house his mother and grandmother lived in when he was a baby. The front door, with its blistered and peeling paint, was reached by a worn step. A lonely blue vase stood on the sill of the downstairs window, framed by grubby-looking voile curtains. The bottom half of the upstairs sash window was open, like a big, black letterbox.

He'd read everything about the day he became known as Miracle Boy in his newspaper clippings. He could imagine the policemen on the pavement, looking up at his mother and pleading with her to come down and open the door. He saw his mother leaning out of the upstairs window with him in her arms. The paper said he was wrapped tightly in a blanket, like a parcel.

Did his mother just drop him, or did she throw him? The pavement was quite narrow, but even so, she must have swung her arms for him to land on the roof of the police car parked at the curb. Not only that, but then he'd bounced into the road. She must have thrown him with some force. It wasn't a car that was passing, as Mrs Eaton's mother said, but a van. The newspaper said it was being driven by a retired butcher who worked part-time making meat deliveries. His name was Frank Shaw. It's not every day a parcel of baby bursts through your windscreen. It must have been quite a shock, enough to cause him to swerve across the road and hit a lamppost; probably that lamppost, or maybe the one further down.

The poor man died of a heart attack almost immediately, the newspaper said. What would the Shaw family say if they met him now? Would they blame him? Raymond hoped not. Ever since he'd learned about the events of the day, Mr Shaw had been added to the ghosts of his past; the ones he felt he owed something to.

At what point did his mother jump? The police said they'd turned their back on her to run to the scene of the accident. No one saw her leap. She must have climbed out onto the window ledge first. Had she always intended to jump, or was it only when she realised the magnitude of what she'd just done? He'd never know. He suspected that even if she could speak she wouldn't be able to tell him.

He could have died here. If the van had passed a split second later, he might have been lying in the road and been run over. His soul might have been the one taken rather than Mr Shaw's. It was pure chance. Life was pure chance.

This was his last visit to this place, he decided. There was no memory, not even a trace. No matter how many times he read the newspaper cuttings, it didn't feel like the story was about him. Everything was in front of him now. Finally, unbelievably, he had great expectations.

*

Raymond was called into the office by Uncle Stanley on his return home from school on Friday. His house-father wasted no time on preamble.

'You're leaving, Raymond,' he announced. 'It'll take about a week to sort out the paperwork and then you'll be off to the Bests. I'm really pleased for you, lad.'

He extended his hand and Raymond shook it.

As Raymond left the office, he saw Shirley at the other end of the corridor. She raised her thumb and her eyebrows. Raymond stuck his thumb up in response to her silent question. Shirley's open smile was so un-Shirley-like that Raymond was touched.

All Over Now

Raymond was on the horns of a dilemma. Wendy hardly spoke to him on the way to the youth club, but every time he caught her eye she blushed and put her head down. He gripped the packet in his pocket, which was battered from all the handling he'd subjected it to. Soon they'd be at the club and she would disappear to transform herself into the siren of the Whispering Wall. He noticed Shirley glancing at him and felt the weight of expectation on his shoulders. Should he or shouldn't he? It was no big deal, was it? They all did it. At least, they said they did.

When they arrived at the youth club, the girls disappeared as usual. Raymond bought himself a Pepsi and stood in the doorway connecting the two rooms of the club so he could watch Stuart and Nigel play table tennis and, at the same time, keep an eye on the main room. After a while the newly made-up Backville girls began to drift into the room and Raymond went to stand by the bar. Wendy was taking her time.

Maybe she was taking special care with her appearance just for him. Maybe she was as jittery as he was.

He finished his drink and wondered about buying another. There was still no sign of Wendy. Monica passed him on her way to the bar and he turned to her.

'Have you seen Wendy?' he asked.

'She was in the bog getting tarted up last time I saw her,' Monica said, adjusting her décolletage. 'Do you think this top suits me?'

'Yeah, it's nice,' he replied and averted his eyes from the cornucopia of white flesh on display.

He looked around the room. Shirley was sitting at a table chatting with a girl he didn't know, so he decided not to ask her if she knew where Wendy was. He bought another Pepsi and began to suck on the bottle. Seeing Theresa heading for the door, he followed her. When he caught up with her, he asked if she would check to see if Wendy was in the toilets. She agreed and he waited at the top of the stairs. After a minute, she came to the door of the girls' toilet, shrugged her bony shoulders and said, 'There's nobody in here.'

Raymond was nonplussed. He wandered back into the main room of the club and leaned against the bar. More minutes passed and Raymond couldn't decide whether he was annoyed or relieved. Shirley came up to him.

'What's up?' she asked.

'I don't know where Wendy is,' Raymond said.

Shirley glanced around the room said, 'Oh oh!'

'What do you mean?' Raymond demanded.

'Nowt,' Shirley said. 'I'm sure she'll be here in a minute. She might not be feeling well. She's probably still in the toilet.'

'No, she isn't,' Raymond said. 'I asked Theresa to look for me.'

'She's probably gone outside for some fresh air, then,' Shirley said.

Raymond left Shirley and went downstairs and out into the street. It was still light and he could see along the whole length of the road. There was no sign of Wendy. He made his way back up to the bar and carried on waiting. Various people spoke to him over the next half hour or so, but he answered in monosyllables.

And then he saw Wendy. She was in the doorway, about to enter the room. She was Wanton Wendy from the top of her backcombed hair to her elevated heels. Her face was flushed and her eyes were bright. Standing next to her, with his arm around her shoulder and his hand gripping her upper arm with an unmistakable air of ownership, was Brian Walker. He saw Raymond staring and bent his head to whisper in Wendy's ear. She smiled.

Everyone standing between Raymond and the couple at the door seemed to melt away and a hush settled over the room, leaving only the Rolling Stones pounding out 'It's All Over Now' to fill the vacuum. Raymond took three paces forward and confronted the couple in the doorway.

'Wendy?' he said, regretting the crack in his voice.

His face felt hot and his fists down by his side were clenching and unclenching as if attached by wires to his turbulent thoughts.

'Can't you see?' Brian said, while pulling Wendy even closer to him. 'She's with me now.'

Wendy didn't look Raymond in the eye, but tilted her head towards Brian's shoulder. Raymond took a step forward and raised his fists. Brian immediately let go of Wendy and adjusted his stance in preparation for a fight. At that moment, Shirley appeared between them and threw her arms around Raymond.

'No!' she cried and began to pull him away. 'It's not worth it, Raymond. Leave it.'

'Let him be,' Brian snapped behind her. 'Miracle Boy's about to run out of luck.'

'You lay one finger on him and you'll wish you'd never been born,' Shirley spat over her shoulder while man-handling Raymond away from the scene.

Wendy was also playing her part to diffuse the situation by pulling at Brian's arm and pleading with him to leave Raymond alone. Then the flustered vicar appeared and told everyone to calm down and not spoil the evening. Once Brian was out of the way of the door, Shirley pushed

Raymond towards it and told him she was taking him home. Raymond's resistance was only token, although his hurt pride urged him to go back and fight. By the time they reached the pavement, his anger started to subside and he resigned himself to walking home with Shirley.

'Did you know?' Raymond asked Shirley after a period of silence.

'About Brian?' she said. 'No. It's no surprise, though. I told Wendy you were leaving.'

'What?' Raymond exclaimed and turned to face Shirley. Shirley was calm.

'Think about it,' she said. 'This time next week you won't be here, but Wendy will – and for a long time after that. Don't say you would have come back to visit her. Have you ever gone back to anywhere you lived before? No. Nobody does. Besides, you were only going to do it with her because that's what she wanted.'

It was true. He couldn't deny it, but that didn't give Brian the right to make a fool of him.

Shirley seemed to read his mind.

'Brian's a git, but he's not all bad, Raymond. How did you expect him to feel when you got your name and picture splashed all over the newspaper? He's just like the rest of us – stuck in a place he doesn't want to be, but unable to do owt about it. I'm really pleased you're leaving. I think you deserve it and can make the most of it, but it's different for Brian. Do you know how many lads leave the homes and end up in prison? Loads. That's where Brian's heading, and he knows it. He's angry because he can't stop it happening.'

'I know,' Raymond admitted.

'I know you do,' Shirley said. 'That's what I like about you. Sometimes, we all have a laugh about the books you read when you leave them lying around in the playroom. Nobody's got a clue what they're about, but you must get summat out of them, because you understand deep stuff.

On the other hand, you can't see what's under your nose half the time. Miracle Boy's a good name for you. Most of the time you fool everybody into thinking you're harmless, and then you do something incredible. Come on, let's get home. I want a smoke before we get in.'

When they got to Backville Manor they went straight round the back to Smokers' Corner. Normally, they would hear sounds from the house, but it was as silent as a grave-yard.

'I'm going to miss moaning at you when I take my fag breaks,' Shirley said.

'Me too,' Raymond said.

'So you think I'm a moaner, then?'

'A bit.'

'Cheeky bugger,' Shirley said and blew smoke out of the side of her mouth. 'I'm hard-faced, I know. The thing is, I can't let anybody take advantage of me. You know the reason why. I can never forget what happened at Hillcrest. Uncle Richard used to find excuses to send us to bed early and we knew what was going to happen. It was awful, lying there in the dark, jumping at the slightest sound, knowing he was going to come and make you do things you didn't want to do. I wanted to die. One day I'm going to find out where his grave is and spit on it.'

'Let me know when you do,' Raymond said. 'I'll come with you.'

'You're all right, you know, Raymond,' she murmured.

Raymond accepted, with good grace, the implication that she might not always have thought so. She was all right too. He watched her as she finished her cigarette in silence and stamped on it. Without the glow of hot ash, he could hardly see her face in the deep shadow.

'Those johnnies,' she said. 'It's a pity to waste them, isn't it?'

'What?' Raymond said, taken aback.

'In your dreams,' she said with a throaty chuckle. 'Give them here. I can swap them for a packet of fags.'

'Oh,' Raymond said and began to fumble in his pocket.

'Bloody hell, Raymond,' she said when he handed her the crumpled packet. 'Have you been chewing on this? You're so funny sometimes. I'm really sorry I'm never going to see you again when you go. Come here and give me a cuddle. No trying to cop a sneaky feel, mind.'

'I wouldn't dream of it,' Raymond said, feeling awkward as she wrapped her arms around him.

'Oh, you would dream of it, Raymond,' she said. 'That's what you're good at – making things happen inside your head until they come true.'

Shirley held on to him for what seemed like a long time. Her head was on his shoulder with her face turned away from him and she began to sob quietly. He put his arms around her and held her tight. He knew her tears weren't for him. He understood what they were for, but he wouldn't have been able to explain it to anyone in words.

*

Raymond's last day at Backville Manor started in ordinary fashion, with breakfast and the usual chores. Stuart and Nigel said their perfunctory goodbyes to him before leaving for work and Raymond retired to the dormitory to make his final preparations. Before he snapped his suitcase shut, he wandered over to Bernard's bed and slipped his mystery painting, the one Bernard liked so much, under the pillow. Then he walked over to Brian's bed, unfastened his silver wristwatch, and pushed it under Brian's pillow. The alarm clock on the windowsill made no sound as it watched him.

Without a backward glance, Raymond carried his suitcase downstairs and placed it in the hallway. Then he knocked on the office door.

'Come in,' Uncle Stanley called out.

'Ah, Raymond,' he said when Raymond entered. 'All set?'

'Yes,' Raymond said. 'All packed.'

'Good,' Uncle Stanley said. 'The driver will be here shortly. You just need to sign this paper for your savings from your pocket money. After that, I suggest you say your goodbyes and then you'll be ready for the off.'

Raymond signed the receipt for his small savings and pocketed the money. Then he shook hands with his housefather, who wished him good luck. Leaving the office and heading to the playroom, he marvelled at the thought that it would be his last visit to that place, where the games played were not those intended by the architects of children's homes.

Farewells were awkward when the other party wanted to be in the leaver's shoes and, sensing this, Raymond didn't make a big show as he went round to each inmate and said a brief goodbye. Bernard sulked in a chair by the window and kept his head down, so Raymond just patted him on the shoulder. Wendy gave him a whispered goodbye and weak smile. Mary and Theresa wished him luck. Monica sighed and stared out of the window. Elsie lisped a wet 'Tho long', while Derek grunted, clearly peeved that Raymond had beaten him in finding a way out of Backville Manor.

Shirley held out a book. It was *Great Expectations*.

'You left this in the bookcase,' she said.

'I know,' Raymond said. 'I meant to.'

'Don't you want it?' she asked.

'No,' he said. 'Someone else can have it. So long, Shirley. I'm gonna miss you.'

'Get lost, you daft sod.'

Brian was nowhere to be seen.

Raymond was making his way to the kitchen when he heard a knock on the front door. He opened it to find Mr Pickup standing on the step.

'Just a minute,' he said to the corporation driver and went into the kitchen.

'See you, Auntie Maude. I'm off now,' he said to the only occupant.

His homely house-mother wiped her hands on her apron and came towards him. She gave him a warm hug and wished him luck.

That was it. There was nobody else to say goodbye to, except Brian, and he was conspicuous by his absence. Raymond made his way to the front door, picking his suit-case up on the way. Mr Pickup was waiting by his black car and he took Raymond's suitcase from him and put it in the boot. Raymond could see the inmates of Backville Manor staring through the playroom window and he gave a small wave.

When he turned to get in the car, Brian was standing on the doorstep.

'Shirley told me last night you were the one who nicked me gear from the outhouse and buried it,' Brian said.

Raymond looked at Brian's stony face. Surely, he didn't want to fight now.

'She said you did it to keep me out of trouble,' Brian said. 'I believe it of you. I'm sorry I gave you a hard time. I can't get that time back now, but I wish I could. Good luck, mate.'

Brian held his hand out and Raymond clasped it.

'Thanks,' Raymond said. 'You'll be right behind me. You'll see.'

'No I won't,' Brian said. 'There'll be no early release for me. Me dad's away for a long stretch this time and me mum won't have me back. At least now I know where me gear is we can have a party tonight to celebrate you leaving. It's a pity we haven't got any bangers to hang from the roof.'

He pulled his hand away and turned to mount the steps and go back into the house. Raymond watched him disappear and then turned back to the car. Mr Pickup was seated at the wheel, but he'd left the passenger door open. Remembering all his backseat journeys, Raymond knew that this was a privilege, and he climbed in and closed the door behind him. He looked at Mr Pickup, who was looking back at him. The lines around his mouth etched into his leather skin, which Raymond had never noticed before, were caused by his smile. Mr Pickup winked.

'Now this is the kind of job I like,' he said as he started the car.

The corporation driver didn't stop talking all the way to the Bests' house.